DATE DUE

FEB 16 2014	
NOV 2 7 2014	
DEC 1 3 2014	
MAY 2 7 2017	

WORLD LITERARY PRESS

ISBN-13: 978-0989050845
ISBN-10: 098905084X

HAVE NO SHAME

Cover Photography © Susan Fox / Trevillion Images
Cover Design Regina Starace

World Literary Press
PRINTED IN THE UNITED STATES OF AMERICA

PRAISE for *Have No Shame*

"A gripping and poignant novel dealing with a subject once taboo in American society."
Hagerstown Magazine

"Have No Shame is a powerful testimony to love and the progressive, logical evolution of social consciousness, with an outcome that readers will find engrossing, unexpected, and ultimately eye-opening."
Midwest Book Review

"A historical novel of love and its triumph, told with a unique and compelling voice."
Bestselling Author, Kathleen Shoop

"[HAVE NO SHAME] Perfectly catches the South at the dawning of the Civil Rights Movement ... an adventure that twists and turns unpredictably to a tense climax that renders this novel a true page-turner. Undoubtedly the best novel I have read in a long time."
Author, Roderick Craig Low

"... a delightful eye opener and a rather poignant book that everyone everywhere should put on their 'must-read' lists."
Readers' Favorite

"A dynamic and heartwarming tale of young love, giving testament to those who struggled so we can live in an integrated society."
Author, Rachelle Ayala

"Overall Have No Shame is a stunningly impactful read."
Rabid Reader Reviews

PRAISE for *Traces of Kara*

"TRACES OF KARA is psychological suspense at its best, weaving a tight-knit plot, unrelenting action, and tense moments that don't let up, and ending in a fiery, unpredictable revelation."
Midwest Book Review

"What sets Melissa Foster apart are her compelling characters who you care about...desperately. This is psychological suspense at its most chilling. I dare you to read the first chapter and not be hooked."
International Bestselling Author, M.J. Rose

"[TRACES OF KARA] Hannibal Lector, Freddie Kruger and the Tami Hoag villains combined with the emotional bond of Jody Picoult, Jane Fitch, and Steel Magnolia."
Author, Rachelle Ayala

"TRACES OF KARA is a twisted, eerily atmospheric tale with an ending that will shock you."
Author, Barbara Taylor Sissel

"TRACES OF KARA is a thriller that offers the readers unexpected twists and turns as one page follows another [and] will keep readers absorbed throughout its pages."
Readers' Favorite

"TRACES OF KARA is a minute by minute thriller...[it] will test your bravery, loyalty and make you want to hug your own family."
Stephanie, Beauty Brite Blog

"TRACES OF KARA is a tense and engrossing read."
IndieReader

PRAISE for *Megan's Way*

"A wonderful, warm, and thought-provoking story...a deep and moving book that speaks to men as well as women, and I urge you all to put it on your reading list."
Mensa Bulletin

"MEGAN'S WAY is a fine and fascinating read that many will find hope in."
Midwest Book Review

PRAISE for *Chasing Amanda*

"CHASING AMANDA – the MUST READ THRILLER OF 2011. Intelligent, entrancing, luminous."
Author, Dean Mayes

"Secrets make this tale outstanding."
Hagerstown Magazine

PRAISE for *Come Back To Me*

"COME BACK TO ME is a hauntingly beautiful love story set against the backdrop of betrayal in a broken world."
Bestselling Author, Sue Harrison

"COME BACK TO ME is passionate, romantic, and moving. A vivid story of loss and hope—a fine read for a wide audience."
Midwest Book Review

LITERARY AWARDS

Megan's Way

Beach Book Award

Readers' Favorite Award

New England Book Festival, *Honorable Mention*

Next Generation Indie Book Award, *Finalist*

Chasing Amanda

Dan Poynter's Global EBook Awards

Readers' Favorite Award (2 categories), *Finalist*

Come Back To Me

Next Generation Indie Book Awards, *Finalist*

Readers' Favorite Award, *Finalist*

Kindle Book Review Best Indie Books Award, *Finalist*

Dan Poynter's Global EBook Awards, *Finalist*

Author's Note

Some stories just beg to be written, and Alison and Jackson's story, *Have No Shame,* is one of those stories. I could not turn away from their voices if I had wanted to. I know there is ugliness in this beautiful world of ours, and for that reason, I feel that stories such as this one are so very important to be told.

I was lucky enough to be brought up by a woman who believes that love knows no boundaries, and I try to raise my children with the same conviction. In this very short life we live, we are lucky to find true love, and my hope is that society will accept—and even strive for—happiness for all, regardless of color, sexual orientation, or religious beliefs.

I hope you enjoy *Have No Shame*, and I thank you for picking it up.

Melissa Foster

Attention Readers

Choose Your Reading Format

You will notice that this book is presented in two formats: With Southern Dialect in Narrative, and Without Southern Dialect in Narrative. After querying over 400 readers about their reading preferences, and receiving an overwhelming response, it became apparent that readers are very passionate about their reading preferences, and in this ever-changing world of ours, we are lucky enough to be able to give readers what they want. Therefore, you may choose which version you'd like to read. Both versions are included in this paperback.

For everyone who has ever been touched by the harshness of society, and for my mother, for teaching me that the heart is color-blind, just as it should be.

Chapter One

It was the end of winter 1967, my father was preparin' the fields for plantin', the Vietnam War was in full swing, and spring was peekin' its pretty head around the corner. The cypress trees stood tall and bare, like sentinels watchin' over the St. Francis River. The bugs arrived early, thick and hungry, circlin' my head like it was a big juicy vein as I walked across the rocks toward the water.

My legs pled with me to jump from rock to rock, like I used to do with my older sister, Maggie, who's now away at college. I hummed my new favorite song, *Penny Lane*, and continued walkin' instead of jumpin' because that's what's expected of me. I could just hear Daddy admonishin' me, "You're eighteen now, a grown up. Grown ups don't jump across rocks." Even if no one's watchin' me at the moment, I wouldn't want to disappoint Daddy. If Maggie were here, she'd jump. She might even get me to jump. But alone? No way.

The river usually smelled of sulfur and fish, with an underlyin' hint of desperation, but today it smelled like somethin' else all together. The rancid smell hit me like an invisible billow of smog. I covered my mouth and turned away, walkin' a little faster. I tried to get around the stench, thinkin' it was a dead animal carcass hidin' beneath the rocks. I couldn't outrun the smell, and before I knew it I was crouched five feet above the river on an outcroppin' of rocks, and my hummin' was replaced by retchin' and dry heavin' as the stench infiltrated my throat. I peered over the edge and fear singed my nerves like thousands of needles pokin' me all at once. Floatin' beneath me was the bloated and badly beaten body of a colored man. A scream escaped my lips. I stumbled backward and fell to my knees. My entire body began to shake. I covered my mouth to keep from throwin' up. I knew I should turn away, run, get help, but I could not go back the way I'd come. I was paralyzed with fear, and yet, I was strangely drawn to the bloated and ghastly figure.

I stood back up, then stumbled in my gray midi-skirt and saddle shoes as I made my way over the rocks and toward the riverbank. The silt-laden river was still beneath the floatin' body. A branch stretched across the river like a boney finger, snaggin' the bruised and beaten body by the torn trousers that clung to its waist. His bare chest and arms were so bloated that it looked as if they might pop. Tremblin' and gaspin' for breath, I lowered myself to the ground, warm tears streamin' down my cheeks.

While fear sucked my breath away, an underlyin' curiosity poked its way through to my consciousness. I covered my eyes then, tellin' myself to look away. The reality that I was seein' a dead man settled into my bones like ice. Shivers rattled my body. Whose father, brother, uncle, or friend was this man? I opened my eyes again and looked at him. *It's a him*, I told myself. I didn't want to see him as just an anonymous, dead colored man. He was someone, and he mattered. My heart pounded against my ribcage with an insistence—I needed to know who he was. I'd never seen a dead man before, and even though I could barely breathe, even though I could feel his image imprintin' into my brain, I would not look away. I wanted to know who had beaten him, and why. I wanted to tell his family I was sorry for their loss.

An uncontrollable urgency brought me to my feet and drew me closer, on rubber legs, to where I could see what was left of his face. A gruesome mass of flesh protruded from his mouth. His tongue had bloated and completely filled the openin', like a flesh-sock had been stuffed in the hole, stretchin' his lips until they tore and the raw pulp poked out. Chunks of skin were torn or bitten away from his eyes.

I don't know how long I stood there, my legs quakin', unable to speak or turn back the way I had come. I don't know how I got home that night, or what I said to anyone along the way. What I do know is that hearin' of a colored man's death was bad enough—I'd heard the rumors of whites beatin' colored men to death before—but actually seein' the man who had died, and witnessin' the awful remains of the beatin', now that terrified me to my core. A feelin' of shame bubbled within me. For the first time ever, I was embarrassed to be white, because in Forrest Town, Arkansas, you could be fairly certain it was my people who were the cause of his death. And as a young southern woman, I knew that the expectation was for me to get married, have children, and perpetuate the hate that had been bred in our lives. My children, they'd be born into the same hateful society. That realization brought me to my knees.

Chapter Two

It had been a few days since that awful night at the river, and I couldn't shake the image from my mind; the disfigured body lyin' in the water like yesterday's trash. At the time, I didn't recognize Byron Bingham. I only knew the middle-aged colored man from town gossip, as *that man whose wife was sleepin' with Billy Carlisle.* Daddy told me who he was after the police pulled him from the river. I know now that the purple, black, and red bruises that covered his skin were not caused from the beatin' alone, but rather by the seven days he'd spent dead in the river. I tried to talk to my boyfriend, Jimmy Lee, about the shame I'd carried ever since findin' that poor man's body, but Jimmy Lee believed he probably deserved whatever he got, so I swallowed the words. I wanted to share, but the feelin's still burned inside me like a growin' fire I couldn't control. It didn't help that some folks looked at me like I'd done somethin' bad by findin' Mr. Bingham. Even with those sneers reelin' around me, I couldn't help but want to see his family. I wanted to be part of their world, to bear witness to what was left behind in the wake of his terrible death, and to somehow connect with them, help them through the pain. Were they okay? How could they be?

I walked all the way to Division Street, the large two-story homes with shiny Buicks and Chevy Impalas out front fell away behind me. A rusty, red and white Ford Ranch Wagon turned down Division Street. There I stood, lookin' down the street that divided the colored side of town from the white side. Even the trees seemed to sag and sway, appearin' less vital than those in town. A chill ran up my back. *Don't go near those colored streets,* Daddy had warned me. *Those people will rape you faster than you can say chicken scratch.* I dried my sweaty palms on my pencil skirt as I craned my head, though I had no real idea what I was lookin' for. The desolate street stretched out before me, like the road itself felt the loss of Mr. Bingham. Small, wooden houses lined the dirt road like secondhand clothes, used and tattered. How had I never before noticed the loneliness of Division Street? Two young children were sittin' near the front porch of a small, clapboard house, just a few houses away from where I stood. My heart ached to move forward, crouch down right beside them, and see what they were doin'. Two women, who looked to be about my mama's age, stood in the gravel driveway. One held a big bowl of somethin'—beans, maybe? She lifted pieces of whatever it was, broke them, then put them back in the bowl. I wondered what it might be like to help them in the kitchen, bake somethin' delicious, and watch those little childrens' eyes light up at a perfect corn muffin. The short, plump woman had a dark wrap around her hair. The other one, a tiny flick of a woman with a stylish press and curl hairdo, looked in my direction. Our eyes met, then she shifted her head from side to side, as if she were afraid someone might jump out and yell at her for lookin' at me. I felt my cheeks tighten as a tentative smile spread across my lips. My fingertips lifted at my sides in a slight wave. She turned away quickly and crossed her arms. The air between me and those women who I wanted to know, thickened.

I felt stupid standin' there, wantin' to go down and talk to them, to see what the children were playin'. I wondered, did they know Mr. Bingham? Had his death impacted their lives? I wanted to apologize for what had happened, even though I had no idea how or why it had. I realized that the colored side of town had been almost invisible to me, save for understandin' that I was forbidden to go there. Those families had also been invisible to me. My cheeks burned as my feelin's of stupidity turned to shame.

A child's cackle split the silence. His laughter was infectious. I couldn't remember the last time I'd heard uninhibited giggles like that. It made me smile. I bit my lower lip, feelin' caught between what I'd been taught and the pull of my heart.

A Buick ambled by, slowin' as it passed behind me. I startled, rememberin' *my place*, as Daddy called it. Daddy'd keep me right by his side if he could. He didn't like me to be around anyone he didn't know, said he couldn't take care of me if he didn't know where I was. I turned and headed back toward town, like I'd just stopped for a moment durin' a walk. The elderly white man drivin' the shiny, black car squinted at me, furrowed his brow, and then drove on.

I wondered what my daddy might think if he saw me gazin' down Division Street, where his farmhands lived. Daddy's farmhands, black men of all ages, were strong and responsible, and they worked in our fields and gardens with such vigorous commitment that it was as though the food and cotton were for their own personal use. Some of those dedicated men had worked for Daddy for years; others were new to the farm. I realized, surprisin'ly, that I'd never spoken to any one of them.

A long block later, I heard Jimmy Lee's old, red pick-up truck comin' up the road behind me. The town was so small, that I could hear it from a mile away with its loud, rumblin' engine. I wondered if someone had spotted me starin' down Division Street and told him to come collect me. He stopped the truck beside me and flung open the door, flashin' his big baby-blues beneath his wavy, brown hair. Jimmy Lee was growin' his hair out from his Elvis cut to somethin' more akin to Ringo Starr, and it was stuck in that in-between stage of lookin' like a mop. I liked anything that had to do with Ringo, so he was even more appealin' to me with his hair fallin' in his face.

"Alison, c'mon."

"Hey," I said, as I climbed onto the vinyl bench seat. He reached over and put his arm around me, pullin' me closer to him. I snuggled right into the strength of him. It was hard to believe we'd been datin' for two years. We'd met after church one Sunday mornin'. I used to wonder if Mama or Daddy had set it up that way, like a blind date, but there's no proof of that. Jimmy Lee's daddy, Jack Carlisle, was talkin' to my mama and daddy at the time, so we just started talkin' too. Jimmy Lee was the older, handsome guy that every girl had her eye on, and I was the lucky one he chose as his own. I'd been datin' Jimmy Lee since I was sixteen. He was handsome, I had to give him that, but ever since findin' Mr. Bingham, some of the things he'd done and said made my skin crawl. Others thought he was the perfect suitor for me. I wondered if that, along with my daddy's approval, was enough to make me swallow these new, uncomfortable feelin's that wrapped themselves like tentacles around every nerve in my body, and marry him.

I twisted the ring on my finger; Jimmy Lee's grandmother's engagement ring. In eight short weeks we'd be married and I'd no longer be Alison Tillman. I'd become Mrs. James Lee Carlisle. My heart ached with the thought.

The afternoon moved swiftly into a lazy and cool evenin'. I was still thinkin' about the women I'd seen on Division Street when we stopped at the store for a few six-packs of beer. Jimmy Lee's favorite past time. Like so many other evenin's, we met up with my brother Jake and Jimmy Lee's best friend, Corky Talms, in the alley behind the General Store. I think everyone in town knew we hung out here, but no one ever bothered us. The alley was so narrow that there was only a foot or two of road between the right side of Jimmy Lee's truck and a stack of empty, cardboard delivery boxes, boastin' familiar names like Schlitz, Tab, and Fanta, lined up along the brick wall beside the back door of the store. On the other side of his truck, just inches from the driver's side door, a dumpster stood open, waftin' the stench of stale food into the air. Just beyond that was a small strip of grass, where Jake and Corky now sat. And behind them were the deep, dark woods that separated the nicer part of town from the poor.

I sat on the hood of Jimmy Lee's truck, and watched him take another swig of his beer. His square jaw tilted back, exposin' his powerful neck and broad chest. The familiar desire to kiss him rose within me as I watched his Adam's apple bounce up and down with each gulp.

Jimmy Lee smacked his lips as he lowered the beer bottle to rest on his Levi's. His eyes were as blue as the sea, and they jetted around the group. I recognized that hungry look. Jimmy Lee had to behave when he was away at college, for fear of his uncle pullin' his tuition, which I knew he could afford without much trouble. Jack Carlisle was a farmer and owned 350 acres, but his brother Billy owned the only furniture store in Forrest Town, Arkansas, and was one of the wealthiest men in town. Jimmy Lee might have been king of Central High, but now he was a small fish in a big pond at Mississippi State. The bullish tactics that had worked in Forrest Town would likely get him hurt in Mississippi, and Billy Carlisle wasn't about to be humiliated by his nephew. Jimmy Lee was set to become the manager in his uncle's store, if he behaved and actually graduated. I was pretty sure that he'd behave while he was away at college and make it to graduation, but I rued those long weekends when he returned home, itchin' for trouble.

"Jimmy Lee, why don't we take a walk?" I suggested, though I didn't much feel like takin' a walk with Jimmy Lee. I never knew who we'd see or how he'd react.

He wrapped his arm around my shoulders and pulled me close. "How's my pretty little wife-to-be?" He kissed my cheek and offered me a sip of his beer, which I declined, too nervous to drink. I felt safe within his arms, but those colored boys were out there, and my nerves were tremblin' just thinkin' about what Jimmy Lee might do. I took my hands and placed them on his cheeks, forcin' his eyes to meet mine. Love lingered in his eyes, clear and bright, and I hoped it was enough of a pull to keep him from seekin' out trouble. Jimmy Lee was known for chasin' down colored boys when he thought they were up to no good, and I was realizin' that maybe he just liked doin' it. Maybe they weren't always up to no good. Ever since findin' Mr. Bingham's body, I noticed, and was more sensitive to, the ugliness of his actions.

I took inventory of the others. My brother Jake sat on the ground fiddlin' with his shoelace. His golden hair, the pale-blond color of dried cornhusks, just like mine, though much thicker, was combed away from his high forehead, revealin' his too-young-for-a-nineteen-year-old, baby face. Jake seemed content to just sit on the grass and drink beer. He had spent the last year tryin' to measure up to our older sister's impeccable grades. While Jake remained in town after high school, attendin' Central Community College, Maggie, with her stellar grades and bigger-than-life personality, begged and pleaded until she convinced our father to send her to Marymount Manhattan College.

I wished more than ever that Maggie were home just then. We'd take a walk to the river like we used to, just the two of us, climb up to the loft in the barn, and giggle until Mama called us inside. We'd do anything other than sittin' around watchin' Jimmy Lee blow smoke rings and think about startin' trouble.

Corky cleared his throat, callin' my thoughts away from my sister. He looked up at me, thick tufts of dark hair bobbin' like springs atop his head as he nodded. I bristled at the schemin' look in his brown eyes. He smirked in that cocky way that was so familiar that it was almost borin'. With muscles that threatened to burst through every t-shirt he owned, one would think he'd be as abrasive as sandpaper, but he was the quiet type—'til somethin' or someone shook his reins. He came from a typical Forrest Town farm family. His father was a farmer, like mine, but unlike Daddy, who saw some value in education, Corky's father believed his son's sole purpose was to work the farm. Everyone in town knew that when Corky's daddy grew too old to farm, he would take over. Corky accepted his lot in life with a sense of proud entitlement. He saw no need for schoolin' when a job was so readily provided for him. I swear Corky was more machine than man. He worked from dawn 'til dusk on the farm, and still had the energy to show up here smellin' like DDT, or hay, or lumber, or whatever they happen to be plantin' or harvestin' at the time, and stir up trouble with Jimmy Lee.

Corky took a long pull of his beer, eyein' Jimmy Lee with a conspiratorial grin.

I tugged Jimmy Lee's arm again, hopin' he'd choose a walk with me over trouble with Corky, but I knew I was no match for a willin' participant in his devious shenanigans. Jimmy Lee shrugged me off and locked eyes with Corky. Tucked in the alley behind the General Store, trouble could be found fifty feet in any direction. I bent forward and peered around the side of the old, wooden buildin'. At ten o'clock at night, the streets were dark, but not too dark to notice the colored boys across the street walkin' at a fast pace with their heads down, hands shoved deep in their pockets. I recognized one of the boys from Daddy's farm. *Please don't let Jimmy Lee see them.* It was a futile hope, but I hoped just the same.

Jimmy Lee stretched. I craned my neck to look up at my handsome giant. Maggie called me Pixie. Although she and Jake both got Daddy's genes when it came to height, I stopped growin' at thirteen years old. While bein' five foot two has minor advantages, like bein' called a sweet nickname by my sister, I often felt like, and was treated as if, I were younger than my age.

Jimmy Lee set his beer down on the ground and wiped his hands on his jeans. "What're those cotton pickers doin' in town this late?" He smirked, shootin' a nod at Corky.

"Jimmy Lee, don't," I pleaded, feelin' kinda sick at the notion that he might go after those boys.

"Don't? Whaddaya mean, don't? This is what we do." He looked at Corky and nodded.

"It's just…" I turned away, then gathered the courage to say what was naggin' to be said. "It's just that, after findin' Mr. Bingham's body…it's just not right, Jimmy Lee. Leave those boys alone."

Jimmy Lee narrowed his eyes, put his arms on either side of me, and leaned into me. He kissed my forehead and ran his finger along my chin. "You let me worry about keepin' the streets safe, and I'll let you worry about—" he laughed. "Heck, worry about somethin' else, I don't know."

Corky tossed his empty bottle into the grass and was on his feet, pumpin' his fists. My heartbeat sped up.

"Jimmy Lee, please, just let 'em be," I begged. When he didn't react, I tried another tactic and batted my eyelashes, pulled him close, and whispered in his ear, "Let's go somewhere, just you and me." I hated myself for usin' my body as a negotiation point.

Jimmy Lee pulled away and I saw a momentary flash of consideration pass in his eyes. Then Corky slapped him on the back and that flash of consideration was gone, replaced with a darkness, a narrowin' of his eyes that spoke too loudly of hate.

"Let's get 'em," Corky said. The sleeves of his white t-shirt strained across his massive biceps. The five inches Jimmy Lee had on him seemed to disappear given the sheer volume of space Corky's body took up. He was as thick and strong as a bull.

I jumped off the hood of the truck. "Jimmy Lee, you leave those boys alone." I was surprised by my own vehemence. This was the stuff he did all the time, it wasn't new. I was used to him scarin' and beatin' on the colored boys in our area. It was somethin' that just *was*. But at that moment, all I could see in my mind was poor Byron Bingham.

Jimmy Lee looked at me for one beat too long. I thought I had him, that he'd give in and choose me over the fight. One second later, he turned to Jake and clapped his hands. "Let's go, Jake. We've got some manners to teach those boys."

"Don't, Jake," I begged. "Please, leave them alone!"

Jake looked nervously from me to Jimmy Lee. I knew he was decidin' if it was safer to side with me, which would lead to instant ridicule by Jimmy Lee, but would keep him out of a fight, or side with Jimmy Lee, which would not only put him in Jimmy Lee's favor, but also make his actions on par with our father's beliefs. He'd happily fight for a few bonus points with Daddy to balance out his poor grades.

My hands trembled at the thought of those innocent boys bein' hurt. "Jake, please," I pleaded. "Don't. Jimmy Lee—"

They were off, all three of them, stalkin' their prey, movin' swiftly out from behind the General Store and down the center of the empty street. Their eyes trained on the two boys. Jimmy Lee walked at a fast clip, clenchin' and unclenchin' his fists, his shoulders rounded forward like a bull readyin' to charge.

I ran behind him, kickin' dirt up beneath my feet, beggin' him to stop. I screamed and pleaded until my throat was raw and my voice a tiny, frayed thread. The colored boys ran swift as deer, down an alley and toward the fields that ran parallel to Division Street, stealin' quick, fear-filled glances over their shoulders—glances that cried out in desperation and left me feelin' helpless and even culpable of what was yet to come.

Jimmy Lee, Jake, and Corky closed in on them like a sudden storm in the middle of the field. The grass swallowed their feet as they surrounded the boys like farmers herdin' their flock.

"Get that son of a bitch!" Jimmy Lee commanded, pointin' to the smaller of the two boys, Daddy's farmhand. The whites of his eyes shone bright as lightnin' against his charcoal skin.

Corky hooted and hollered into the night, "Yeeha! Let's play, boys!"

Bile rose in my throat at the thought of what I knew Jimmy Lee would do to them, and I couldn't help but wonder if he might take it as far as killin' those boys—if even by accident. I stood in the field, shakin' and cryin', then fell to my knees thirty feet from where they were, beggin' Jimmy Lee not to hurt them. Images of Mr. Bingham's bloated and beaten body, his tongue swollen beyond recognition, seared like fire into my mind.

Jimmy Lee moved in on the tremblin' boy. I was riveted to the coldness in his eyes. "No!" I screamed into the darkness. Jimmy Lee threw a glance my way, a scowl on his face. The smack of Jimmy Lee's fist against the boy's face brought me to my feet. When the boy cried out, agony filled my veins. I stumbled and ran as fast and hard as I could, and didn't stop until I was safely around the side of the General Store, hidden from the shame of what they were doin', hidden from the eyes that might find me in the night. There was no hidin' from the guilt, shame, and disgust that followed me like a shadow. I sank to my knees and cried for those boys, for Mr. Bingham, and for the loss of my love for Jimmy Lee.

Chapter Three

Every mornin' began the same way. Before sunrise, Daddy would creep downstairs, listen to the weather on the radio, and walk softly into the kitchen. I'd lay in my bed, listenin' to his mornin' noises—the refrigerator door openin' and closin', a mug drawn from the cabinet, the sink water runnin', the kettle settlin' on the stove—and then, I'd roll over and fall back to sleep feelin' the safety of his familiar rituals.

Mama and I were in the kitchen when Daddy came in from the fields. I swear he has a sixth sense, because every mornin' he came inside just as breakfast was bein' prepared. It wasn't until years later that I learned that Daddy watched the sun, and when it had risen to just above the roof, he'd know it was time for breakfast. Today he patted my head, as he'd done every mornin' for as far back as I could remember, and though I was too old to be patted, his touch brought comfort.

"Good mornin', Pix," he said. His tired eyes lit up at the smell of the warm eggs and hot, buttered biscuits. The deep lines that etched his forehead softened as he reached out and gently touched the small of Mama's back, and whispered in her ear. She turned to face him, her eyes wide. Her hand flew to her gapin' mouth. All of the color drained from Mama's face.

"Mornin' Daddy," I said, watchin' Mama press her lips into a tight line and rub her neck. I knew better than to ask for specific details of whatever they were wrestlin' with, so I kept my question light; the kind of question Daddy didn't mind answerin'. "Is everything okay?"

"Sure is," he said. He washed his hands, then sat down at the table.

Mama set our plates on the table then wiped her hands on a dishcloth, removed the apron from her waist, and set it on the counter. Her fingers remained clenched around the fabric. She didn't make a sound. She just stood there, one hand on the crumpled apron, the other coverin' her eyes.

"Mama, aren't you gonna eat?" I asked. I glanced out the window. Jake's bicycle was already gone. He had class in an hour, and it was a long ride to school.

"Eat up, Pixie," Daddy said.

Mama was a quiet woman who rarely let her opinions be known, and I was used to Daddy speakin' in her place. I picked up my fork and swallowed my questions.

"Is Jake at class?" I asked, just to break the silence.

My father nodded, and shoved his third biscuit into his mouth, chewin' fast. "He's comin' back early. We're down one hand today. Some dumb boy got himself beat up."

I put my fork down as my stomach lurched and twisted. "Who?" The smell of the river came back to me like a bad dream.

"I dunno. One of them coloreds."

I set my napkin on the table and stared at him. "You don't know who it is, but you know he's missin'?"

My father glared at me. "Alison, know your place young lady." He took a sip of his coffee. The tension in his cheeks softened. He reached out and patted my hand. "Sorry, Pix. Albert Johns, if you must know. Why are you so interested?"

Albert Johns. I repeated his name over and over in my mind. I could no longer listen to Daddy refer to the coloreds in town, or the ones who worked for him, as "them coloreds." I'd been ignorin' how Daddy'd spoken of them forever, as if they were invisible. But now, havin' come face to face with a dead colored man, a man who I was sure had died at the hands of a white man, I could no longer pretend they didn't matter. They were people. They had names, and families, and feelin's, and thoughts.

I looked down. I'd overstepped that thin, gray line Daddy saw so clearly. "I'm just...it's just...after what happened to Mr. Bingham, I just wanted to know his name."

My father set down his fork and wiped his mouth with a napkin. I could feel Mama's eyes on me from behind. "The boy isn't dead, Pix, he's beat up. Probably did somethin' to deserve it."

"Yes, sir," I mumbled. "May I please be excused? I need to get ready to go to the library before Mama and I start bakin' for the day."

Daddy nodded. "Sure, Pix. Come over here and give your daddy a hug."

"I'll drive you in today, Alison." Mama's eyes were dark and serious.

"Okay," I said, thankful that she'd saved me from what was sure to be an uncomfortable ride with Daddy—me holdin' in my new feelin's about the coloreds and him tryin' to talk to me about marryin' a boy I wasn't sure I wanted to be marryin'. I wrapped my arms around Daddy's neck. His earthy smell warmed me, his whiskers tickled my cheek.

"Are you sure, Hil?" Daddy only called Mama by her full name when they were in contention, which wasn't often. She was always Hil, not Hillary. Her features softened as he spoke.

She nodded. "I have to go into town for some sugar anyway. I'm makin' a cake for tonight's Blue Bonnet meetin' so we need more. Go get ready, Alison, and don't forget your sweater. It's gettin' chilly."

Mama drove faster than her usual careful pace, her left elbow rested on the open window, her fingers pressed firmly against her forehead. You'd think a small-framed blonde might look out of place drivin' a beat up, old, pick-up truck. I always thought she made Daddy's truck look better. Mama didn't need to drive an expensive car to get noticed. People were drawn to her natural beauty. When it was warm out, she'd whip a scarf around the front of her hair, and tie it under the back, the scarf trailin' down her back. The end result looked perfectly planned. Today her waves blew free.

She hadn't said a word since we'd left home, and as we neared town I asked her if she was okay.

"Mm-hmm," she answered, then forced a smile. "I'm fixin' to stop at the drugstore first."

As I wandered through the drugstore door behind Mama, I caught a whiff of Mr. Shire's familiar aftershave. Ever since I was little, he'd worn Old Spice, a fragrance Daddy said smelled like a waste of good money. I loved the peppery-vanilla and warmed-wood smell. "Are you ready for your weddin', Alison?" he asked. Mr. Shire reminded me of any generic grandfather; a sweet, gray-haired man who tsked at the ways of youth *these days*.

"Yes, sir, almost. I'm wearin' Mama's weddin' dress, and the church is all set. We just have to coordinate who's makin' what for the reception. Thank you for askin'." Thoughts of the weddin' left an acrid taste in my mouth. I glanced at Mama as she shopped and contemplated talkin' to her about my misgivin's about Jimmy Lee, but I wasn't sure she'd understand. My own father talked about his farmhands as though they were a commodity, not individual people, and she was married to him. I decided I'd better hold my tongue for a while.

Mama returned to the counter with an armful of bandages, bottles of antiseptic, and medicated creams. She quickly slipped down the condiments aisle and returned with a bag of sugar.

"What's all that for?" I asked.

She looked at me, then at Mr. Shire. "Oh, just stockin' up. You can never be sure when you'll need first aid items."

We made one more stop on the way to the library that mornin'. She pulled up behind the furniture store and told me to wait in the car.

Seconds later she was up the back steps, carryin' the bags she'd just purchased. She knocked on the door, her back to me. A colored woman opened the door and peeked out. Mama shoved the bag into her arms, lookin' behind her as she did so. The woman pushed the package back at Mama, shakin' her head. Mama pushed it back into the woman's arms. *What was she doin'?* If Daddy knew that she used our money to buy things for a colored family, he'd...I don't know what he'd do, but I wouldn't want to be anywhere near the house when he found out.

The woman nodded fast and hard. Mama took the woman's hand in her own and leaned in close, sayin' somethin' that I couldn't hear. The colored woman looked down, hugged the bag to her chest, and nodded.

When Mama came back to the truck, I stared straight ahead. I wanted to ask her who that was, and why she'd given her the bag of first aid supplies, but I couldn't find the right words without soundin' disrespectful. I had so many questions racin' through my mind. *How often did she come here? Does Daddy know? How long has she known that woman? What other colored people does she know? Were they friends?* I turned to face Mama, gatherin' the courage to ask.

She stared straight ahead as she drove away from the store, and said, without lookin' at me, "Your father is never to know about this. You hear me, Alison Jean? Never."

Pride swelled within me. Mama had trusted me with a dangerous secret. "Yes, ma'am." Maybe I could talk to her about Jimmy Lee after all. I learned more about Mama in that five-minute stop at the furniture store than I had in my entire eighteen years of livin' in her house.

She reached out and touched my leg, her eyes focused on the road. "Good girl," she said.

Chapter Four

I sat on the deep front porch mullin' over my conflictin' feelin's, tryin' to enjoy the sunshine and the gentle breeze, but the air carried with it whispers of the colored boys' cries for help. I rocked, tellin' myself to think of somethin' else, but the porch creaked, remindin' me of the way I impotently pleaded for Jimmy Lee to take me instead of hurtin' those boys. I covered my ears, wishin' the memories away. Shame warmed my cheeks. What would Daddy think of me?

The sound of tires on dirt and gravel brought my eyes to Jimmy Lee's truck pullin' into the driveway. Somethin' I wasn't used to rose within me. At first, it was like I'd eaten somethin' bad and it was stuck in my throat, pushin' its way out, but then, it melted to a heat that filled my chest and spread to my limbs.

Jimmy Lee stepped from his truck, swaggerin' all tall and handsome across the front walk and up the steps. He wrapped his arms around me, kissed my head. "Hey there, beautiful. How's my girl?"

There it was—the sweet that evened out his sour. I stood in his arms, against the chest that was so familiar. I felt safe, and I breathed him in.

"Ready to go to town?" he asked.

We held hands as we walked to the truck. Jimmy Lee's hand engulfed mine, like Daddy's did. Daddy's hand was calloused from workin' in the fields. Jimmy Lee's was tainted with the blood of those boys. *Daddy would never beat up anyone.* I dropped Jimmy Lee's hand and climbed into his truck, happy to be free from the memory of the fields. "As long as we stay away from the old high school crowd. I swear, ever since I found Mr. Bingham's body, they act like I'm the one who did somethin' wrong." Jimmy Lee didn't say anything, but he patted my leg as if to say, *It's okay. I'm here.* We used to talk more, and I wanted that now. I needed it. I needed to feel his comfort and love, and try to wipe away the darkness that was creepin' into my heart.

"Remember last June, before graduation? How my friends stopped hangin' out with me? I was the odd girl out because of datin' someone older? I was the literal third wheel that got kicked to the curb," I admitted, sadly.

He drew his eyebrows together and I watched tension darken his eyes. Then his gaze lightened and he said, "I remember. It's worth it though, right? You didn't need to go anywhere with them. You had me."

"Yeah," I said. "But now, it's happenin' all over again. It's as if by findin' Mr. Bingham's body, I carry some sort of bad luck. I never knew bad luck could be contagious, but others seem to think so." Jimmy Lee turned on the radio, and I continued, "Do you remember a few years back, when the Holsten's farm flooded? The neighbors helped them through, but after that year, when the next crop season began, everyone disassociated with them. I'm beginnin' to wonder about the strange relationships that our small town is made up of, and it scares me."

Jimmy Lee didn't respond. He tapped his hand on the steerin' wheel to the beat of the music. I tried again to bridge the gap between us, to gain his understandin'.

"I feel like findin' Mr. Bingham is like that—like I'm bad luck and that's why they're shunnin' me now. I saw Sheila Porten at the store the other day and she didn't even say hello to me. We graduated together! Do you think they somehow blame me for findin' him?"

He stopped tappin' the steerin' wheel and cast his winnin' smile upon me; his white teeth beamin' like pearls, a sparkle in his eye. "Nah, they're just jealous that they didn't find 'im."

"You're such a jerk, Jimmy Lee. That's just awful. Who would want to see that?"

"A dead nigger? Most of the town," he laughed. His eyes danced with delight at the nastiness of his own comment.

I clenched my teeth against the unfamiliar venom that wanted to spew, and leaned against the door. In silence, we drove out to the river in the next county, which we'd done often enough for me to know what he had in mind. He had to return to school the next day, and the last thing I wanted was to be intimate with him again before he left. Sometimes I regretted givin' into him the first time. Oh, I can't blame him for that. I wanted to do it just as badly as he did. He was everything I had dreamed of, strong and decisive like Daddy, and on a successful enough career track that I knew Daddy would be pleased. I just wish I had understood then what I understand now. Somehow, and I'm not sure why, sex complicated things. Sex was no longer somethin' that we fought the urge for. Now it was expected.

Jimmy Lee reached over and grabbed my hand, a lusty look in his eyes. He hadn't started drinkin' yet, and he was always kinder when he was sober. I liked his gentler side and felt my heart softenin' toward him.

"Soon, we won't have to sneak away to the river to be alone," he said with a grin.

I feigned a smile, then turned and looked out the window, watchin' the town fall away. I wish I had talked to Mama about my feelin's. I was battlin' myself, wantin' to be with him and not wantin' to at the same time. I wish I understood what was goin' on inside my crazy heart.

The wind blew the tips of the long grass this way and that, the smell of manure from nearby fields hovered in the air. Leaves rustled in the trees as we walked toward the water. Jimmy Lee carried a blanket under one arm and held me with the other. The smell of him rose to meet me, musk and pine, liked he'd rolled around on the forest floor. I felt a tug down low, and gritted my teeth against my growin' desire for him.

Jimmy Lee spread the blanket out below a tree and lay down, relaxin' back on one elbow. He beckoned me with his finger in a playful way. I continued toward the water.

"Can't we just walk a little first?"

"Walk?" he asked.

"Yeah, you know, one foot in front of the other? Come on." I headed down river, hopin' he'd follow. The last thing I felt like doin' was lyin' naked beneath him. I was too confused, too sickened by the way he'd viciously attacked Albert Johns, leavin' the poor boy in a field, lyin' in pain, broken ribs an' all.

Jimmy Lee came up behind me and wrapped his arms around my middle. I flushed, ashamed of how my heart fluttered at his touch.

"We don't have much time," he whispered in my ear. "I want to be with you."

It was hard to turn away from him. As much as I loathed what he'd done, I still loved him.

He took my hand and led me back to the blanket, lowerin' me to my knees. I closed my eyes, willin' myself to be in the moment. Allowin' myself to. His fingers trailed down the buttons of my blouse, unbuttonin' them one by one, then caressin' the skin beneath. Shivers ran up my chest, a collision of desire and the frigid air. He pulled my blouse down off my shoulder, kissin' each bit of skin as it was revealed. His lips were soft and tender.

"I'm cold," I complained, partly to slow him down, and partly because it was chilly kneelin' there in the breeze.

"I'll warm you," he said. The scent of him wrapped itself around me. He leaned against me, pushin' me back until I was lyin' beneath him. I could feel him pressin' against me. With one hand he reached behind his back and pulled his t-shirt over his head, his hungry eyes lookin' right into mine. His knees pushed my legs apart and I wanted to hate his touch, wanted to *want* to push him away because of what he'd done to those boys, but that hatred melted under his touch and I longed for him to be closer to me. His hand slid down my side and hiked my skirt up around my waist. He kissed my neck, sendin' a shiver down my spine. His fingers hooked my panties, drawin' them down. I hated myself for wantin' him.

A bird sang out from the tree, bringin' my brain back to the surface. The breeze on my naked chest was causin' me to shiver. I opened my eyes, listenin' to the flow of the river, the bristlin' of the leaves above us, Jimmy Lee's heavy breaths against my neck, and I began to tremble. *Byron Bingham. Albert Johns.* Thoughts tumbled like stones into my mind, knockin' me out of my reverie. I must have gone rigid, because Jimmy Lee lifted his head and looked at me with a quizzical, lust-filled gaze, like he wasn't really seein' my face, but he was lost in the frenzy of what he was doin'. I pushed at his chest.

"Stop," I whispered. My voice was lost in the image of Byron, strangled by the thought of Albert.

Jimmy Lee laughed, tugged his jeans down.

I turned away, a tear slippin' down the side of my face. "Stop," I whispered again, or maybe I just thought it in my mind.

He thrust himself inside of me, groanin', one hand clenchin' my breast, the other clamped onto my hip.

"Stop, stop." I whispered. My body shook with each poundin' thrust of his body. Anger rushed through me. I clawed at his back, screamin', "Stop! Stop!" I kicked and fought against him, and he pumped harder, faster, as if he didn't hear me.

"Almost," he said. "Al…al—"

"Stop!" I found my voice and screamed until my throat was raw, my nails stripped chunks of skin from his back.

He gave one last, long thrust then fell on top of me, pantin'. I pushed him off, cryin' and shakin' as I did so. I thought I was gonna throw up, pass out, die. I crawled away. He lay there, spent, lookin' at me with a stupid grin on his face.

I pulled my clothes on, sobbin', strugglin' to stay upright, and stumbled through the grass, toward the water. The breeze stung my skin. The birds sang out in a beautiful tune that I could not reconcile with the awful feelin' bloomin' inside me.

"What?" he called after me with his palms held up toward the sky, confusion in his spent eyes.

Hate blinded me. I wanted to go home. I wanted to run away. I wanted to find someone to beat *him* up. The grass and trees swirled around me, pointin' their branches like fingers at my guilt of knowin' what he'd done. As he climbed back into his jeans, I ran past him, clambered back into the truck, and slammed the door, sobbin'. Curled up against the door like a child, I covered my face and waited for him to get back into the truck and take me home. I smelled like him, like sex. I had never felt so powerless and alone.

On the way home, I remained huddled against the door. All I could think of was Mama, and how she'd kill me if she knew I was havin' sex with Jimmy Lee, and how Daddy might slaughter me if I told him I wasn't sure we should get married. Jimmy Lee kept lookin' over at me.

"You okay?" he asked.

I opened my mouth to answer, but all I could do was cry. How do you tell your fiancé that he makes you sick to your stomach? Anger simmered within me when he didn't ask me again, or try to figure out why I was pullin' so far away from him. I never thought Jimmy Lee would force himself upon me. He'd been rough with me before, but not like this, not like he ignored what *I* wanted. How do you tell him that the world you've lived in for eighteen years suddenly looked different, that you noticed sneers that you previously accepted as normal, or maybe that you—ashamedly—had also doled out? Jimmy Lee was hummin' to the radio, his thumbs tappin' on the steerin' wheel like he was fine and dandy, while my world was spiralin' out of control and I could barely keep my head on straight.

My father's truck was gone when we arrived home. Jimmy Lee leaned over to kiss me but I pulled back and hopped out of the truck.

"That's it? No goodbye kiss? I'm goin' back to school. Won't you miss me?" He looked so hurt, and the last thing I wanted was an argument.

"Sorry," I said, and reluctantly climbed back into the truck. I scooched across the seat and pecked his cheek.

"That's more like it," he said.

Anger bubbled up again, but this time, I found my voice. "Jimmy Lee, I asked you to stop, and…" I saw it then, a look in his eye that said it all. Not only was I wastin' his time tellin' him somethin' he didn't want to hear, but he could no better understand what I was sayin' than I could understand what he'd done to those boys. "Nevermind," I said, and slammed the door.

As I walked toward the house, I could feel my heart breakin' into a million little pieces. I couldn't bear to face Mama. I knew I'd break down in tears and have to tell her the truth. She'd surely kill Jimmy Lee if she knew he'd forced himself on me. Or had he? Had I led him on? Confusion drove me around the house to the backyard. I didn't dare look at the windows of the house, or toward the barn or the garden. I didn't want to accidentally see Mama. I ducked beneath the dryin' line hangin' from the massive oak tree in our backyard, and hurried toward the cellar doors, thinkin' about how livid Daddy would be if I backed out of the weddin'. All he ever wanted for me was to be happy, like him and Mama, and I don't think Daddy could understand how I could be anything *but* happy with Jimmy Lee.

It was time to get my feelin's in check. I pulled open the cold, metal doors and descended the stairs into the dark dirt cellar where Mama kept jugs of water, first aid kits, towels, and all sorts of canned supplies in case of tornadoes. The damp, earthy smell was cold and seemed appropriate given what I'd done. I quickly slithered out of my clothes and doused a towel in water. I scrubbed his kisses from my neck, his touch from my breasts. The water was cool, raisin' goose bumps on my arms and across my chest. The blood rushin' in my ears reminded me of his lousy, lust-filled grunts, and I cried louder, tryin' to drown them out as I spread my legs and wiped his chlorine-like scent from within the soft folds of my skin. In my mind, my fightin' him replayed over and over, and with it came more hatred, more disgust with myself. I started scrubbin' his sweat from my stomach, legs, and arms. I was pressin' too hard, deservin' of the pain, and hopin' it would wipe all the ugliness of the last few weeks away. I scrubbed 'til my skin was red and raw. By the time I'd finished, my body shook and shivered, my heart ached from loneliness, and my mind ran in circles. There was nothin' left for me to do but slip my soiled clothin' back on, sit on the cold step, and sob until I had no more tears to free.

I washed my face, bundled the dirty towels together, and took them with me to the burn barrel by the barn, where I hid them beneath the debris. I hoped it might even burn away the memories of the afternoon, the alleyway, and the field where Jimmy Lee had stolen precious moments of those boys' lives.

The barn loomed before me, a big, wooden structure almost as big as our house. I walked through the double doors; the familiar smell of hay and the sharp odor of stored wood and fuel assaulted my senses. Memories rushed in. Oh, how I wished Maggie was here to help me with the way I was feelin' about Jimmy Lee. I could almost feel her pullin' my arm toward the stall where our old cow, Hippa, used to live. Mama had painted a mother and baby cow on the wall inside of the stall. It had chipped and cracked with age, and by the time Hippa died, a few years ago, it was nearly indiscernible. I'd cried for days when Hippa died. By then Maggie was too old to be attached to a cow, I guess. She didn't cry, but when Daddy told me that it was just a fact of life on a farm, and that I should be used to it by then, Maggie took me up to the loft and held a memorial service for Hippa. Just the two of us.

Maggie went away to college while I was still in high school, and I wondered if she'd want to hang out with me anymore, or if she'd be too grown up. I longed to talk to someone about Jimmy Lee, and I had no one to turn to. Thoughts of Jimmy Lee made my stomach clench all over again. I went out the back doors of the barn and sat against one of the tractor's tires, shaded between a thick, old maple tree and the barn, out of sight from the fields and the house. I laid my head on my arms, and tried to wash away the thoughts of what I had just endured.

The calm of the breeze and the familiar sight of the newly planted rows of cotton should have filled me with ease. Instead, I grew even sadder. Nothin' felt right. The life I thought I had swirled around me with the realization that Daddy, who I treasured, was treatin' people like machines, Mama, who I believed to be honest and good, was keepin' secrets from Daddy, and my boyfriend, whose strength I used to adore, I now loathed. It was as if they all mixed together and whirred in circles, like a tornado of a mess unravelin' around me. I didn't know how to move forward. I didn't want to move back. So I remained there, stiff and confused, with no outlet other than my own tears.

"S'cuse me, Miss, are you okay?"

I jumped at the unfamiliar man's voice, and pushed to my feet. I'd never been approached by a colored man before. I was even more startled because this young man wore a military uniform. He stood so straight I thought he might salute me. My stomach tightened, my senses heightened. I fought the urge to run away.

"I'm fine, thank you." I took a step backward. *They'll rape you faster than you can say chicken scratch.* I whipped my head around. My father's truck had not yet returned. I suddenly regretted my decision to hide behind the barn.

The man removed his hat and held it against his stomach with both hands. He looked down, then up again, meetin' my eyes with a tentative, yet respectful, regard.

"I'm lookin' for a Mr. Tillman?" His uneasy gaze betrayed his confident tone.

"My father?"

"Yes, ma'am. I have a message for him."

I stood up straighter, suddenly feelin' as though I needed to exert my strength and take control of the situation, as Daddy might. "Farmhands show up at five in the mornin'. It's gotta be seven o'clock *at night* by now. What are you doin' here?"

He smiled, then shook his head. "My apologies. I'm not a farmhand, ma'am. My younger brother is Albert Johns."

Albert Johns. The night came rushin' back to me. The way Corky had egged on Jimmy Lee and Jake. *Oh, God, Jake.* What had he done? I hadn't even seen him since last night. "I...I'm sorry," I said.

"Yes, ma'am. Thank you. I came to let Mr. Tillman know that my uncle, Byron Bingham, he passed away recently, and the funeral is tomorrow. My brother Albert got beat up real bad, so he won't be here tomorrow on account of his injuries and the funeral. I wanted to come work in his place after the service, to make up for his absence."

"Your uncle?" My chest constricted. The oxygen around me slowly disappeared. I gasped for air, my heart palpitatin' so fast I thought I might pass out. I reached for the tractor, missed, and stumbled.

"Ma'am?" He rushed to my side, grabbin' my arm just before I hit the ground, and lowered me slowly to the earth.

I waited for my breathin' to calm.

"I'm sorry, ma'am. I didn't mean to—are you okay?" A flash of fear washed over him. He squinted, glancin' around to see if he'd been seen touchin' me, and backed away quickly.

The magnitude of that one act of assistance suddenly burst before me like fireworks. I understood the fear in his eyes, and it killed me to know that if someone had seen him—Daddy, Jake, or Jimmy Lee—he'd be runnin' for *his* life right now.

I nodded, unable to find my voice. Mr. Bingham's bloated face floated before me. My eyes dampened. "I'm so sorry," I whispered, unsure if I was apologizin' for what had happened to his uncle, or to his race for how his people were treated. I rubbed my arm where he'd grabbed me.

"Yes, ma'am. Thank you." He watched me with concern. "I'm sorry if I hurt you. I just didn't want you to fall."

"You didn't hurt me. I've just never been touched—I'm sorry, I've never even spoken to a colored person before." The realization of that statement sickened me. It also wasn't quite true. Once, when I was a little girl, maybe five or six, I'd seen a colored girl in the street by Woolworths. I asked her if she wanted to come in with me and get a soda pop at the counter. Mama had dragged me away. I remember cryin' because I had no idea what I'd done wrong. That was the instance that drove home the meanin' of *knowin' my place*. I'd never spoken to a colored person again—child or adult.

He dropped his eyes, noddin' his head as if he'd expected my response.

I looked behind me. If Daddy caught me I probably wouldn't be allowed out of his sight for weeks. The coloreds in town never would have spoken to me, even if I had been cryin'. They knew better. But this man who stood before me, he had a gentle confidence about him that made me want to know more about him.

"Yes, ma'am. I understand. I don't want to cause no trouble." He lifted his eyes to meet mine. "I heard a noise, and I thought you mighta been Mr. Tillman. I'm sorry to have startled you. I meant no disrespect." A friendly warmth lingered in the gentle way he spoke. He looked right into my eyes, as if he was interested in, even waitin' on, what I had to say next. There was a little liftin' of the edges of his lips, not quite a smile.

"Aren't you afraid to talk to me? You know what happens to colored men when they talk to white women, right?" I realized after I'd spoken that I'd said that because it's what was probably expected of me, not because it was somethin' that I felt.

He pursed his lips, holdin' tight to his hat. "Yes, ma'am," he said. Before I could respond he added, "I know what happens here in Forrest Town when colored men speak to white women, but that's not what happens everywhere."

I knew there had been racial riots in some of the bigger cities, even if Daddy did turn off the radio the minute I walked into the room. Kids at school had talked about civil uprisin's, but I'd never seen them, or, I suddenly realized, cared enough about them to ask for details. I lifted my eyebrows in question.

"Yes, ma'am. I serve with white men. Do you think we don't talk?"

"Men, not women," I smirked.

"No, ma'am. I've been to other states. My people talk to white women in other areas."

I was not accustomed to bein' told I was wrong by a colored man. I thought of Mama—the way she'd hidden her conversation with that woman at the furniture store, and the supplies she'd given her—and it gave me pause. Were there places where that was allowed? Why was it so wrong, anyway? I looked again for Daddy's truck, thinkin' about *why* I had to *know my place*. What had this man ever done to me?

"Does your mother work at the furniture store?" I asked, wantin' to know if he somehow knew Mama.

He cocked his head, as if he were weighin' the answer. "Yes, ma'am, her and my aunt."

"Do you know Hillary Tillman, my mama?"

"No, ma'am," he answered.

I was still mullin' over my own misgivin's about what she'd done, keepin' a secret from Daddy an' all, but I still wanted to know how Byron Bingham's family was, how Albert was feelin', and how badly he was hurt. I realized, too, that I wanted it not to be a bad thing to want to speak to this man. I measured my fear of him, not the fear that I knew I should have, but the real fear that rattled in my mind. I quickly realized that there wasn't much fear up there. The fear that did exist was driven by my father's warnin's, and overpowered by my own curiosity. My chance to get the answers to all of my naggin' questions about Mr. Bingham's and Albert's family was starin' me in the face, and I wanted to have that conversation more than I wanted anything else in the world, as long as Daddy didn't find out.

"How is he? Albert?"

He took a step toward me. I scooted backward, still sittin' on the ground.

"He's beat up real bad, but he'll be okay."

I'm sorry seemed so unsubstantial, so I remained quiet, thinkin' about that night, the fear I'd felt, and knowin' that the fear Albert Johns had felt must've been ten times worse. I took a deep breath and asked him if he knew who had beaten up his brother.

He shook his head. "He's not talkin'."

I let out a relieved sigh, and then felt guilty for wantin' to protect Jimmy Lee, Corky, and Jake after what they'd done. "What about your uncle?"

He turned away, his eyes suspiciously glassy when he turned back. His face was tighter, stronger than it had been the moment before. He stared past me, into the fields as he nodded, wringin' his hat within his hands.

"I found him, you know." The words were out of my mouth before I had a chance to stop them, and they were oddly wrapped in what sounded like pride. I cringed, wishin' I hadn't opened my mouth in the first place.

"That didn't come out right," I offered. "I mean, it was horrible."

"Yes, ma'am. I know you found him." This time his eyes locked with mine.

I came to my feet. Strangely, I wasn't afraid. At that moment, the only thing I felt was a need to talk about the things I wasn't supposed to, with someone who might also want to talk about them, and if that someone was a man I wasn't supposed to talk to, then so be it.

"Let's walk," I said.

He looked at me with curiosity, his eyes jettin' around our property. "I'm not sure that's a good idea."

"Maybe not, but I want to talk about Albert and Mr. Bingham. I want to know how your family is, and I'm afraid we can't do that here. I don't know when Daddy will be home." I straightened my skirt. The incident with Jimmy Lee all but forgotten, I pushed away the residual anger that I felt toward him and decided to deal with those awful thoughts some other time.

The young man, who looked to be a little older than Jake, didn't follow me. He put his hat on and said, "I'm sorry, ma'am, but this is Forrest Town. I'm not sure goin' off alone is the best idea."

"Afraid?" I knew it was mean to present such a dare. Maybe even dangerous. I understood what could happen to him if we were caught, and yet, selfishly, I wanted to get my answers.

He bristled, threw his shoulders back, and said, "No, ma'am." Then he looked back up the yard toward the driveway. "Maybe a little," he confessed.

"I won't tell if you won't. C'mon." I grabbed his arm, his muscles tensin' beneath my grasp. Doin' somethin' so many would see as wrong was exhilaratin'. I pulled him through the fields, through the line of trees that edged our property, to the creek that ran right through the outskirts of town. Maggie and I had spent hours there when we were young, throwin' leaves in and followin' them downstream as they drifted in the water.

We walked in nervous silence, until we could no longer see the roof of my farmhouse. I pushed away Daddy's warnin'. My excitement about talkin' with him was not hampered by fear of what might happen if we were caught. In fact, just the opposite. Elation danced within me! For once I wasn't standin' by Jimmy Lee's side, wonderin' who he'd hurt next. I didn't feel as though I had to hide my face, like I did when I ran into old friends from highschool, because I'd found a dead body. This man was fightin' for our country. He wasn't fightin' against our own men. He already knew that I'd found his uncle, and he didn't look at me like I was somehow tainted because of it.

"My name is Alison," I said as we walked by the creek.

"I'm Jackson," he answered. He walked a careful distance from me, and I appreciated the space. Each time I glanced at him, he was lookin' either down or straight ahead. He had a gentle face and full lips. Every so often, lines would form on his forehead, like he was thinkin' of somethin' important. I wondered how scared he really was, and I wondered why I wasn't.

When we reached the "Y" in the stream, where it bloomed in one direction and narrowed in the other, I leaned against a tree and watched him.

"I'm really sorry about Albert," I said.

Jackson sat down on a big rock near the water's edge. He picked up a stick and poked it in the water. "Yeah," he said, shakin' his head. A bead of perspiration spread across his brow.

"So you want to work for Daddy?"

"My family needs the money. I'm home for a week, so—" he shrugged.

I hadn't thought about him goin' back. "What's it like? The war, I mean? Vietnam?"

He turned to me and somethin' changed in his eyes. They grew darker, more serious. "It's like havin' a million guys all chasin' you at the same time, only they have guns, and so do you, so you can kill them before they kill you. And every day you realize you're damned lucky to have survived." He turned back toward the water and tossed the stick in. "As a matter of fact, it's a lot like livin' here, only here, you're not the one with the guns."

I sat down beside him. He inched away, stiffened. We sat in silence for a few minutes.

"Sorry about your uncle," I whispered. I realized how much death this man must have seen, and it sent a shiver down my spine.

"Me, too," he said. "He was a good man."

"Do you know why he was killed? I've heard rumors about his wife's—indiscretions—but in this town you never know what's true." Rumor had her sleepin' with Jimmy Lee's uncle. I had no proof of the truth of that situation, but everyone in town believed it. I leaned on my elbow, watchin' him fold and unfold his hat.

He nodded, glanced my way, then turned back toward the water.

I waited; each second drew my curiosity about him further toward the surface. I felt my cheeks flush. I was slowly becomin' more upset with Daddy, with this town, and with the way people treated one another. This was life. This was what we were given. I knew that if Daddy was here, he'd ask me who I thought I was to think things should be any different, and I wondered what Mama would say. I thought of her face when she came back to the car behind the furniture store, her eyes fastened on the road like it was a path to escape her secret. I wondered what she was thinkin' at that moment. What would happen if Daddy knew? How long had she been talkin' to that woman? What started it? Why on earth did she trust me with such a volatile secret?

"You okay?" Jackson asked.

I looked down at my hands, clenched into fists around the edge of my skirt. "Um, yeah," I said. "I'm just thinkin', that's all."

"I got way too much time to think when I'm away."

I nodded, not knowin' how to respond to his comment. "How is your aunt?" I watched him carefully, wonderin' if he'd get mad or lie to me.

"She'll be leavin' after the funeral. Run out of town." He stood and walked a few paces back toward my house, shakin' his head.

I watched each determined step, hopin' he was not goin' back. There was still so much I wanted to know. The muscles in his back constricted beneath his uniform. I hurried after him.

"I'm sorry. I shouldn't pry, I'm sorry."

He stopped walkin'. "It's not you. It's this whole thing, this town. I come back to be with my family and my uncle is dead, my brother is beaten to a pulp—"

I ached for his pain, and touched his arm out of instinct and empathy. His muscles tightened beneath my fingers. I pulled back.

"I'm sorry."

"Don't you see?" his voice rose. "You touch me and we both freeze."

I stepped back. "I'm sorry. I didn't mean anything by it."

"It shouldn't matter if you did. Don't you see that? We can't talk because our skin is different. It's crap. I have seen the other side. I've been places where I can talk to white folks. I come back here and it's like travelin' back in time. It may not be easy or perfect in other cities, but it's not—" He drew his arm wide, like he was presentin' the fields beyond where we stood. "It's not like this."

I had no idea what to say, and until that week, I wouldn't have ever agreed with him. But now, everything had changed. My feelin's about colored people had changed, and along with that came my inability to accept everything Daddy said as bein' right.

"I agree with you. It shouldn't matter."

"What?" His eyes grew wide.

"I agree with you. I mean, I'm embarrassed to say it, but I didn't used to. I was taught what everyone else 'round here was taught, that coloreds and whites don't interact—unless they're workin' for you. But I've been thinkin' about everything. You know, coloreds and whites...and it just doesn't make sense to me anymore." I turned my back to him, ashamed and angry. "Findin' your uncle changed me. I see everything differently now. When I found him, I wanted to know who his family was, and why he had to die." I didn't recognize the self-confidence in my own voice, and no matter how firmly I spoke, the words themselves surprised me. "He was a person. His family, your family—they matter."

Jackson walked toward me, each step a force of its own. I stumbled backward. He spoke through gritted teeth. "You want to know why he died? Because some white jackass wanted to sleep with my aunt, and she was too afraid to say no." His nostrils flared with anger.

He stood so close that I could feel his warm breath on my nose. His chest rose and fell, inches from mine. "You have no idea what it's like."

Time stood still. We stood like that for several minutes, listenin' to each other huff our frustrations away. Eventually he turned away, his shoulders rolled forward. I was too frightened to speak, though, strangely, I was not afraid of him. I was scared for the pain and anger that his family had endured.

"Tell me," I said quietly.

The air around us was quiet, save for the trickle of the creek and the rustlin' of leaves.

I bit my lower lip, hopin' that I wasn't pushin' him too far. "Tell me what it's like for you and your family. I want to understand."

Chapter Five

"You missed dinner." My father sat in his readin' chair by the front door watchin' David Brinkley on the evenin' news on our small black and white television. He motioned to Jake to turn it off as soon as I came in. I usually didn't notice that small shelterin' act. I was so used to it, it was like the white noise of a fan. Today it stood out like a sore thumb and I resented Daddy for the first time in my life. I heard Mama washin' dishes in the kitchen, and guilt settled around my grumblin' resentment toward Daddy for thinkin' he could keep me from knowin' what's goin' on in the world. Between the guilt and the resentment, I felt strangled, and struggled to maintain my sense of normalcy within my family.

"Yes, sir. I'm sorry. I was out for a walk." I looked down at the worn hardwood beneath my feet and concentrated on the uneven lines between the boards.

"Your mother said she didn't see you after you came back from your visit with Jimmy Lee today. Everything alright?" he asked.

I lifted my eyes and took in Daddy sittin' in his favorite upholstered chair. Daddy worked long days, and by this time of night everything looked slightly askew, from his dirty, gray t-shirt to his five o'clock shadow which grew in uneven patches of blond and brown. His hair had an indentation all the way around from the baseball cap he favored when he was out in the sun, like a halo had slipped and gotten stuck in his thick, buttery hair.

Jake turned off the television, sat back down on our plaid couch, and put an open textbook in his lap. His knuckles were black and blue. He noticed my gaze, and tucked them under his book. Workin' on a farm, Daddy and Mama wouldn't think anything about Jake's bruised knuckles. I knew better. Jake raised his eyebrows, as if he were challengin' me to reveal what he'd done. I smirked in return, contemplatin' my answers. *Yes, I met a colored man and don't understand why I shouldn't talk to him.* Or, I could go with somethin' a bit more detailed, *Jimmy Lee made me do somethin' I didn't want to, so I hid from Mama, and met a man who I know I'm not allowed to talk to, but I sure want to.* Or, I could expose Jake for what he must've done. I wondered how Daddy might react if he knew Jake had caused his farmhand not to show up for work, though I secretly feared that Daddy might praise him for what he'd see as an indiscretion. Instead, I went with a safe answer.

"Yes, Daddy. It was just such a nice night that, after Jimmy Lee dropped me off, I went for a walk. I won't miss dinner again. I'm sorry."

"It's not a problem. Just makin' sure you're okay," he answered.

Mama walked out from the kitchen, wipin' her hands on a dishtowel. Mama, Jake, and I had the exact same shade of blond hair, like cornhusks kissed by the sun. Tonight hers was swept away from her face with a red and white paisley scarf. She looked beautiful, even if tired. I waited for my reprimand, and when she didn't chide me for missin' dinner, I wondered how so much could have changed in the span of just a few hours. I guessed that holdin' Mama's secret had a few benefits that I was only beginnin' to discover.

"Maggie's comin' home," she said with a wide grin.

"When? Oh, Mama, can I go to get her at the train station with you, please?" I begged.

"Settle down, Pix," Daddy said. "She's not comin' until Friday, and your mama will be needin' you to help her prepare supper."

"But Daddy, I can miss—"

"Now, now. You'll help your mama, just like always. Jake'll go with me."

I bit back my frustration. I no longer wanted to be treated like a child. The world was out there and I'd had a taste of understandin' what I hadn't cared enough to even think about before findin' poor Mr. Bingham. Doesn't that count for somethin'? I had to remind myself that, for Mama and Daddy, nothin' had changed. Mama might have shared her secret with me, but I was still their sheltered daughter who believed whatever her daddy told her.

Mama nodded, as if to tell me to agree. I was enjoyin' this sudden collusion between us. Mama and I were close when it came to bakin' and fixin' meals, but watchin' her and Maggie always stoked the jealousy bug in me. I was glad that I was the one Mama trusted with this secret.

"Yes, sir," I said.

Daddy reached for my hand and winked. "That's my girl," he said.

"Daddy, I have to study. I can't go." Jake purposefully shook his bangs into his eyes, hidin' from lookin' into Daddy's eyes. He blamed Maggie for our father not allowin' him to go away to school, and I knew he carried too much resentment to want to drop whatever he was doin' and go pick her up. He thought that Daddy had used all of his money on her education instead of his, but to me it was clearly more than that. Maggie was more aggressive than Jake; besides havin' perfect grades, she possessed a mouthiness that was hard to ignore. She would've been like a caged tiger if she'd stayed here in town, whereas Jake fared just fine as a typical Forrest Town boy—from what I'd seen lately, a little too well.

I climbed the stairs to my bedroom on the second floor and thought about all that I had learned over the past twenty-four hours. I thought about Jackson, and all that he'd said. He'd described what it was like for him when he'd left; *I was scared to death of bein' in the military with them white folks.* He had no idea what to expect. Jackson only knew what he'd grown up with in Forrest Town—segregation to the nth degree. When he'd told me that, sadness took hold of my heart in a way that I never thought I'd feel for a colored boy. I just wanted to reach out and hug him, steal that fear away from him. The military had opened his eyes to the ways of the world outside of Arkansas. The white guys he'd met were from all over the world, right out of high school, like he'd been when he'd enlisted three years earlier, and some much older than him. They told him stories of integrated areas and he'd said that at first he didn't believe them. His eyes grew wide when he told me this, and he got me thinkin', wonderin' what it would be like in those places, and if it could possibly be true. He thought they were pullin' his leg, too, makin' fun because he was colored. He quickly came to see otherwise. He said that when they're fightin', it's as if every soldier were color-blind—unless you were Vietnamese.

Though it was cool outside, my small bedroom was warm and welcomin'. My bedroom has always been a safe place for me. Probably because I shared it with Maggie for so many years. Maggie's bed was on my left when I walked in, untouched since she'd gone back to school after her holiday break. My bed was across from Maggie's, with our small desk to the right. I walked over and opened the window at the foot of my bed. Then, I sat down, lookin' at the photographs we'd taped to our wall throughout the years, and wishin' things could go back to how they were before she'd gone away. Life had been so easy. We went to school, came home and played, and were oblivious to the inequities of life. What might it be like to be so far away from home, away from the eyes of Forrest Town? I wondered. I lay back on my pillow and thought about how Mr. Bingham had died because he'd tried to defend his wife's honor. Jackson said his mama told him that Mr. Bingham had confronted Billy Carlisle and told him to leave his wife alone. That was eight hours before he'd disappeared.

Clara Bingham was also threatened that night, by Billy's wife, or at least that's what Clara told Jackson's mama. Clara had been in hidin' ever since, somewhere Jackson wouldn't reveal, with plans to leave town for good as soon as Mr. Bingham's body was safely put to rest. She'd waited to hold the funeral until Mr. Bingham's brother could come into town from Mississippi.

I wondered what Daddy would do if the tables were turned, and some colored man held the power to make Mama do things she didn't want to. Would he defend her honor and die in the process? I knew the answer and the thought of losin' Daddy only made my heart ache even more for Clara.

The more I thought about the family, and the impendin' funeral, the more I wanted to attend the service. But I knew that tellin' them I was sorry for their loss and standin' with them, without shame, to hear the final words before his body was laid to rest, wouldn't make up for the loss of his life. Of course, I wouldn't dare attend. The chance I'd taken that evenin' with Jackson was ten times worse than anything I'd ever done before, and yet, it didn't feel one ounce wrong to me.

A knock on my door brought my thoughts back home.

"Come in."

My door pushed open and Mama stood in the hallway. She glanced toward the stairs, and then slipped inside, closin' the door behind her.

"Hi, honey," she said, and perched herself on the edge of Maggie's bed, her hands folded in her lap. I sat up, smoothed my skirt, and crossed my ankles, as she did.

"Hi, Mama. I'm sorry I missed dinner."

She shook her head. "That's okay. I'm not here about that."

She adjusted herself on Maggie's bed, then came to sit beside me. She took my hand, and I knew for sure I was in trouble.

"Honey," she began, "you know I'd never go against your father's beliefs if it wasn't very important, right?"

I nodded, afraid to breathe. She'd let me in on her secret, now what? She began rubbin' the back of my hand.

"Well, you know I love your father, no matter what I tell you, right?"

I nodded again, wantin' to shove my fingers in my ears and yell, *Na na na na na, I can't hear you!* Even though I was enjoyin' the secret between us, I sorta wanted to keep the image of my mama as I'd always seen her, as a woman with no secrets. Learnin' her secrets put me in a place of keepin' more secrets from Daddy. Although it was gettin' easier to do, I found doin' it a bit scary, like I was drivin' a wedge between us.

She dropped my hand and lifted my chin with her finger, lookin' deep into my eyes. "I shouldn't have brought you with me this mornin'. I was upset. It was wrong." She took a deep breath, then continued. "The thought of that sweet boy bein' beaten—" She turned away.

I wrapped my right hand in my left, excited and nervous about this newly forged relationship that was growin' between us.

"Does Daddy know how you feel?"

She looked at me again, and shook her head.

So many questions rattled around in my head, I didn't know where to start. Talkin' to Jackson gave me strength. He had been just as relieved to get his anger off his chest as I'd been to talk about what I'd been feelin'. I took a deep breath, sat up straight, and asked Mama if she'd brought the woman things before.

"No. There was no need." Her eyebrows drew together. "Until now."

"Who is she?" I asked.

"She's Albert's mother. Millie Johns."

"How long have you known her?"

"I'm not gonna lie to you, Alison. I've known her for as long as Albert has worked for us. His mother sought me out, one day, while I was in town shoppin'. She told me that Albert was her youngest." Mama laughed under her breath, in a way that I read to be some sort of a secret joke that only another mother might understand. "Her older son was away at war, the others had moved away from Forrest Town, and Albert was all she had left."

"But why would she seek you out? Why would she do that?"

Tension drained from Mama's shoulders. She cocked her head and looked at me with so much love it made my heart ache. She brushed my hair away from my face, and said, with so much emotion that I wanted to crawl into her lap, "Because when you have children, you'll do anything to keep them safe."

Chapter Six

The next mornin', I lay in bed listenin' to Daddy make his way toward the stairs. He peeked into my room, as he always did, and on the occasion I was awake, he winked at me. Today he blew a kiss my way and headed down the creakin' stairs. I tried to go back to sleep, but half an hour later I was still too wound up from the evenin' before. I got up and rushed through my mornin' routine—showered, brushed my hair and teeth, chose my outfit.

Mama was in the kitchen when I came downstairs. "You're up early. Are you hungry?"

Only for more information. "No, thank you. Where's Jake?" I asked.

"He was headin' into town before school. He already left."

I thought of the bruises on his knuckles, the way he'd followed Jimmy Lee into that fight like a puppy vyin' for attention. The muscles in my neck pulled tight. "He's never 'round anymore."

"That's what happens when children grow up." Mama sounded sad. I felt bad for her, but was lost within my own emotional hayride. "Are you gonna see Jimmy Lee later, before he goes back to Mississippi?"

"No, he's leavin' too early." Guilt pushed at my heart, but I didn't let it in. Jimmy Lee had hurt me, emotionally and physically, and he was the last person I wanted to see. After what he'd done to Albert, I wasn't sure I could ever look at him in the same way.

I stood and walked to the window, starin' into the fields. The farmhands were takin' a break, sprawled out on the grass at the edge of the field. I thought about tellin' Mama about Jackson comin' to work later that afternoon instead of Albert, but was afraid to reveal my secret.

"I'm goin' outside to wait for Daddy. He's runnin' me into town to pick up more of that molasses. He loved those cookies."

"Your father has a meetin' at the bank this mornin'," Mama said.

"Yes, ma'am, I know. He said I could take the bus back home. I'm stoppin' at the library anyway. He'll probably beat me back home." I kissed Mama's cheek. "Love you," I said, and headed for the door.

The mornin' air was chilly, and as I sat in the rockin' chair, the smell of dew-soaked grass in the air, I considered the farmhands showin' up at five in the mornin'. How cold they must have been durin' the fall, and scorchin' hot in the summertime. There must've been many times that they were too tired or sick to come to work, but out of fear of bein' fired, they showed up anyway. I wondered what Jackson's family was doin' right then. Were they sittin' around a kitchen table cryin' in anticipation of the impendin' funeral? Or perhaps they were reminiscin' about the life of Mr. Bingham. I thought about Clara, hidin' out wherever she might be, her life altered in a way she may never recover from.

I thought of Jackson and my stomach tightened. Could he be killed for bein' alone with me? I wasn't sure, though from what Jimmy Lee did to Albert—broken ribs and countless contusions—I'm sure that wasn't so far fetched. When Jackson and I had left each other the evenin' before, he followed the stream in the opposite direction of our property to the end of town, and I went back home the way we'd come. How hard must it be to live every moment watchin' over your shoulder for somethin' as natural as just bein' alive?

"You're early, Pix." My father climbed the porch steps, his stained t-shirt and overalls a wicked mess of dirt. That's when the guilt hit me. As much as I disliked his disregard for the colored farmhands, I was still a Daddy's girl, and I wanted nothin' more than for him to reach out and pat my head, as he always did.

He held his palms up. "Been fixin' the tractor. Think your mama will mind?" he asked.

"I think Mama'll tell you to hose off out back," I laughed.

"You're probably right," he said as he touched my head. "I'll be ready in twenty minutes."

As he walked inside, I looked up at the clear sky, glad there was no rain in the forecast. Our family's income relied on the farm, and too much rain could wipe out our crops. My father listened to the weather on the radio every mornin'. The familiar tinny sounds made their way upstairs to my room. Some mornin's I'd lay in my bed and listen, tryin' to nod back off, until Mama woke me an hour later. When Maggie was still home, on really cold mornin's, I'd crawl into bed with her and steal her warmth.

I spent hours millin' about the library, readin' the backs of so many books I couldn't keep track. I loved to sit between the rows of shelves, pullin' book after book into my lap, and takin' my time nosin' through 'em, lookin' for the one that held voices that called out to me in a way I couldn't turn away from. I'd run my fingers over the covers imaginin' what I'd find inside. I was struck by how different I was from Maggie, who'd snag two or three books, leaf through the first few pages, and be ready to leave. To me, each book held the promise of a secret world, and disappearin' into that world is simply delicious.

Later that afternoon, the bus dropped me off two blocks from our house. I carried my library books down the long dirt road, the tips of my shoes covered in dust. I heard the pedalin' of a bike behind me, and I walked to the edge of the road to let it pass.

Jackson pulled up next to me and dropped his feet from the pedals. I whipped my head around, makin' sure no one was watchin'. If Daddy had found out about us meetin', he'd be sorely disappointed in me. I worried about him comin' around the corner in his truck and scoopin' me right off the road. God only knew what he'd do to Jackson. The thought sent a shiver up my spine. Luckily, there was no one in sight right then. My nerves were afire with trepidation, and somethin' else that I hadn't felt in quite some time—anticipation? As wrong as it might be, every time I thought of our first meetin', I got hot all over, like blushin' gone haywire. There was no mistakin' the growin' attraction within me, but I knew I needed to get my feelin's in check and get back on track with what Daddy was expectin' of me.

It took all my strength to continue walkin'. "We can't talk," I said, and walked faster toward home. The last thing his family needed was more trouble.

He stepped off his bike and hurried beside me. "Meet me later?"

I wanted so badly to know how the funeral went, if his aunt had escaped town safely. I didn't respond to him.

"Please?"

I glanced up and saw the same kindness that I'd seen the day before, the same open, hopeful smile, so different than what I'd seen in Jimmy Lee lately.

"Where?" I asked.

"Same place, by the creek. Later, after I work for your dad."

"It's too dangerous." My heart slammed against my chest. I stole a glance at him, still walkin' as fast as I could. His smile slowly sank, his lips pressed into a disappointed line.

"You're the first person 'round here who—oh, never mind." He climbed back up on his bike, his muscular thighs burstin' against his dark work pants. "I guess you are just like everyone else."

I watched him pedal away, dirt kickin' up behind him in a billowin' puff of smoke. I hugged my books to my chest, wishin' I'd agreed to meet him.

By the time I reached my house, Jackson was already helpin' Daddy in the barn. His bicycle lay sideways across the grass next to Daddy's truck. I went around the back of the house and found Mama takin' clothes off of the dryin' line and hummin' a little tune. I plucked a few of the clothespins off of Daddy's t-shirts and laid them in the basket, watchin' her move through her chores as she had every day of my life. Had I not known her secret, I'd never have pictured Mama doin' anything more than tendin' to our meals, clothin', and school needs. Mama was becomin' someone else right before my eyes, and I wondered what other secrets she held. The more I thought about what I might not know about her, the more I wanted to share my burdens with her.

"Mama?" I asked tentatively. "What if you knew who hurt Albert Johns? Would you do somethin' about it?"

She stopped hummin', her eyes shot to the barn and back. When she answered, her voice was very quiet. I leaned in close to hear her.

"That wouldn't do any good. There's no punishment for beatin' up a colored boy."

Or killin' a colored man. "But, how would you live with yourself? Knowin' what someone had done and that they didn't get punished?"

Again her eyes shot across our property. She folded the sheet she had been holdin' and came to my side. Mama took my hand in hers and walked me around to the other side of the house, out of sight from the barn. She reached in her apron pocket and pulled out an elastic band, wrapped it expertly around her fingers, then gathered her hair behind the nape of her neck, and fastened it in one quick movement.

"Honey, no justice will be served for this. There's nothin' we can do or say that will make this attack be justly punished." Again, she eyed the barn. "I shouldn't have taken you with me. It was wrong of me. Please, if you do one thing, please just live your life and forget about this nonsense."

"It's not nonsense, Mama, and I can't even believe you are callin' it that."

Mama remained quiet for so long, I feared I'd be punished for talkin' back to her. When she looked back into my eyes, I saw so much more there than anger. They were drenched in defeat.

"Honey, you're too young to understand the dangers that make up this kind of thing."

"I'm not, Mama." I paced beside her, adrenaline rushin' through my veins. I had never stood up to either of my parents before, but I couldn't stop myself. "Do you think that just because you and Daddy turn off the radio I don't hear about what's happenin' in the world? Look at Mr. Bingham. He was murdered and the police didn't even care." The honesty felt good, even if it scared the hell out of me.

"Alison, lower your voice." Mama peered around the side of the house toward the barn. "Please, just keep yourself out of this mess. You have a good life ahead of you. Marry Jimmy Lee, have children, let this kind of thing work itself out."

"Work itself out? Well, can I do what you did? Can I help them?"

"No." She didn't hesitate or soften her tone. Mama grabbed my arm and squeezed tight. She'd never before laid a hand on me. She meant business, and it frightened me. "You are never to do what I did, do you hear me? Alison Jean, promise me."

I tried to pull my arm away, but as confident as I had suddenly become, I had no strength to back it up. I relented. "Okay, I promise." In my mind, I was already plannin' my traipse down to the creek, more determined than ever to see how Jackson's family was holdin' up. I knew in my heart that I was doin' the right thing, and though Mama feared for me, and was probably correct in doin' so, I had to do what I felt was right.

I helped Mama with the dishes, nervously lookin' for Jackson through the window. He had no way of knowin' that I would meet him. I'd denied that I would, after all. A plan formed in my mind. While Daddy listened to the radio in the other room, and Mama finished the dishes, I stepped out on the porch where I'd left my library books. I grabbed a pencil, tore a piece of paper from my notebook, and scribbled, *I will be there.* Then I peeked in the window to make sure Daddy was still seated in his chair, which he was, and I ran out to where Jackson's bike was layin' on the ground. My hands shook as I lifted the seat and tucked the slip of paper underneath. I hoped he'd understand what the note meant, and I hoped we wouldn't get caught.

Chapter Seven

The sun hovered just above the horizon, illuminatin' the sky in beautiful shades of blue, purple, and pink. I had been waitin' for Jackson, watchin' the sun set, and was ready to give up when I felt, more than heard, him behind me. My heartbeat sped up and set my legs tremblin'. I turned around and my eyes lingered over his sweat-laden muscles pressin' against his drenched t-shirt. I felt a blush creepin' up my cheeks, and I was powerless to move. The air between us was suddenly thick, uncomfortable.

"You came?" he asked in a low voice.

I nodded, feelin' the heat of his gaze, the same longin' desire I was tryin' so desperately to hide. I turned away and sat down on a wide tree stump, hopin' to quell the heat on my cheeks. He knelt at the creek bed and washed his hands in the fresh water.

"Did it go okay?" I asked.

He looked back and that heat of attraction hit me again. I smoothed my skirt, then patted my hair, worryin' about if I looked pretty enough. I didn't know what to do with the feelin's I was havin'. The same heart racin' excitement I'd felt for Jimmy Lee so long ago, only somethin' deeper. I wasn't only interested in Jackson's looks, like I was with Jimmy Lee at first. I wanted to know everything about Jackson. I wanted to touch him, take my time, savor the feel of his hand, our fingers interlaced. I wanted him to whisper my name in my ear and set my nerves on end. I looked away, embarrassed. What I wanted was so wrong that it was even more excitin'. *What on earth was I doin'?*

"Your pop's real nice," he said.

My heart sunk. *My father will kill me.*

"Albert should be back by next week, when I leave."

Another kick to my heart. He was leavin'.

Jackson wiped his hands on his pants and sat on the stump next to me. My senses were in overdrive. Goose bumps rose on my arms. My hands fiddled like nervous fish in my lap. *Stop over dramatizin' things.* Surely I was just mad at Jimmy Lee, confused, but I could not deny the desire to relax my shoulder, to let it touch his. Was I turnin' into one of those easy girls Jimmy Lee talked about?

"How was the funeral?" I asked, tryin' to stop thinkin' about the richness of the color of his skin, the way it glistened with sweat, so smooth I wanted to touch it.

"Sad. My aunt was there, and no one bothered her. I guess they figured they'd done enough, killin' her husband and runnin' her out of town. And now she's gone."

Reality appeared in the form of Byron Bingham's bloated face in my mind. I shivered, the former heat of attraction lost in reality. "Where will she live?"

He shrugged. "What does it matter? She's lived here for thirty years, now she doesn't." He clenched his teeth, the muscles in his jaw pulsated. "I think she went to Mississippi with my other relatives."

"Then at least she won't be alone." I had the urge to soothe him. If he were one of the guys I had known durin' school I'd probably have put my arm around him and told him it would all be okay, but there was an invisible line between us, and I was afraid to cross it.

He turned to face me, the sound of the water tricklin' fell away, his breathin' fillin' each pulse of my heart. I was unable to resist the urge to be closer, if only by emotional pull. I turned my shoulders toward him and lifted my gaze. Our eyes held.

"True," he said, wringin' his hands.

I watched his lips move, heard his words, but my mind was workin' what it might feel like to kiss him, what it might taste like. I stumbled over my words, finally askin', "And Albert? How is he?" A tinglin' sensation traveled up my arms again. I inched away from him, hopin' to slow my racin' heart.

"He's hurtin', but good. Scared. You know." He sighed, a long, loud sigh, his eyes lookin' at me, my own desires reflectin' back. He pushed up from the stump, turnin' his back to me like he, too, was fightin' an urge more powerful than he could manage. "Life in Forrest Town. It is what it is."

"So when you're done, with the war, I mean, where will you go?" I spoke just above a whisper, afraid of the answer. "Will you come back here?"

He laughed, but it wasn't a real laugh. It was more of somethin' that I read to mean that he wasn't stupid enough to come back, no matter what he might be leavin' behind. "Not if I can help it. My friend Arthur invited me to New York, said he could get me a good job there. A real job, not in the fields or maintenance work, like what I could get here."

He held his hand out to help me off the stump. I took his hand and stood, holdin' my breath, not knowin' if I should let go or hold on. I wanted to hold on. He withdrew his hand, and I swear his eyes lingered on mine for a second. Then again, my heart was beatin' so hard I might have just imagined it.

We walked side by side along the bank of the creek. Each step measured, each breath calculated, so I could feel the energy that rode between us like an invisible tie.

"How's your mama doin'. I can't imagine what she's goin' through. My mama would be a mess."

"She's thinkin' that she's thankful that your mother is kind, even if your father is—" He wiped his forehead with his arm and sighed. "Even if your father is just like everyone else."

"You know about that? About my mama?"

He put his hands on his hips and said, "Sure I know. I'm real thankful, too. Your mama is a really good person."

Fear suddenly gripped my chest. "Oh no, who else knows?"

"No one who's gonna say anything."

I crossed my arms and paced, my skirt swished in the silence. "No one can know about my mama," I said. "I can't even think about what could happen to her." My voice rose, my words tumbled out fast and harsh. "You don't understand. If Daddy finds out, he'll—"

He put his hands gently on my upper arms. Even through my sweater my skin warmed beneath his palms. He looked into my eyes and spoke just above a whisper. "Hey, hey. Did you forget who you're talkin' to? I *do* understand. If anyone does, I do. My brother, Mama, my aunt. We all do."

I don't know why I did what I did next. He didn't pull me forward. He didn't push me away. My body relaxed into him and it felt like the most natural motion in the world. I leaned into his chest, my head restin' on his sweat-damp shirt. He smelled of hay and perspiration. His chest trembled beneath my cheek, his hands moved slowly around me, comin' to rest, hot and sure, on my lower back. I closed my eyes, feelin' his heart pound against my cheek. Tears burned at the edges of my eyes. The warmth of his body and the tenderness of his touch were so different than when Jimmy Lee held me. With Jimmy Lee I was an afterthought, an imposition in his precious day, or a means to a climactic end. Jackson welcomed me, drank me in. He didn't rush my need for comfort or push me away. He didn't throw me down and push into me. He simply held me, as if I belonged right where I was.

Chapter Eight

Friday afternoon, Maggie pushed through the front door wearin' clothes I didn't recognize, and an expression to match. There was tension in her smile, and her normally laughin' eyes were different, more serious. I rushed into her arms, and she swung me around.

"Pixie! Oh, how I missed you." She set me down, held my shoulders, and pushed away from me, surveyin' me from head to toe. "Girl, you are one pretty, little thing! Gosh, look at you, all grown up!" She pushed my blond waves from my shoulder and cupped my cheek. "When you were little, one bat of those blue eyes used to get you everything you wanted from Daddy. I bet now they worry him somethin' fierce. Boys must look at you everywhere you go."

My cheeks burned. "I missed you."

She grabbed my hand and touched my engagement ring. She squeezed my hand and said, "You're sure about this?"

"Waddaya mean?" I asked, wonderin' if I was wearin' the changes in my feelin's on my sleeve. Could she see the difference in me as clearly as I could feel it?

"I haven't seen you since you got engaged. Someone needs to look out for my little sister." She squinted, "So, are you sure?"

I'd been meetin' Jackson down by the creek for several days, and though we had never embraced again, I was fully aware of my growin' attraction toward his gentle nature and his knowledge of the world, which was so much bigger than mine. I found myself sittin' on the stairs listenin' to the news on the radio in the evenin's. I wanted to answer Maggie with the truth: *Not really. He's different than he was, and my heart is pullin' me toward someone else.* Instead, aware of our parents watchin' us, I said, "Yeah, and Daddy says he has a promisin' future."

"Of course he does," Maggie feigned a smile in his direction.

"Enough of this. Come over here and give me a hug." Mama's cheeks were plumped up, pink with happiness. She opened her arms wide, and Maggie sank into them. They could have been sisters. I wished I had the beauty that they possessed. I wasn't ugly, but they had a certain somethin' that shined through dirt, worry, and fatigue. *One day*, I hoped. One day, I'd find that beauty in myself.

"Pants?" Jake smirked.

"They're all the rage in New York, little brother." Maggie twirled in a circle, hands by her head. She looked down at her slim figure in cotton pants that tapered to the knee then flared at the bottom. "It's a whole different world out there, Jakey-poo."

Pants? Jakey-poo? It was like listenin' to Maggie, only bigger—more outspoken than before—and she had an air of not carin' what we thought. My eyes shot to Daddy, whose arms were crossed, his right hand rubbin' his chin. I had a feelin' that he was tryin' to figure her out just as I was. I was definitely intrigued.

Mama had baked a meatloaf, fresh biscuits, and green beans. Maggie's favorite.

"Tell me about New York." I was excited to hear about the big city. She was so far away and all I could think about was how scared I'd be, movin' away from Mama and Daddy and startin' a life without knowin' they were right around the corner.

Maggie's eyes lit up. "It's like nothin' you've ever seen. There are a million people, and I swear the noise never stops." Maggie poked at the vegetables. She had yet to take a bite.

"Do you have many friends?" I asked. Sometimes I wondered if it was easier to make new friends than to try and reignite friendships with those I'd left behind because of datin' someone older. I wasn't even sure I'd want to rekindle those relationships, given how much I'd changed. Reinventin' yourself to be seen as the person you wanted to be, rather than the person everyone had known since the day you were born, sounded excitin' to me—and terribly scary.

"Does she ever not?" Jake smirked. My parents gave him a *not now* look. "What? Well, doesn't she?"

"That's enough, Jake," Daddy said. "Maggie, tell us about your classes. Are you learnin' a lot?"

She nodded, drawin' her eyebrows together, as if she were thinkin'. She looked at Jake and said, "I have lots of friends. Everyone is real nice."

"That's good, honey," Mama said, and patted Maggie's arm.

Maggie tilted her eyes toward Mama and smiled.

"How about your classes, Maggie?"

Maggie set her fork down. She looked at Daddy, pulled her shoulders back, and said, "They're alright, Daddy." Her words were flat. I detected a lie.

Tension thickened in the room.

"Grades? Are you doin' okay?" he asked, starin' into her eyes.

She held his gaze. "Yes, I'm doin' fine." Maggie picked up her fork again, droppin' her eyes to her plate. I watched her draw in a deep breath and blow it out slowly through her full lips. "There's so much more to New York than school and grades, and there's so much more to life, Daddy."

The room grew silent. I watched Daddy's face tighten. I looked at Maggie, flabbergasted. What was she doin'? I knew our parents had saved every penny to send Maggie to New York, and Daddy had fought sendin' her "into the big city" with ferocity. Maggie had been too much for him. She knew when to turn on the charm, "Don't worry, Daddy, I'll make you proud," and when to push, "Come on, Daddy, what's wrong with a woman gettin' an education?" In the end, I think Daddy got tired of fightin' and let her go.

My father cleared his throat. "Meanin'?" he asked.

"Meanin'—" Maggie's eyes danced around the room, much to my chagrin, they settled on me. I loved Maggie but I hated bein' pitted between her and Daddy, and somehow, things always ended up that way. I played with my fork, holdin' her stare. The air electrified between us. I knew nothin' good was about to happen. Maggie's lips spread into a wide grin. "There's so much goin' on out there. Music, clothin'," she grasped the edge of the table with both hands, her voice risin' in excitement. "People. The people are talkin', livin' like they love life, sharin' time, information." She turned to face our father, shakin' her head. "This town, Daddy," she laughed under her breath. "It's…it's way behind the times—"

"That's enough Maggie," he interrupted her.

Maggie stood up, then walked around the table and stood behind my chair, grabbin' my shoulders with both hands. Her grip was strong, thrillin'. "Things are happenin', Pix, big things. Things you could never imagine."

"Like you losin' your mind?" Jake laughed.

"Margaret Lynn, sit back down." My father's voice was calm, steady, forceful. Mama sat in silence, the edges of her lips slightly raised, her pride-filled eyes on Maggie, her napkin clenched in her hand. I shook in my seat, afraid of what Daddy might say. I had no idea what Maggie meant by the things she said, but I wanted to know so badly that I had to clench my teeth to remain silent.

Maggie walked around the table, swingin' her hands dramatically from side to side, her chin tilted upward. "There's a whole world out there. I know you've heard about it," she lowered her chin and locked eyes with our father. "On the radio?"

"I said that's enough Margaret." If fumes could come from a person's ears, the dinin' room would have been filled with smoke.

"Civil rights," she said, as if she were answerin' her own question

Civil rights? Civil rights was not a topic discussed in the Tillman household. We knew what we heard on the radio in those moments before Daddy turned it off. Daddy was quick to shoot down our questions. *Things are just fine 'round here. We don't need no trouble brought on by some trouble-makin' coloreds. When somethin's not broke, why fix it?* I knew there were marches and speeches goin' on in other places, and Jake and I knew better than to ask questions or bring up what we'd heard in school or picked up by scannin' the newspapers. Maggie was another story. She reveled in challengin' Daddy.

Maggie leaned against her chair, watchin' Daddy with a dare in her eyes. Tension thickened in the small room. Silence ensued, until finally Maggie looked like she might burst.

"The civil rights movement is on, Daddy, and—" She drew out the word "on" like it was magnified.

"That's it, Margaret Lynn. I'll have no more of this disrespect." My father threw his napkin on the table and stood up.

"You can't shelter them forever, Daddy," Maggie taunted him.

I cringed.

"There's a whole world out there, and they should know about it. They should live it, Daddy."

My father grabbed Maggie by the arm and dragged her outside. We remained at the table. Mama cleared her throat, wiped her mouth with her napkin, and lowered her eyes. A piece of me wished she'd stand up for Maggie, but I knew if there was one thing Daddy didn't stand for it was disrespect, and if Mama had spoken up, Lord only knew what argument might follow. I'd been watchin' Mama carefully since seein' her with Albert's mother, and I'd decided that she picked her battles. She may have been one of the smartest women I knew, and at that moment, while Daddy yelled at Maggie out on the front porch, and Maggie yelled back, I wished she'd taught Maggie that same tact. I don't think I could have left the table if I wanted to. No one spoke to Daddy that way. Daddy wasn't a hittin' man, but the threat of losin' Daddy's favor was enough to usually keep my words in check. Bein' in Daddy's favor was like havin' the sun shine down on you, radiatin' with warmth and smothered in love. Mama and Jake never sassed him, either. Mama was just raised that way, and I think Jake took his cue like I did, from whatever lay behind Daddy's eyes when he was angry—a silent threat that hung in the air, and though I was never quite sure what was at the end of that threat, I was afraid for Maggie.

That evenin', as Daddy listened to the news on the radio and Mama read on the couch, Maggie and I remained in our room. Maggie paced, her arms crossed, her face tight.

"As much as I love comin' home to see you, Pix, I hate comin' here because of how backwards this town is." She didn't give me a chance to respond. "Daddy wants to keep you here." She grabbed my left hand. "Marry you off." She pushed my hand into my lap and paced again. "It's just…there's so much—"

"Haven't you learned your lesson yet, sis? Daddy's gonna come up here and whoop your tail." Jake stood in the doorframe, arms crossed.

Maggie spun around. "My lesson? Is that what you think this is about Jake? You're just as bad as Daddy. Do you think I don't know what you do out there?" Her hand shot out toward the window.

Jake clenched his jaw.

"Huh? Do you? You think you're some groovy guy because you follow the other thugs in this town, beatin' up coloreds and laughin' while you walk away."

Jake came away from the doorframe and stood tall, squintin' at Maggie, his jaw muscles workin' overtime.

"It's not right, Jake. And look," she pointed at me.

I opened my eyes wide. *Me?* As much as I loved Maggie, I didn't want Daddy yellin' at me like that. *Please leave me out of this.*

"Look at her, think of her," Maggie continued. "Do you really want her to have a life like," she paused, and then continued just above a whisper, "like Mama? Caterin' to some man her whole life? Alison is smarter than that. She's got her whole life ahead of her."

"She's not that smart." His eyes never left Maggie's. As much as his comment hurt, I knew Jake was achin' inside by Maggie's comment, since Daddy had kept him home. I swallowed my own feelin's in hopes of the whole hurtful conversation blowin' over.

"I know you hate me because they sent me to school, Jake, but the truth is, they didn't send me over you. They sent me to get rid of me. I'm nothin' but a pain to Daddy. You," she rubbed her forehead, "you're his meal ticket when he's old and can no longer run the farm. You're plenty smart enough to go to school outside of this crappy place, but he'll never let you go."

Jake's eyes changed from angry to interested in the space of a second. Maggie sat down on her bed, and covered her face. I thought she was cryin', until she lifted her face from her hands and I saw her reddened cheeks and a fierce look in her eye.

"I have to get out of here." She stood up and began throwin' her clothes into her suitcase.

"What? Why? You can't leave," Jake said.

I grabbed her arm, alarm bells goin' off in my head. I needed her. "Maggie, please don't go. You just got here. Just stay, please." *I have no one to confide in.*

She shook me off and backed onto my bed, then pulled me down beside her. Jake sat down on Maggie's bed, breathin' hard, like he was ready to jump up and stop her if she tried to leave.

"Pixie, I know you don't get this, and I know you are probably scared to leave this place, but trust me, please." Her eyes bore into my heart. "You're too young to get married. This isn't Mama's generation. You can get an education, have a life other than this, more than this."

I looked from her to Jake. Deep creases ran across Jake's forehead. He fidgeted with his hands in his lap. I looked back at Maggie, not sure what I felt, what I should say. So, instead, I remained quiet. Maggie filled the silence.

"Look at me," she pleaded. "In New York, coloreds and whites talk, on the streets, in the shops. It's not like here. Women are not only homemakers or garment workers, they're secretaries and they work in the stores. They go out and dance. They don't sit around on some dirty, old farm waitin' for the next rainstorm to create chaos in their lives, or walk down the aisle at seventeen."

"Eighteen," I whispered.

"Eighteen. Pfft." Maggie drew in a deep breath and blew it out loudly. "Do you love him? I mean really love him? Does he make your stomach quake, even now, after two years? Do you long to see him when you're apart?"

I was afraid to answer honestly.

"Do you?"

I felt Jake's eyes on me, and worried that he'd run and tell Jimmy Lee if I told the truth. "I don't know."

"What?" Maggie asked.

"I don't know, okay? It's just...he's all I know." I stood up and went to the window, thinkin' about Jackson's arms wrapped around me. I hadn't even kissed him, and yet I still felt a longin' to see him that was stronger than I'd felt for Jimmy Lee in a long time. "Sometimes, he does things I don't like," I said. *Like beatin' up Albert and makin' me do things I don't want to.* I let out a relieved sigh. It was out there in the open, someone besides me heard what was rattlin' around inside my head.

Jake's eyes were as wide as a child's seein' Santa Claus come down the chimney.

"Please, Jake, don't say anything. Please?"

Maggie grabbed his arm. "If you say one word, I will kill you."

"Maggie!" I said.

"Quiet, Pix. This is important. This is your entire life. If you love him and know it here," she thumped her chest, "then I'll shut up. But if you don't, there's no way you're gonna marry him, unless it's over my dead body."

"Dramatic, don't you think?" Jake pulled his arm from her grip.

"You don't get it, Jake. Once she's married, she's stuck."

Was she gonna break up me and Jimmy Lee? Was she fixin' to try to call off my weddin' that was takin' place in two months? I twirled the ring on my finger. Fear gripped my heart. My father would be furious.

"I said, *I don't know*," I interjected. "Maybe I do want to marry him." I went back to the window, breathin' fast and hard, my palms sweatin' against the wooden sill. The moon shone high in the sky, and my mind sought the image of Jackson, the nubby thickness of his hair, the softness of his eyes. Jackson and I had developed a system. If I were able to meet him right after he was off work, I'd leave my library books on the front porch, and if I had to meet him after supper, I left them on the rockin' chair. I had done my readin' on the front porch just before dinnertime, and purposely left my book on the rockin' chair. Now I wondered how I'd ever get out to see him—and I wanted to more than anything in the world. My only hope of sneakin' out was while Maggie was asleep, and I'm not sure she'd ever go to sleep at the rate our conversation was escalatin'.

"If you don't know, that means you aren't sure," Maggie said.

"Don't push her, Maggie. Just because you like it out there doesn't mean she will."

They both stared at me and I wondered how it was possible that our parents hadn't come up stairs with all the noise we were makin'.

"I'm so tired. Can we just be done already?" I asked.

Maggie threw her hands up. "Whatever you want, Pixie. I just want you to be happy."

"I am happy," I lied. Jake left our room, leavin' me filled with guilt, which burned in my stomach like a bonfire.

"He's scared. Daddy will never let him leave."

I flopped onto my bed, starin' at the ceilin'. After the rush of adrenaline that carried our discussion, my body was heavy and tired. I listened to Maggie in the bathroom, brushin' her teeth and washin' her face. Daddy's radio silenced, and my mind ran in circles, thinkin' of my upcomin' weddin', which I'd been so carefully ignorin'.

Heavy footsteps ascended the stairs.

"Goodnight, Maggie." My father peeked into my room and smiled. "Goodnight, Pix," he said.

I listened for Maggie's response. It saddened me to know Daddy was answered with silence. "Goodnight, Daddy," I said.

Maggie came back into the room, closed the door, and climbed into her bed. She lit a candle on the nightstand, then turned off her light. "Don't let Jake make you stay, either. He's afraid he'll be left all alone." There was an edge to her voice, a warnin'.

I looked at her then, her silhouette strikin' in the flickerin' light. "I never said I wanted to leave."

Maggie squinted in the darkness. "Oh, Pixie, is it too late? Have they ruined you for life?"

I didn't understand why Maggie was pushin' me away from Jimmy Lee and Forrest Town. Or maybe I did. Maybe what I was just startin' to figure out, Maggie had figured out long ago. I was torn between annoyed and curious. "Jake doesn't care if I'm here or not," I said.

"No, he just doesn't want to seem like he needs you. Everyone needs someone, and we're all he's got right now. He hangs out with guys who do nothin' but get in trouble."

"Hey, Jimmy Lee is one of those guys."

"Sorry," she said quietly, then she sat bolt upright in her bed, mischief in her eyes. "Pix, the world is about to change more than you could ever imagine." She leaned toward me and whispered. "The white people here are assholes, Pix. The schools are not supposed to still be segregated."

She spoke so fast I could hardly keep up.

Two seconds later she was perched atop my bed, sittin' cross-legged, her eyes bright with enthusiasm. "Things are happenin', and they're gonna happen here, too. There's this group, the Black Panthers, and they're just gettin' together out in California, but my friends say they're formin' in New York, too. They're gonna help the coloreds gain equal rights."

"Didn't Martin Luther King do that?"

"Look around you," she said.

I looked around the bedroom.

"Not here, out there." Maggie pointed to the window. "You tell me, did good old Mr. King fix things here in backwoods Arkansas? Can coloreds eat at the diner and go see movies in our theaters?"

Maggie was scarin' me. What she said was true, it was like Mr. King's words were empty in our town—the white folks still ruled the roost. I assumed they always would.

Maggie stood up and paced, energized by her own vision. "I'm joinin' 'em, Pix. As soon as I get back to New York, I'm gonna help."

"You can't do that. It'll be dangerous. I hear about race riots on the radio when Daddy listens." I grabbed her arm. "Please, Maggie. Please don't do it."

She sat back down next to me. "I'm a woman. I'll be behind the scenes, helpin' the families and children. Oh, Pixie, I can barely walk by Division Street anymore without feelin' sick to my stomach. Those poor kids haven't a clue how they're bein' held back."

It occurred to me that Maggie wanted to fight for exactly what my heart was achin' over. She hadn't said anything about white folks datin' black folks, but if this whole movement went as she hoped, couldn't that naturally follow? Maybe not, and maybe never in my daddy's world. "Daddy will never let you do it." Fear prickled my arms. I couldn't stand it if anything happened to Maggie.

"Daddy won't know." She stifled my response with her glare. "Don't you care about what's goin' on 'round here?"

More than you know. I thought of Jackson standin' out by the creek in the pitch black waitin' for me, riskin' his life just to talk to me, and the excitement that chased me as I ran through the fields toward him. "I care. I do care."

"Then you won't tell Daddy."

Lyin' to Daddy was new to me. Before meetin' Jackson I'd only lied twice—once two years ago about if Jimmy Lee had ever tried to touch me in ways that weren't appropriate (I wanted Jimmy Lee to touch me, so I didn't feel that was really a lie, or inappropriate), and the other time just the other day about where I had been when I missed dinner. I wasn't about to tell Daddy that I was with Jackson.

"Okay, but promise me that you won't do anything dangerous."

Maggie nodded fast and furious, then took me in her long, sinewy arms and hugged me tight. She pulled away and said, "Okay, good. Good." She hopped over to her bed and dove under the covers.

I lay in bed waitin' for Maggie to fall asleep, and hopin' Jackson wouldn't leave. The hours had passed by so quickly that I was sure he had. But still, I had to try to see him, drawn to him like a thirsty man to a river. The spark of electricity, the pull in my stomach I'd felt when Jackson held me, came rushin' back and made me shiver. The right and wrong of bein' together made it that much more titillatin'. How I craved to share my secret!

I wondered if I was missin' some clue, an indication that Jackson would one day become just as hurtful as Jimmy Lee. Did all boys eventually evolve into selfish, aggressive men? My father didn't seem that way, but then again, he treated his farmhands like machines. Wasn't that just as bad?

I don't know how long I laid there, worryin' on the thought and cravin' his touch at the same time, but when I looked over, Maggie was fast asleep.

I turned to face the wall, still in my skirt and blouse, and fought the urge to see Jackson. I didn't want to put him in danger.

Ten minutes later I snuck out the back door and ran through the field, my heart thumpin' like a jackrabbit. *Please be there. Please be there.* I slowed as I neared our meetin' spot, listenin' to the soft voices of nature. Inhalin' the scent of the creek, my nerves pulled tight as a spool of yarn. Maggie's words and the hope of freedom for the Johns family flitted through me.

I flicked on my flashlight. "Jackson?"

Silence.

I walked toward the water, illuminatin' the dark night. "Jackson?" I called again. He was gone. Had he even come and waited for me? Fear shot through me like a bullet. *Jimmy Lee. Oh, God, no.* I turned and ran toward home. If Jimmy Lee got wind of us, he'd kill him. My foot caught on a ditch and my body fell forward, landin' on the earth with a thud. My hands and knees stung. I cried out as I pushed myself up. The darkness consumed me. I brushed myself off, prayin' Jimmy Lee didn't find out about Jackson.

My flashlight grew dim. I reached for it just as it went dark. Dead. *A sign?* I was too frightened to think straight. I had to find Jackson. *Please, Lord, please let him be okay.*

"Alison."

My heart jumped into my throat. I spun toward his voice. Jackson's worry-filled eyes stole my breath. He reached for my tremblin' body and pulled me close, one hand on the back of my head, like Mama used to do when I was a little girl, the other hand on my lower back.

"Shhh."

I shivered from the cold and couldn't stop the river of tears. The relief in my heart was too big. I opened my mouth to speak, but a coherent string of words didn't come. I'd already pictured his bloated body mirrorin' Mr. Bingham's and couldn't reconcile the image with the livin', breathin' man before me.

My palms pressed into his chest, confirmin' the surety of him. His heart beat hard and true against my hands. I touched the warm skin of his cheeks.

"Alison," he whispered.

I put my finger to his soft, succulent lips. Real life fell away—Mama, the farm, Jimmy Lee—none of it mattered or existed. None of it belonged to me any longer. The only thing that remained was Maggie's determination to make our embrace okay, and how deliciously safe I felt. Jackson brought his hands to the back of my head, his thumbs pressin' against the hollow beneath my ears. He leaned into me, his body tense, his gaze slidin' right into my soul. I put my lips to his, tastin' his sweet breath. His tongue slipped slowly into my mouth, lingerin' inside me, caressin' the roof of my mouth, the sides of my teeth. I'd died and gone to heaven. A light rain trickled upon us, drippin' down our faces like tiny, little blessin's.

He kissed my cheeks, my neck. "Alison."

I pulled him down to the ground, our bodies now a part of the field. He pushed my hair from my face. "Alison," he said again, lyin' beside me.

Desire swallowed my voice. Love poured from his fingertips as they trailed my blouse. "We can't," he whispered.

I pushed him onto his back. "We can," I said, and brought my lips to his, alightin' warmth between my legs. I reached for the buttons on his pants. He grabbed my wrist, shakin' his head.

I lowered my lips to his fingers, drawin' them back from the ridges of my wrist, and moved them slowly into my mouth, one by one. I wanted to taste every inch of him. His body trembled in anticipation. He closed his eyes. I watched him bite his lower lip, fightin' his desires. *Know your place*, my father's voice whispered. I was surprised how easily I was able to ignore it.

I pushed his shirt up around his neck and kissed his chest, gently movin' his arms away when he reached for me. Tears fell onto his chest as I ran my tongue down his stomach. He sucked in a breath, liftin' my head, meetin' my eyes.

"I'm leavin'. In a week, I'll be gone." His eyes pleaded somethin' between desire and fear.

"We have now."

He shook his head, and pulled me alongside him. He leaned over me. "I want more than now."

I moved beneath him. "I'll wait for you." I didn't know if I meant those words or not, but at that very second, their meanin' felt as real as the ground beneath me. I reached for his cheek. He grabbed my arm and brought it between us. Our eyes met over my ring.

"You're not mine to have."

We stared at each other for interminable minutes. The rain sprinkled the ground around us.

"I am, here," I laid my hand on my heart, "where it matters."

Sadness laced his eyes. He turned away.

"I won't get married." I said, and in the heat of that moment I meant it. "When you get out of the military, we can go to New York, with your friend, and my sister."

Hope swelled between us like a heartbeat. Jackson rested his forehead on my chin. I arched my neck and kissed his worry lines away.

When he entered me, I gasped from pleasure, every nerve inside me sprang to life. He moved slow and careful, watchin' my eyes, askin' if I was okay. His body shook, though his muscles strained beneath my hands. He kissed my cheeks, my eyes, licked my lips, in ways Jimmy Lee never had. We moved together like a perfect chorus to a familiar song. The brown of his eyes basked in love so true I could feel it wrappin' around us like a blanket. Suddenly his body shivered and shook. He grit his teeth and let out a few fast, hard breaths.

My future became clear. I could no longer be with Jimmy Lee. My heart belonged there, with Jackson. No matter how wrong Daddy might think we were, and for as long as it might take until we could safely be together, I would wait for him.

Chapter Nine

I awoke in a panic Saturday mornin'. What had I done? How would I get myself out of my impendin' marriage? I ran down the stairs and bolted out the front door. I needed air.

Mama and Maggie were headin' toward the house from the garden out past the barn. The mornin' sunlight illuminated Mama's golden hair. Her striped, blue dress hung past her knees, the only thing that differentiated her age from Maggie's. Maggie's short shift stopped mid-thigh. I wondered what Daddy might think. Maggie threw her head back and laughed. I longed for her strength and confidence.

I heard Daddy's tractor in the distance, and looked for Jake's bike. It was gone. Jake had been spendin' more and more time away from home, and I wasn't sure if that was a good or bad thing.

"Pixie!" Maggie's voice broke through my worry.

Headin' in her direction, I yelled, "I like your boots." I'd only seen knee-high boots in fashion magazines. Maggie wrapped the crook of her arm around my neck.

"Now I'm one of the cool girls," she said with a pose.

"Until Daddy sees you. He won't let you wear those."

Mama lifted her eyebrows in confirmation.

"Come on, Pix, before we go I want to show you somethin'." Maggie grabbed my hand and ran toward the barn. She called over her shoulder, "We'll be back in a bit!"

I pulled the bottom of my skirt as low as it would go to cover the backs of my legs. The hay tickled my skin. Maggie wiggled beside me, pushin' the hay flat beneath her thighs. "This loft used to be much more comfortable," I laughed.

"We're orderin' your weddin' invitations today," Maggie said.

I looked out the small window that overlooked the fields. "I know," I said.

"So, if you're gonna back out, now's the time."

"Maggie!" I swatted at her arm. "I can't back out. Mama's already booked the church. Everyone knows about it. Daddy would kill me." *Please help me back out.*

"So what?" Maggie pulled out a pack of cigarettes from her pocket and withdrew one cigarette. My eyes about popped out of my head as I watched her hold it elegantly between her lips and light the tip with a match.

"What are you doin'?" My eyes swept the entrance of the barn, afraid our parents might catch us.

Maggie took a long drag of the cigarette and held it in my direction with a nod.

"No, no way. You're gonna get in so much trouble." She exhaled and smoke wafted around us. I inched away, fannin' the air.

She laughed. "I forget how young you are—and how sheltered. Everyone smokes, Pix."

Maggie looked so sophisticated, jealousy wrapped itself around my muscles and squeezed. She held her hand out again in my direction. I reached for it, fumblin' to hold the cigarette the way she did, and dropped it on the hay below us. Maggie scooped it up and tamped down the embers.

"Careful! You'll burn the barn down." She held the cigarette butt toward me and I moved my lips over it, sucked in a breath of awful-tastin' smoke, and hacked until I fell over on my side, my face hot. My lungs burned. I knew then that I'd never be the same risk taker that Maggie was. I spat the ashy taste onto the hay. Maggie burst out laughin', and I was only seconds behind her. The next thing I knew, Maggie had put out the cigarette and we were rollin' around, throwin' hay at each other.

Maggie climbed on top of me and held me down, my arms pinned beneath her knees. We were laughin' so hard my stomach hurt.

"Truth," she said. "Do you want to marry him?"

"Truth?" I sobered.

"Truth."

I looked at Maggie for a long time, wantin' desperately to make her happy, to side with her in whatever her dreams and goals might be. I ached to be as cool as she was, and as worldly, but I knew I didn't have it in me. I didn't even possess the strength to confide in my own sister and admit that I didn't want to marry Jimmy Lee. I shrugged.

"Uh-uh. That doesn't work, Pix." She pressed her knees harder into my arms.

"Ouch!"

"Mama and Daddy can't make your life into what you want, Pix, only you can. This is about you. Tell me."

I turned my head, gazin' out the window, and prayin' for strength. "I don't know."

Maggie slid off of my arms. I rubbed the pulsin' soreness from them.

"That's better," she sighed. "Now that we know the truth, tell me more."

"I don't know what you mean."

"Do you want to marry him? Are you sure he's the only person, the only man you want to be with? Ever?" She turned "man" into a two-syllable word.

I bit my lower lip.

"Pixie, I've been your age. I know what's goin' on in that body of yours, the way your hormones are dancin' 'round in ways Mama and Daddy would kill you for."

My cheeks burned with embarrassment.

"Yeah?" There was that mischievous smile again. "So, tell me."

"I can't," I said, movin' away from her.

"Have you done it?" she asked.

My jaw dropped open. "Sheesh, Maggie. A little direct, aren't you?"

"Real, maybe," she smirked. "Come on, I'm your sister. Okay, I'll start." She crawled over to where I was sittin' and leaned against my back. Maggie must have known that it would be easier for me to talk to her if I didn't have to look her in the eye. "I did it when I was your age. Remember Mr. Crantz?"

"That substitute from Mississippi?" I was mortified. "He was so old. Gross."

"He was not. He was twenty-seven, and he was adorable."

"Gross."

"Okay, your turn."

I didn't say anything.

"Pixie, what are you afraid of? That I'll run and tell Mama and Daddy? Uh, no. This is me you're talkin' to."

I locked my eyes on the tips of my fingers, tappin' them up and down on the hay.

"Are you careful at least?" she asked.

I nodded against the back of her head.

"Always?"

No. "Yes." Another painful lie. My stomach tightened.

She let out a relieved sigh. "Good, because the last thing you need is to get pregnant." She spun around and in the next moment was sittin' next to me. "Is that where you were last night?" The high-pitched excitement in her voice matched my fear of her knowin'.

"What are you talkin' about?"

"Gosh, Pix, do you think I'm dumb? You went to bed with your clothes on. Anything you're doin', I've already done—many times over."

I doubt that. I put my head down on my knees.

"You don't have to tell me, but you know if Daddy finds out you're dead meat." She went to the window and tapped on the panes. "See the path? Daddy will see that one day and you'll be in a lot of trouble. You need to be more careful."

I looked at the flattened plantin's, a clear path leadin' to a large flattened area where we were last night. I crossed my arms to stop them from shakin'.

"Pix," Maggie said, turnin' my head with her hand so I was facin' her serious eyes. "You can't get caught. You hear me?"

The truth in her words was more significant than she knew.

"Girls?" Mama's voice sang into the loft from below, stealin' my chance to tell Maggie what was really goin' on. "Let's go."

Before we climbed down the ladder, Maggie whispered in my ear, "Don't confuse sex for love."

Chapter Ten

The pungent smell of flowers greeted us at Mrs. Watson's front door. I looked around for a vase of newly picked stems, but saw none as we walked through the threshold of the old farmhouse. Lace doilies covered every surface of the dark furniture. Mrs. Watson bustled around us in her skirt and newly-pressed blouse.

"I can't believe the big day is so close!" Mrs. Watson clapped her hands together. Though she was only in her mid-sixties, she moved slowly. Mama wondered who would take over the invitation business when Mrs. Watson no longer wanted to sell them. From her enthusiasm, I wondered if that day would ever come.

When she leaned in to hug me, I realized that the overpowerin', sweet smell was comin' from Mrs. Watson's perfume.

"You've grown up so much, Alison." She embraced Maggie. "Oh, dear, when are *you* gettin' married?"

Maggie looked at me and rolled her eyes, then turned on a charmin' smile and said, "I don't know, but I'll be sure to order my invitations from you when I do."

Mama glared at Maggie.

"Of course you will." Mrs. Watson led us to the livin' room, nicely appointed with braided rugs and a dark wing chair at the front, which she stood behind as she pointed to the couch. "Please, sit."

Mrs. Watson's gray hair was piled high on her head like a puff of frostin'. She sat down in the wing chair, settin' a thick, paper catalog on her lap, and a permanent smile across her thin lips. "Alison, this is a big decision for you. Do you have a color scheme in mind?"

I couldn't take my eyes off of her nose. I had never noticed the way it pointed and turned toward the right, just slightly at the tip. I blinked away my stare. The idea of plannin' a weddin' with Jimmy Lee turned my stomach. Instead, I thought of what I might want if I were to marry Jackson. "Yes, ma'am. Beige and white, please."

She sat up straighter and moved her feet in closer, knees so tight they could hold a penny between them. "Beige? For a weddin'?"

"Alison likes things simple," Mama offered.

Maggie kicked my foot. I looked at her out of the corner of my eyes and she mouthed, *You can still get out of this.*

"Girls, pay attention," Mama said.

I snapped my eyes back to Mrs. Watson's nose. "Yes, ma'am. I like things simple."

She said, "Well, it is your weddin', dear," but her tone said, *It will be ugly, but it's your choice.* She flipped through the catalog, sighin' and glancin' up at me. "We don't have much with beige." Flip, flip, flip. "I don't believe I've ever ordered beige invitations before."

I wanted to run out of the room. I didn't care what she wanted, and with Maggie sittin' beside me, I couldn't stop thinkin' about what she said about love and sex. Maybe I was mixin' up sex and love with Jackson. Ugh! My life had become much too complicated.

Finally, after what felt like an hour, but in reality was only minutes, Mrs. Watson said, "Here we go, beige," with feigned enthusiasm. She pointed to two invitations, one with brown letters and one with a lighter shade, though not exactly beige. The embossed flowers were so tiny that they looked like bugs crawlin' on the paper.

Maggie grabbed my hand and squeezed. "Pix, do you like these?" The laugh she held at bay bubbled behind the back of her free hand.

"I, um, I'm not sure. They're not really beige, are they?"

"Well, we could go with gold," Mrs. Watson offered.

"Gold?" Mama asked.

"Yes, gold."

"That's a little flashy, don't you think, Mama?" I said.

Maggie chimed in, "Well, you could change your whole weddin' to be gold and white. You could even put gold glitter on the cake."

The ridiculousness of the comment tickled my ribs and I stifled a snort, which spurred Maggie's laughter.

"And you could wear gold shoes!" Maggie chortled.

Laugher burst from my lips. Maggie fell over in my lap in a fit of giggles. Mama tried to rein us in.

"Girls!" she chided. "Girls, don't be disrespectful."

My belly hurt from laughter. I saw the sparkle in Mama's eyes, right before she swallowed hard and turned a stern face and a strong apology to Mrs. Watson. Maggie and I folded our hands in our laps and choked back our giggles.

We were led out the door five minutes later with instructions to return only when sincere decisions were to be made.

We drove into town in silence. Mama glanced at us every few minutes with a look of disbelief. I waited for her to lecture us, especially Maggie, who really should have known better.

Mama parked the car in front of the drugstore and turned in her seat to face Maggie. "Gold shoes?" she said, then laughed.

I held my breath, waitin' for her to stop laughin', but she didn't, which made me laugh, then Maggie chimed in, "Don't forget the gold gloves!"

Mama threw her head back with a loud laugh, mouth wide, eyes tearin' up. She wrapped her arm around her stomach and bent over the steerin' wheel in a fit of giggles. Never before had I witnessed Mama laugh so unabashedly, and though I didn't know it was possible, Mama looked even more beautiful.

"Aren't you mad, Mama?" I asked.

She cleared her throat, looked in the mirror and patted her hair, then said. "Mad? No. Embarrassed? Yes. You know the whole town will be talkin'. She'll probably pray for the two of you in her Monday night prayer group, to rid you of the evil influences that abound." Mama climbed out of the car and we followed her.

"Mama, can we wait out here?" Maggie pulled me toward a wooden bench in front of the buildin'.

Sugar maple trees lined the sidewalk. The street bustled with Saturday shoppers from neighborin' towns. Saturdays were "town" days for most local folks. Errands were run and friends visited. I watched with new interest the way the colored folks kept their eyes low and pulled their children toward them as they hurried down the sidewalk. For the first time, I noticed the glances they cast behind them as they walked toward the back of the diner, and the way the little children hung onto the front glass window with longin' in their eyes. Then I noticed somethin' that turned my stomach. The slight lift of the chin from the white folks as they passed the coloreds, a snub so small it's not surprisin' I missed it for so many years. A snub so small I was certain the coloreds felt it like a momentary disappearance of the air they breathed.

I thought of Clara Bingham bein' chased out of town, and wondered if she was missin' this side of Forrest Town or if she was happy to bid farewell to the chin snubs. I hoped she'd found a better place in Mississippi, but if you only know one place for so many years, I can't imagine it would be easy to start over somewhere else.

Maggie watched a little colored boy standin' on his tiptoes, beggin' his short and stout mother for ice cream. She tried to pull the toddler from the window, speakin' in crisp whispers. Maggie's smile faded and she stood and grabbed my arm.

"Come on," she said.

In the diner, Maggie purchased a vanilla ice cream cone with money I didn't know she had. She walked back outside, bent down, and handed the cone to the boy with the enormous, dark eyes and tight, black tendrils. The little boy reached for it with a squeal. His mother pulled him out of Maggie's reach and into her arms.

"No, thank you," she said, her eyes dartin' from side to side.

An elderly couple slowed to watch as the mother took a step backwards.

Maggie stepped closer, the ice cream held out in front of her. "Take it. It's a gift for the baby."

The child reached for the cone, "Want it!"

His mother stepped further away from Maggie. "Thank you, ma'am," she said, her eyes on Maggie's feet. "No, thank you. Please." Her eyes begged to be left alone. A murmur rose from the bystanders.

Maggie's lips formed in a tight line. She turned to the gatherin' crowd. "It's an ice cream cone. He's a child." She thrust the ice cream toward the woman.

The woman hurried away. The child screamed in her arms, his hands outstretched over his mother's shoulder.

Maggie walked right up to the group of people who lingered with mumbles of "wrong" and "nigger lover."

Just as Mama stepped out of the drug store, Maggie thrust the ice cream cone at the bystanders and said through gritted teeth, "They're people. People! Not niggers, or any less worthy than you." She pointed at a heavy-set man. "Or her." She pointed at a toddler in a white woman's arms.

"Margaret Lynn!" Mama's face was as red as the sunset, her eyes as angry and ashamed as if Maggie had walked outside naked. She grabbed Maggie's arm in one hand, holdin' a bag of groceries in the other, and pulled her toward the car repeatin', "I'm sorry. I'm so sorry," to the crowd.

I followed on Mama's heels, in awe of Maggie's courage.

Chapter Eleven

The clinkin' of forks to plates in between stretches of chewin' filled our dinin' room that evenin'. Tension mounted with every bite for everyone, it seemed, except Maggie. My father had yet to look at either of us. Jake stared at Maggie, his nose down, irises ridin' atop the whites of his eyes. Only Maggie ate without any noticeable tension. Her shoulders didn't ride up high, each cut of her knife was slow and careful. Every so often she looked up and smiled at me, shrugged at Daddy. I wondered what had happened in New York to make her not care about what our father thought, or what he might do. I worried that although Daddy wasn't a whippin' man, he might stop payin' for Maggie to come home to visit, or even worse, not pay for her to go back to New York. All afternoon she'd acted as though nothin' had happened in town. She and Mama baked bread while I worked on the weddin' list, which was only about twenty-five people long, because I couldn't think past the pencil-thin man in overalls who had called my sister a nigger lover. He had it wrong. I was the nigger lover.

My father sat at the end of the table with the sleeves of his t-shirt pushed up, revealin' his milk-white skin beneath and the tan line that all farmers sported. He chewed slow, determined, as if each bite held his full concentration.

"Daddy, there's an art course that's gonna be given at the University of Mississippi that I'd like to take. I could work off the money on the farm." Jake's eyes were hopeful.

My father looked at him, then wiped his mouth with a napkin and set it on the table next to his plate.

Jake looked at Maggie, then shifted his eyes to his plate. "One of my teachers told me about it," Jake continued. I had a feelin' it was Maggie who told Jake about the class, but I knew better than to ask right then.

My father looked at me, then back at Jake. "Art class? What a waste of money. Art class," he laughed. "What on earth can someone do with an art class under his belt? Draw cartoons?"

"No, sir." Jake sat up tall. "I can do lots of things. I can learn to design buildin's or—"

"Pipe dreams, son. You stick with your business courses. You'll do just fine."

"Daddy, what if Jake doesn't want to be a—"

My father cast harsh eyes on Maggie. He leaned forward, his elbows on the table, and said in a serious, dark tone, "I know what's best for my children, includin' you."

Maggie set her fork down and crossed her arms, meetin' Daddy's stare.

"I heard about you today, little missy. Disgracin' the family like that. You should be ashamed of yourself."

Maggie looked at Mama, who had conveniently begun clearin' her plate, avoidin' Maggie's pleadin' look.

My father shook his fork in Maggie's direction. "I don't want you girls goin' into town while Maggie's home. There's no good gonna come from what you did today."

"No good? Ashamed? Daddy, please, I tried to give a child an ice cream." Maggie picked up her fork and poked at the green beans on her plate.

My father stabbed a piece of meatloaf. "You listen to me, Margaret. You will not go into town. You're leavin' tomorrow night, and I don't need anymore strife from you."

Maggie pushed her chair from the table. "It was an ice cream. He was a child, a little boy no different than Jake was as a child. How dare you—"

"How dare I?" Daddy yelled. His chair shot out behind him as he sprung to his feet. A lump grew in my stomach heavy as lead.

Please stop, Maggie, I silently pleaded.

"Those people are not the same as Jake, or you, or me, or any of us." He swung his arm around so hard I thought he might hit her. "Don't you sass me, young lady." He stood with his face two inches from Maggie's.

Tears burned in Maggie's eyes. "Know my place, right Daddy? I'm a white girl so I should act like one?"

Shut up, Maggie. Shut up! I clenched my hands into fists, prayin' as hard as I could for Maggie to stop needlin' Daddy. She didn't catch my prayer.

"I've seen other parts of the world, Daddy. I know about civil rights and I know that this damned town you live in is ass-backwards, and I'll do whatever I can to fix that."

My father's hand connected with Maggie's cheek with a crack so sharp she stumbled backward. Mama flew between them, arms spread out wide.

"Ralph! Stop!" It was a command, not a plea. She pushed Maggie behind her with the order to go upstairs. When Maggie remained, too stunned to move, a pink mark blossomin' on her cheek and hatred glowin' in her wide eyes, Mama said in a strong, even tone, "Go."

My father reached for Mama's arm. I watched in horror as Mama's eyes narrowed. Fear laced every fiber of my bein'. I couldn't watch Mama get hit. Jake's hands were on the table, elbows bent, like a cat ready to pounce.

Mama lifted her chin just as those white folks had on the street, castin' a silent warnin' between them that could only be read by husband and wife. My father hesitated, then lowered his hand. His chest heaved up and down, his teeth clenched. To my relief and sorrow, he stormed out the front door. I flinched when the screen door slammed against the frame, makin' a mental note to bring my books indoors before bed. There would be no sneakin' out tonight.

That night Maggie and I lay atop her blanket, our hands entangled, our breathin' matched, the silence of the house pressin' in on us.

"I'm scared," I whispered.

"You shouldn't be scared, Pix. You should be angry." Maggie spoke with little to no emotion, as if she'd accepted the anger that had replaced our previously happy family.

"I don't know what to feel. Ever since I found Mr. Bingham, my whole life has gone crazy."

"What was it like? Findin' him?" she asked.

I thought about the moment I realized that what I'd thought was a lump of refuse was really a body. The memory seeped back in from the crevices of my mind where I'd tucked it away. I cried as I told Maggie about the bruisin', his bloated body, and the way his eyes looked up toward the sky with a permanent shock of terror that I couldn't look away from. I must have squeezed Maggie's hand, because she yelped and turned on her side, facin' me. She took her finger and moved my hair off of my forehead, the way Mama used to do.

"I'm sorry you found him, Pixie. That must have been horrible."

A tear slipped down my cheek.

"I wish I could bundle you up and take you back to New York with me. I hate leavin' you here."

The weight of my life tumbled around me. Jackson swam in my heart and Jimmy Lee clawed at my mind. Maggie was pushin' herself out of our family faster than a chicken chased by a fox, and Mama was standin' up in ways I'd only imagined in my dreams—and it all felt so wrong. I put my hands on Maggie's arms and curled into her, wishin' I could climb beneath her skin and soak in her strength. She wrapped me in her arms and held me as I sobbed.

Maggie didn't ask me why I was cryin', she didn't try to fix what was wrong. She honored my sadness with patience, allowin' me to lie against her beatin' heart until my eyes were red and swollen, with no more tears to shed.

Chapter Twelve

By mid-afternoon, Mama was already wrist deep in apple peels. The kitchen was alive with the aroma of cinnamon and baked apples. It was Wednesday and Jackson would be returnin' to his military service on Friday. I needed somethin' to keep my mind off of him leavin'. Three days had passed since Maggie returned to New York with promises of weekly letters and bein' home before the weddin'. And it had been exactly four days since I'd seen Jackson. I just couldn't muster the courage to sneak out after what I'd witnessed between Daddy and Maggie. My heart pulled and fought me to see Jackson again, and I cringed with sadness every time I thought of him lookin' for my library books on the porch. He must hate me by now, I was sure of it. But after the rift between Maggie and Daddy became a fissure that I wasn't sure would ever close, I knew I wasn't ready to take a stance and chase away my Daddy's love to be with Jackson.

Mama focused on the apple she was slicin'. She sighed, long and low.

I pretended not to notice, figurin' she'd tell me what was wrong when she was good 'n ready.

She finished corin' and slicin' the last apple, then removed the first batch of baked apples from the oven. I mixed the brown sugar, cinnamon, and honey in a big bowl, dippin' my finger in for a taste of the sweet nectar before addin' the butter.

While Mama mixed the apples and the sauce together, I leaned against the counter, lickin' my fingers and wonderin' what I could do to mend Maggie and Daddy's relationship.

"Honey, wash your hands, please."

I turned on the water and glanced out the window over the sink. Albert had come back to work, although he wasn't workin' in the fields yet. He and Daddy stood by the barn. My father pointed to the tractor, and I looked in that direction, catchin' sight of Jackson comin' in from the furthest field alongside several other colored men, their arms heavy with containers of DDT, their faces glistenin' with sweat. Smiles lifted their lips as they chatted back and forth, throwin' a rag like a ball between them. They stopped their playful banter as they neared the barn.

"Mama, shouldn't we bring those boys some lemonade?" Seein' Jackson opened the door to my heart that I'd closed out of fear.

"Your father has water for them."

"But, couldn't we bring them lemonade? On a day like today it might be more refreshin'." I eyed the bowl of lemons on our counter.

Mama put her hand on my shoulder and said, "It's probably best if we don't."

I spun around and asked her why.

For a long time she just looked at me, measurin' her response. "Well, when you were younger, your father didn't want you takin' them anything, because he worried for your safety; but I think if we do it together, it'd probably be just fine."

I made quick work of cuttin' and squeezin' lemons into several pitchers of ice water, dousin' them with sugar, and makin' sure the end result was sweet and refreshin'. We put the pitchers on trays and carried them outside just in time to greet the men as their day came to an end.

I didn't trust myself bein' too near Jackson for fear of blushin'. I knew Mama would see the desire in my eyes. Fifteen young colored men grabbed glasses of lemonade. I was too young to be called ma'am, and yet these men, some just about my age, with fatigue in their eyes and sweat on their brows, treated me as if they knew the place Daddy had spoken of so often—my *place*.

Some of the men were as slim as the day was long, holdin' their glasses out for more of the cool drink. Their long arms bubbled with baseball-sized muscles. They gulped down a full glass worth in one swallow and set their glass back on the tray with a sincere measure of gratitude.

Jackson stayed a respectable distance from me, acceptin' a glass from Mama's tray with a generous thank you. I watched him out of the corner of my eye. His eyes were cold and distant, locked on the fields beyond the house. *Our fields*, as I'd come to think of them. I swatted at a bug, awkwardness graspin' at my movements. *What had I done?* Four days was too long. I hadn't talked to Jackson since we'd made love, and now I worried that I'd never have a chance.

I coughed, played with my hair, spoke too loudly, and still he didn't look over. I told myself that Jackson would never take a chance of bein' caught eyein' me, then worried that he hadn't wanted to. There was no secret smile, no symbolic gesture, and the absence of even the smallest acknowledgment hurt like a paper cut, swift and deep. Today, my books were goin' on the rockin' chair.

Chapter Thirteen

As soon as the house was silent, I tiptoed to my parents' room and peeked in. They lay still, Daddy's arm arced over his head, the other across his stomach. Mama slept with her back to him. I made my way silently downstairs and out the back door. As soon as the night air hit my lungs, any hesitation I'd felt the days before turned to determination. I might not be ready to give up Daddy's love, but the hurt I felt that afternoon when Jackson shunned me made me realize that I wasn't ready to give him up, either.

The rows of plantin's were thick and soft beneath my feet as I ran toward the creek. When I finally reached the end of the field's grasp, I saw Jackson sittin' on a rock beside the water, his back to me and his strong frame hunched forward. I ran to him, brushin' his shoulder. He flinched beneath my touch.

"Hi," I said, out of breath.

He nodded. He didn't move toward me, he didn't reach for my hand.

I crouched before him and touched his knee. "Hey, you okay?" When he didn't answer, I said, "I missed you."

He nodded again, then sat up tall. "I'm leavin' tomorrow."

"Tomorrow? That's only Thursday. I thought you were leavin' Friday." It was too soon. *One day.* One day wasn't enough.

He shrugged. "Tomorrow, Friday, what's the difference?"

"A day. A full twenty-four hours."

He stood and crossed his arms. "Right, and what's the big deal about that?"

I shook my head. "What do you mean? Don't you want to be with me?"

"Me?" he raised his voice. "Yes, I want to be with you, but you've made it clear how you feel. I haven't heard from you in days."

My stomach tightened. I touched his arm, desire warmin' my throat. "I'm sorry." It was the truth, I was sorry. "I couldn't get away." *I'm too weak.*

"I'm sorry? Is that all it takes for you? Well I don't know how you treat Jimmy Lee, but that's not enough. We..." He lowered his voice and pulled his shoulders back, like he was recoverin' from sayin' Jimmy Lee's name and bringin' him into our conversation. "We were close, and then you disappeared. How do you think that made me feel? I look at your porch everyday, hopin' your books are there, and everyday I'm shut down like a used-up mule."

Hearin' him say Jimmy Lee's name was strange. I hadn't thought about Jimmy Lee in days. I was too busy worryin' about how to keep my family together, and the steps I needed to take to protect myself from losin' them.

"I'm sorry. I really, truly am. I've been confused."

"Yeah, well you'll have four months to get unconfused, because that's how long I'm gonna be gone, and when I'm out of the service, I'm goin' straight to New York."

"Wait, I thought we were goin' to New York together?" I heard the falseness of my words as they left my lips. I wouldn't run away with him and leave my family behind. I couldn't.

He touched my arm, then, and said softly, "Alison, you're not goin' anywhere. You're one of them. What we had—"

Hot tears fell down my cheeks. He wiped them away, and I grabbed his hand and brought it to my lips. I kissed his palm, then rested my cheek on it. "I love you."

"Maybe, but if this is how you love, it's not enough for me. I've been oppressed my whole life, held back by the ropes of color. I want to love for real. I want to know that whoever loves me will love me regardless of my color, regardless of what others think, and you can't do that, not here."

"I could lose my family."

"I know." He leaned down and kissed my forehead. I grabbed his waist and held on. His words were true, but they didn't stop the ache in my heart. The cool night air stung my lungs as I sucked in a deep breath, hopin' to dislodge the lump from my throat. "I can do it. I do love you."

"I know you do, but I watched you these last few days, avoidin' the fields, avoidin' me. I couldn't think past your name, Alison. I can't eat, I can't sleep. It's killin' me."

Our bodies trembled, mine from the fear of bein' without him, and his, I was sure, from the truth his words carried.

"No," I cried, shakin' my head and pullin' away. "I want to be with you. Maybe I can do this."

"Alison, you're gettin' married in a few weeks. *Maybe* means you can't do this."

"No," I cried. "Be with me, I'll show you. One more time, before you leave?"

He shook his head. "You're not mine. You never will be."

"It hurts too much. I want to be." I wiped my eyes with my arm. "Will you write me? Through Albert? We can find a way, like my mama does with your mama?"

Again, he shook his head. I dropped to my knees, the harsh sting of rejection stealin' my strength. "I just made a mistake. I should've given you a message. I should've met you. I'm sorry. I was afraid. My sister had a fight with Daddy, and I was afraid he'd tell me to leave, too, if he found out."

"You're right. He would have, and I would never forgive myself if he did. I love you. I will always love you. But I won't steal you from another man, and I won't be your hidden lover." He came down on his knees. His lips met mine, soft and delicious.

When our lips parted, my eyes remained closed. I knew that the moment I opened them what we had would be forever changed.

"I don't blame you one bit," he whispered.

I opened my eyes and saw tears in his.

"Maybe I'll see you when I visit Maggie?" I knew it would never happen.

"Maybe," he said. He held my hand and we sat there, on the side of the creek, the tricklin' water movin' by like the past few days, sure and steady.

I touched his face, his eyes, his hair, his ears. I wanted to memorize every bit of him. His musky smell, his taste, sweet and ripe, the feel of his palms, soft like butter, yet peppered with callouses across the tops. I let my hands drop to his wide, solid hips. His hands moved down my shoulders, my arms warm beneath his touch. Moonlight streaked through the umbrella of trees, illuminatin' the grass beside us. I wanted to fall asleep there beside him, and wake with his gentle caress. I wanted to make baked apples for him, and to take his mother a batch without havin' to hide. More than anything, I wanted our love not to be forbidden.

He pulled me to my feet, our chests touchin'. I pressed into him and felt his desire firm against my hip. He kissed away my tears.

"You deserve a beautiful life," he said. He turned and walked away, followin' the creek toward town.

"Jackson," I called after him. He turned, and our eyes met. Mine, pleadin' for him not to go, his knowin' he had no choice. I blew him a kiss. He reached toward the sky and caught it, then put his hand to his heart. *Run after him.* My legs were rooted to the ground by my Daddy's love. He disappeared into the darkness, takin' a piece of my broken heart with him.

Chapter Fourteen

The weeks before the weddin' passed painfully slow, like molasses from a Mason jar. Each breath took an insurmountable effort to push past my feelin' of loss. I had created my own darkness by pushin' Jackson away instead of followin' my heart, and God knew how much I loved him, but I held a mantra in my mind that it was the right thing to do.

I found myself longin' for Maggie's presence, but she hadn't returned home from college at the end of her term. She stayed in New York to work as a secretary for a law firm. She'd written me a letter and confessed that she'd joined the Black Panthers, as she'd hoped to, and that the law firm that she was workin' for was really into makin' changes with civil rights. She made me promise not to tell Daddy. She said she was makin' a difference, and I was happy for her, but every time I looked at her empty bed or brought up her name at the dinner table, a wave of despair settled in around me. Daddy wouldn't even say her name, and in his silence, sadness pressed forward. The blue in his eyes dimmed with hurt. I couldn't imagine what it would feel like to have him feel that way because of me.

One day I snuck over to the side of the field where Albert Johns was workin', and I'd asked him if Jackson had sent any letters for anyone. He'd taken two steps backwards, whippin' his head around like we were doin' somethin' against the law—in a way we were, though the law was unwritten. Albert looked at me like I was crazy for talkin' to him, and that's when I knew there would be no letters. As much as I missed Jackson—and I surely did—I thought I'd made the right decision, no matter how sad it made me.

With my love for Jackson put on hold, and without Maggie around to sidetrack my thoughts, I finally gave in and chose a light pink for our weddin' invitations, which seemed to please Mrs. Watson. Jimmy Lee had graduated from college, and although I was too sick the mornin' of his graduation to attend, I was proud of him. I had high hopes that once he returned and was a workin' man, instead of a schoolboy, he'd stop his crazy antics and settle down.

Chapter Fifteen

The mornin' of my weddin' arrived with a bout of nausea. Mama said it was just my nerves, and Maggie, who'd arrived the evenin' before, held my hair back as I threw up the previous night's dinner. My father had yet to say two words to her.

"You're sure about this, Pix?" she whispered when Mama left the bathroom.

"I'm not you. This is best for me." The inability to see Jackson made it that much easier to convince myself to start fresh with Jimmy Lee. Even if I didn't love him the way I loved Jackson, and maybe I never would, I knew it was best if I stayed in my safe cocoon of a life. I didn't have what it took to be on my own the way Maggie did. The comfort I drew from Daddy's warm embrace, and his conditional admiration, no matter how unrealistic, was somethin' that I cherished. There was no doubt in my mind that I needed Daddy in my life.

We moved into the bedroom to prepare for my weddin'. I sat at the dressin' table with my puffy eyes and pink nose, soakin' in the tenderness of Maggie's efforts as she combed through my hair.

"Okay, but you know, the offer is still open for you to come to New York with me." There was a sparkle in her eye that made me want to follow her anywhere. The thought of seein' Jackson in New York excited me, then saddened me. I'd made my bed, and it was time to sleep in it.

"I'm good, thanks, though."

"Will you at least visit me?" she asked.

"Right after we're settled."

"Promise?"

"Promise." And so it was set. I'd take the train to New York at the end of the summer. I was sure Jimmy Lee wouldn't mind. He knew how close Maggie and I were. Maggie told me all about her job with Mr. Nash's law firm. He was a civil rights activist and had warned Maggie about the Black Panthers, but she assured me that they had never done anything violent, he just worried they might. She said she'd remain safely behind closed doors with the families.

"I won't protest, don't worry. I just want to do my part," Maggie said.

"I wish I could do somethin' like that here, help the colored families to do little things, like eat in the diner."

"Little things?" Maggie said sarcastically. "That's a huge thing, Pix."

"Girls, need any help?" Mama came into the bedroom in a flurry, nervously lookin' around the room. She looked gorgeous in her blue dress with her hair brushed shiny and full away from her face.

"We've got this, Mama," Maggie said, zippin' up my dress.

I stood in the middle of the room in Mama's weddin' dress, which was less like a frilly weddin' dress and more like a long, white ball gown. She'd hemmed it, and it fit like a sleeve, though noticeably tighter than it had when I'd first tried it on.

"Is it too tight?" I worried.

Mama ran her hand down my side, trailin' the silky gown's seam. "You're just carryin' five pounds of happy," she said. "Brides gain or lose weight right before their weddin', because they're happy. They've caught their man and they relax a little bit." She patted my cheek. "Glory be, you are a sight, Alison. Jimmy Lee is one lucky man."

Why the statement saddened me, I wasn't sure. I thought I had moved past my indecision—or maybe I just hoped that I had.

"Yes, he is, and he'd better remember that every day of your long life," Maggie smirked.

Mama embraced me. "My little girls are all grown up. Why, I'll have no one left 'round here."

"We're only movin' into town, Mama. It's not like you'll never see me. Besides, you have Jake here, remember?"

A shadow crossed over Mama's face, and I wondered what she was thinkin' just then. She kissed my cheek and said, "I'll go make sure your Daddy is ready. He's all thumbs when it comes to tyin' his tie."

There are times in our lives when everything comes together and we know we are exactly where we are supposed to be. My weddin' day was not one of those days. I stood at the altar, facin' Jimmy Lee, handsome in his black suit and crisp, white shirt. My stomach quivered as I looked into his eyes, recitin' my vows. "I promise to love, honor, and cherish…" *Love, honor, cherish.* I could love him, yes, I knew I could. I had before, and once he stopped chasin' down innocent boys, I'd surely love him again. *Honor.* I respected Jimmy Lee, well, at least most of the time I did. We'd had a long talk last week about how I felt that day at the river, when he was too rough, and he apologized and I could tell he meant it. It was easy to forgive him, we'd been together for so long that he knew just how to say all the right words to make me feel better, even if he didn't do that unsolicited anymore. Did anyone after two years? Yes, I could honor him. *Cherish* was a more difficult concept for me to wrap my heart around. The pulse of my heart fought me on *cherish.* When I thought of the curved edges of that word, they were Jackson's arms I felt around me. When I said the word out loud, I'm reminded of Jackson's soft lips on mine, the way his body felt against me, the way he moved in slow, careful movements, lookin' at me, not through me. *Cherish* was not a word my heart embraced with Jimmy Lee, but I said it all the same. It was my place, after all, as his wife.

Jimmy Lee slipped the ring on my finger and my marriage became real. I was no longer Daddy's little girl or Maggie's little sister. I was Mrs. James Carlisle, and when Jimmy Lee kissed me to seal our union, I prayed to feel the same rush of love I felt for Jackson. I prayed for the heat to rush from the center of my stomach up to my chest and down my thighs. I hoped the kiss might rekindle the spark I once felt for him. I came away from that kiss, that start of our marriage, wonderin' how I would ever find what I was hopin' for.

Chapter Sixteen

We didn't take a honeymoon because his uncle said Jimmy Lee needed to begin trainin' for his position with the furniture store. Jimmy Lee hoped to plan a trip to Niagara Falls once we had enough money saved. I didn't mind waitin'. I knew it would be forever before we could afford it, even if his uncle was fixin' to pay for half of the trip.

We fell into our married life like two kids playin' house. Every mornin' Jimmy Lee went to work and I cleaned, baked bread, planned dinners, and quickly grew bored. I wondered how Mama did it for all those years. After a few weeks, Mama suggested that I think about gettin' a job in town, where I could walk to work, somethin' part-time.

"I make enough money," Jimmy Lee argued. "You don't need to work."

We were eatin' dinner at our small kitchen table. I had spent the entire day inside, and I wasn't used to bein' so confined. I was tired all the time and hardly ever felt like eatin'. I was sure that it was because I missed the activity of daily life. I stared at the same white walls of our apartment day in and day out. I tried takin' walks, but it wasn't enough. I needed somethin' more to pull me out of the funk I'd fallen into. Some days, it was hard for me to climb out of bed and when I finally made it to the kitchen to fix Jimmy Lee's breakfast, the smell of his eggs cookin' made me sick to my stomach.

"I know you do. I just need a little somethin' to do, Jimmy Lee. I'm in this apartment all day and night."

"Mama doesn't work. Your mother doesn't work." He took a bite of the biscuits I'd made the evenin' before, which weren't nearly as flakey as Mama's, but he didn't seem to mind.

"I know yours doesn't, but mine does, on the farm, and besides, they had us to take care of. It's just me here, all day, by myself."

"We're not havin' no baby, Alison. Not yet, at least."

I sighed. Why didn't he ever listen to me? "I don't want a baby, Jimmy Lee, I just want a part-time job where I can talk to people and get out of the apartment for a few hours each day." Nausea rose in my throat. I swallowed against it. *Nerves.*

He wiped his mouth and stood to leave. "Do what you want to, but just make sure you're home every night early enough to make dinner. I work hard. A man needs to eat."

Already plannin' my outfit for my day of applyin' for jobs, I agreed. Even his chauvinistic comment couldn't damper the renewed energy the idea brought with it.

Each store held the promise of somethin' new and excitin'. My legs were tired as lead, but as I looked in the windows of each shop, new energy filtered in. I looked back toward our apartment and wondered what Daddy would think of my workin' part time. I asked myself, *What would Maggie do? Maggie wouldn't have thought about Daddy in the first place.* I checked my blouse and hair in my reflection in the window of the diner, thinkin' about the little boy and the ice cream cone he wasn't allowed to accept. I took a deep breath to quell my nerves, and walked through the door, and nearly bumped right into Mrs. Tempe, who was holdin' an orange and black Help Wanted sign.

"Oh, I'm so sorry."

"Alison! Why that's okay, darlin', I was just headin' up front to hang this old sign. Marla left on account of her movin' outta town next week." Her yellow and white waitress uniform fit snug against her thick curves. Her short, brown hair curled so perfectly in tiny rings around her face it was like she had invisible rollers holdin' them in place.

"I didn't mean to run you over like that," I said.

"Oh, honey, you couldn't run me over if you tried, you're such a tiny, little thing." She waved her hand up and down. "I guess I oughta call you *Mrs*. Carlisle now, huh, sugar?"

"It's strange, havin' a new last name. I'm not really used to it yet."

"By the time you get used to it, you'll be over it. That's how fast it happens. One day you wake up and you realize that you didn't notice the switch, when you went from Alison Tillman to Alison Carlisle. Those few days you have to think before you sign your name pass faster than castor oil through a baby." She patted my arm. "What are you here for today? A nice cake for that handsome husband of yours?"

"A job." The words slipped out before I could form a proper response.

"A job?" She leaned in close and whispered. "Are you havin' money troubles already?"

"Oh, no." Worry soared through me. Is that what people would think? I couldn't embarrass Jimmy Lee like that. "I'm just bored, really. Jimmy Lee is at work all day and I've got nothin' to do in that tiny little apartment."

She drew her eyebrows together. "Yes, that does happen, doesn't it?" She looked around the diner. "With Marla gone, I am in need of a capable set of hands, and yours'll do just fine. It's only a few hours here and there."

"That would suit my needs perfectly. Thank you!" I bit back my enthusiasm and asked tentatively, "Do you think people will really think we're havin' money trouble? I don't want people talkin' like that."

She waved her hand in the air. "What do you care what others think? A young, pretty girl like you?" She put her arm around my neck and said, "Better to have a little sanity break every now and again than to lose your mind worryin' about small town gossip, right?"

There was a knock at the back door and I waited as Mrs. Tempe gathered the wrapped food that was spread across the counter, placed it in a paper bag, and headed for the door. I sat down next to a heavyset man on one of the orange stools at the counter. The stools spun if you pushed them hard enough. I had driven Mama crazy on those stools more times than I could count.

I watched Mrs. Tempe at the back door. A small colored boy, who couldn't have been more than eight years old, dug deep into his pockets. His spindly arms were all elbows and wrists. He handed her a fistful of money and stood on his tippy toes, peerin' around her. His eyes caught mine, and I couldn't read what they held—embarrassment? Curiosity? He looked away quickly, leavin' me feelin' embarrassed for bein' *inside* the diner. Jackson sailed into my mind. The thought of him standin' at the back door of any diner bothered me. I'd been pushin' away the thoughts of him so effectively that the memory took me by surprise.

The door thumped shut, joltin' me out of my own mind and back to the present. Mrs. Tempe's hips swayed from side to side with her hurried gait as she picked up dirty dishes from the booth where two women sat. They whispered among themselves, and Mrs. Tempe's lips pressed into a firm line. She slapped a check down on the table, spun around with determination, and carried the dishes behind the counter, where she passed them wordlessly to Joe, the cook, who masterfully slid them out of sight.

She punched numbers into the cash register, mumblin' about *hoity toity* women and the nerve of them. "Those people have to eat, too," she whispered to me with a speck of frustration.

The coloreds in our town had always gone to the back door of the drugstore and the restaurants. I had known that my whole life, but until that moment, I hadn't felt suffocated by the knowledge. I blinked several times, tryin' to make my thoughts of Jackson go away, but they remained as present as the floor I stood upon. There was no denyin' my growin' discomfort. My eyes were opened to the segregation around me and I knew I had to do somethin' to help those who where treated differently. *Maggie would be proud.*

Mrs. Tempe must not have noticed my momentary lapse of focus. She gave my wrist a sweet squeeze and said, "Can you start tomorrow? Ten a.m.?"

Chapter Seventeen

All dolled up in my prettiest dress, with Jimmy Lee's favorite meal in the oven, I was ready to break the news of my bein' employed. *Employed.* A thrill rushed through me. I'd never held a job before, besides helpin' out on our farm. Dinner was perfectly timed. At exactly five forty-five the table was set just so, candles were lit, and my speech was practiced. I tapped my foot as I watched the minutes tick by. *I'll save every penny toward our honeymoon,* I rehearsed. Anticipation made me jumpy, and I paced our small kitchen.

By six fifteen my back ached and I knew the biscuits were gonna be too soggy for Jimmy Lee to enjoy, so I quickly piled his meal into a bowl and set new biscuits in a separate dish. I'd lather the chicken, vegetables, and gravy on top when he walked through the door.

By six thirty my frustration had stolen my pleasant mood and I felt too sick to eat. I blew out the candles, and wrapped Jimmy Lee's dinner.

The sun dropped from the sky and I closed the curtains against the darkness. I thought about walkin' down to the furniture store, but I knew Jimmy Lee would worry if he came home and I wasn't here. I curled up on the couch and read, until my eyes became too heavy to remain open.

The key jigglin' in the lock woke me from where I'd fallen asleep on the couch. I stood too fast and my head spun. I grabbed the side of the couch as Jimmy Lee stumbled in through the door and toward the livin' room. The stench of alcohol was so thick I turned away.

"Where have you been?" I asked.

Jimmy Lee staggered backward and sat down at the kitchen table. "Where's dinner?" he slurred.

I looked at the clock; it was one thirty in the mornin'. I could not tame my spiteful snark. "I put it away."

"I told you a man gets hungry." He took his jacket off and tried to place it on the back of his chair. It missed, landin' on the floor.

I folded my arms across my chest, breathin' hard. "Why didn't you tell me you were goin' out?"

"Why should I?"

Why should you? "Maybe because we're married, and I made your favorite dinner." *Damned tears.* I swiped at them with my hand. "I lit candles and everything."

"So light them again," he slurred.

I stomped into the kitchen and pulled his dinner from the oven, removed the foil wrap, and dropped it before him with a *clank*. He flinched.

"Where were you?" I asked again.

Jimmy Lee shoveled the food into his mouth like he hadn't eaten all day.

"Jimmy Lee?"

He stopped his hand in mid air and lifted his eyes, still hunched over his food like a protective animal.

"I got a job," I spat.

He shoved the food into his mouth, his eyes locked on mine. He chewed slow and solid. I sat in a chair to stop my legs from tremblin'.

"At the diner, part-time."

He dropped his eyes to his plate and ignored me.

I stewed, too tired to argue. "I start tomorrow," I said over my shoulder as I went to the bedroom. Tears streamed down my cheeks. It seemed that's all I did lately. Cried. I paced the bedroom floor, wonderin' why I ever wanted to get married in the first place.

It wasn't until the next mornin', after Jimmy Lee had gone to work and I was separatin' the laundry, that I noticed the bloodstains on his shirtsleeves and the thighs of his pants. Fear gripped me by the throat. *Which colored boy paid the price of his drinkin' this time?*

Chapter Eighteen

I'd been workin' at the diner for three weeks, much to Jimmy Lee's chagrin. He'd taken to comin' home late several nights each week, complainin' about my needin' to wash my uniform in the evenin's, and yappin' about me workin' at all. Although I enjoyed my job, I was tired all the time. A knock came from the back door. Jean (Mrs. Tempe asked me to call her that, *Makes me feel younger,* she'd said) still wouldn't allow me to bring food to the colored folks. She said the white folks could get feisty if their food had to wait, and she didn't want any trouble for me. I watched with a longin' to be involved each time she handed over the meals, wrapped tight and kept warm, into the waitin' and thankful dark hands. The more I witnessed them callin' at the back door, the more I wanted to help them get rights to the front. I called into the kitchen for Jean, grippin' my stomach. The smell of eggs was particularly strong, and I bit back my breakfast from makin' a second showin'.

"She ran to the market. We're out of paprika." Joe's basketball-shaped, bald head poked through the food window, which hid his plump body.

Another knock came from the rear of the diner. Joe handed me a big, brown bag and said, "Take this to them, will ya'?"

I swallowed against the dizziness that seemed to plague my too-fast movements lately. The heavy door swung in and I stepped aside. Albert Johns' mother stood before me. I remembered her gentle face from the furniture store. I must have looked surprised, because her eyes changed from smilin' to concerned.

"Sorry it took so long," I said, and handed her the paper bag.

She stood with her frownin' lips pressed tightly together.

I held my hand out to receive her money, and wondered what I'd done wrong when she didn't offer payment. *Great, my first time takin' food to the coloreds, and already I messed it up.* "Ma'am? You're supposed to pay now," I whispered, flush warmin' my cheeks.

She slipped a hand into her dress pocket, then pressed the money into my palm, grippin' my hand. Hard.

I looked down at my hand, then back at her.

She whispered, "You hurt my boy."

My throat tightened. *Jimmy Lee*. I shook my head. "No, ma'am, I never touched Albert."

She stared at me with the darkest eyes I'd ever seen. "Jackson."

The world spun before me. I held tight to her hand as the world went black and cold. Everything moved in slow motion, my legs gave way. I saw the concrete step comin' too close, too fast.

"Pregnant?" Mama's voice hung in the air. Dr. Davis stood beside me, his white hair and spectacles comin' slowly into focus. I tried to sit up, but my head felt like it'd been run over by a truck.

"Mama?" I whispered through the haze that clouded my mind.

"Jean called me. She said you passed out," Mama explained.

"Lay back, Alison," Dr. Davis said, gently pressin' my shoulders back down on the couch. "You knocked your head pretty hard when you passed out."

"Passed out?" I asked. I realized that I was in the office of the diner.

Mama leaned over me, her eyes wet with tears. She leaned in close to my ear and asked me when I'd had my last period.

I blinked, not sure I'd heard her correctly. Understandin' sent me bolt upright, ignorin' my throbbin' head. "You think I'm pregnant?" *Oh no, Jimmy Lee will be so upset.*

"Well, when was your last menstrual cycle?" Dr. Davis asked.

"I don't know. It's hard to think. With all the stress of the weddin' and all, I guess it was sometime before the weddin'."

"Why don't you come by my office this afternoon and we'll do a quick blood draw."

Mama lifted her eyebrows. "Have you been sick in the mornin's? Tired?"

Oh, God.

Two days later Mama drove me to Dr. Davis's office to discuss the results of the blood test. I prayed that I was just sick or tired, anything but pregnant. There we sat, on metal chairs in his claustrophobic office, the two of them speakin' as if my pregnancy was a good thing. My mind spun in circles. I hadn't slept in days, the sight of food sickened me, and the thought of tellin' Jimmy Lee I was pregnant nearly sucked all the air from the room.

"You can eat like you normally do, but try not to gain too much weight. The baby needs you to be healthy, so be sure to drink your milk and eat plenty of protein."

"Crackers will help with the nausea." Mama squeezed my hand, a glint in her eye. "Oh, honey, wait until Jimmy Lee finds out."

"Are you sure, Dr. Davis?" I asked, pickin' at my fingernails.

"Sure as the day is long."

Mama rattled on the whole way home about how she'd make me maternity clothes, and we'd have a baby shower when it was time. I could use my old crib if I wanted. She had it stored in the attic. I lay my head back on the passenger seat headrest and wondered how on earth I was gonna tell Jimmy Lee.

"I know you were fixin' to see Maggie, but I think I'd wait a bit. You're just three months pregnant, and it's probably best to wait another month or two. Just to be sure everything is okay."

I wondered if Maggie would be disappointed in me.

"But then I can take the train to New York?" I needed to hear her say it again. I needed to be sure. I didn't want to miss seein' Maggie.

Mama laughed. "Of course. You can do anything when you're pregnant, but it's best to wait until you have some of your energy back. The first three months can be very tryin'."

"You're tellin' me? I just passed out and konked my head."

Mama squeezed my hand. "Will you quit your job now? So you can rest?"

My job? I hadn't thought about quittin' my job to rest. I loved my job. "No, actually, it really helps keep me sane. I can't stand bein' alone all day in the apartment."

"Well, you won't be alone much longer."

I knew she meant well, and I could feel the light radiatin' from her with the thought of bein' a grandmother. Mama loved babies. I, on the other hand, couldn't help but worry about bein' a mother. I was barely able to hold my marriage together. How would I ever care for a baby?

That evenin', before Jimmy Lee came home, I drafted a letter to Maggie and walked it down to the post office.

"We talked about this. How could you let this happen?" Jimmy Lee wasn't drunk, but the smell of alcohol on his breath was becomin' the norm.

"This wasn't all me, Jimmy Lee." I sat on the couch, my feet curled under me, watchin' him pace across our small livin' room floor.

"How? When? We're careful."

He was right. Since we'd been married, we'd been more careful than ever.

"I don't know, okay? It just happened. We are havin' a baby, Jimmy Lee, and we just have to deal with it."

Jimmy Lee lit a cigarette and sat down beside me. I pulled back. Even his cigarette smoke bothered my stomach lately. He took a long drag and turned his head to blow the smoke in the other direction.

"Okay," he said, and leaned back against the couch.

"Okay?" I asked.

"Yeah, okay. You're gonna have to deal with it. It's not like we have a choice."

I'm gonna have to deal with it? "Maybe you can come home earlier some nights?"

He turned angry eyes toward me. "And do what? Leave Corky to hang out alone? I'll do what I see fit," he snapped.

The memories of the afternoon he'd forced himself upon me came rushin' back, followed by a shiver of a memory of bein' with Jackson, then a rush of fear from the confrontation with his mama. She was right. I'd hurt her son. I only wish she knew how much I'd also hurt myself. None of that mattered anymore. That part of my life was over. I was Mrs. James Carlisle, and a mother-to-be. I vowed to try to be the best mother ever.

Chapter Nineteen

I'm not sure what disappointed me more, the extra weight that went to my boobs and made them heavy instead of perky, or Jimmy Lee's increased drinkin'. Several weeks had passed since I found out I was pregnant, and all of my clothes were too tight. Mama altered the larger waitress uniforms Jean gave me, but I still felt like a packed sausage as I waddled through the diner.

There was a knock at the back door, and ever since I saw Jackson's mother, I had steered clear of answerin' it.

"Can you get that, hun?" Jean hollered from the office. She'd been givin' me more and more responsibility lately. *You're gonna be a mama. You can handle anything now.*

With not a single patron in the diner, I had no excuse not to answer it. I grabbed the paper bag from the counter and headed for the back door. What if it was Jackson's mother again? The metal doorknob was cold beneath my sweaty palm. I peered slowly around the edge of the door. To my relief, a small boy stood on the step with his hand outstretched and three dollars and fifty cents in his tiny palm.

"Hi, sweetie. Here you go," I said, and handed him the bag.

A gap-toothed smile graced his lips. Before I could say anything more, he turned on his heels and ran away, his pencil legs movin' as fast as they could down the alley, disappearin' around the corner.

A week later the same little boy showed up, and I realized that his father bought lunch from the diner every Friday. The third Friday, I was ready. When the little boy put the money in my palm, I pressed a cookie into his.

Later that afternoon I was walkin' through my parents' house thinkin' about the smile on that little boy's face, when Daddy took me in his arms and squeezed me so tight I could barely breathe. "Pixie! Look at you, plump as a mother hen."

"Thanks, Daddy. I think."

"Are you sure you want to go to New York in your condition? It's a lot of travelin'."

"Yes, Daddy. I haven't seen Maggie in ages and I miss her."

Daddy kissed the top of my head. "I worry about you is all. Don't let her put those crazy notions of hers into your sweet little head, ya' hear?"

"Don't worry, Daddy. I'll come back just as I left, as your perfect, little, pregnant girl." As I said those words I wondered, not for the first time, if bein' Daddy's perfect girl was the right kind of girl for me to be. I used to be filled with pride 'bout bein' his perfect, little girl, but now I realized that bein' that girl meant not helpin' the coloreds, and my heart battled that stance at every turn.

"Woman," Mama interrupted.

I sure didn't feel like a woman. Jake sidled up next to Mama.

"I thought I heard your voice," he said, and hugged me. "Look how fat you are."

I punched him in the arm. He laughed. Behind us, the farmhands piled into a rusted and dented truck. Albert looked back over his shoulder before climbin' into the back with the rest of them. The way he shook his head made my heart sink. I wanted to run over and tell him that I didn't mean to get pregnant by Jimmy Lee and that I wished it was Jackson's baby, but I knew that even thinkin' that thought was wrong.

"I got somethin' I wanna show you," Jake said, and I followed him into the house, hidin' my face behind the curtain of my hair.

Upstairs in his room, he opened a notebook and showed me a sketch of the inside of the barn, complete with mine and Maggie's feet hangin' over the loft, and the crack in the window.

"Oh, Jake, this is wonderful. How did you get such detail? Every strand of hay is perfect. I can practically smell the DDT on it."

He shrugged.

"Did you show Daddy? I'd bet if you do, he'll let you take those art classes you want."

"No way," he said and snagged the notebook back from me.

"But—"

"You've seen what he does. You saw how he treated Maggie. No way will I go up against him. No way." He tucked the notebook into his desk and changed the subject, askin' me what it felt like be pregnant.

"I feel like a fat girl. Don't change the subject."

He laughed.

"Seriously. Nothin' fits, I waddle, and I can't do anything about it." If he could change the subject, so could I. Maybe Jake could help me figure out what to do about my husband disappearin' every night. "Jake?"

He stood with his back to me.

"Jimmy Lee is drinkin' all the time, and he comes home late every night. Are you hangin' out with him and Corky?"

He turned around and sighed.

"Jake, you can tell me. I won't get mad at you. Promise."

He shook his head. "Corky hasn't been out in two weeks. He cut his hand at the farm and is on some big time medicine. Can't drink while he's on it, so he just stays inside at night."

"So, have you been with him?"

Jake shook his head. I suddenly felt like there was a lead balloon in my stomach instead of a baby in my womb. I lowered myself to sit on his bed. "Jake, what's goin' on? He said he's been out with Corky all this time."

Jake shrugged, and started for the stairs.

I couldn't tether my risin' voice. "What's goin' on? What's he doin'?"

Mama opened the front door and hollered up the stairs. "Is everything alright up there?"

I stood with my arms crossed, starin' at Jake.

"Fine," I said to Mama. I heard her step back onto the porch as I pushed past Jake and hurried down the steps.

All I could think about on the way home was where Jimmy Lee was goin' and what he was doin'. I stopped at the furniture store, somethin' I hadn't done in the weeks since we'd been married.

"Why, Alison, what a nice surprise."

Mr. Kelly had worked at the furniture store forever. A widower who had a gift for makin' himself seem important, he stood before me in a crisply-pressed, three-piece suit, his shoes perfectly shined. His chin maintained a constant tilt up, as if he was always lookin' down his nose at you.

"Hi, Mr. Kelly. Thank you. Is Jimmy Lee here? I'd like to talk to him."

He cocked his head as if I'd asked him if he had seen a five-legged cow. "No." He offered no explanation.

"Do you know when he'll be back?" I asked, bitin' back my mountin' anger.

"I think you'd better ask his uncle."

His uncle? "Okay. Is Mr. Carlisle here?" The storeroom door opened, and Jackson's mother stepped into the showroom. Her eyes dropped to my ever-expandin' belly. She dropped her eyes to the floor and clasped her hands in front of her waist, waitin' silently for Mr. Kelly's attention.

"Yes?" he said, chin lifted.

"I'm sorry, Mr. Kelly, sir. I was just comin' to tell you I was leavin'," she said.

My legs locked. I fumbled with my purse and forced myself to move clumsily toward the door. "Thank you. I'll...I'll find him. Thank you."

Chapter Twenty

The empty shoebox lay on the bed, the lid on top of my clothin', which was strewn across the floor. My belongin's were scattered around the bedroom like we'd been robbed. Jimmy Lee sat on the bed with his back to me, Maggie's weekly letters unfolded on the pillows like public newspapers.

"What's this shit?" he spat.

Maggie's letters spoke of the ways she was helpin' the colored folks, and the things she was plannin'. I never thought Jimmy Lee would actually rifle through my belongin's, and yet, maybe I did, and that's why I'd felt the need to hide them. "What are you doin'?" I hurried to the bedside and grabbed at Maggie's letters, pullin' 'em toward me. "You had no right."

He grabbed my wrist. "No right? I'm your husband. What is all this shit?" He pushed me away. My back hit the dresser. He grabbed one of the letters and read it aloud, "I'm so happy that you want to know what you can do to help with the civil rights movement." He turned scorn-filled eyes toward me. "Civil rights? What are you doin', Alison?"

I clamored for the letters. "Give me those. They're my private letters. This is none of your business." I hated myself for not throwin' the darn things away, but the thought of discardin' anything from Maggie saddened me. Now, I wish I hadn't been so darned sentimental. I'd never make that mistake again.

He pushed me again; my back slammed against the wall and I fell to my knees, protectin' my stomach, and cryin' out in pain.

"This *is* my business. You wanna help those niggers? You? *My* wife?" He gathered the letters in his arms and tossed them in a bag. "You're not goin' to New York. You can forget it."

I pushed to my feet, holdin' the dresser for support. "I'd rather be there than here with you," I cried. "I'm goin' to see my sister, and you can't do a darn thing about it. My father already bought the ticket."

"I never should have married you! You're a…a…charity case."

"Charity case?" A lump lodged in my throat like a baseball. "My family has more class than yours ever will, the way you beat up those poor kids." I pushed past the hurt in my back and the fear that made my entire body quake, and gathered my courage like a shield. "I know you and your uncle killed Mr. Bingham, too." It was a guess, a weighted guess based on the things I'd learned about my husband and his uncle in recent weeks. I had hoped it wasn't true, but the moment the words left my lips there was no question.

He was on me in seconds, pinnin' me to the bed, my belly between us like an unwelcome border. Through gritted teeth he said, "Don't push me, Alison. You don't know shit. That nigger deserved to die."

I struggled against his weight. "Get off of me. You'll hurt the baby."

"My wife ain't gonna help no cotton-pickin' niggers. You got it?"

Hate soared through me. My wrists felt like they were ready to snap beneath his weight.

"Got it?" he hollered. His knees dug into my thighs. "Or it'll be the last thing you ever do."

I had to do somethin'—to get out of there before he hurt the baby. "I got it. Okay, I get it," I seethed.

He pushed his knees deeper into my thighs, until I cried out in pain. Then he climbed off of me with one last thrust , grabbed the bag of letters, and left the bedroom. I curled into a ball, my arms around my belly, and cried, wonderin' what in the hell I should do next.

Chapter Twenty-One

I sat on the porch of my parents' house the next afternoon thinkin' about my life, and how it was spiralin' out of control. I spent my days avoidin' bein' alone and my nights avoidin' my drunken husband who thought I had to *deal with* havin' our child on my own, like he wasn't plannin' on helpin' at all. I felt so alone. I searched for my daddy's truck and found it parked near the fields. It was almost quittin' time. I longed for him to call me his little girl and hug me tight. I needed to talk to Mama. She'd know what to do about Jimmy Lee. Loneliness was stranglin' me, and I needed to find a lifeline before it was too late.

The farmhands walked toward the barn in pairs. I watched Albert, wonderin' if Jackson was out of the service yet, and then felt guilty for wantin' to know.

The screened porch door creaked open behind me. "Daddy's got your train ticket purchased and ready for your trip next month. Are you waitin' to see him?"

"No, actually. I wanted to see you." We sat on the rockin' chairs, side by side. "Mama, do you still see Albert's mother?"

She looked out at the field, then down at her lap. When she finally lifted her eyes toward me, she said, "Yes, and Alison, I know Jimmy Lee and Jake hurt that boy. No doubt they were egged on by Corky or some other troublemaker."

"You know about Jake?"

She nodded. "Surely you noticed how little time he's spendin' at home these days. I had a long talk with him." She pressed the wrinkles in her dress against her thighs. "Jake tries to please your daddy, but he battles himself, too. He's a sensitive boy, always has been. He knows what he did was wrong, but inside," she put her hand over her heart, "he's all confused. And now he's avoidin' me for settin' him straight."

"But what about Daddy?"

"Your father doesn't know, and Jake isn't gonna run to your father. He's...more sensitive than that." She inhaled and blew it out slowly.

"He's just like Daddy."

"No, he isn't. Jake's nothin' like him. He just doesn't know any way to connect with your father other than followin' in his shoes."

I didn't understand. If she knew about Jake and Jimmy Lee, why did she allow me to marry him?

"So, you just overlooked what Jimmy Lee did altogether?"

"No," she said. "I was very upset, and I had a talk with his mother. But, the truth of the matter is, that here, in this town, things aren't gonna change anytime soon, and in life, we must pick our battles."

I got up and paced the front porch. "But you let me marry him, so what you really mean is turn our backs on what's happenin', right?"

Mama stood behind me, her hand on the small of my back. "No, I mean do what we can, but not ruin our families in the process. You love Jimmy Lee, who am I to ruin that? We can't change how people like your father and Jimmy Lee feel about equal rights. We can't change how Jimmy Lee was brought up, but we can stop the cycle. We can make changes in the next generation and be kind on the other end of things."

I turned toward Mama, my eyes wet. "I am the next generation."

"Yes, you are."

"But what if that's not enough? I can't look past it. I hate my husband more every time I see him." My hands flew to my mouth, coverin' it before anymore could slip out, and hidin' the shame I felt for havin' admitted my secret.

Mama reached out and took my hand in hers. "Alison Jean, you don't mean that."

A tear slipped down my cheek, fallin' onto my blouse as I nodded my head. "Yes," I whispered. "Yes, I do."

"You must learn to deal with that hatred. Think of what he provides for you, what made you fall in love with him in the first place."

"Mama, I keep thinkin' about Maggie. She's makin' a difference, and workin' hard at bein' involved, and I'm here in this…this…cocoon of a town, pretendin' things aren't goin' on around me." I turned and watched the men at the barn. "My husband is hurtin' boys, and men, just because their skin is a different color."

"Oh, Alison. You're not Maggie. Maggie is a different woman all together. She could no sooner settle down and have a baby than you could go to New York and change the world. You're sewn from different fabric."

Maybe Mama was right. Maybe I was just dreamin', and I didn't actually have the strength to do anything or evoke any changes in life.

"I guess." I sighed, resignin' myself to the life I'd created. "How do you get past it, Mama? When you are with Daddy, how do you forget how he treats them?"

"Your father isn't beatin' up anyone. He treats them fairly, he gives them secure jobs. He just holds them at a different social level than us. That's very different."

"Is it?" I asked.

Chapter Twenty-Two

I had looked forward to the train ride to New York, but after several hours of travelin', the movement made me sleepy. I dozed on and off, thankful that there was not a passenger sittin' next to me, though we picked up more at each stop along the way. The nearer we came to New York, the more color the leaves boasted. Glorious red and orange leaves waved from their branches. The crisp sky looked less dense than the Arkansas sky, and I wondered if that was because of the heat that seemed to linger in the south, or if it was just the unhappiness in me liftin' itself off my shoulders. Jimmy Lee fell silent after our fight. He didn't argue about me goin' to see Maggie, and I didn't press him about goin' through my personal things. It was like there was a silent agreement between us to leave each other alone for a bit, and for that, I was thankful.

When I first stepped on the train, I was scared of travelin' so far by myself. I wasn't sure what to expect, though Maggie had assured me that no one would bother me. I brought a few books and when I wasn't gazin' out at the pretty landscape, I was nose down, escapin' into the private world of John and Abigail Adams. *Those Who Love* had been recommended by Maggie, and I found myself enthralled with the love in those pages.

Each time the train stopped, I'd look around at the people goin' off and comin' on the train, and I'd wonder where they were headin'. I didn't dare talk to anyone. All in all, I found the train relaxin', like I was in the pages of my own adventure book.

Mama had sewn a small pillow for me to rest my head on, and another for my lower back, and surely I would have been in worse shape without them, but still, I was achy and uncomfortable as we neared my destination. I was surprised to see two colored men board the train and sit in the same car as me. I couldn't help but keep glancin' at them. *Were they worried about sittin' where the white folks sat?* I didn't think so. That must be what Jackson and Maggie had been talkin' about. Things were different up here.

It was no wonder Maggie didn't come home more often—by the time we reached New York, the twenty-two hour trip felt as though it would never end. Crowds of people disembarked, walkin' fast, as if they all knew exactly where they were goin'. I felt as out of place as a pig in a horse trailer, and as lost as a blind cow.

"Pixie!" Maggie's voice carried through the station like a familiar embrace. I saw her runnin' toward me, dropped my bags to the floor, and fell into her open arms. "Let me see you!" She ran her eyes up and down my swollen body. "You are so beautiful," she said.

My feet hurt, my belly was as big as a house, and I knew how awful I must have looked. Though I'd been tryin' to ignore it, loomin' on my shoulders was Jimmy Lee's rage. Even the relief of seein' Maggie and her compliments didn't take away the hurt of my life.

"Come on," she said, gatherin' my bags. "Let's get you to my place. I wanna hear all about your new married life."

Cars raced by as we walked block after block toward Maggie's apartment. Her hair had grown shaggier, and her skin shone bright. The walk didn't seem to dampen her energy one bit, though it zapped what little I had left quicker than I realized. I had never seen so many people in one place. Several times I stopped and stared, in awe of the mixin' of the races, and the sheer number of people on the street. Maggie tugged me forward, anxious to get to her apartment. I felt like a cow bein' herded toward a barn. Everyone seemed to be goin' somewhere in a hurry. I didn't notice the chin-snub that was so common back home, and that, more than anything else, made me wonder about this new place Maggie had made her home.

When we finally flagged down a streetcar with the money Daddy had given me, I fell into the black vinyl with a long-overdue sigh of exhaustion and took it all in. I ran my hands along the smooth, shiny seats. I'd never seen anything like it before. Daddy would be mad that we gave money to someone to drive us around. I could just hear his voice, *That's what God gave you legs for*. I smiled to myself, missin' him but knowin' I'd have to keep yet another secret about what we used his money for. We took the streetcar for several blocks, and I marveled at the height of the buildin's. Never before had I seen anyplace with so much concrete. Everything here was new to me, and I tried to make sense of this world that Maggie lived in. There was hardly any grass anywhere. Where did all those people get their eggs and beef? Maggie explained that in New York, everything came from markets, and there was no farmland in the city. I couldn't wait to tell Mama about everything. I soaked it all in, memorizin' the way the buildin's looked, and even the insane honkin' of the horns. Every buildin' seemed to have a stream of people walkin' in and out. Cars' engines revved and lights flashed, and I was drawn into the energy of the area. By the time we reached Maggie's apartment buildin', my reservation had been replaced with curiosity.

We climbed five flights of narrow stairs up to the top floor of a very old buildin'. Plaster peeled from the walls, from cracks wider than my pinky finger, and snaked around the corners.

"Maggie, are you sure this is safe?" I asked, out of breath as we neared the top of the staircase.

"You're such a farm girl," she laughed. Maggie unlocked three locks and let us into an apartment, which was about the size of our bedroom back home. There was a tiny stove and refrigerator to the left of the door, and a window that looked across a span of about ten feet, and directly into the brick wall of the buildin' next to us.

"My view of New York," Maggie laughed. "Pix, wipe that pity off of your face. This is the most freedom I've had in twenty years."

"It's just that it's…"

Maggie twirled around, her arms almost hittin' the wall. "Small? Old? Ugly? I know, and I still love it!"

I sat down on the only piece of furniture in the room, a ratty, old couch. I sank all the way down to metal.

"Careful, that's our bed you're sittin' on," she said.

I stood and Maggie lifted the cushions to show me the convertible sofa. "The guy next door was givin' it away when I moved in. It suited my purpose just fine." Maggie poured us each a glass of lemonade and sat down beside me.

"Wow, you really are pregnant." She rested her hand on my stomach.

"Yeah, I guess I am."

"I guess I had you pegged wrong, Pix. I got the feelin' you weren't even sure about gettin' married to Jimmy Lee. Are you happy? Does he treat you right?"

I nodded, feelin' the burn in my cheeks, tryin' to feign a smile. My sister saw right through my façade. She squeezed my hand and put an arm around my back.

"Oh, Pixie," was all she said. I laid my head against her shoulder and breathed in the floral scent of her perfume. Tears bubbled up from within my chest and I tried to bite them back, tensin' my muscles and swallowin' the sound of my sobs. I must have cried for a full five minutes before I pulled back and wiped my eyes, snifflin', my cheeks growin' redder by the second.

"What is it? You can tell me, Pix."

"He found your letters. He—" I couldn't bring myself to tell her about him attackin' me. She'd be furious. She'd never have been that weak.

Maggie brushed my hair off my shoulders and held my hand. "Okay. Okay, so he knows…what? You're involved? I'm involved?"

"I don't know. That you're involved, and that I wanna be."

"Damn." Maggie drew in a breath and let it out quickly. "Well, then, we gotta figure out what's next. Do you think he'll tell anyone? This could be very dangerous if they know what's comin'."

"What's comin'?"

"Pix? Did somethin' else happen? Did he do anything to you?" Maggie skipped right over my question.

I turned away.

"Pixie, if he touched you, so help me."

I nodded with my back to Maggie.

"Damn him. Well, you're not goin' back there. No way, Pixie."

I spun around. "I have to go back. He's my husband. Mama and Daddy are there."

"What kind of husband hurts his wife?" Maggie paced, her arms crossed. She stopped and put her hand to her chin. When she got that determined look on her face it could only mean one thing. The wheels of her mind were churnin', plannin'.

"He didn't really hurt me. He just, he...he held me down and called me a Negro lover."

"Oh, I'll show him a Negro lover all right," Maggie fumed. "I can't let you go back there."

"I'm goin' back, Maggie. I have to." I laid my hand across my stomach. "I'm havin' his baby. It's my duty."

"Damn it, Pixie, now you sound like Daddy. Your place is not to be held down by an ignorant redneck."

In my heart I knew she was right, but in my mind, I couldn't take his baby away from him even if he didn't want it. He'd grow to want it. Mama said all men did, that they were just scared of the responsibility, but once they see the little baby's face, they melt like butter. I was learnin' that marriage was hard, and stayin' in my marriage was what was expected of me by Mama and Daddy, no matter how much it hurt or how hard it was. I found myself stuck between runnin' from a man I no longer loved or respected and confessin' my failure as a wife to Daddy, or stickin' with my weddin' vows, for better or worse, and remainin' the sparkle in Daddy's eyes.

Maggie stomped across the floor and took my face in her hands. I had nowhere to look besides into her angry eyes.

"Pixie, you listen to me. I know you, and you know this isn't right. It's not okay for you to be treated this way."

"He was just angry. It'll pass. He's never hurt me before." *At least not physically.*

"It'll pass? Pix, you're not a little girl anymore. You're gonna be a mother. You need to think about more than just yourself." Maggie put her hand to her eyes. "What happened? How did he go from sneakin' out with you to this?"

If only she knew.

"Promise me that if he touches you again, you will leave immediately. Go stay with Mama and Daddy. Come here. Hell, go anywhere you need to, but do not stay with him. I swear to God I will kill him if he touches you again."

I gave her my word, then wondered if I were strong enough to keep it.

Maggie pulled a flyer out from beneath a stack of papers. "There's a meetin' tonight about the boycott in Forrest Town."

"Wait, you didn't tell me about a boycott there. You said they were makin' headway with civil rights, but you never mentioned Forrest Town. Maggie, I said I wanted to be involved, but a boycott, where I live? I don't think that's smart."

"I didn't tell you because I thought you'd cancel, Pix. They've been workin' on this for months. They were gonna have the meetin' last month, but I asked them to wait."

"You tricked me!"

"No, I opened a door so you could make a decision for yourself. You don't *have* to do a damn thing. There are groups comin' from all over; Mississippi, Chicago, New York. Pix, this is huge. They'll be boycottin' the major stores and—"

"Wait," I said, panic thumpin' against my chest. "Boycottin' the major stores? Why? Jimmy Lee's furniture store? It's the biggest store in town. Why are you doin' this to me?"

"Oh, my God, Pix, have you lost your mind? Doin' this to you? Think about it, they don't let coloreds work in the showroom, only in the stockroom, and for peanuts!" She paused, lettin' her words settle on my shoulders like a weight. "Hell, they don't even let them shop in the front of the stores or eat in the diner. If we don't take a stance now, when will it happen? Do you see any changes occurrin'? Do you see Jimmy Lee openin' his shop to Division Street families?" Maggie ran her hand through her hair. "Do you want your baby to grow up like we did? Afraid to talk to the little colored girls in town? Come on, Pixie, do the right thing."

The tiny room was closin' in on me. *Jimmy Lee's store, boycotted?* "If the coloreds boycott, how will that help make any changes?"

"Not just coloreds, Pix. This is bigger than you and me and Division Street. There are whites from all around who are takin' part in enforcin' integration." Maggie spit her words out fast, smackin' the back of her hand in her palm for emphasis, as if everything she said was the most important. "Think about it. No one will come from other cities to shop there. People will be afraid to cross the picket lines, afraid of fights and trouble."

"Maggie—"

"I know what you're thinkin'. Not trouble like violence trouble, but trouble like yellin' and name callin'."

That didn't feel right. I'd heard about the riots, the fights, coloreds gettin' beaten. "How can you say that? You don't know," I said. "You have no idea what might happen, and you know what they do to coloreds there, for nothin' more than breathin'—this could cause all sorts of trouble for them. And what about you? What will you do in all of this?"

Maggie sat down and crossed her long legs, her short skirt barely coverin' her thighs. "Alison, listen to me. You can live in your little daddy bubble all you want, but I can't. I thought you wanted to help."

I sat next to her. "I did, but—"

Maggie shook her head. "You did when it was removed from where you were, when you could hear about it, but not really be affected by it. I get it, you know? I was that person. But now," she looked around the apartment. "Things are different. I have friends who are colored. I have met wonderful men and women who are colored. I can no longer turn a blind eye to things. Even if things are better here, and in bigger cities, I can't pretend they're that way everywhere."

I closed my eyes and just breathed. I couldn't make any decisions, my mind was too full of information, right and wrong, segregation and integration, tangled together like a convoluted web of confusion.

"Why don't you rest for a few hours before we leave for the meetin'."

Nothin' could have sounded more invitin' at that very moment. I closed my eyes and drifted off to sleep.

Chapter Twenty-Three

The only thing that separated night and day in New York was the color of the sky. There were just as many people walkin' around the streets at night, comin' in and out of stores and restaurants, as there were durin' the day. Some were dressed in fancy clothin', others wore everyday jeans. Comin' from a family where goin' into town was a big deal, seein' children millin' about at eight o'clock at night with their parents made me wonder what type of parents those people were. Children sat in restaurant windows, their parents smokin' at the dinner table. Daddy would have none of that. Daddy was all about family bein' home, safe, together. Forget the fact that we couldn't afford fancy restaurants. Even if we could, I think Daddy would want Mama's down home cookin' warmin' our bellies.

"Don't these kids have to get to bed? Don't they go to school?" I asked

Maggie laughed at my ignorance. "Of course. It's just different here." She pointed to a brightly lit sign above the restaurant that said, *Anyone with cash is welcome*. "You don't see that back home, huh?"

Maggie pulled me down an alley and then down two more quieter streets. I began to worry when I realized we were suddenly alone. The noise of the city fell away behind us, and suddenly everything seemed too big. Two colored men came around the corner, headin' in our direction. I grabbed Maggie's hand.

"Relax," she said with a smile. "You're not in Arkansas anymore."

I watched them descend a stairway and disappear, and then I let out a breath I hadn't realized I was holdin'.

Two minutes later, we were headin' down the same set of stairs. I clung to Maggie's arm, beggin' her to turn around. "Trust me," she answered. The stairway led to a small, dead-end alley. Maggie knocked three times on a dark-green, wooden door. She knocked two more times in rapid succession, and the door swung open.

A colored man with an enormous Afro and crooked, yellow teeth stood before us. Maggie embraced him. I closed my mouth tight, my eyes dartin' around the inside of the buildin'. The alley behind me was dark, the room before me was not much lighter. I wanted to run, to find a modicum of somethin' familiar, but there I stood, mesmerized by the sweet and pungent aroma that filtered out the door.

"Marlo, this is my sister, Pixie. Pixie, Marlo."

"H...hi." My voice shook. It took all of my will to follow Maggie into the dark, low-ceilin'ed room. Cigarette smoke and somethin' more acerbic filled the air. Music played low in the background, the beat fast and inconsistent. My hand was glued to Maggie's arm. She pulled me forward, embracin' each person, colored or white, introducin' me as her little sister. I'm not sure what I expected, but the closeness of the coloreds and whites, sittin' on the same couches, white girls with their legs stretched across the colored girls' laps, passin' cigarettes back and forth, took me by surprise.

"Drag?" A stick-skinny, dark-haired girl held out some sort of thin cigarette toward me.

"No," Maggie said, and pushed her arm away. "Darla, this is Pixie, my little sister. She just 'bout choked when she tried smokin' with me." Maggie winked at me. "She's not smokin' and she never drinks, so she won't be playin' any of those reindeer games." They laughed like schoolgirls.

"Sit down. Take a load off," Darla said. I wiggled in between her and the end of the couch. The biggest colored man I'd ever seen came over and sat on the arm of the couch. I leaned toward Darla, my heart goin' *thump, thump, thump* real hard.

"That's Bear," she said, and tapped Bear on the back.

"You're scarin' her. Move your ass," she said.

Bear grinned at her, then turned very serious, threatenin' eyes toward me. "I scare you?"

I swallowed hard, instinctively reachin' for Darla's arm as if she were Maggie.

"Relax," Maggie smacked Bear's arm. "He's teasin' you, Pix."

"I thought I was gonna have a heart attack," I whispered harshly to Maggie, which only made Bear laugh harder than he already was. I inched closer to Darla.

"She's straight off the train from Arkansas," Maggie explained. "Be nice, will ya'?" Maggie sat at my feet and said, "He's sweet as a teddy bear, hence the name Bear. Nothin' to worry about, Pix."

I grabbed Maggie's shoulder and hung on tight. Bear got up to answer the door, and I breathed a sigh of relief.

"Can we go home, please?" I whispered to Maggie.

Maggie squeezed my hand and shook her head. "I'm here, you're fine. Trust me."

The door opened and I heard it slam closed. Several colored men blocked the doorway, murmurin' somethin', then makin' a hole between them. Two white men in business suits entered the room, movin' toward the front of the crowd. All eyes were on them, includin' mine. I wondered if they were courageous or stupid. In Forrest Town this mixin' of the races, where there were more coloreds than whites, might render these men in trouble. They showed no fear, which made me wonder again if this was the type of thing Jackson had been referrin' to.

Marlo held his hands up and shushed the crowd. "Let's come to order, please, we have a lot of ground to cover today. Mr. Nash and Mr. Grange are here to fill us in on what we can expect, legally, from the boycott."

We listened as the lawyers described violent riots, with protesters of all races bein' beaten, some near death, colored men goin' missin', and even reports of women bein' manhandled. Arrests, they said, were sure to happen, by the hundreds. I clawed Maggie's shoulder. She put her hand on mine and patted it. I could feel her digestin' all of the dangers as her shoulders tensed beneath my fingers. Darla reached over and laid her hand on top of ours. I looked at her, and she mouthed, *It's okay. Change is good.*

There was beauty in the mixin' of the races in the room. I sensed a meshin' of strength and hope. What was missin' was fear. The coloreds in Forrest Town carried fear in their tentative gaits, embarrassment clear in their rearward glances when they headed toward the back doors of the buildin's. The lack of that type of fear was evident in that jam-packed room where I sat clingin' to my sister's shoulder. I still didn't trust this change, though the enormity of the hope rose above the horrific odors of perspiration and cigarettes that lingered like thick fog in the tiny room. I laid my hand across my belly, and slowly came to realize how much I wanted my baby to grow up in a world of hope, not a world of oppression—even if that oppression might not be pushed upon a white child, it still had an unforgivable impact.

"We're scheduling the boycott for Forrest Town for late fall. As you know, the white children go back to school in September, but the colored children are forced to pick cotton in the fields, and they don't return to school until after picking season. We want to hit at a time when those white folks *need* the colored labor. The goal is to stop all purchase power in the white stores and all picking power on the farms. This will have the greatest impact." Sweat glistened on Mr. Nash's forehead, the pits of his white shirt soaked through.

His words hit home, and I worried about my daddy's farm, and how he would make it through the winter without his income from the fields. There had been years when he had to borrow money for cotton seed, and I remembered those years with less food on the table and restrictions on how often we could go into town with the truck. One year we all helped Daddy cut down all the trees in the lower five acres of our property and brought it to the mill to sell. My memory of that year was dull. I scarcely remember anything more than constant fatigue. I worried about Jimmy Lee's job and his uncle's furniture store, but that worry was too cloudy with hurt to be anything more than an obligatory thought.

"Forrest Town families rely on the income from the fields, both colored and white families. Retailers rely on the income stream from neighborin' towns. Without it, the stores will shut down."

The voice came from behind me and stole my very breath. *Jackson*. I turned toward his proud voice, my hand slippin' from between Maggie and Darla's safe grip. I stared into a thick crowd of bodies, my heart slammin' against my ribs, and I wondered if I'd somehow merely wished his voice. Then, the crowd split, and Jackson, in all his handsomeness, stood before me. His eyes were locked on the lawyer in the front of the room. Each step he took brought with it a memory; his scent, his touch, the thick deliciousness of his kiss. The urge to reach for him was strong. I clasped my hands in my lap, hopin' to quell my sinful thoughts. The love that I thought I had given up, forgotten about, maybe even only dreamed existed, reared its powerful heat within me.

"There'll be coloreds who won't take part. They won't work against us, but they'll be too 'fraid of what comes with fightin' segregation." He stood beside Mr. Nash, his shoulders and chest thicker than when I'd last seen him, five months ago. His face was stronger, his eyes more determined and focused than I'd remembered. Under my hand, somethin' in my stomach moved. *My baby*. Jimmy Lee's baby. The doctor estimated twelve weeks when I had the blood drawn. Twelve weeks. My weddin' night. There was no turnin' back, now just shy of five months. I'd made my choice, and now I felt sick to my stomach instead of excited by the first movements of the child that grew within me.

"Are you okay, hun? You're shakin'." Darla put her hand across my shoulder.

Maggie spun around. "Pix, you alright?" she whispered.

I didn't mean to shake my head instead of nod, but that's what happened. Maggie helped me stand from my perch on the couch. Darla put an arm around my waist as they led me away from the group. I turned and looked over my shoulder, meetin' Jackson's confused eyes.

The small bedroom in the back of the apartment where the meetin' was takin' place smelled like cigarettes and hummed from the voices outside the door. I laid on the bed, Maggie and Darla crouched beside me.

"What's goin' on? Do you need a doctor?" Maggie asked.

"No, I'm just tired. All that travel must have worn me out worse than I thought." Their concerned stares were too much to take. How could I tell my sister about my secret love for Jackson? I was sure that even the thought would get me a one-way ride to hell. "Can we just go home?" I asked.

Maggie shook her head. "It's a really long walk. I think we're better off restin' here until after the meetin' and bummin' a ride. I don't have fare for a streetcar."

I closed my eyes and listened to the noises of the meetin', remindin' myself that I was supposed to love Jimmy Lee. *I love Jimmy Lee. I love Jimmy Lee* played in my mind. I turned toward the dirty, gray wall and thought, *I love Jackson Johns. I love Jackson Johns. I'm in so much trouble.*

The door opened and when Jackson's voice floated over my back and into my ears I held my breath. "Is everything alright?"

I couldn't turn and face him. I was afraid to be that close to him. I didn't trust myself.

"Yeah, my sister just got here from Arkansas. She's exhausted." Maggie rubbed my back, then said, "Hey, Jackson, do you know Alison? You worked on our farm a bit when you were home, remember?" She tapped my shoulder. "Pix? Turn around and say hi."

No, no, no!

"Uh, no, we never met," Jackson lied.

Maggie pulled my shoulder and turned me just enough to see him. I blinked back the love that wanted to drip from my eyes. I covered my belly, ashamed of the child that grew within me, ashamed of what that child represented between us—my weakness, the love I threw away to save face with my own father.

Jackson walked over to the bed and looked down at my stomach. I thought I had forgotten the hold that look of desperation had on my heart. His dark brows furrowed, his eyes softly takin' me in. Behind the concern of his serious cheeks, I felt a warmth, a carin' smile that dared not show for fear of revealin' whatever emotions lie in wait. "When is your baby due? Alison, right?"

I nodded.

"She's due in March. Little Pix here got pregnant on her weddin' night!"

"Maggie!" I flushed.

"Yeah?" Jackson crossed his arms. His next words were caressed with sadness that I think only I noticed. "You are certainly blessed."

"Hey, Jackson, do you want to meet up with us tomorrow, after Pixie, uh, Alison, is feelin' better? I want to talk about what she can do back home, in town, to help prepare."

"Maggie? What if I'm not feelin' better?"

"I can come to your apartment," Jackson offered, holdin' my gaze.

"Yes, perfect. We'll figure it out then," Maggie agreed.

Jackson reached for my hand. "Until then, Alison?"

I shook his hand, in the eyes of Maggie and Darla, the hand of a carin' stranger. Warmth spread through my body, and I knew I was in trouble.

Chapter Twenty-Four

The next afternoon, trepidation pinched my nerves. By noon I had already cleaned Maggie's apartment, washed down her counters and bathroom, and still had more nervous energy than I knew what to do with.

"What is with you, Pix? One minute you're shaky and weak, the next you're like Mama, only hyper."

"Nervous, I guess. I'm not sure this boycott is the best idea." I kept my back to her as I wiped down the inside of the front door.

"It's scary, but just think of the families you will help. For generations to come, people will talk about the ones who made it happen."

"But, arrests? Missin' men? I mean, it sounds pretty scary to me. You know what Jimmy Lee and Daddy will do if they find out I'm helpin', right? They'll lock me in the cellar for good." My mind drifted back to the day Jimmy Lee found Maggie's letters and the attack that followed. I shivered.

"They'll never know."

I turned to face her. I swear my belly had grown overnight. It protruded like a small watermelon carried by my widenin' hips. "Yeah? Jimmy Lee already thinks I'm wantin' to be involved in civil rights, remember?"

"We'll have to go covert, then. Can I send you letters at work instead of at your apartment?"

I thought about that route. "Maybe."

"And as for Daddy, well, why would he find out? Daddy stays on the farm. He's not a busy body or attune to town gossip. Jimmy Lee might be a different story. You'll probably have to figure out a way to meet with some of the colored supporters without Jimmy Lee findin' out."

"Supporters? Division Street? Do you really think that's a possibility?"

"Jackson's mama has been coordinatin' the meetin's. She works at the furniture store, in the warehouse, too. And since Albert works for Daddy, maybe you guys could meet at one of their houses."

"Oh, yeah," I smirked. "I can just see me waddlin' down toward that end of town. People would notice me from a mile away."

"What about outside of town?"

"How would I get there?"

"What about at the river, that's not far from the apartment, you could say you're takin' a walk, or do it while Jimmy Lee is at work."

I could do that.

By the time Jackson arrived, a knot had tightened across my shoulders in anticipation of his visit. Maggie let him in and I busied myself pourin' lemonade and settin' out the cornbread I had baked.

"Smells like my mama's kitchen," Jackson said as he sat on the couch.

Seatin' would be a problem. The couch was small and there were no other chairs. I set the tray on the small table and lowered myself to the ground facin' the couch.

Jackson stood, "Please, sit here."

"I'm fine," I said. "I'm pregnant, not injured."

"Alison!" Mama's shock rode on Maggie's face. She turned to Jackson. "I'm sorry, her manners must have slipped away with her pregnancy."

Jackson laughed, and it brought warmth to my cheeks. I felt like a schoolgirl experiencin' her first sip of moonshine, only I'd already tasted the sweet nectar and longed for more. *Would I flush every time I was near him?* I wondered, or was it the old everyone-wants-what-they-can't-have syndrome that Mama had warned me about so many times?

"I'm sorry. Thank you, Jackson," I said.

Jackson and Maggie concocted a way for me to communicate with the families. Jackson would call his mother, and she'd spread the word among them. She'd get a message to me through the back door of the diner, and so the system was born. I couldn't take my eyes off of Jackson. I could feel him purposefully not lookin' at me, and when he did stray my way, his eyes met mine, never lowerin' to my stomach, never lettin' on that he had any feelin's for me whatsoever. I couldn't blame him. I had been the one to throw away the brief, albeit immense, love we shared. I'd been the one to marry a man I didn't truly love, and now I'd have his spawn. I loved the baby inside me, or at least I thought I was lovin' it more and more with each passin' day. It still didn't feel very real to me. But that love was tamped down the moment I saw Jackson. The baby felt like a bridge between us that I knew we could never cross. I must be losin' my mind, because I had no business thinkin' in those terms at all.

"How does that sound, Alison?" Maggie asked.

I had been so busy wallowin' in self pity that I had no idea what they'd been talkin' about.

"Um, what part? The river?"

Maggie laughed. "The whole thing. I know how you feel about the river."

"We're worried that with findin' Mr. Bingham," Jackson's voice softened, "it might bring back too many hard feelin's." He looked at Maggie. "Maybe we should choose another location. I don't feel really safe with her goin' there anyway."

"No, I'm fine," I said, knowin' full well that it would be harder than milkin' a horse to return to the river. Not only did Mr. Bingham's body linger in my mind, but a shadow of Jimmy Lee's nastiness remained. "Actually, can we meet at the creek at the end of our property? It runs parallel to the apartments behind the woods. I think it's even closer than the river, so it might be easier for me." Maybe it was bad of me to suggest the creek, since it was where Jackson and I had spent our first afternoon together, but I couldn't help it. I wanted to see how he'd react, and besides, it was more convenient.

Jackson shot a look at me and rearranged himself on the couch. The way he twitched in his seat told me that, like me, he was thinkin' about the first time we walked down by the creek. As cruel as that might seem, it warmed my heart to see him squirm. He couldn't forget our time together any better than I could. "I don't—"

"I think we should do whatever will make Alison feel safest," Maggie looked at me protectively. "Pix, do you remember Mr. Kale? The old man who used to run the post office?"

"Sure. Candy Kale the lollipop man? Why?"

"His son is part of the Panthers' support group and he'll be there at each meetin'."

"Is that safe for him? I mean—"

"Yes," Jackson answered. "He's well protected. I worry more about you, Alison. You're with child. I'm not sure this is the best thing for you to take part in."

"I want to do this. I want my baby to be born into an integrated world and brush arms with everyone, not be afraid to play with other children just because of the color of their skin. Every time I see a white water fountain and a colored water fountain it makes me sick. Don't get me wrong, I'm petrified to do this, but I think I have to." I took a deep breath and said, "I can't be weak any longer. It's time Daddy knew what I believed in." I wanted to prove to Jackson that my feelin's still rode deep, and that I was gonna make a change in my priorities. I realized that as soon as Daddy knew what I was fixin' to be a part of, there'd be no keepin' those thoughts from Jimmy Lee, and I was slowly comin' to realize that my baby bein' born into an integrated lifestyle did not go hand in hand with Jimmy Lee raisin' this child. I had no idea what I'd do about it, but the thought was ridin' heavily on my shoulders.

"Whoa, Pix, you can't tell Daddy what you're doin'. No way."

I knew she was right. "I know, okay. I didn't mean that literally. Sheesh, he and Jimmy Lee would kill me." Jimmy Lee's name slipped out before I could catch it, and Jackson looked away. "I meant that I want to do this. I've been a coward with all of the important aspects of my life, and I don't wanna be anymore."

Maggie ran her eyes over my belly, then gave me a look that said she was proud of me, but also…that it might just be too late. I twisted the weddin' ring I wished I wasn't wearin'.

On the way out the door, Jackson hugged Maggie, and then she went to the kitchen to wrap up a piece of cornbread for him to take home. Jackson pulled me close and whispered, "Even with his child inside you, I still love you."

Too shocked from the embrace to reciprocate, I stood there like an idiot, paralyzed by his admission. Maggie returned and handed him the cornbread. "We should do this again," she said.

I couldn't tell if the tiny flutter in my belly was caused by butterflies or the baby.

"There's a get together Thursday night. A bunch of people are holdin' a live performance of enactin' desegregatin' America."

Jackson caught my worried look. I saw him searchin' my eyes for a response to his confession, but I had no words to say. They were tethered to my achin' heart and refused to break free.

"Don't worry, the word isn't out," Jackson finally said. "There are just about thirty of us and it's in the projects. There's music, but there'll be no words. I'd love for you to come see it."

"What are the projects?" I had so much to learn.

Jackson lifted one eyebrow, and smirked. "It's like Division Street back home."

"Is it safe?"

"Safer than Division Street." Again, his sarcasm cut me like a knife.

"I promised to work late Thursday night—big court day Friday. But you should go, Pix. Jackson, will you take good care of her?"

"No, really. I would feel funny."

"Nonsense. I'll pick you up at eight." His tone left no room for negotiation.

Chapter Twenty-Five

"You're goin' tonight, Pix. This is good for you, to break out of that small town fear. I was scared the first time I went, but really, Jackson will take good care of you."

That's what I'm worried about. Maggie wasn't buyin' my fake sick routine. She was goin' to work and I'd have all day to stew over bein' alone with Jackson.

"Besides, remember when we used to walk by the church near Division Street on Sundays and the gospel just pulled us in? Remember how we moved to the music, and if anyone drove by we'd pretend we were just messin' around? You don't have to do that anymore. Now you can enjoy it. I promise you, you'll return a changed woman."

I think I already am.

The knock on the door made my heart leap into my throat. My hands trembled as I reached for the knob.

I pulled the door open. *I can do this.* Jackson stood before me in a dark-green t-shirt and jeans. His eyes met mine, and I swear a current of electricity passed between us.

"You look radiant," he said.

I looked down at my maternity blouse and skirt, feelin' like an overgrown balloon, and turned to hide my blushin' cheeks. "Let me grab my bag," I said.

Jackson came inside and closed the door behind him. He stood in the entryway, respectfully givin' me space.

"I'm glad you agreed to come."

"Mm-hmm." My voice was caught in my throat. It took all my courage not to fall into his arms.

"Listen, we should talk," he said. "The way we left things, I'm really sorry. I understood where you were comin' from. Things were too dangerous for us." He paused. I listened with my back to him as I put Maggie's house key in my purse. "You did the right thing. I'm happy for you."

"Don't be." *Oh, my goodness, where did that come from?* I spun around and fumbled for words. "I mean, don't be happy. No, not that, it's just...oh, I don't know how to say it."

Jackson took a step closer to me. I could smell his aftershave, a different, sexier scent than the smell of him after he'd worked all day.

"What is it?" he asked. He placed his hand on my upper arm, and my heart swooned with its warmth, incitin' memories of his tender touch as we dropped to the field months before. I could still feel his body tremblin' under my hands, his muscular thighs bare against my own.

I looked down at the floor, hidin' my blush. He lifted my chin with his finger. "Alison, you can tell me anything. I won't think poorly of you. I won't try to take you away from the life you have."

"But—"

"I meant what I said, that I love you even if you are carryin' Jimmy Lee's baby. I haven't been with another woman since we parted, and I don't want to. It's you who touched me with your open heart."

He touched my cheek, and I closed my eyes again, relishin' in his touch. When I opened them, he was smilin'.

"I believed what I told you, that things needed to change. I was goin' in this direction anyway, but I didn't really have the courage then to do what I'm doin' now. You gave me that courage. You made me realize that no matter what I thought in my heart, no matter what I might have felt, this issue was so much bigger than that. Love can't conquer all."

"I was afraid to lose Daddy," I explained.

"Shh," he said, and dropped his hand. I wished he hadn't. "I understand. Your father, your family, that's your world. My world isn't backwoods Arkansas. My world is everywhere. I want to know that anywhere I go, I can go with the one I love."

"I'm sorry."

"Don't be. You helped me to understand myself better. I know I can't have a partial relationship." He rubbed his hands on the thighs of his jeans, then said, "Alison, there was a big Supreme Court case in June, and it, combined with our boycotts and protests, has the ability to change everything."

"What do you mean? Martin Luther King tried to change everything and Forrest Town is still segregated."

"Come, sit." He guided me to the couch. "The Lovings, they're an interracial couple who married in '57 in Virginia."

My eyes grew wide. "That was ten years ago."

"Illegal, right? Well, they were sentenced to a year in prison in '59, but it was suspended for 25 years if they agreed to leave the state. Mildred, the wife, she wrote in protest to Attorney General Robert F. Kennedy. Kennedy referred her to the American Civil Liberties Union, and that's when everything started to change.

"The ACLU filed a motion on their behalf, and a slew of lawsuits followed, eventually reachin' the Supreme Court. Get this, five years later, the Loving's case still hadn't been decided, so they began a class action suit in the D.C. district court—and even that was shot down."

"I really don't understand all this legal stuff."

"What it comes down to is that they didn't give up. They appealed, and in June, the 12th of June to be exact, the court overturned their convictions, dismissin' Virginia's argument that the law was not discriminatory because it applied equally to, and provided identical penalties for, both white and colored people. The Supreme Court ruled that the law against interracial marriages violated several clauses in the Fourteenth Amendment. They won. They won, Alison, and they've opened doors for more interracial couples."

"But what does that have to do with Arkansas?"

He grabbed my hands. "Things are changin'. Maybe not now, maybe not tomorrow, but they are. Look around you. You've seen how different New York is from Arkansas."

"Yeah, it scares me a little," I admitted.

"It scared me, too, when I first got here, but I can't ever go back to livin' how it was in Forrest Town."

I tried to process what he'd said, but Mr. Bingham's dead body kept floatin' into my mind.

"I can't imagine Forrest Town ever bein' any different."

"Baby steps. That's all we can do. We can try, and if we fail, we fail."

"But what if failin' means you get killed?" The reality of that possibility loomed between us, thick and uncomfortable.

"I fought for this country. Doesn't it make sense that I'd fight for my hometown, where my family lives?"

We walked through the dark streets of the projects, passin' old men and women sittin' on the concrete steps, cigarette smoke cloudin' around them, open bottles of alcohol by their feet. Children moved about, carefree and seemin'ly undaunted by what I found desolate and depressin'. There were small clusters of young colored men and women hootin' and laughin'. I grabbed Jackson's hand, then wrapped my free arm around my belly protectively.

Jackson leaned into me. "Don't worry, nothin's gonna happen."

We turned down an alley and entered a courtyard with a small, grassy area. Eight or ten men and women were performin', their arms swayed in the air and they jumped about with great, dramatic flair, but they didn't speak. I had never seen such a performance. Some moves were as graceful as a dancer's, while others were sharp and angry. The crowd moved to a strange musical rendition of guitars and tambourines.

People sprawled on blankets on the grass or leaned against the buildin'. Many held cigarettes, and I recognized the same sweet aroma that I'd smelled at the meetin', which Maggie explained was marijuana. The moon shone down on the performers like a spotlight, and we sat on the grass and watched the performance unfold. It seemed everyone held either a can of beer or a bottle of alcohol, and it reminded me of the night that Albert was beaten, further confirmin' my desire to be part of the Forrest Town desegregation efforts.

Darla came and sat next to me, pullin' me into her thin chest in a deep embrace. "So glad you made it, Pixie," she said with a coy smile. "I hope you don't mind, Maggie shared your nickname with me. I love it. It suits you perfectly." She touched my belly. "You're such a tiny, little thing."

"I don't feel so tiny," I answered. I wasn't used to people touchin' my stomach. I'd lived such a solitary life with Jimmy Lee that my shoulders relaxed, the knot in my stomach loosened, and it felt good to let Darla in. It had been so long since I'd had a friend, that I was almost afraid to believe in it.

"Aw, come on. You're a pixie. It suits you." Darla sat next to me and began swayin', her arms held high above her head. I turned to find Jackson starin' at me. He nodded, and then put his own arms up in the air. I followed, tentatively, lettin' the soothin' guitar rhythm move me.

"Pix, you made it! Groovy to see you!" I opened my eyes to find Marlo, yellow teeth and big hair, crouched in front of me. His stringy arms hangin' by his side.

Darla shrugged. "I said Pixie suited you. So I shared, shoot me."

"It's okay, Darla," I said, coverin' my blushin' cheeks.

"Nah, don't be embarrassed. Know why they call me Marlo?"

"Uh, it's your name?" I said.

"Are you kiddin'? My parents would never call me that. My name is Martin Riley Logan, after my pop. Never been called Marlo 'til I met these fine folks. They gave me an identity all my own."

I liked that. Maybe it was time I had my own identity.

"Right on, sista'," Marlo went off to greet another friend.

I turned toward Jackson. "Thanks for bringin' me. I'm really glad I came. This is so different than anything I've ever been around."

"This is the new world, Alison."

He wrapped his arm around my shoulder. I stiffened.

"I'm sorry," he said, withdrawin' his arm. "I didn't mean anything by that. I just got too comfortable."

I looked at Darla, worried she'd seen and would think I was some sort of loose woman. Her eyes were closed, her hands wrapped around a beer bottle. She swayed back and forth, seemin'ly oblivious to the rest of us. Completely absorbed by the music.

"I overreacted," I said. "I just don't want to cause undue trouble. That's all."

In protectin' my own emotions by tryin' to remain at a distance from him, I'd hurt his feelin's. I reached for his hand. To hell with what others thought. Jackson was my friend, and if this wasn't someplace we could show that, there would never be a time or place where we could. Even if for only a few minutes, I wanted to feel the sense of bein' with him, alive, in public. Jimmy Lee was so far away that it was like he existed in some dream I'd conjured up long ago.

After the performance Jackson and I held hands as he walked me home. My back and legs were tired, but I felt free from the shadows of the past. Strangely, I didn't feel as though I was cheatin' on Jimmy Lee by holdin' Jackson's hand, and the worry of what Daddy might think was fleetin' rather than all-consumin'. I did wonder what Mama might think, if she saw me now. She'd be disappointed, of that I was certain. Not because the color of Jackson's skin, but because of the vow that I had taken with Jimmy Lee.

We stopped at a coffee shop, and I waited out front at a small, round table while Jackson went inside to grab two cups of hot chocolate. Car horns honked as they passed. How different New York was from Forrest Town. If I were home, I'd be sleepin' beside Jimmy Lee, waitin' for the next uneventful day to unfold. A cool breeze wrapped itself around me. *Jimmy Lee*. I was havin' his baby. What was I doin' here with Jackson? I watched him through the glass storefront, payin' for the hot chocolate. He looked over and smiled. I turned away. Why was life so complicated? Why had I not stood up for what I felt back home, all those months ago? How would I ever get out of the pickle I was in? Maybe I couldn't. I'd chosen my life, what right did I have to try and change that now?

"Here you are," Jackson said as he set down the hot cocoa. "You alright? You look kind of, I don't know. Sad?"

I sipped the cocoa, lettin' the warmth of it soothe my worries. "I'm alright. This is all so new to me."

"That it is," he said, and reached for my hand.

I looked around. No one there knew me, no one would run back home to tell Jimmy Lee that they'd seen me, but I worried about Maggie—what would she think? I withdrew my hand.

"Alison, I don't want you to get the wrong impression. I'm not tryin' to take you away from your husband."

"You're not?" *Now I feel stupid.*

"I love you. I do, but I'm not a kid. I know what trouble it would cause for you to leave your husband and come to New York, or for me to come back to Forrest Town—I'd never survive. It'd be my body they found next in the river."

"Don't say that," I said.

"It's true."

How we'd gone from bein' apart to bein' this close in one evenin', I had no idea. We drank our hot cocoa, then walked the rest of the way home in silence. The lights were on in the apartment. Maggie was home. A relieved sigh blew through my lips. I didn't want to be in the position to have to decide where to go from there.

Jackson took my hands in his.

"What now?" I asked.

"Now, we work to make things better for the folks back home."

"Right, through your mama. But—"

Jackson put a finger to my lips. "Don't. I know what happened. She told me."

"But you told her—about us? How could you?"

"How couldn't I? I trust Mama. She raised me. She loves me."

"She hates me."

Jackson shook his head. "She hurts *for* you. She knows there was no way we could be together, but I needed to tell someone." He looked down, rubbed the back of his neck. "The hurt was so deep, Alison. I wasn't eatin', wasn't sleepin'. Mama knew without me tellin' her. All I did was confirm who I was pinin' for."

I wanted to run away and hide in a hole. His mother knew how much I had hurt him. I was just as bad as Jimmy Lee. I'd hurt one of her boys. What would my own mother think?

Jackson touched my cheek. "Alison, now we go back to our lives. You have your baby, I have my life."

I was thrown right back into that night at the creek, when I chose Daddy's love over him. Fear tiptoed up my nerves and clasped around my heart. That all-consumin' emptiness I'd felt as he walked away shrouded around me. I squeezed his hand; my heart pullin' my lips toward his, my mind tellin' me to beware. I shook my head. "I don't want to lose you again."

His eyebrows drew together. Jackson shook his head, his confusion stretchin' between us like a bridge I wanted to cross.

I pulled him gently toward me and kissed him, long and slow, like he'd kissed me all those months ago. His hands slid around my waist, my pregnant belly pressin' against him. I ran my hands up the back of his neck, feelin' the pulse of his heart against me. The world fell away. "I want to be here with you," I whispered.

He kissed my cheek, my neck, then whispered in my ear, "Don't make promises you can't keep."

"I can't promise, but I can try," I whispered. All I knew was that I wanted to be right there forever. I never wanted to go back to Forrest Town. I didn't want to see, much less be with, Jimmy Lee. I didn't want to watch Jake vyin' for Daddy's attention, or see the hurt look in Daddy's eyes when I spoke of Maggie. I didn't want to think about Clara bein' forced into a sexual relationship with Jimmy Lee's uncle, that would lead to the death of her husband and her fleein' from her family and friends to save her own life. I wanted to remain in New York, in Jackson's arms, far away from the reality of life that scraped at my very bein' every second of the day.

The doorknob rattled, startlin' me out of my fog. I stepped away from Jackson.

"There you are, Pix!" Maggie was dressed in an oversized t-shirt I didn't recognize and cotton pants. "I was worried. Jackson, did you take good care of my little sis? Wanna come in?" She swung the door wide open.

My cheeks burned as I slipped by her and into the apartment. I sat on the couch, my arms wrapped around my middle, and my heart tied in knots.

Chapter Twenty-Six

The week after I returned from New York, I was settin' out the chocolate pie Jean had made, when there was a rap at the back door of the diner. It was Friday, and I grabbed a lollipop from the counter and headed toward the back door, lookin' forward to the one happy moment in my world of disappointment. Jimmy Lee hadn't asked me about my trip, and he hadn't been spendin' much time at home. Seein' the little boy's face light up would be a real treat.

I pulled the door open and Mrs. Johns stood before me, her thick middle bubblin' over the belt of her dress. I blinked a few times, lookin' from side to side, our previous confrontation rushin' back. My heart slammed against my chest as if seekin' escape.

She dropped her eyes to my swollen middle.

I put my hand over my belly. "Ma'am?"

She reached into her purse, shakin' her head and pursin' her lips.

Oh, God, oh, God, oh, God.

She took a step toward me, leanin' in so close that I could smell the coffee on her breath. She took my hand in hers, then curled my fingers around somethin' and pressed in tight. "Be careful," she whispered. She turned and hurried down the steps, disappearin' around the side of the buildin'.

"Was there an order?" Jean asked from behind me.

I slipped my hand into the pocket of my uniform. "Uh, no, she was mistaken. Her husband didn't order anything today, I guess." I kept my back to Jean, worried my eyes might reveal my lie.

As Jean's footsteps retreated, I hightailed it into the bathroom and locked the door. The sealed envelope was small and stained. I ran my fingernail along the underside of the flap and withdrew the single-paged letter. I brought the paper to my nose and inhaled, hopin' for a scent of Jackson. There was none.

Dear Alison,

I know you're scared, afraid you'll be caught writing to me, or that Mama will be caught giving you the letters. Have faith. Be strong. I will wait as long as I have to, until your trying can become your promise.

Love, Jackson

Jean jiggled the doorknob. "Alison? I gotta go, hun."

"I'll be right out." I looked around the tiny bathroom and saw no place to hide the letter. Afraid of bein' caught with it, I tore it into tiny pieces, wrapped it in toilet paper, and flushed it down the toilet.

For days I'd wished I'd kept the letter, if only to see the easy slant of his handwritin' or to be sure I remembered each word correctly, but gettin' caught weighed heavily on my mind. I watched the face of every person who came into the diner, and watched Jean for an inklin' of her knowin' the truth.

Main Street was empty as I walked toward my apartment. I had no idea if I could safely send letters to Jackson, but it didn't matter. I was high on the fact that he hadn't forgotten about me or moved on, or even hated me for what I'd done before.

Mama was expectin' us for dinner at five thirty, and Jackson's letter had filled me with purpose, strengthenin' me over the days since receivin' it. I felt as if I might finally be becomin' a woman rather than a little girl goin' home to see Mama and Daddy.

Chapter Twenty-Seven

Six o'clock came and went, with no sign of Jimmy Lee. I phoned Mama to let her know we'd be late, and she said she'd hold dinner for us. Each passin' minute fueled my annoyance. Between Jimmy Lee's drinkin' and his disregard for me, I'd wondered if he'd show up sober for the sake of my parents. I hadn't thought he would not show up at all.

I dialed the furniture store's phone number and asked Mr. Kelly if I could speak with Jimmy Lee.

"Oh," he said with surprise. "Hold on just a moment, please."

Silence stretched long and painful. Just when I thought he'd forgotten about me, Mr. Kelly came back to the phone. "Alison, did you speak to Mr. Carlisle the last time you came in?"

"No." I tried to keep the annoyance out of my voice, and failed miserably.

"I think you need to speak with your husband about his whereabouts."

What did he think I was *tryin'* to do? "Yes, thank you. Is he there?"

"No, he's not." He paused, then hissed into the phone, "Perhaps you should try The Waterin' Hole."

The line went dead. *The Waterin' Hole?* I stared at the telephone, as if it held the answers of my husband's whereabouts. The Waterin' Hole was the nastiest bar around. Located at the edge of town, it was rumored to be where bored husbands went to fill their sexual needs with some of the dirtiest, lowest women in Forrest Town. It was too far to walk at that time of night, but even if it was closer, I wouldn't stoop so low as to go traipsin' after my husband like the pathetic wife, even if I was startin' to feel that way. No, I couldn't believe it. There was no way Jimmy Lee would lower himself to that. He wasn't bored. I was home all the time, with dinner ready, and a clean house. I wasn't sure what made me feel sicker—that I was always home waitin' for him or that he might actually be with another woman.

I dialed my parents' number and told Mama we would not make it for dinner after all. I feigned fatigue and said Jimmy Lee was workin' late. The more I thought about where he might be, the easier it became to believe him that he'd been spendin' time with Corky. They both like to drink and chase coloreds. That thought didn't sit any better in me than him bein' with some nasty other woman.

"Do you want me to come by with some dinner for you?" Mama asked.

"No, I'm just gonna go to bed."

"Are we still bakin' tomorrow?"

Damn, I'd forgotten. "Yes, of course. I'll be there 'round noon."

That night, I penned my first letter to Jackson. I had no idea if he would receive it or not, and I knew if Jimmy Lee found out we'd both be dead, but with hurt coursin' through my veins, and nowhere else to point my anger, I let it fuel my writin'.

Dear Jackson,

I'm changing. I can feel it in everything I do. When I serve meals at the diner I can barely look into the eyes of the men who I know have made things hard for the people of Division Street. When I inhale, there's a charge of hope in the air that I'm sure only I can feel, and that pulls me forward and takes me to the next task at hand. I want things to be different for my baby—I want things to be different for me, and yet, I know how selfish that sounds, but as much as integration will change things for coloreds, it carries over into a freedom that impacts everything in life for all of us, and I look forward to that change.

I'm seeing Daddy this weekend, and I pray I'll be strong enough to start being myself, instead of his little girl. I'm not sure if you can understand that, but I don't know how else to say it.

Stay safe.

Love always, Alison

Chapter Twenty-Eight

The faintest outline of dark circles shadowed Mama's eyes as she rolled the crust for the pecan pie.

"Mama?" I asked.

She stopped rollin', wiped her brow with her forearm, and lifted her eyebrows in answer.

"Can I talk to you about somethin'?"

Mama set down the roller and pulled out two chairs from the kitchen table. I sat down, fidgetin' with a dishtowel. My father's tractor roared as it neared the house. Jake sauntered into the kitchen.

"Alison, wow, you're as big as a house," he said, and grabbed an apple from a bowl on the counter.

"Thanks," I said, wishin' he hadn't come in so I could talk privately with Mama.

"Hey, what do you think of this?" Jake placed a hand-drawn picture of our farm on the table, every detail precise, from the cracks in our front porch to the perfect dips and mounds of plantin's in the fields. He'd drawn the entire picture with a pencil, shadin' each crevice to the nth degree.

I picked up the paper and looked closer. "Jake, this is amazin'."

Mama sat back with a smile across her lips. "He's good, isn't he?"

"More than good. Jake, how did you learn to do this?"

He shrugged. "Mama showed me a few things."

"Mama, really?"

Pride filled Mama's eyes. "He's a natural. I just showed him a thing or two, tweakin', you know. He's really gifted."

"Have you shown Daddy?" I asked.

I caught a wave of discomfort pass between them. Jake reached for the picture as the noise of the tractor quieted. Jake folded his drawin' and shoved it in his back pocket as the screen door creaked open.

My father crossed the kitchen and lifted me to my feet, then bent down and hugged me close. "I've missed you. You look radiant. How's my grandchild?"

I blushed. "Fine, Daddy."

"You look just as beautiful as your mother did when she was pregnant with you."

Mama pushed her hair behind her ear, revealin' a flirty grin, then went back to work on the pie crust.

"Thanks, Daddy."

He smacked Jake on the back. "About ready to go into town?"

Jake's mouth tightened.

"Daddy, have you seen—"

"Alison, come help me," Mama interrupted.

"Uh, okay," I said, confused.

Jake gave me a harsh look. "C'mon, Daddy, let's go."

"Wait. I gotta get a drink for the crew." My father grabbed a big, plastic pitcher from the cabinet and ran the water in the sink.

"I've got ice water ready for them in the fridge," I said.

"This'll be fine," he said.

"Daddy, why don't you give 'em the cold water? They'd probably appreciate it." I spoke before thinkin', and Daddy turned and looked at me like I'd spoken another language all together. "I mean, it's not that cool out, and they've probably been workin' for hours and all."

"Why don't you let me worry 'bout the farmhands, and you worry 'bout the pies, okay?"

"Okay, Daddy. Sorry."

Mama shook her head. If I hadn't been lookin' to her for support, I might have missed it. I mixed the sugar and butter in a large bowl, annoyance tightenin' my nerves until I had to speak.

"Daddy, why don't I take the water out? I don't mind gettin' the water with ice."

"Alison Jean," Daddy said, leavin' no room for negotiation.

I stirred the butter until it was creamy, faster, harder, pourin' my energy into it as I gathered the courage to take a stance. I took a deep breath and turned to face Daddy, holdin' onto the back of a chair for support. "Daddy, they deserve ice water. It's just ice. It's not like you're cookin' 'em dinner."

Mama set her hand on my shoulder, pressin' gently.

My father narrowed his eyes. I thought of Maggie, and Jackson, and every person in the Panther meetin', and I held his stare, white knuckles wrapped around the edge of the chair.

"What's this about, Alison?"

"About? Nothin', Daddy, it's just," I dropped my eyes. *Be strong.* I wrapped my arm around my middle. "They're people, Daddy, and now that I'm havin' a baby, I'd hate to think of someone not givin' my child a drink of cold water when he or she needed it. It just seems…unnecessary."

Mama squeezed my shoulder. "Honey, why we'd better get this pie ready, or we won't have any for dinner."

My father walked out of the kitchen with the pitcher of tepid water and a frown on his unshaven cheeks.

"Sheesh, sis, what the heck?" Jake hissed.

"Me? How about you and your picture? Why can't Daddy see it?" Goin' up against Daddy left my nerves full of adrenaline, and maybe even anger, but I had done it. Maggie would be proud of me. Heck, I was proud of me.

"You know how your father is," Mama said. She put a hand on Jake's arm. "He doesn't want to see Jake waste his time. He knows Jake's talented, but your father believes self-worth comes from hard work, and in his eyes, art isn't hard work."

Jake pulled his arm free and headed for the door.

"Jake!" She stopped him with her tone. "I know it's hard work. Your father's just old school. You can't teach an old dog new tricks, is all."

"Right." Jake pulled the picture from his pocket and tore it into shreds, throwin' it behind him as he stormed from the house.

"Mama, I didn't mean to cause trouble," I said quickly.

Mama just shook her head. Creases formed across her forehead. She put the spoon she was holdin' down and leaned on the table.

"It's not you, honey. All you're doin' is what's right."

All you're doin' is what's right. Mama's confirmation fed my confidence. With Daddy and Jake gone, I willed myself to speak a little more openly with her.

"Mama, what do you think about this whole civil rights movement?" I kept my eyes on the bowl before me.

She sighed. "Another boy was beaten last night. It's really gettin' outta hand."

I wanted to spill my hurt over Jimmy Lee not comin' home, and connect the dots that it might just be him beatin' those boys, but given that everyone in my family seemed to be havin' issues of some kind, I thought it best to hold my tongue.

"A fourteen-year-old," Mama continued. "He was walkin' home from the drugstore with aspirin for his mother." She rubbed her arms as if she'd suddenly gotten a chill. "I think in general, it's a good thing. It's a dangerous thing, but a good thing." She walked to the window and watched Daddy drive the tractor toward the barn. "You know, Alison, we haven't talked about Maggie. Tell me about Maggie. How is she?"

When Mama turned back to me, I understood the shadow in her eyes that I hadn't been able to decipher earlier—she was lonely. How empty her life must feel with the house so empty, all at once, losin' both your daughters, and havin' a son who did everything within his power to stay away from home.

"She's good. She likes her classes, and her job. She's involved in things that keep her busy."

Mama took my hand and led me to the table, where she sat with her elbows propped up beside the bowl I'd been usin'. Then she sat back and folded her arms across her chest, then set them in her lap.

"You're as jumpy as Jake was with Daddy. What's wrong?"

"I miss her, you know? I mean, she and your father, they never saw eye to eye, but me and Maggie—"

"She drives him batty, that's for sure."

She nodded. "She knows what she wants and I admire that. Maggie's not afraid to go after her dreams, no matter what it involves."

"Or, who's in her way," I said.

"Right, or who's in her way."

"Or, who she might lose," I added.

Mama nodded. "I didn't think I'd miss you girls so much," she admitted. "One minute the house is full of laughter, little feet scamperin' up and down the stairs, my name bein' hollered, then the next minute, Maggie's off to school and you're sneakin' out of the house."

She lifted her eyes and caught me by surprise.

"You knew?"

"I'm your mother. I know everything."

"But, why didn't you—"

"I was young once, too. I remember what it was like, your heart poundin' so hard in anticipation of that secret kiss. Oh, yes, I remember. I wouldn't have taken that away from you for anything in the world."

Embarrassment softened my voice. "Thank you. I'm sorry."

"Don't be sorry. Although, you do owe me. There was one time, just before your graduation, when your father woke up as you came in the door, and I had to convince him it was the wind." Mama took my hand and said, "It's not easy bein' a mother, Alison. I worried sick over you, even before you started sneakin' out. I worried about you walkin' down our street, headin' to the store, while you were at school. And now, I worry about you workin' your way through your life without me by your side."

The way Mama looked at me made me wonder if she knew what was goin' on with Jimmy Lee. The more Jimmy Lee didn't come home, the less I cared. But naggin' and pullin' at my mind was the thought of him beatin' up colored boys. I didn't have proof, and even if I did, there wasn't anything I could do about it, so I kept it tied inside my mind like a bug in a web beggin' to be set free.

"Do you think I can do it? Be a good mother I mean? Like you?"

"Like me?" she laughed. "I'm not a very good mother, Alison."

"Yeah, Mama, you are."

"I'm weak. I let your father make the rules." She folded the edges of a napkin.

"You have to. You can't fight him." I thought about Daddy, his ability to define our lives without any force or harsh words. Daddy's leer was enough to let you know your place, and his lovin' smile was enough to want him to remain on your side.

Mama shook her head, the edges of her eyes damp. "I'm so thankful Maggie did what she did. I should have stood up for her long ago. I should have stood up for Jake, and you."

"Me? Mama, I've had a great life. I don't think you did anything wrong."

"Alison," she took my hand in hers and lowered her voice, "I let your father teach you to believe that you *had a place*, and that's just wrong." She looked away and then back at me. "I let him push away my dreams, and that was okay, that was a different time all together, but then I let him push away Jake's dreams, and your own blessed thoughts."

"I don't know what you mean." I swear my heart stopped and the world silenced as Mama searched my eyes for the truth. I knew exactly what she meant, but I didn't dare tread down that path. I wanted the illusion of Mama bein' happy to remain in my heart forever.

She patted my hand. "Okay, well, I should have stepped in and made you realize that such a *place* should not exist."

What are you tellin' me?

"Alison, how are things with Jimmy Lee?"

Mama wasn't a nosey woman. The fact that she was askin' me meant that she'd caught wind of somethin'. I shrugged. "Okay, I guess. He works a lot."

She looked deep into my eyes and drew my tears right out. I held my breath. *Don't cry. Don't cry.*

"Oh, Alison." Mama wrapped her hand around the back of my neck and pulled me to her bosom. "Shh."

"It's so hard, Mama. He's never home, and when he is, he's drinkin', and I just don't know what happened, how things went so wrong."

She stroked the back of my head. Tellin' her the truth brought my shoulders down where they belonged and air to my lungs. I breathed like I hadn't breathed in months, with lungs so full of oxygen I felt like my brain worked for the first time in forever. I pulled back from her and wiped my eyes. "I'm sorry. I shouldn't have said anything. That was very unwifely of me, but Mama, it's so hard. Some days I feel like I might burst, sittin' in that apartment waitin' for him, not knowin' if he'll be drunk or if he'll even come home before midnight."

Mama listened, without interruptin' me.

"I don't even think he loves me anymore, Mama. Most days I'm not even sure why I married him."

"I know why you married him, Alison. You'd have done anything to keep peace within this house. I just shouldn't have let you do it."

I stood and paced. "You couldn't have stopped me, Mama. I was runnin' from myself as much as tryin' to keep peace. I was afraid of what I might do if I didn't marry him."

Chapter Twenty-Nine

So much had happened over the past few weeks that I felt like everywhere I turned a crisis was waitin' on me. Though it felt good to unload my marital worries on Mama, I wondered if puttin' that burden on her was fair. I knew she'd worry 'bout me now more than ever. I was feelin' so alone lately, maybe I secretly wanted that worry. Did that make me selfish? I wondered.

The mornin' rush had eased into a calm afternoon at the diner. I was puttin' in a few more hours than I usually did, but I figured it's better than sittin' home worryin' 'bout my husband's whereabouts. When the knock came at the back door, I was happy for the distraction.

I opened the back door of the diner and shivered against the tricklin' rain. A gust of wind blew through the alley and up my legs. I handed the large, brown, paper bag to Jackson's mother, his letter tucked deftly inside between two napkins.

"Tonight, eight o'clock," she whispered from beneath her umbrella.

I nodded, and as I turned to go into the buildin', she touched my hand. When I turned to look at her, fearin' an outburst about how I'd hurt her son, she looked at me with a smile behind her eyes. I retreated back inside the diner and closed the door, leanin' against it as I calmed my racin' heart.

My eyes jumped from one customer to the next. I half expected them to jump up and point at me, yellin', *"Negro lover!"* I smoothed my uniform over my burgeonin' belly and went back to work.

As I walked home that afternoon, I wondered how I would get out at eight o'clock. Maybe Jimmy Lee wouldn't even be home yet. With the way things had been goin', that was a real possibility. I decided to face the problems with Jimmy Lee head on. I turned around and headed for the furniture store, knowin' that there was a good chance he wouldn't be there. I just kept hangin' onto the hope that he did show up for work on most days, and that I was just askin' on the days he'd skipped out. If he was there, I was fixin' to ask him if he'd be home on time, and if not, then he needed to fess up to whatever was goin' on to keep him away from home. I walked seven blocks in the pourin' rain. By the time I reached the parkin' lot I was determined that if Jimmy Lee wasn't at work I'd walk down to that godforsaken bar and find my husband. There wasn't an ounce of jealousy left in me concernin' Jimmy Lee, but the notion that he would choose to be with those heathens instead of me set my feet in motion. Even with my umbrella, my sneakers were soaked through to my toes, and my legs were frigid.

I peered around the corner of the buildin', lookin' for Jimmy Lee's truck. Relief brought a laugh to my lips. Maybe Mr. Kelly was wrong after all. Jimmy Lee might drink, but maybe he wasn't doin' those other things behind my back.

The metal door on the side of the buildin' squeaked open. I ducked around to the front and leaned against the brick beneath the green and tan awnin'. The side door slammed, echoin' against the rain.

Yellin' filled the air. I strained to hear what was said, but between the now sheetin' rain and the distance, I only caught angry tones—and those angry tones belonged to Jimmy Lee and his uncle. I hurried back down the street toward the diner. I heard Jimmy Lee's truck start, so I turned into the alley beside the drugstore and waited for him to pass.

Wheels squealed on the wet pavement. Jimmy Lee's truck sped past. I breathed fast and hard, panicked. Jimmy Lee would arrive home and I would not be there. I went into the drugstore and searched for somethin' to use as an excuse.

"Hi, sweetie, what can I get for you today?" Mr. Shire's wrinkled face was too happy for the frantic worry that raced through me.

"I, um, gee, I can't really remember," I said.

"Oh, honey, that happens a lot with pregnancy. You just take your time. Here, let me get you a paper towel to dry off." He disappeared behind the counter and returned with a handful of paper towels. "It's a wet one today, isn't it?"

I wiped the rain off my arms, chest, and face. My eyes searched the shelves, finally landin' on a beautiful, pink bottle of Pepto Bismol. "That's what I came for, a bottle of Pepto." I reached for it while Mr. Shire rattled on about his wife's stomach ailments when she was pregnant.

"Are you gonna be alright walkin' home in this mess? You're welcome to wait here for a while 'til the rain lets up."

And deal with Jimmy Lee's wrath when I get home even later? "No, thank you. I'll be fine."

Jimmy Lee's truck wasn't in the parkin' lot when I arrived home. I went upstairs and found the apartment just as I'd left it. A warm shower served to chase away the chill that had settled in my bones. It was already three thirty and I prayed the rain would stop before the evenin' arrived.

I answered the phone on the second ring, hopin' it would be Jimmy Lee.

"Alison? This is Mr. Kane. I wondered if I might escort you tonight to the meetin' of the Blue Bonnet Club."

"The Blue Bonnet Club?" Had I missed somethin'?

"Yes, the *women's guild* meetin' tonight? My wife Mitzi will be goin' and she suggested we pick you up along the way." He lowered his tone when he said *women's guild*, and I realized that he was coverin' for the meetin' at the creek later that evenin'. I felt as dumb as a stump.

"Yes, of course, that would be lovely. Thank you."

"We'll pick you up at seven forty-five."

The rain had stopped, leavin' the creek runnin' high and the surroundin' ground soft and mucky. I stood in my rain boots among a growin' crowd, some of whom I recognized, and some I did not. Since Jimmy Lee didn't return home, I left him a message and decided that what I was doin' was far more important than worryin' about where he'd sped off to.

Mr. Kane stood beside me in his huntin' coat, his rifle in his right hand, pointed at the ground. I questioned the safety of my very presence as the din around me grew louder and more people emerged from the woods. I worried each one would be Daddy, or worse, Jimmy Lee.

Mitzi Kane stood beside me, her fleshy arm around my shoulder, a constant source of comfort and confidence with her whispers of encouragement, "We're doin' the right thing. This has to change. Maggie would be so proud of you."

Mrs. Johns came through the crowd with two boys in tow. I recognized Albert, a light-colored scar led from the corner of his eye to his hairline, a painful reminder of what my husband and brother had done to him. I wanted to reach for his hand, touch his arm, do somethin' that would let him know that I cared, but I didn't dare. We might be among mixed races, but this was not New York, and I thought I'd be better off keepin' my hands to myself than makin' waves. I moved from Mitzi's grasp and stood before Albert.

"I'm sorry," I said softly. "I'm sorry they hurt you."

He nodded, his eyes cast toward his feet.

Jackson's mother put her arm around the other boy, who I recognized as my Friday afternoon lollipop boy.

"This is Tinsel," she said. "And I'm Patricia."

How I had wanted to know Jackson's family, to sit at their kitchen table and talk with his mother about her children, cookin', and life, as I did with my own mother. Jimmy Lee's parents rarely spoke to me, and I longed for the warmth that I saw in Patricia's eyes, so different than when we had met at the diner.

My voice shook. "It's a pleasure to meet you both." Fear and happiness coalesced, creatin' a bubble around us, in which I wanted to stay. I wanted to get to know her better, but stronger than my curiosity was my desire to right the wrongs done by my race, in Forrest Town.

A young girl stood behind Patricia and, behind her, a man who must have been six foot five rested his hand on her shoulder. When he looked into my eyes it was Jackson's image that was starin' back. My heart skipped a beat.

He nodded. "Ma'am."

"I'm Alison," I said.

"Michael Johns," the man said, in a voice so deep it startled me.

It took all of my concentration to look away from Jackson's father, when what I really wanted to do was give the man a hug and tell him that I was sorry for hurtin' his son. Instead, I cast my eyes to the left, recognizin' the clerk from the department store, the gangly man who ran the gas station, and the always-smilin' librarian, Lilly. I was thankful for the distraction. The moonlight shone down on the sea of people. Most of the men carried weapons, spinnin' around every few seconds to scan the woods.

Mr. Kane sidled up beside me. "There are more comin'. We have scouts on the other side of the woods, they'll send someone in if there's any hint of trouble brewin'."

"Alison?"

I had a difficult time reconcilin' Mama's voice to my surroundin's. I turned slowly, and found her standin' behind me, her eyes wide, her hair perfectly combed. She wore her Wednesday night Blue Bonnet best.

Suddenly, I no longer felt afraid.

Chapter Thirty

"What are we gettin' at the market, again?" Jimmy Lee was drivin' me to the store to buy fixin's for dinner.

"I'm makin' chicken and biscuits."

Jimmy Lee had come home after me the evenin' of the meetin', and we'd barely spoken in the days that followed. I lived in constant anticipation of receivin' Jackson's next letter, and there was no avoidin' the guilt that followed the rush of excitement. I was a married, pregnant woman, and even if I'd married Jimmy Lee for the wrong reasons, even if I didn't love him, I had to know in my heart that our marriage wasn't failin' solely because of my love for someone else—a warped need to not let Daddy down on all accounts. He'd be devastated if our marriage ended, but if it were my fault, he might never get past it.

"Nice." Jimmy Lee reached for my thigh and gave it a squeeze. "You look pretty today." That was the first compliment he'd given me in months, and I hadn't realized how much I missed the soft edges that he hid so well. I realized then, that even with him bein' kinder to me, I still yearned to be with Jackson.

"Thank you," I said, runnin' my fingers through my hair. "Do you wanna go to your parents' house for Thanksgivin' or mine?"

Jimmy Lee didn't answer.

We passed the diner, and I longed to go inside, march right to the back door, and whip it open. I longed for Patricia to hand me another letter. A quick note, some sort of acknowledgment that Jackson had received my letter.

"Alison!" Jimmy Lee fumed.

"Gheez, what, Jimmy Lee? You scared me."

"I asked you three times. You were off in La La Land. I said, I have to go out tonight, so have dinner ready early."

"Where are you goin'?" Annoyance pecked at my nerves.

"It doesn't matter," he said.

"It does matter. We're married, and I never see you." I crossed my arms over my chest, bitin' back my hurt.

"You see me. I'm here now, aren't I?"

"That isn't what I mean. Ever since we got married, we never hang out anymore, we never go on dates, we never do anything but wake up together."

He eyed my belly. "I think we do more than that."

I rolled my eyes and turned away. Then realized it was now or never.

"Jimmy Lee, where do you go at night, when you go for drinks? Where are you goin' tonight?"

We stopped at a red light and Jimmy Lee turned toward me, one hand on the steerin' wheel, the other restin' on his open window. "What I do does not concern you." He faced forward, then said in a cold, even tone, "Someone has to keep these streets safe."

Chapter Thirty-One

Women huddled by the butcher, whisperin' among themselves. The cashier leaned in close, whisperin' to the customer in line when I walked by. I glanced out the front window where Jimmy Lee was lightin' a cigarette, and then headed for the frozen vegetable aisle. I neared the butcher counter and the gossipin' women quickly dispersed.

"Hi, Charlie," I said to the butcher as I passed.

"Alison. Where's that husband of yours?" He looked up and down the aisle.

"He's waitin' outside."

What was goin' on? Did everyone know about the meetin' last night? *Oh, God.* I hurried through the store and picked up the groceries I needed, then headed for the cashier.

"Hi, Millie." Millie Lapas, a thin-lipped girl who'd been in my English class, looked me up and down.

"How are you Alison?"

I patted my belly. "Fat and happy, I suppose."

She smirked, dartin' her eyes at the women who were now huddled by the dairy aisle.

"How are you really doin'?" she whispered.

"Fine?" *What on earth?*

"I just figured, with that boy pressin' charges and all that, you know?" she raised her eyebrows.

I shook my head in confusion.

"Oh, it's none of my business. I'm sure it wasn't Jimmy Lee." She swatted the air.

"What wasn't Jimmy Lee?" I asked. Jimmy Lee leaned on the front of the truck, cigarette in hand.

Millie stopped ringin' up my items and leaned across the counter. "You know, that boy he beat up?"

Albert? I wrapped my arm around my belly, wantin' to protect my baby from hearin' whatever might come next.

"You don't have to hide it, Alison. Everyone knows he beat up that colored boy, Thomas Green. Left him near 'bout dead."

My knees grew weak. "Wh...what?"

"His uncle and his daddy will get him off." I hated myself for parrotin' my vicious husband.

"I raised you better than that."

I flushed. "I don't know what to do. He's a monster. He was a monster before I married him. Mama, what do I do?"

"I can't tell you what to do. I can only tell you that you need to make sure that you and that grandchild of mine are safe. That's your job, Alison."

I don't know what I expected, but it sure wasn't such a hands-off approach. I wanted her to give me the answers.

"What would you do?" I asked.

Mama took a deep breath and blew it out slowly. "Come, let's walk," she said, and we headed out toward the edge of the property.

"I thought he might change after we were married," I explained. "I thought he was just, I don't know, bein' a schoolboy or somethin'. But he's only gotten worse."

"Alison, what we're doin', it's terribly dangerous. Not just because your father or your husband might find out, but most folks around here, they're just fine with the way things are. In fact, they want things to remain exactly how they are."

"I know that."

"Jimmy Lee's uncle, Billy, he's the ring leader. I didn't know 'bout this before you married Jimmy Lee, and I'm not certain 'bout it now, but I think he might even be part of the KKK."

"The KKK? Are they even around here?" I'd heard about the KKK in other towns, but not here, not in Forrest Town. If Mr. Carlisle was part of that awful group, then chances were, so was Jimmy Lee. It was fallin' into place like pieces of a puzzle. Jimmy Lee disappearin', boys gettin' beat up. Of course Mr. Carlisle would cover for him. I shook my head, but the awful reality clung to my mind like meat to a bone.

"Oh, yes. Mr. Carlisle doesn't wear a white hood and carry a burnin' cross, he's more clever than that. He goes undetected, but let that leave no question. They kill people—and leave them in rivers to rot." The look in her eyes made me shiver.

"I'm gonna be sick." I leaned over and coughed, holdin' onto Mama's arm.

"Sit down, here, under the tree."

I settled in beside Mama, my back against the tree, my head on her shoulder.

"So you really think Jimmy Lee killed Mr. Bingham? Mama, I can't go back to him. I can't sleep next to him in that apartment."

"You have to."

I looked at her as if she was crazy.

"If you leave now, he's gonna figure it all out. He'll track your every move, and his uncle will be sure of it. Right now, you're protected. You're his wife. He thinks you'll cover for him no matter what it takes, and you will."

"But—" I must be thick headed, because it struck me then that if Jimmy Lee and his uncle were involved with the KKK, then chances were, so was his father.

"But nothin'. Listen to me. This is real, Alison. This is life and death. If Mr. Carlisle thinks we're plannin' to help the colored folks, he'll take us all out. I have no doubt."

"That sounds really paranoid," I said.

"Maybe, but think about it. Jimmy Lee found your letters from Maggie."

"How do you know that?"

"Maggie told me."

"Oh, God."

"She was worried about you," Mama explained.

"So, you knew what Maggie was up to this whole time?"

"I've known what Maggie was up to since she was five. Why do you think I encouraged your father to send her to New York? I have friends there who keep an eye out for her."

Who is this woman? "You have friends in New York?"

Mama blinked, her cheeks flushed, as if a fond memory had wormed its way into her mind. "A friend who relocated there after high school. If Maggie had stayed here, she'd have gotten herself killed, or put in jail. She was a wildfire waitin' to burn. Once she sets her sights on somethin', she pushes until she's right in the thick of it. In New York, she can burn all she wants and people will rally around her—she's one of thousands, not a seed in the miniscule flowerbed of Forrest Town."

The truth of her words hung between us. I realized that what I'd seen of her was merely what she wanted me to see. I wondered if she worried that once the outside layer was removed, the others might unravel.

I knew that, when Mama was young, she had painted beautiful pictures, like the one inside the barn, but she'd given that up before I was born, and I'd never seen her pick up a paint brush a day in my life. Now, I wanted to know how that felt—givin' up somethin' you loved. I wondered if it were strangely like how I had felt about Jackson, the night at the creek when I'd let him go.

"Mama, why'd you give up paintin'?"

Mama stared off into the fields. "Oh, honey, I wasn't that good, not like Jake, and things were so different then. Women didn't go traipsin' off to some big city to follow their dreams."

"Couldn't you follow them here? Take classes, continue to paint?"

She shook her head, and looked at me as she had when I was a little girl dreamin' of things that were far more magnificent than I would ever see. "I tried. I painted a bit when Maggie and Jake were younger, but life takes over, and Daddy and I had no money. Grandma and Grandpa left us some, but not much. Sometimes what you want to do isn't really what you're meant to do. I like my life just fine. Besides, I'm old, honey. Now it's your turn."

"Old? You look like my sister." We laughed, and it felt good to let down my guard for a minute. Lately it felt like I was hidin' behind a coat of armor. Mama's forehead grew tight again, and I knew our moment was over.

"Listen, Alison, you need to be very careful. Stand by your husband. Don't give him any reason to believe that somethin' bigger than what he's already goin' through is goin' on. To everyone in town, you are the wife of a wayward husband—to your husband, you're his savin' grace. Men fall hard, and he will. He might get mean, and if he does, you leave immediately. Call me and I'll come get you, but I don't think he's gonna go in that direction. Most bullies—and that's what he is, a bully who beats up kids—they turn into whiny babies. Once the seriousness of this comes forward, he'll cling to you like a child, and the town will rally around you out of pity."

"No, they won't. You should've seen the spears they shot at me in the market. You'da thought I was the one who beat up Thomas Green. And besides, I don't want pity."

Mama leaned back against the tree, once more. "There are bigger things on the horizon. Pity isn't so bad. You're young, you're just startin' out in your life. Pity will endear them to you and you will come out on top."

"Are you worried, Mama? About the boycott?"

Her eyes darted back toward the house and fields. She nodded. "Yes, but you and I, we aren't gonna be in it. We're behind the scenes, and we'll stay there. Maggie's gonna stay in New York. I'm more worried about someone findin' out about it ahead of time. If anyone finds out we're involved," her eyes met mine, and held them, "well, let's just not let them."

"Then why should I stay with Jimmy Lee? Can't I come home? I feel like a lamb tied to a tree."

"I'm not givin' you up like a sacrificial lamb," she laughed. "If you support Jimmy Lee, he'll have no reason to doubt your motivations. If you argue with him, work against him, leave him, he'll have reason to be concerned and may go nosin' around. The last thing you do to a snake is hit it with a rake. It'll turn on you faster than you can run away." She leaned forward and softened her tone. "You know I love you, and I'd bring you home today, but there are many lives at stake here, and we're too deep in to turn back."

"Do you wish you could? Turn back, I mean?"

"From bein' involved? No, but with other things—"

"Meanin'?" I could see somethin' else festerin' in the worry of her hands on the edge of the rocker.

"I wish I could turn back time and stand up for my children more."

Chapter Thirty-Three

The hammer came down a week later, swift and skillful. Mama came into town and was havin' a cup of coffee at the diner when we heard shoutin' outside.

"What are those boys up to now?" Jean said as she walked toward the front window. "I swear, there's more fightin' in this town—" She peered out front and called for me, wavin' her hand to hurry me along.

"What is it?" I set down my order pad and excused myself from my customer. Mama got up from the counter and followed me to the window.

Down the street, Jimmy Lee stood red-faced, chest heavin', before two men in dark suits who stood in front of Mr. Mackey's law office. Mr. Carlisle was rushin' up the sidewalk from the direction of the store. Jimmy Lee's voice rang out, echoin' between the buildin's. I could not make out the words, or maybe I didn't want to.

"Oh, sweetheart, your man's in a bit of trouble, isn't he?" Jean took my hand and walked me toward one of the booths.

I glanced at Mama. *Pity. How could she have known?*

"It's okay, Alison. You just sit here and we'll find out what's goin' on." Jean looked at Mama.

"Yes, right. I'll go see if I can calm things down."

"Mama?" I worried that Jimmy Lee might get upset if she intervened. Mama held her hand up, as if to say she had it under control. She pulled her shoulders back and walked out the door toward the ruckus.

Customers rose from their seats and gathered in the front window, watchin' the scene unfold. I remained seated, my head bowed. I would accept that pity with grace, just as Mama had advised.

A knock at the back door startled me.

"I've got it, hun. It's gonna be Tinsel, come for his daddy's food. He's so cute." She hurried off and I knew that if it wasn't Tinsel, if it was Patricia, I'd have missed my chance at a letter from Jackson. I sat and listened to my husband's life fallin' apart out front and my worry mounted about what was transpirin' out back. Mr. Bingham's ravaged body came to me, strengthenin' my resolve. My husband deserved whatever they doled out to him.

The bell over the door jingled as Mama came back into the diner. She walked strong and tall toward the booth, and slid in across from me. She leaned in close and whispered, "They're pressin' charges for what he did to Thomas Green. Those are attorneys, here to meet with Thomas' family. I didn't hear too much, but from what I gathered, Jimmy Lee caught wind of their visit and, well, you know, sort of lost it."

"What should I do?"

"Nothin'. You do just what you're doin'. Tonight, don't bring it up. Let him stew. He'll talk when he's ready. Be as invisible as you can. The more you pry, the angrier he'll get. He needs to know you believe in him and that he's not alone."

"But I don't believe in him. What he did was wrong."

"I know." She took hold of my hand. "Now is not the time to show your strength, now is the time to make your husband love you."

The shoutin' outside the diner quieted. Jean moved toward the front of the diner. "Okay, people. Sit down and eat. The show's over." She wrangled customers back to their seats and brought me a cup of tea.

"I'm okay, Jean, really."

"You have a lot on your family's dinner plate right now, Alison. Why don't you take the afternoon off and go relax."

"Relax?" I no longer knew what that word meant.

Before I even got inside the apartment that afternoon, Jimmy Lee was askin' me questions.

"Finally. Where have you been?"

I set my purse on the table and stood by the door, weighin' his mood. "I was at work." It took all my strength not to let him know how embarrassed I was, or how angry.

"Those niggers hired lawyers."

Should I act surprised? I was glad he'd been caught. I didn't have a clue how to respond, but I didn't have to decide, because in his next breath, he told me everything.

"They're pressin' charges for beatin' up that little shit, Thomas Green."

And Mr. Bingham?

"My uncle's lawyer says it'll never stick," he fumed.

His eyes were glassy, open wide like a crazed animal, his hair disheveled. I almost felt sorry for him—until I thought of Mr. Bingham, Albert, and Thomas. I walked over to the couch where he sat and lowered myself down on the far end. I hoped the charges would stick, and I swallowed the urge to tell him so.

"So, now, I go to work and I come home. He said they'd be watchin' me, or some shit like that."

"Okay," was all I could manage. *Home?* At least he wouldn't be at that dirty bar, if, in fact, that was even where he'd been hangin' out.

"Alison, I know I haven't been the best husband in the world, and I'm sorry."

How did Mama know? "It's okay," I whispered.

"No, no it's not. I haven't been home, and you're all pregnant and everything. I promise I'll be better. No more goin' out for drinks, no more late nights. I'll be home every night on time."

Because you have to be.

Jimmy Lee sprang to his feet when someone knocked on the door, his eyes wide and fear-filled. Every muscle in his body clenched.

He looked out the window. "Police."

Police! I hadn't thought the situation through. Of course they'd come for him. Panic pounded in my chest and the tiny hairs on the back of my neck prickled. "What do we do?"

He put his hands on his hips, then crossed them over his chest, and blew out a long breath. "Answer the door."

We stood a foot apart, eyes locked on each other. He reached for me and I clamored into his arms, unexpected tears fillin' my eyes.

"I love you," he said.

"I love you, too." I was shocked by my need to hold onto him. I felt like a piece of me was bein' arrested with him. He pulled away from me and went to the door.

"Ma'am." Officer Chandler stood in the doorway, noddin' at me as he spoke; his partner stood silently beside him. "Jimmy Lee, we gotta take you in."

Jimmy Lee nodded. I ran to his side and wrapped my arms around him. I might not be in love with him, but at that moment, I realized that I did love him, and it hurt like hell to listen to Officer Chandler give him his Miranda Warnin' and to see Jimmy Lee's shoulders roll forward and his head hang low.

Jimmy Lee stared at the floor. "Yes, sir. I understand. Yes, sir." He spoke without lookin' at me. "Alison, call Uncle Billy."

I picked up the phone as the door closed behind them. I stood with the phone in my tremblin' hand, the magnitude of what he'd done pressin' in on me. I was married to a felon. My husband was goin' to jail.

Chapter Thirty-Four

"Mr. Carlisle? This is Alison. Jimmy Lee's just been taken to the police station." Tears flowed steady and warm down my cheeks as I pressed the phone to my ear. Why was I so darn upset? It made no sense. I should be happy that he was out of my way. There would be no threat to me as long as he was gone, and still, I was torn, and scared, and alone.

"Thank you. We'll take care of it," he answered.

"Should I go to the police station?" I was already thinkin' ahead about callin' Mama and havin' her drive me there.

"No, you stay put. We'll take care of it and bring him home." Jimmy Lee's uncle spoke confidently.

I hung up the phone and called Mama.

"Hello?" My father's voice caught me off guard.

"Daddy?"

"Pixie?"

He knew. I could hear it in his tone. "Hi, Daddy, is Mama there?"

"Are you okay? Do you want me to come get you, bring you home for a bit?"

Yes, God yes! "No, I'm okay. I just need to talk to Mama."

"They'll get him off, Pix, you know they will. He'll be back home before you know it."

That's all I need. Daddy was bein' positive because that's what he thought I wanted. I felt guilty acceptin' Daddy's careful coddlin' when I knew I should be fessin' up to the truth of my feelin's.

"Those damn Negros, they're bitin' off more than they can chew with Jimmy Lee Carlisle."

"Daddy! They didn't do anything wrong." *Damn it. Why can't I do what Mama told me to do?* I listened to Daddy's heavy breath come through the phone. "Sorry, Daddy, I mean, I don't know what I mean. I'm all confused. Can I please just talk to Mama?"

My father didn't say a word. He set down the phone and I listened to his heavy footsteps retreat on the wooden floor.

"Alison? Are you alright, honey?"

"Yes. I think I made Daddy mad, though. They arrested Jimmy Lee. They took him in!" My words fell fast and panicky from my lips. "He told me to call his uncle, Billy, which I did. What should I do now?"

"Alison, take a deep breath. Calm down. It's gonna be fine."

"Okay," I said, and then did as she asked.

"What's his uncle doin'?"

"He told me to stay home and he'd take care of it. I have no idea what that means—get a lawyer, I guess. Mama, Jimmy Lee is in *jail*." I rubbed my belly. "I'm not ready for this. This is too much."

"Alison, grab a chair and sit down."

She waited while I settled myself onto a kitchen chair.

"Now, listen to me. You let Mr. Carlisle handle this and you go along with your life just as if Jimmy Lee was still home. You eat breakfast and lunch, go to the diner, whatever it is you do, do it."

"But, everyone knows. Daddy already knew!"

"Yes, they do, and that won't change no matter what you do, so the best thing to do is just go on with your daily life. Do you want me to come over?"

"No. Daddy needs you there. I'm just scared, Mama. I feel like I'm caught in a trap. I've got all this stuff goin' on behind his back, and now *this*. I wish I could just go to sleep and wake up to everything bein' normal again."

I pictured Mama pushin' her hair behind her ear and crinklin' her forehead, stuck between wantin' to take care of her daughter and tellin' her to do the right thing. I didn't look forward to that kind of maternal quandary.

"Normal wasn't great, Alison, it just felt that way because you were blissfully ignorant, like we all were. We walked around with blinders on, but you do have a choice." She lowered her voice. "You don't have to be involved in any of it. You can turn away and never look back."

She wasn't bein' condescendin' or makin' me feel like I was weak. Mama was doin' what any mother would—offerin' genuine support that carried through her tone and wrapped itself around me like her lovin' arms. Even so, she didn't know how wrong she was.

Chapter Thirty-Five

My heart leapt with the ringin' of the phone. I sat up in bed, still encased in a sleep-induced fog.

"Pixie, are you alright? Mama told me about Jimmy Lee." Maggie didn't give me time to respond. "About time, huh?"

"Maggie." I sat up and tried to wrap my mind around why I was hopin' it was Jimmy Lee. "He's my husband. This isn't really *good* news." *Except, it kinda is.*

"I'm sorry, you're right, but it does clear the path. The boycott is right around the corner, and it'll be easier with him out of the way."

"You shouldn't be callin'. You can't afford it," I said.

"This is different, Pix. It's one phone call. I'd go into debt to make sure you're alright. Don't ya' know that yet?"

I was comforted by Maggie's words, and wishin' I could chance a phone call to Jackson. Maggie's call was one thing, but a call to Jackson would leave a trail that could only end in trouble when Jimmy Lee saw the phone bill.

"The meetin' went well. We've got a system set up to disseminate information, and I don't think anyone knows about the effort. Mr. Kane was brilliant. What's happenin' up there?"

"They're plannin' a march in South Carolina over the weekend, to help integrate one of the schools. I'm thinkin' about goin'."

"Maggie! You promised you wouldn't do anything dangerous." I threw my legs over the side of my bed. The apartment was silent around me, the sun peerin' in through the bedroom curtains. I thought of Jimmy Lee sittin' in a jail cell, and though I had been emotional about him bein' taken away yesterday, I felt no sorrow today. I didn't miss him. I didn't worry. I knew his uncle would take care of him. I finally began to see how little room there had been for me in his life from day one of our marriage, and now I no longer cared.

"It's fine, Pix. I won't go if it looks like there's gonna be trouble."

"There'll be trouble alright, Maggie. Hey, you knew about Mama. Why didn't you tell me?"

"I was worried about you. You and Daddy are so close."

"Were so close."

"Oh, Pix, no. What's happened?" I pictured Maggie's eyebrows comin' together, and that worried look passin' over her face.

"Nothin' *happened*, really. I'm just not the same little girl I once was, and some of the things Daddy does, well, they're irkin' me more and more. I'm havin' a hard time keepin' my mouth shut."

"Oh, no, Pix. Don't do what I did. It's not worth it. Daddy doesn't mean to be the way he is. He's just doin' what he was brought up to do and to believe. Don't let this come between you." She paused. "I miss him. I miss our family."

"I know. I do, too," I said, and I meant it. "I wonder if they're gonna nail Jimmy Lee for beatin' up Albert too, or killin' Mr. Bingham?"

Maggie was silent for a moment. "I hope they do," she said, then quickly added, "I'm sorry. I know he's your husband, but—"

"It's okay. I'm so conflicted about all of this, but if I weren't married to him, I'd want the right thing to happen. How's Jackson?" I squeezed my eyes shut, prayin' she wouldn't think too much about why I'd asked.

"He's doin' really well. He's goin' to the march, too. He's enmeshed more deeply than I am on the outside, so he keeps us all up to date on the movements he attends."

My heart sank. "He goes to marches and things?"

"Yeah, he goes to most of them. He's got a huge followin' and he's really rallied the folks across five states. Who knew a leader would come out of Forrest Town? Crazy, right?"

"Yeah, crazy. Hey, Maggie, I gotta run. Patricia is bringin' me the meetin' information when she picks up her husband's lunch today at the diner. Love you, and call me the second you get back from the march. I know you can't really afford it, but just a quick call. I wanna know you're okay."

The order for lunch wasn't called in that mornin', and I was surprised when there was a knock at the back door. I swung the door open, expectin' to see Patricia, but she wasn't the one who showed up that afternoon. A middle-school-aged boy with darker skin was bent over, leanin' on his knees, pantin' like he'd been runnin' for too long. He looked up at me with eyes so big and white they were unsettlin'.

"Mr. Green, the father of the boy who was beat up, is missin'," he said.

"What do you mean missin'?"

He stood, pushin' his hands into his sides as he panted out an answer. "Didn't come home last night. Everyone's worried."

Oh, no. My heart slammed into my ribs, chasin' a chill up my arms. "Where's Patricia?" I asked, then looked back over my shoulder for Jean, who was busy at the cash register.

"She's at home, 'fraid to leave. Everyone's lookin' for him." He looked frantically up and down the alley. "I gotta go." He ran away, leavin' me starin' after him, frightened and feelin' useless. I prayed that Mr. Green was okay, but I knew otherwise. *Mr. Bingham. The river.*

"Jean," I called as I made my way to the front of the diner. "I'm not feelin' so well, do you mind if I go?"

She was at my side in seconds. "Are you okay? Want me to get Joe to drive you home?"

"No, I'm okay, just a little off. I think I need to rest. This whole thing with Jimmy Lee has me tied in knots." *Jimmy Lee.* If somethin' happened to Mr. Green, then at least this time it wasn't at the hands of my husband.

"Sure, sugar, you go. You don't work again 'til Monday, so you rest up."

Chapter Thirty-Six

Please don't be there. Please don't be there. I didn't see anything along the way to the river—literally. I didn't notice if there were cars goin' down the street or people millin' about in town. I had tunnel vision, clouded by the image of Mr. Bingham, my nerves rememberin' the fear that consumed me when I found him. I shook and trembled as I made my way through the woods, passin' trees and steppin' over logs as if on autopilot. *Please don't be there.*

I don't know what made me think that I'd find Mr. Green in that same location, or why I thought I'd find him at all, but somethin' told me I would. I pushed through the last bush and into the clearin'. Tears burned my eyes and I squeezed them away. *Please don't be here.* Scenarios raced through my mind. What if I found him? Who would I tell? Would we all be next, everyone who was at the meetin'?

The river flowed steady and fast from the recent rains. I climbed over the rocks to the edge, flashes of memory comin' at me hard and fast. I looked down river, then up. A tangle of somethin' massive in the branches of a tree that sprouted from the water's edge sent a stab of fear through me. *Please don't be him.* I moved cautiously toward it. *Please don't be him.* Twigs and grass covered a mound of somethin' brown. I stopped dead in my tracks. What was I doin'? I can't do this again. I can't take it. I turned toward the woods, but knew I had to continue on. Adrenaline pushed me forward, fear made each step like walkin' through quicksand. I crouched by the water's edge, prayin' it wasn't him. I poked at the mass of muck and twigs. The mass didn't budge. I used the stick to clear away a spot in the center of the mass, revealin' brown fur. I dropped to my knees, coverin' my face with my hands, and let the tears fall. I glanced back up at the mass, and it was then, through my blurry eyes, that I saw the long, thick neck craned backward, the horse's head positioned at a painful angle, buried deep under the water.

I walked down river, away from town, partially to get closer to where the woods met my apartment, and partially to calm my revved up nerves. I wished Jackson was there. What I needed more than anything was someone to hold me and tell me everything was gonna be okay, because as it stood, I couldn't see anything bein' okay any time soon.

Vultures circled overhead, givin' the white sky and chilly air an ominous weight. I stopped at the edge of the woods, listenin' to the flow of the river and the birds cawin' overhead. I placed my hand on my expandin' belly and closed my eyes, tryin' to envision what my life would be like once my baby came. Darkness prevailed. I saw my lonely apartment, and Jimmy Lee's drunken comments and disheartenin' absence. I took a deep breath and blew it out slowly. I put my other hand on my belly and envisioned what my life might've been like if I had gone to New York with Jackson—if the baby within me had been his. The glow of his face filled me with warmth and comfort, his soft and supportive eyes danced with light, a smile graced his plump lips. The smell of his sweat came back to me, the feel of his hands on my body gave me goose bumps. Beneath my fingers, my baby moved, bringin' with it renewed thoughts of security. I wanted my baby to have what I had growin' up—two parents who loved each other, safe goodnight kisses, and a sense that the world was safe. I wanted that more than I wanted to breathe fresh air. I opened my eyes, reality all around me in the place I stood, the reason why I was there. I had to decide once and for all, before it was too late. Was I stayin' with Jimmy Lee, as Mama said, to help with integration efforts, for the greater good of the community, and for all babies who would come forth after that time, or could I close my eyes and walk away, without a care for what happened outside my own thin walls?

I pondered that thought as I navigated my way through the woods, toward home.

Street noises filtered in through the trees as I neared the apartments. A blood-curdlin' scream came from somewhere off in the distance. I stopped. Listened. More screamin'. Footsteps rushin' through the brush. All at once people were runnin' into the woods, hollerin' in the direction of the outcry. I followed the panicked trail toward the screams.

A deep voice hushed the screamin' woman and broke through the panic. "Get back. Everyone, get back."

I peered past the group of people and followed their craned necks up toward the umbrella of trees. Mr. Green's limp body hung from a rope like a deer bleedin' out. I turned away, grabbin' a nearby tree for support. *Why did this have to happen?* Fear pierced my thoughts—was it because of our meetin'? Did someone know? I racked my brain tryin' to remember if Mr. Green was at the meetin', and came up empty. Jimmy Lee had beat up his son. A shudder ran through me as comprehension of what was sure to be the truth set in.

A young mother turned away, hurryin' out of the woods with her child in her arms. Two white men turned and walked away at a calm, even pace, one mutterin', "Got what he deserved. "

Every muscle in my body stiffened. I willed myself not to run up to those men and smack them across their pompous cheeks. Enough was enough.

A colored man scurried up the tree and cut the rope, droppin' Mr. Green's limp body into the arms of three colored men waitin' below.

"There's a note," one of the men said. He pulled a piece of paper out of the pocket of Mr. Green's flannel shirt. His dark eyes scanned the note, and then he dropped his hand to his side without utterin' a word. The man standin' next to him took the note from his hand.

"It's a warnin'. It says, '*Back off or you're next.*'"

"Back off what?" a colored woman asked.

Back off? Of the charges to Jimmy Lee? Of the boycott? I turned and ran home as fast as my pregnant body would carry me. Mr. Green's lifeless body solidified my decision. There was only one way that I could ever move forward with my life without livin' in regret's unforgivin' shadow.

Chapter Thirty-Seven

I flew in the apartment door, grabbed the phone from the table, and dialed Maggie's number. Her phone rang and rang. I hung up and tried to reach Mama. There was no answer. I walked in circles, wishin' I could go to the jail and talk to Jimmy Lee. His uncle said he'd take care of it. I lowered myself to the couch. *He'd take care of it. Mr. Carlisle. Of course.*

"The same way you took care of Mr. Bingham for your brother?" I stomped across the floor. *The hell with this.*

I yanked open the bedroom closet door. The shoebox, where I used to keep Maggie's letters, sat empty on the top shelf. I dug the bag of summer clothes out from the back and emptied it onto the bed. I found the pair of dark blue shorts and unzipped the tiny pocket, then withdrew the small piece of paper, and walked back to the phone. Starin' at the receiver, I gathered my courage, rememberin' the mornin' after I'd returned home from New York. After Jimmy Lee had gone to work I'd hidden Jackson's phone number in the closet. I couldn't bear throwin' it away, and Jackson had made me promise to use it if I was ever in trouble. I reached for the receiver, and unclenched my shakin' hand. The slip of paper fluttered down onto the bed. I dialed Jackson's number, watchin' the rotary move painstakin'ly slowly back to zero with each pull of a number.

"Hello?"

My voice stalled in my throat. *What was I doin'?*

"Hello?" he said, again.

"It's…it's me," I said softly.

He was silent for a beat. "Alison?"

"Mm-hmm."

"Alison, what's wrong? We said we wouldn't take the chance of callin'. Are you alright?"

"They killed another man. Jimmy Lee got arrested for beatin' up Thomas Green and now Mr. Green's been hung." Tears streamed down my cheeks. I held the receiver so tight my knuckles hurt. "There was a note in his pocket that said somethin' like, 'Back off or you're next.' And his uncle, Billy, he told me not to go to the jailhouse." I spoke so fast I could barely breathe. "He said he'd take care of it, but Jimmy Lee didn't come home, so I guess he's still in jail, and I have no idea what else Mr. Carlisle might have meant. I thought he meant he'd get a lawyer or somethin'. Oh,

God, Jackson, what should I do?" I gasped a quick breath. "I think Jimmy Lee had him killed."

"Okay, okay. Damn it. But you're alright? Where are you?"

"I'm fine. I'm at my apartment."

"Maggie and I are leavin' in an hour to go to South Carolina. Damn it. Can you call Mr. Kane? Let him know what's goin' on? Alison, how can you be sure this isn't because they caught wind of the boycott?"

"I can't, but I've wracked my brain and I don't remember Mr. Green bein' at the meetin'. I'll call Mr. Kane. He'll know if he was there. He knows everyone who attends."

"Can you go stay at your mother's?" Jackson asked.

"I don't know."

"Alison, I don't want you to be alone. If there's any chance that Jimmy Lee knows what we're up to, you'll be in danger."

He was right. "Okay, I'll stay at my parents'. I wish you were here." I wished so hard, my stomach ached.

"Me too, but we couldn't be together anyway, so what good would it do?"

"Why do you have to be so practical?" Wishin' that, just for once since leavin' home, someone would make everything in my life okay.

"Because I want to stay alive."

Chapter Thirty-Eight

"Life got you a little freaked out, sis?" Jake asked when he came to pick me up in Daddy's truck.

"A little."

"Want me to take you to see Jimmy Lee?"

It hadn't dawned on me that goin' to see him was an option. I was still the obedient, little girl Daddy raised. I didn't really want to see Jimmy Lee, but part of me thought it was my wifely duty to act as if I cared, and another part of me wanted to try and figure out what was goin' on in his head.

"You'd do that?"

Jake drove toward the jailhouse and handed me a paper he'd had tucked under his leg.

I unfolded the paper and was surprised to find an application to Mississippi State. "Where'd you get this?"

"Mama got it for me."

"No, she did not."

Jake grinned. "Daddy doesn't know. She said it wouldn't be easy to get in, and I'd have to work to afford it, but she said they had great art courses."

"Jake, what will Daddy say? You can't leave him." *We can't all leave him.*

"I probably won't even get in, but Mama says I have to try. I don't know what's come over her, but she's been different since you left."

"How do you mean?"

"I don't know, just different. She's all…like, tellin' me to follow my dreams, and she takes pies she bakes outside to the field hands and stuff." Jake laughed, then said, "You shoulda seen Daddy's face the first time she took them a snack. He shot her a look, and she just went on like she didn't see it."

I couldn't believe Mama was takin' such blatant strides. I wondered what other changes I might find when I got back to the farm.

The jail smelled like old leather and summer sweat. I wrapped my arms around myself as I sat and waited to be taken back to see Jimmy Lee.

Jake leaned in close beside me. "You okay?"

I nodded, unable to speak. What would I say to Jimmy Lee? What if his uncle came in and saw me? I shuffled my feet and clasped my hands together.

"Would you really go to that school?"

Jake shrugged. "Maybe. I don't know. I want to."

My world was changin', and I was either gonna change right along with it, or remain in an unhappy marriage and raise my child with a racist husband.

"Mrs. Carlisle?" A bald, overweight officer spoke with a stern voice as he held the door open. His eyes dropped to my pregnant belly.

"A woman in your condition shouldn't have ta worry yourself none. None of us want your husband in here. He was just cleanin' house."

Cleanin' house? Was the entire police department corrupt?

"He'll be out of here soon enough." He turned and winked.

The door closed with a *clank* behind us as we made our way down the narrow, gray hallway. At the end of the hall, we turned right and the officer stopped in front of a solid door with a small glass window. He opened the door and stepped aside.

Inside, Jimmy Lee sat at a metal table. He wasn't wearin' handcuffs, as I'd imagined. He didn't look especially tired or even unhappy. He stood and opened his arms.

"Alison," he said, and pulled me close.

"You're okay?" Completely taken aback by his warmth, I gently pushed away.

"Sheesh, yeah, I'm fine. Piece of cake."

The door closed, leavin' us alone in the stark room.

Jimmy Lee sat down and I lowered myself into the cold, metal chair across from him.

"Your uncle told me not to come, otherwise, I woulda been by yesterday."

"That's okay. It won't matter. There won't be a case by tonight," he said smugly.

"Whaddaya mean?"

"We took care of things. I don't think the Green's will be botherin' us anymore."

The room began to spin. *Took care of things.* I didn't want to believe it. I grasped for some other explanation. "They're droppin' the charges?"

"In a way."

I held my purse in both hands to keep them from shakin'. "In what way? Either they're droppin' the charges or they're not." *Tell me you didn't have him killed. Please, lie to me if you have to, just please tell me.*

"Oh, they'll drop the charges all right. Stupid niggers."

The word made my skin crawl. "Do you have to do that?"

"What?" He held his palm up toward the ceilin', as if he had no idea what I was referrin' to.

"That—callin' 'em stupid." *Shut up. Shut up. Shut up.* I knew I was travelin' down a dangerous path. My life was speedin' out of control, like a train wreck waitin' to happen. My pulse raced, my hands worked at frayin' the edges of my purse, and I wanted to jump up and run from the room—heck, I wanted to run from Arkansas.

"They are stupid," his voice escalated as he rose from the chair. "Dumb niggers think they can keep me down? No way would Daddy or Uncle Billy let that happen."

Your father? Your uncle? How long can you rely on them to take care of you? Had I relied on Daddy takin' care of me for too long? On some level, was I still relyin' on the security of him too much? I forced my emotions inside, and asked when he'd be comin' home.

"I'll be out by midnight."

"Midnight?"

"They're settin' bail tomorrow, but I think somethin' is gonna change that plan."

Mr. Green's dead body.

"I'm stayin' at Mama's tonight. I don't really wanna be alone."

Jimmy Lee nodded. "Okay. I'll get you when I'm out."

"Not at midnight."

"In the mornin', then."

"Yeah, mornin'. Okay." I let Jimmy Lee take my hand in his. My stomach twisted and turned. My husband was responsible for a man's death, and I had to keep my mouth shut. My Daddy's voice haunted me—*Know your place*—but the image of Mama sneakin' up to the back door of the furniture store rivaled that thought.

Chapter Thirty-Nine

Jimmy Lee didn't come to collect me the next mornin', and my phone calls home went unanswered.

"Let the man be. He'll come when he can," Daddy said dismissively. "He's in a mess of trouble. He might be meetin' with lawyers or somethin'."

"I guess, but he coulda called," I said.

My father sat at the head of the kitchen table eatin' his eggs as quickly as he could. "Are you alright, Pix? You don't look very well."

"I'm just tired. My husband is in jail, Daddy, and Mr. Green is dead." I watched his eyes narrow. "Aren't you affected at all by Mr. Green? I mean, he was hung from a tree, Daddy. I saw him. It was awful." I pushed my plate away.

He went to work on his biscuit. "It's not my business," he said between bites. "And it ain't yours, either."

Mama walked behind my chair and set a glass of orange juice in front of me, pattin' my shoulder, remindin' me to go easy. My entire life was spent goin' easy. No wonder Maggie blew up.

"My husband beat that kid, of course it's my business." I set my eyes on Daddy, ignorin' the heat from Mama's stare.

He set down his fork and looked up at Mama, but spoke directly to me. "Your husband did whatever he felt he had to do. Know your place, Alison. Don't cause undue trouble. There's enough of that goin' 'round right now."

I stood and paced, then threw my napkin on the table. "Right now, Daddy, I'm so sick of knowin' my place that I could puke." I stormed out of the house and sat on the front porch.

Five minutes later, Mama joined me.

"Mr. Kane called. The Blue Bonnet meetin' is scheduled for tonight instead of Wednesday."

A silent message passed between us; *Mr. Green's death had sent up alarms.*

Twice as many people showed up that night as had the previous week. Mr. Kane explained that supporters from other towns were already arrivin', with others on their way. Many had already arrived in neighborin' towns. The boycott had been rescheduled. We had three days to prepare.

Mr. Kane leaned on his shotgun and announced with a low, serious tone, "Now, we're suggestin' that women and children stay inside their homes durin' this protest. We don't know what we'll come up against, but if Mr. Green is any indication, it may be very dangerous."

"How many is comin' from other towns?" A short colored man asked. The crowd murmured in agreement with his question.

"We don't know, but it looks like hundreds of protesters, includin' the Black Panthers."

The Black Panthers? Maggie? I hadn't heard from her since she'd left for South Carolina. How would they make it here in three days? I wondered how the South Carolina protest went.

"What can we expect, in town, I mean?" my voice quaked.

"We're gonna march down Main Street with signs and picket the businesses. None of the supporters are fixin' to show up at work, at least none that are takin' part in the protest."

"They'll shoot y'all. You know that. They hung Mr. Green; the police, they're all part of it. I saw it. I heard it with my own ears." Mike Taylor, who worked in the lumber mill, pulled at the straps of his overalls.

"Shot? We can't be part of that!" The voice came from the back of the crowd.

Mr. Kane nodded. "Now, now, settle down. Mr. Taylor, you're right, but there are a few police who aren't tainted. And Mr. Nash is bringin' the press, so everything will be documented. People will know."

"But people know about everything that's goin' on. That doesn't stop it from happenin'," someone else called out.

Albert came burstin' through the woods and into the center of the group. He bent over, out of breath. "South Carolina, the march. It—" he panted, catchin' his breath.

"What?" I urged him.

He turned to face me. "It went real bad. Six people died. More injured."

"Maggie? What about Maggie and Jackson?" I asked, fear snaggin' hold of my emotions and my voice.

"Don't know. I don't think it's good, though. Several men are missin'. A ton got arrested."

A collective gasp came from the crowd, followed by a shoutin' of questions and worried comments.

I grabbed his arm, then let it go quickly. "How'd you find this out? We have to find them."

"Pastor Peters got a call. They're tryin' to track down everyone. The Panthers showed up with guns. Everything went haywire. That's all I know."

I grabbed hold of Mr. Kane's arm. *Guns!* "What should we do? We can't do this."

Mama stood before Albert and set her hands on his shoulders. "Albert, listen to me. You tell me any information you get, do ya' hear me?"

"Yes, ma'am." His forehead glistened with sweat, fear shadowed his eyes.

"How, Mama? How can he do that?"

"Calm down, Alison." She turned back toward Albert. "He knows how."

Albert nodded.

I understood that there was much I was not privy to.

"Listen, Alison, we're goin' home. You are not to leave the farmhouse—understood?" She turned to Mr. Kane. "Are the others ready for this?"

"Chicago, Mississippi, DC, yes, they're all ready."

Mama nodded, then faced the angry group. "Then, so are we. Change isn't easy, and it's not a game. But if we're gonna make this happen, now's the time."

I couldn't believe what I was hearin'. Her daughter was missin' and she was tellin' everyone to risk their own lives? Why? I couldn't see the value in the protest if death would be the outcome.

On the way back to the farmhouse I argued with Mama. "How can you tell them to do this?"

"Maggie and Jackson will be fine. Maggie promised that she wasn't gonna get involved if things got violent. She and Jackson probably took off when things got ugly."

Her words were confident, but in her eyes, worry swam.

"What if they didn't? What then, Mama? What if they find Maggie and Jackson hangin' from trees?" A cramp strangled my belly like a vice. I called out in pain.

"What is it?" Mama pulled the truck over and slammed it into park.

"Nothin', just a cramp. I'm okay." I breathed deeply and leaned far back in the seat, givin' my baby as much space as I could in my tight ball of a stomach.

"Alison, this is too stressful for you. I don't want you comin' to these meetin's anymore."

"I'm fine. Let's just get home." Another cramp called my attention, this one not quite as strong. I closed my eyes and took a few deep breaths until it subsided.

By the time we reached my parents' house a dull pain the size of Mississippi had formed in my lower back. Mama helped me inside and reminded me not to mention Maggie to Daddy. She assured me that she would let me know as soon as Albert was in contact with her.

My father was sittin' in his chair beside the front door when we arrived. "Did Jimmy Lee call?" I asked him.

"Nope. How was Blue Bonnets?" he asked.

Mama leaned down and kissed his cheek. "Oh, just fine. You know how we women like to gab."

"Pix, you look green around the gills, you okay?"

"Yeah, too much pastry," I lied. "I'm gonna go upstairs and lie down." I started up the stairs then turned and asked, "Daddy, can you please call the jail and ask if Jimmy Lee was released?" I didn't care so much about talkin' to him, but I did wonder if he was out of jail yet.

"Oh, he was released alright. He's just takin' care of things, I'd imagine."

"How do you know?" *And why the hell didn't you tell me?*

My father called over his shoulder to me. "I don't rightly know. I just assume his uncle got him out, and frankly, it's none of my business."

"Urgh!" I stomped upstairs, frustration consumin' my ability to think clearly. I went into my bedroom and shut the door.

Jake opened it behind me and slipped in. "I know where Jimmy Lee is," he said, and closed the door behind him.

"Where?" I was too worried about Maggie and Jackson to really care where Jimmy Lee was, but I had to look like I cared, just as Mama had said.

"There's gonna be a boycott or somethin', and Jimmy Lee and his uncle are pullin' together their men to snipe them as they come into town."

Chapter Forty

Two days had passed without a word from Jimmy Lee. Mama had alerted Mr. Kane about Mr. Carlisle's plan to shoot the protesters before they even made it into town, and he alerted the supporters, both local and out of town. I was so nervous that I could barely see straight. I jumped at every noise, and worried that Jimmy Lee had found out what I'd been up to, and I'd be the next body they found hangin' from a tree. Without a word from Jimmy Lee, it was like waitin' for the shoe to drop. I called Jean and asked for a bit of time off work.

"You take all the time you need, sugar," she answered.

No sooner had I hung up the phone than it rang again.

"Alison?"

"Mr. Kane?"

"Yes, can you come over to my house with your mother? Now?"

I looked outside. Daddy was in the lower end of the fields pickin' cotton. Mama was in her garden. "Yes, I think so. What's happened?"

"Not on the phone. Come quick."

I hung up the phone and went outside. My stomach began to cramp as I waddled down the hill toward Mama's garden. I stopped to catch my breath and called out to her. Thankfully, she heard me and came runnin' to my side. She dropped her basket when she saw me grasp my stomach.

"What is it? The baby?" She put her arm around me and held me up.

"Yes, no. Mr. Kane called. We have to go to his house right now."

"What on earth for?" She scanned the fields.

"Daddy's down there." I pointed to where the men were workin'.

"Okay, I'll leave him a note. Let's get you inside. You can wait here."

"No, I'm goin'."

"Alison, you really need to get off your feet."

"I'm goin'."

Mrs. Kane hurried us to a small guestroom off the kitchen.

"Mama?"

Maggie! I spun around and saw Maggie's swollen, black and blue face. Her right eye ballooned so big she could barely open it.

"Oh, my God, Maggie!" Mama and I ran to her. She fell into our arms and cried.

"What happened? Who did this to you?" Mama asked.

"Where's Jackson?" I asked.

Maggie looked up as a tear fell from her good eye. Her lips trembled as she tried to find the words to tell me what her look already had.

"No, oh God. No," I sobbed, crumplin' onto the sofa like my bones'd gone soft.

"I'm sorry, Pixie!" Maggie reached for me.

"No!" I shoved her away. "I don't believe it. It can't be true," I cried. I wrapped my arms around my belly and rocked forward and back, forward and back. "No. No," I repeated.

Mama sat beside me on the small, brown sofa and wrapped her arms around me so tight I couldn't escape her grasp. "Shh," she soothed. "Shh, baby, shh."

If hearts could shatter, I'd have shards of mine litterin' every inch of my insides. I collapsed against Mama's chest, the beat of her heart against my tear-soaked cheek.

"Maggie," Mama said. "What happened? Tell me everything."

Maggie sat down on Mama's other side. "We were marchin', and it was all very civilized, ya' know? Blacks and whites, we had our signs, children even marched. Then, suddenly, from nowhere, the police came at us with these...these shields, tellin' us to get back." She looked up at Mama. "I swear, Mama, I stopped. Jackson did, too, but one of the Panthers, he drew a pistol. God, I had no idea they even had one; then, suddenly, there were several of 'em with guns, and the police were beatin' people, and I got trampled."

"Oh, Maggie." Mama let me go and pulled Maggie to her chest. "My poor girl."

"What about Jackson?" I asked again.

"I don't know. They dragged me into the woods and tied me up, said I was a nigger lover, and they...they beat me, and—" She collapsed into sobs.

"Shh, Mag, no more. You don't have to say it."

She pushed out of Mama's arms. "Someone came and untied me, a woman. Then she ran off. I don't know how long I was in the woods. I finally made my way to a shack, and this couple took me to my friend's car. I asked if they'd seen anyone else in the woods, but they hadn't. I went into town and asked around, but no one knew where Jackson was. There were so many people who disappeared. Some even killed. It was horrible."

"What if he's there, tied up, and hurt?"

Maggie shook her head. "Remember Marlo? He had a group of people search everywhere. He checked the jail, they checked the woods, the river. He said anyone who was missin' was probably—" she choked on the last word, "dead."

I collapsed beside her. *Dead. Jackson's dead.* My body trembled.
"But he's still there? Marlo? Just in case? Right? In case they show up?"

Maggie nodded.

"Why didn't you come home?" I asked.

"Daddy," she said sadly.

Of course.

"What if Jackson is tryin' to get home and can't find Marlo?" I asked
through my tears.

Maggie gave me a pity-filled look.

"We need to get you to a doctor," Mama said.

"No, no way. They'll figure out where I was. We can't chance it. The
boycott is tomorrow!" Beneath the battered face of my sister,
determination shone.

"Oh, no, young lady. You are goin' nowhere near that boycott."
Mama looked from her to me. "You, too. There is no way in hell any of us
are goin' anywhere near it."

"Doc Warden is on his way over." Mrs. Kane stood in the doorway, a
mug of hot tea in her hands and concern in her eyes.

"Doc Warden?" I asked.

She nodded. "He's one of us."

"You said the Panthers were safe," Mama said to Maggie. "You
promised."

"I had no idea. Really, Mama. I didn't know they had guns."
Maggie's bravado had been stolen from her, and it scared me.

Mama shook her head. "I never shoulda allowed this. Maggie, I'm so
sorry, and now poor Patricia has to deal with losin' Jackson."

I felt like I was underwater. All I could hear was the slammin' of my
own heart against my ribcage. Every breath took effort. A cramp seized
my belly and a crushin' blow hit hard to my lower back.

"Mama?" I cried and bent over in pain. "Oh, God, Mama!"

"Lay back, Alison. It's too early for the baby. This is your body
reactin' to the stress." She turned toward Mrs. Kane. "How long 'til Doc
Warden gets here?"

"Any minute."

Doctor Warden opened the door and motioned Mama back into the
room. "I think Alison had a panic attack," he explained, "which set off
some minor contractions. Her baby is fine, but she needs rest. She has
another four or five weeks to go, and I want her off her feet—completely. I
gave her a mild sedative to calm her down."

Mama gave me an *I told you so* look.

"If she's anything like you, that's what it will take to keep her down.
Now, let's take a look at Maggie, shall we?" Doctor Warden was a short,

thin, bespectacled man with wisps of gray hair along the sides of his head. He squeezed my hand before leavin' the room. I listened to their hushed voices and prayed for Jackson's safety as I drifted off to sleep.

Light streamed through the blinds, fillin' the tiny room where I'd fallen asleep. I sat up, my mind still groggy. The events from earlier came back in bits and pieces. Maggie, badly beaten. Jackson gone. *Dead*. I lay back down. Tomorrow was the boycott. None of it seemed to matter anymore. My husband was out preparin' to kill even more people as they rallied around Forrest Town to try and make things better. *Better for who?* I wondered.

Maggie opened the door. She wore a patch over her eye, but looked surprisin'ly better than she had earlier. "Hi, Pix." She sat on the sofa next to me. "Are you okay? I was so worried."

"About me? Have you looked in a mirror lately?"

"Yeah," she whispered. "I'm sorry I got you into this." She played with a bracelet she wore on her left arm. "I can't believe Jackson is gone. We never woulda gone if we'd known."

Mention of his name brought tears. I squeezed my eyes closed against them. I was all too aware of the anger growin' from the pain of losin' Jackson.

"Oh, Pix. I'm sorry to upset you. Jackson was my friend, too. We'll all miss him."

I shook my head. "How do we keep those people from bein' shot by Jimmy Lee and his uncle's posse?"

"You mean the KKK assholes?" Maggie's wit must have come back with the light of day.

I nodded.

"The network is gettin' word out. Mr. Kane has a group goin' miles up the highway to stop 'em before they get close."

"Have you talked to Patricia?"

Maggie shook her head. "Mr. Kane did."

"How is she? I can't stand this," I cried. "Maggie." I longed to tell her how much I loved Jackson. I wanted to tell her about how we used to meet by the creek, and the things he said, and the way he touched me. I wanted to pour my heart and soul into her lap and have her hold it there, safe, forever.

"Are you girls hungry?" Mrs. Kane appeared in the doorway carryin' a tray of soup.

"No, thank you, ma'am," I said, wishin' she'd go away. I swallowed my emotions and knew I'd forever hold my secret.

"Yes, ma'am, I'd love some," Maggie said, and took the bowl of soup from the tray.

Mrs. Kane disappeared back into the kitchen.

"What were you gonna say, Pix?" Maggie asked, and took a sip of the soup.

"Nothin'. I'm just scared for everyone, and now we're stuck here doin' nothin'. Where's Mama?"

"She had to go home. She's tellin' Daddy that you're back at your apartment."

"Are we stayin' here?"

Maggie nodded. "She thought it was safer than goin' back home and raisin' questions with Daddy."

"Do you think they'll reach 'em in time?" I sat up next to Maggie and leaned against the back of the sofa.

"Yeah, they will."

"But what then? Will they call it off?"

Maggie shook her head.

"But—"

"Mr. Kane said they'll let 'em believe the boycott is called off, and then they'll show up."

"But it's too dangerous!" I envisioned Mr. Nash gettin' shot in his car, Bear and the others dead in the backseat. "Is Darla comin'?"

Maggie nodded. "Everyone's comin'."

"Except Jackson," I said, and closed my eyes against the now familiar wave of sadness before it swallowed me whole.

Chapter Forty-One

Maggie and I had been ordered to remain at the Kane's house until Mama came for us, when it was safe. We sat in the livin' room listenin' to Mr. Kane on the telephone, as he gave directions to the contacts for each of the travelin' groups. Mr. Kane's long-time friend was one of the police officers who arrested Jimmy Lee, and he'd confided in Mr. Kane about the timin' of the sniper-style massacre that awaited the protesters.

"That's right, they're expectin' you at ten o'clock, three hours from now. Hang back 'til at least five in the afternoon. By then, they'll figure you gave up, and I'll make sure that's what they think." He paused. "Mm-hmm. Tell them, too. Any word from South Carolina?" Mr. Kane sighed. "Okay, yeah, we have that covered."

"What's gonna happen to everyone here? Did they go to work today?" I felt out of the loop since losin' half the day to sleep yesterday. Maggie's bruises were turnin' a ghostly green and yellow. The swellin' around her eye had gone down significantly from the ice Mrs. Kane had insisted upon.

"They're actin' like it's a normal workday. When the protesters come, that's when they'll leave."

"What about Patricia?"

His eyes softened. "She's angry and scared, but more than anything, she's grievin'. There's been a lot of death around that poor woman lately. Mr. Green was a close friend of their family's."

Mrs. Kane stood with one hand on the couch, one hand on her ample hip.

"Before the ruckus starts, I'm headin' into town to load up on a few necessities. Do either of you girls need anything?"

We shook our heads. "But can we come with you? We promise not to stray. We just want one last look at the town the way it is," Maggie pleaded. It hadn't taken long for her spirits to rise.

Mrs. Kane looked Maggie up and down, a frown on her lips.

"I'll say I fell down. Please? No one knows where I've been," Maggie begged.

Mrs. Kane flattened a wrinkle in her dress and sighed. "I don't know. Your mama would have my hide if anything happened to either of you." She came around the couch and stood before us. "Alison, you heard Doc Warden. You need to rest."

"Yes, ma'am, but—" Even I could hear that my conviction toward goin' to town wasn't as strong as Maggie's, but Maggie was not leavin' me behind.

"I'll stay right with her. We won't get into any trouble. I promise," Maggie piped in.

Mrs. Kane looked at the clock and I held my breath, half prayin' she'd allow us to go along and half prayin' she wouldn't.

"I suppose if we hurry, that's fine. We'll be back here in an hour, safe and sound."

The mornin' sun lit up Main Street just as it did most days. There were people millin' about, and it appeared no one was the wiser to the impendin' boycott. While Mrs. Kane ran into the General Store, Maggie and I went into the diner.

"Oh, sugar, there you are safe and sound." Jean hugged me close. Her jaw gaped when she spotted Maggie behind me. "My word, what on earth happened to you?"

Maggie put her hand up to cover her split lip. "I tripped in the street. I'm a klutz." Maggie was a terrible liar. Her cheeks flushed and her eyes skitted nervously around the diner.

"That musta been some fall. You girls want some coffee? Tea?"

We sat at the counter and I apologized for askin' for time off. I explained what the doctor had said. Jean leaned over the counter and whispered, "With all that's goin' on today, I think y'all should scoot on home right quick."

I grabbed Maggie's hand under the counter and feigned ignorance. "Whaddaya mean?"

Jean rolled her eyes. "Do you think I don't know that you know? Come on, Alison."

"What?" I shot a concerned look at Maggie. "Who else knows?"

"My Aunt Katherine went to the meetin's. I would go if I could, but you know my husband would have me tied to the porch if he had his way. Now you girls get outta here before somethin' happens." Jean came around the counter and put her hand on my shoulder. She whispered in my ear, "Get home and be safe."

Outside the diner, I grabbed Maggie's arm and pulled her into the alley. "What if others know? We could be in real danger."

Maggie held my hands and looked into my eyes in that calmin' way she had about her. "Pixie, no one knows. We're fine."

Suddenly, from across the road, a crowd broke through the trees— black men I didn't recognize, dressed in tank tops and t-shirts, their muscles glistenin' in the sun. There must have been thirty of 'em carryin' somethin' at their sides. I grabbed Maggie's arm. Maggie's eyes danced wildly up and down the road.

"Wicked smart," she said under her breath. "It's the boycotters."

"Maggie, let's go. We gotta go!" I said, pullin' her arm toward Mrs. Kane's car. "Why are they here? They'll be shot." I looked all around for the snipers, expectin' to hear shots ringin' out any second.

"No," Maggie said, as if in a daze. "They're brilliant. The police are all on the highway." Maggie ripped her arm from my grasp and ran toward them, she yelled over her shoulder, "Pixie—find Mrs. Kane! Go! Now!"

I ran toward the drugstore, the heft of my baby weighin' down each step. By the time I reached the store, Mrs. Kane and nearly every store owner on the block had come outside. There were three trucks full of coloreds comin' from the direction of our farm. Alfred was on the bed of the largest truck, along with a mass of other men.

"Good Lord," Mrs. Kane said. "Come quick, child. We must go!" She hurried toward her car.

"I can't leave Maggie!" I ran into the street toward the crowd that now held up signs: *Equality Everywhere; Freedom; Racial Dignity; Stop Racial Wars.* I put my hands under my belly and lifted my girth to alleviate the mountin' pressure in my groin. "Maggie!" I yelled. The trucks had parked and now there were people everywhere I looked, in the road, marchin' down Main Street, standin' on the sidewalks. I was swept away with the pushin' of the crowd.

"Maggie? Maggie?" I yelled again, frantically searchin' for her through the crowd.

Someone pushed me forward and I stumbled, grabbin' onto the man's belt in front of me. He turned around with angry eyes, then softened when he saw me strugglin' to stand. He helped me to my feet and asked if I was okay. We moved down Main Street as a loud, determined group. I worried about the police mowin' us down with bullets. Maggie's voice came from the outside of the crowd. I pushed my way toward her.

"Maggie!" I yelled.

"Pixie! Go home!" She yelled through the tangle of arms and legs.

I was lost in a sea of bodies. Angry store owners retreated behind locked doors. A heavy white woman ran into the street and got in the face of the colored men who led the charge.

"Get out of our town! We don't want you here!" She spat on him and the crowd pushed past her, leavin' her screamin' into the uncarin' air.

Police sirens sounded in the distance. Cars came from the direction of the farms at the far end of town. Whites joined the march. Angry shouts came from the sidewalks, and within the marchin' crowd came a beat of footsteps on pavement and strong voices, "Equal rights, equal pay, equal freedom. Equal rights, equal pay, equal freedom."

I found myself swept up in the cadence and the energy of the crowd. I thought of Jackson and tears stung my eyes. Words thrust from my lungs, "Equal rights, equal pay, equal freedom!"

Suddenly a colored man burst from the crowd and sprinted for the diner. He swung the door open and yelled, "Let our people eat! Let our people eat!"

I stared in amazement, waitin' for Jean to slam the door shut. Jean came out and stood on the sidewalk, arms crossed, a shock of red lipstick across her smilin' lips. Joe's fleshy body filled the doorway, his face set in a harsh, nasty glare. The colored man continued his chant. "Let our people eat! Let our people eat!" Joe shook his head and wiped his hand on the white body apron he wore, then he walked away, spurrin' on the man in the doorway. "Equal rights! Equal Freedom!"

The crowd chanted, "Let our people eat!" Sirens blared, growin' louder by the second until they were almost upon us. Three squad cars skidded to a halt, blockin' Main Street and haltin' the yellin' crowd. "Equal rights, equal pay, equal freedom!"

I caught sight of Maggie pushin' her way through the crowd. I recognized Albert and young Thomas Green's swollen face a few feet from where I stood. They chanted and sweat, their eyes serious, unwaverin'. Thomas limped against a wooden crutch, one arm in a cast. The veins in Albert's neck swelled thick like snakes as he yelled in unison with the group. He turned my way and caught my stare. *Jackson.*

Marchin' toward us was a group of white-capped klansmen carryin' thick sticks. One carried a fiery torch. "Niggers, go home! Niggers, go home!"

I stood, slack jawed, watchin' the group of them stomp down Main Street, the white drapes they wore flappin' in the breeze. Eye holes cut in pointy, white hats that rose far above their heads and covered them clear to their chests. *Mama was right.* Would they kill us all? I scanned the crowd quickly—there was no sign of Maggie. I had to get out of there. I looked for Mrs. Kane, but she, too, had been swallowed by the chaos. How did things go so wrong? I was pushed along with the boycotters toward the KKK, their angry words boomin' louder, above the din of the crowd.

The police stepped from the cars, their nightsticks slappin' hard against their palms. Officer Chandler planted his legs hip width apart. "Y'all break it up now, ya' hear?"

"Niggers, go home!" the KKK chanted.

The crowd continued, "Equal rights, equal pay, equal freedom!"

I spotted Maggie pushin' through the front of the crowd. She crossed her arms and nudged her chin up. I knew that stance. Maggie stood eye-to-eye with Officer Chandler.

"This is a peaceful movement. We aren't hurtin' anyone. We're makin' a statement," Maggie shouted.

"Step aside, Maggie. This doesn't concern you," Officer Chandler commanded.

"Yes, it does," she said. Maggie turned toward the people oglin' from the sidewalk and yelled, "This concerns you!" She pointed at two women comin' out of the furniture store and gawkin' at her. "And you, and you!" Maggie pointed at a white man, then another, standin' angrily and sneerin' at the crowd. "This is our town, and you should all be ashamed."

One of the klansmen moved toward Maggie, his large white fist—the only visible piece of his skin—clasped around a thick stick. Officer Chandler held his arm out, protectin' her. The klansmen moved around the police car and pushed a short, stout, colored picketer. Suddenly there was a rumble of white caps and colored men. Blurs of white sheet flew against flashes of black, spots of red appearin' on the sheets as men were beaten to the ground. I was pushed to and fro, stumblin' to remain upright. Someone grabbed my arm and pulled me back away from the fightin' and into the depths of the group. I heard Maggie's voice risin' and fallin' in an argument with Officer Chandler, as the police moved in on the crowd, pushin' 'em back down Main Street the way they'd come.

Several cars raced into town, screechin' to a halt. People piled out of the cars and shoutin' ensued. Blacks, whites, old, young, men, and women, there were more people than I'd ever seen on Main Street. I pushed toward the front of the crowd, yellin' for Maggie. A sharp pain raced through my lower back and I cried out in pain. The police formed a line and were pushin' the crowd back, the KKK yelled angry barbs, "Coons, go home! Niggers, retreat!"

The ragin' pack of klansmen set their sights on a group of colored men, starin' 'em down through the eyeholes in their ridiculous—and ominous—caps. Suddenly there was a swarm of fists, arms and legs upended, and a rumble on the ground. It was hard to decipher where one white-caped man ended and the next began. I had to look away. The police ignored the beatin's, fuelin' the rage of the group that swarmed the streets. A shot rang out, followed by a hush of the crowd. Then, as if the clouds had suddenly burst upon us, another shot rang out and the coloreds barreled into the police, takin' 'em down and maulin' the KKK.

I caught my breath and felt a strong hand pull me toward the sidewalk. I was bein' pulled and dragged, disoriented as I passed shoutin' people, punches flyin' in all directions. Someone kicked me in the side and I screamed, careenin' forward toward whoever was pullin' me away. I clamored along the ground until we were away from the crowd, and I looked up to find Patricia's terrified eyes, wide-set and serious.

"Get up! Get up!" she hissed.

I stumbled to my feet and she pulled me along, pressure mountin' in my belly, each step a painful, determined force. She pulled me deep into the woods toward Division Street.

"Maggie!" I yelled through my tears.

"I can't help her, but I can help you," she said, and put her shoulder under my arm, bearin' most of my weight as she hurried me away from the fightin'. Shouts and cries drifted away behind us, two more shots rang out.

"I'm sorry, I'm so sorry about Jackson," I said.

"Quiet," she said.

She brought me through the woods and we came out across the road from Division Street.

"Hurry now," she said, and urged me to walk toward her house.

"I can't." Every step felt as though my baby would fall right out of my body. "It hurts."

"It's gonna hurt a lot more if they catch us. Now think of your mama and get your ass movin', child."

We stumbled across the road. Tinsel ran up beside me and turned his wide eyes up to his mother.

"She okay?" he asked, his little arms flailin' up and pointin' at my chest.

I concentrated on breathin', keepin' myself movin' forward.

Patricia didn't answer, just huffed as she helped me toward the house.

Tinsel prodded. "She gonna get us killed? She gonna have dat baby?"

"Tell Arma to boil water," she snapped. "Now!"

Tinsel ran the last fifty feet toward the house.

Chapter Forty-Two

Eight children huddled around the kitchen table, and three women stood by the sink. Worried eyes ran over me, whispers spoken behind close hands as I was led through the tiny kitchen and laid on a mattress in the smallest bedroom I'd ever seen. The walls, adorned with five pictures of young children, nearly touched the sides of the double bed. My eyes were drawn to a picture of a young boy whose kind eyes I'd recognize in the dark. *Jackson.* A deep pain began in my back and slipped across my belly like two giant hands, squeezin' as strong as they could. I wrapped my arms around my stomach and pushed against it.

Patricia rushed from the room, immediately attacked by harsh whispers and strong inquisitions. *Who's that? Why's she here? Dangerous! Too big a chance.* I couldn't take my eyes off of Jackson's face. I cried out as every muscle pulled together, squeezin' my baby within me. Patricia rushed back to my bedside carryin' a pot of steamin' water and towels.

I lifted my head and saw sixteen eyes, wide and curious, in the doorway.

"Get back!" Patricia swatted at them, pushin' the door partway closed. She skillfully pulled my legs apart and said, "You're gonna have this child, and you need to pay attention now."

I couldn't look at her. The pain ran so deep and debilitatin' that I clenched the bedside and grit my teeth, strainin' the muscles in my arms until they rocked my shoulders. "It's too early!" I cried, shakin' my head from side to side.

"Child, you don't decide when this baby comes. This baby is gonna come whether you like it or not, and I'll tell you, you'd better give in to it or it's gonna rip you apart."

I blew fast hard breaths through my teeth. "What about Maggie? My mama?"

"I ain't leavin' your side. Not with my son lookin' down on me." She felt my belly like she'd done it a hundred times before. "Your baby's just about ready. Don't think my boy don't tell me things. I know all 'bout you two." She looked up at the picture of young Jackson, and swallowed hard. "He loves you...he loved you. So, I love you. It's the way it works with kin."

Another hard contraction gripped my body.

"Breathe, child, breathe. You gotta get air to that baby. That's right," she said. "Breathe in, and out, in and out."

"It hurts too much. I gotta get this baby out," I cried.

"Not yet, darlin'. You just let this baby come when it's ready. Don't force it."

"It's too early. Somethin's wrong. I'm not due for another month."

The front door opened and there was a flurry of voices. *Maggie.*

"Maggie!" I yelled, then clenched with another contraction. "Maggie," I said through clenched teeth. "Help me."

Maggie came into the tiny room and climbed around me to the other side of the bed. She sat next to me. "Breathe, Pixie, breathe. That's a girl. In and out."

She thanked Patricia, who made a *what-else-was-I-to-do* face.

"It hurts so much," I whined through the pain.

"I know, Pixie. Think of somethin' good. Think of the barn, and the fun we've had. Think of your weddin' day."

I glared at her.

"Oh, right, no don't think of that." Maggie looked at the photos on the wall, and I watched as she swallowed hard, like she was willin' tears away. "Is that Jackson?" she asked.

Patricia nodded.

"He was a good man."

"Don't count him as gone yet. Not 'til we find him."

Maggie nodded, and then brushed my hair from my sweaty forehead.

"Jimmy Lee's out there with his uncle. They're right alongside the Klan. They're not wearin' white robes, but they're givin' 'em orders. The police have gone haywire."

"That ain't no peaceful march, that's for damn sure," Patricia said.

My belly squeezed and I grabbed Maggie's hand so hard she yelped.

"Can't we do anything for her?" Maggie asked.

"We just gotta let this baby do what it's gonna do."

"What about a doctor? Doesn't she need one? Doc Warden? He might help." Maggie said.

"Doc Warden won't go near that nightmare of a street. He's the only doc we got, and he's too smart to get hisself killed."

The door creaked open and a set of little eyes peeked in. *Tinsel.*

"Boy, you better get your butt outta here. Arma!" Patricia called. A teenage girl came to the door and took Tinsel's hand, leadin' him away.

"Sorry, Mama. I'll keep him out here," she said and blinked her thick, long eyelashes. She closed the door behind her.

"Now, I'm gonna have to take a look down there," Patricia said in a way that left no room for complaint, just as my mama woulda done.

I closed my eyes as she pulled my pants off and then removed my panties. "Oh, child," she said. "You in luck. This baby wants out and soon."

Maggie laughed, and pain tore through me, stealin' any coherent thoughts I might have had. I clenched my eyes shut.

"Breathe, child, breathe!" Patricia commanded. "You gotta breathe or you'll pass out."

"I gotta push. I gotta get it out. It hurts. Please!" I cried.

Patricia used the hot water to wash me down there, and she spread clean towels underneath me.

"Arma!" Patricia hollered. Arma peered into the door with a scared look in her eyes.

"Tell Sharon to heat the towels."

"Yes, ma'am." The door closed with a hurried *clank!*

"How did you," *pant, pant,* "know where I was?" *pant, pant,* I asked Maggie.

"Albert told me he sent someone to tell Patricia that you were sick, and when I couldn't find you, I knew she'd taken care of you." Maggie kissed my forehead. "Pixie, I would never have let you go if I'd known that was gonna happen."

"That's what happens when brothers get angry." Patricia kept one hand anchored to my calf. "I heard that they were the group from up north. They were tryin' to get a jump on the snipers. I guess the jump was on them." Patricia shook her head. "This nonsense has gotta stop. There's gotta be a way."

"This will help. I'm sure of it. There's only a handful of police in this area. They can't hold everyone back." Maggie said.

Another contraction sent the baby's head down between my legs. "Get it out!" I screamed. I could feel Patricia pullin' and proddin' the baby, wigglin' its shoulders until suddenly there was a burst of freedom and the baby slid out from inside me with a whoosh of relief.

"Jesus, Mary, and Joseph." Patricia stared down at the baby.

"What?" I cried. "What? What's wrong?" I grabbed Maggie's hand. "Is the baby okay? I can't hear it. The baby's not cryin'!"

I held Maggie so tight she couldn't move to see the baby.

"Child, you in trouble now." Patricia worked down below cleanin' the baby. She called for Sharon, who rushed in with fresh towels in her arms.

"Goodness!" Sharon shrieked. She handed the towels to Patricia, who caught her eyes and frowned.

"That's enough now," Patricia said in a harsh tone.

Sharon looked at me, then back at the baby. "I heated the towels with the iron, they're nice and warm."

Patricia bundled the baby and told Sharon to come into the room and close the door. "It's a boy. You've got a son," Patricia said. I sensed fear in her tone.

"What's goin' on?" I demanded. "Maggie!" I dropped her arm and struggled to sit up.

Maggie slid off the end of the bed next to Patricia. The baby's cries came in quick, sharp bursts.

"Oh, thank God. Thank God." I cried, and fell back on the pillow.

"Pixie?" Maggie said. She squeezed behind Patricia and Sharon and leaned down to speak to me, inches from my face. "Pixie, who is the father of your baby?" she whispered.

Had she lost her mind? "What kinda question is that? Jimmy Lee is the father!"

"Look at me, Pix. It's me. You can trust me. Who is the father of this baby?" She turned her head toward Patricia and I followed her gaze to my bundled baby held close to Patricia's chest. Patricia leaned forward, and my baby's jet black hair, and skin as smooth and dark as cocoa, came into view. I didn't fully understand what all the fuss was about, until Patricia brought the baby closer to me, and I saw my baby's wide-set nose and full lips. Even through the tiny slit of his eyes I saw the resemblance to his father.

"Girl, you cannot take this baby home. They'll kill you, your baby, and the baby's father." Patricia put her hand on the baby's chest and whispered, "A blessin' and a life sentence, all in one."

"They can't touch his father. He's already dead."

Chapter Forty-Three

Even with the madness takin' place just a mile down the road, with Joshua at my breast, I felt the pieces of my life come together in a way that I never understood they could. The baby I had carried and felt was separate from me, a bein' made not of love, but of duty, had instantly latched onto my heart and made me whole. This wasn't a baby of duty at all. Joshua was made from the very essence of love.

Maggie sat on the side of the bed, her hands on her knees, her face a mask of worry. "I don't understand, Pixie. How? When?"

"Before I got married," I admitted.

Maggie shook her head. "Then, why did you marry Jimmy Lee?"

"You can't blame her," Patricia said. "Love can only endure so much. Imagine your father if she said she was in love with a colored man. Imagine her life. Girl, there was no way this could've come to be." Patricia had cleaned up the baby, and she'd sent Sharon out back with a plastic bag containin' the bloodied sheets, towels, and the afterbirth. She was to bury the whole mess in the back yard.

"You can't take this baby home, Pix," Maggie said. "Jimmy Lee will kill you, you know that."

"What am I supposed to do, leave my baby here?"

"Pixie, remember Mr. Bingham? His wife? Remember what's goin' on down the street? No way, Pix, no way you're leavin' this house with that baby."

"I'm not leavin' my Joshua."

"Joshua?" Maggie asked.

"Joshua."

Maggie leaned against the wall, arms crossed. "You can't even support a baby alone, and what do you think's gonna happen? Jimmy Lee's gonna raise another man's baby? A colored man's?" Maggie covered her face and let out a long, frustrated, guttural groan. "This is a mess."

"That's my grandson. You leave that baby with me. You go on home and tell your husband your baby died."

"Died? No, I won't do it." I held Joshua close against me and cried. "No way. No."

Patricia sat next to me on the bed. "Now you listen here, I have lost one child to this backwards world and I'm not losin' a grandson—or you. Jackson loved you. Do you think he wants you to die because of his seed?"

No. I can't do it. I can't leave him.

"Look into that baby's face. Is that the face of a white baby?" Patricia asked.

I lowered Joshua from my shoulder and looked at his beautiful, dark eyes, the too-dark shade of his skin. I touched his cheek and I felt complete, happy.

"Maggie, I can't do it," I pleaded.

Maggie shook her head as if, for once, she didn't have an answer. She climbed back onto the bed beside me and put her arm around me. I laid my head against her chest, Joshua in my arms, and cried. Maggie brushed my hair away from my face.

"Shh," she soothed. "We'll figure this out."

I shook my head. "How? There's no figurin' this out. Jackson's dead, Jimmy Lee is just plain awful, and—" *Daddy. What about Daddy?* He'd disown me for sure.

"I'm gonna leave you two to discuss this, but our time is short. That nonsense goin' on out there ain't gonna last all day, and someone's gonna be lookin' for that pregnant girl."

Chapter Forty-Four

When I told Jimmy Lee that our baby died, I think he was relieved. He didn't ask to see him. He sat on the couch starin' straight ahead, not lookin' at me, not holdin' me, just starin' ahead like he was watchin' a picture show.

Maggie had come up with a plan to pretend to bury the baby in our family plot on Daddy's farm. She said we couldn't bring Mama into the plan, because we'd be puttin' her in the terrible position of havin' to lie to Daddy, and two liars in the family were enough. Mama was shoulderin' enough burdens for any woman. I didn't want to do it—keep the secret from Mama or pretend to bury Joshua—but I didn't see any other way around the situation. Maggie bundled a doll that belonged to one of Patricia's children, put it in a cardboard box, and taped it up; then, she wrapped the box in blue paper, and even sealed it with a bow. She'd gone back home the night of the boycott to tell my parents what had happened. She said Daddy lugged his biggest shovel down to the plot and dug a hole, stoppin' often to wipe tears with his sleeve. Maggie sat in the truck and watched him, holdin' the box safely on her lap.

Mama showed up at my apartment twenty minutes later.

"Oh, my baby. My poor baby," she cried, holdin' me so tight I could barely breathe. Her wet cheek pressed hard against mine, her chest heavin' with sobs. She pulled back, fresh tears in her eyes. I thought I had no more tears left in me, but seein' Mama's tears, and knowin' that my lies had caused them, made my tears flow like a river.

She reached out and touched Jimmy Lee's shoulder. "Are you okay, hun?" she asked.

Jimmy Lee shook his head. "I'm not sure we were ready for a baby anyway."

"No one's ever ready, but that doesn't make it hurt any less when you lose your child."

He turned to her and said, "I'm not sure. Maybe it does." He stood and walked into the bedroom, leavin' Mama's jaw hangin' open in dismay. When the bedroom door thumped shut, Mama whispered, "Oh, honey. I'm so sorry. He's...ugh...forget about him. What can I do to help you?"

Let me love my baby.

Chapter Forty-Five

The next day after Jimmy Lee went to work, I went outside and walked to the edge of town. Every muscle in my body ached. It felt like a basketball had been ripped out from between my legs. My breasts were full and achy, and I longed to see Joshua. I wanted to hold him in my arms and tell him how much I loved him. I wanted him to hear how much I loved his father, and to know that, even though I could not be with him right then, that I did not abandon him, and above all, that I was not ashamed of him.

Main Street stretched before me with broken windows in the storefronts, glass and debris in the road. I couldn't help but feel like I'd let Jackson down. I looked down at the ground, my arms hangin' uselessly at my sides, and I cried. What kind of difference did we make? I saw no evidence of change, just a haunted street that would forever hold the ghosts of beaten men, and the smell of fear and hatred.

I turned toward the direction of Division Street and my feet drew me forward, as if they were guided by someone other than me.

Joshua.

I ignored the pain and pressure in my lower abdomen, the noise of passin' cars. I had tunnel vision, and at the end of the long stretch of darkness was my baby. *My baby.* The thought of him sent a searin' pain through my breasts. I crossed my arms over them and pressed them against me.

The corner of Division Street was upon me, callin' me forth. I never looked back. I didn't care who saw me. My baby needed me. To hell with Jimmy Lee. He didn't care. He'd never cared. He'd kill Joshua, and he might even kill me. I was never goin' back there. I knew that with all my heart and soul. I. Would. Not. Go. Back.

As I stumbled down Division Street, the houses spun around me. An engine roared behind me. I held onto a tree for support. My legs weakened, my vision blurred. I had the sensation that somethin' wet was drippin' down my legs, but was unable to look down without feelin' like I'd pass out.

Patricia's front door opened, and I saw her standin' on the porch, Joshua bundled in her arms.

"Joshua," I whispered. I barely registered screechin' wheels behind me, a slammin' truck door.

"Alison!"

Jimmy Lee? I turned my head slowly, as if in a fog. Fear ran through me like an electric shock. "Gettin' my baby," I said with as much determination as I could muster, and stumbled toward Joshua.

Jimmy Lee grabbed my arm and held onto me, his fingers diggin' into my skin. "Alison! Stop!"

I pulled and kicked and tried to break free. "My baby! I want my baby!" I cried. I looked at Patricia's house, less than fifty feet away. It felt like a million miles. "Please, my baby, I want my baby," I sobbed.

He dragged me backwards. I kicked and flailed blindly toward him.

"Joshua!" I yelled. The world faded in and out.

Suddenly Patricia was there beside me, yellin', "What are you doin'? She's bleedin'!" Her capable hands pulled at my other arm. I was bein' stretched like taffy, my head lollin' back and forth, the world spinnin' around me—bits of conversation filtered into my ears, muffled as if under water.

"My wife—"

"You'll hurt her!" Patricia's voice was a thin thread, miles away.

My baby wailed incessantly. *Joshua.*

"… stupid nigger!"

Patricia came into focus just as the back of Jimmy Lee's hand connected with her cheek and she tumbled to the ground. I wrenched myself from Jimmy Lee's grasp and crawled along the gravel toward the blurry bundle before me. Joshua lay screamin' within Patricia's grasp.

"My baby!" I reached for him as Jimmy Lee tugged me backwards, leavin' a warm trail of blood beneath me. My fingertips connected with Joshua's blanket and I pulled, hard, until I had him in my arms and tumbled backwards. "Joshua," I whispered over and over. I pressed my cheek against his as he cried and fought me with all his tiny might.

Jimmy Lee's truck roared to life, tires squealin' and comin' to a halt beside me. I felt Joshua ripped from my arms. *My baby!* Hands grabbed me roughly and tossed me into the truck. As we sped away, my baby's cries, and the world around me, faded to black.

Chapter Forty-Six

A light haze filtered in through my eyelashes, as if I were lookin' through gauze. An endless rhythm of beeps surrounded me. I blinked away the haze, my head poundin' out a painful beat.

"Oh, thank God." Mama's tight face came into view. She gently touched my arm. "I was so worried," she said. "It's okay, you're in the hospital. Jimmy Lee brought you."

"Joshua," I whispered.

Mama dropped her eyes. "I know, baby. I know. He's gone, remember?"

I shook my head, my eyes instantly fillin' with tears. Memories trickled back to me. Patricia lyin' on the ground. Joshua in my arms. Jimmy Lee. *Oh God, Jimmy Lee.*

"Where's Jimmy Lee?"

"I'm here," he said from the doorway. "I was just talkin' to the doctor."

"What happened?" I asked.

"I saw you walkin' down the road and I was yellin' to you, but it was like you didn't even hear me. Then I saw the blood drippin' down your leg, and you must have been delirious because you headed down Division Street and you grabbed some woman's baby."

"Joshua," I whispered.

Jimmy Lee looked at Mama. "She must still be out of it."

I shook my head. Mama rubbed my arm. "She lost so much blood," she said. "Alison," she said softly. "You hemorrhaged, from the delivery. They were able to stop the bleedin', but you have to take it easy." She closed her eyes against the tears poolin' in her eyes. When she opened them, she touched my cheek. "I'm so sorry, baby. Thank goodness you're alive. We almost lost you."

"Joshua," I said again.

"He died, remember?" Jimmy Lee spoke sharply, then turned and paced. "Can't they do somethin'? Make her go to sleep or somethin' so she doesn't torture herself like this?"

I grasped the edges of the mattress, the IV line in my arm pinched my skin. "I'm not torturin' myself."

"He's dead, Alison," Jimmy Lee insisted. "Dead, okay? He's not comin' back."

I shook my head against the pillow.

"Alison, we buried him in the family plot, remember? You rest, honey." Mama turned to Jimmy Lee. "Why don't you go home and rest, too, Jimmy Lee. You've been through a lot lately."

"I'm not leavin'," he said.

I could still feel the soft weight of Joshua in my arms. My baby didn't know me. He might not ever know me. My breasts ached, engorged with milk my baby would never drink. I looked at Jimmy Lee and felt the same disgust I'd felt since the day he forced himself upon me at the river. I turned away, my mind burnin' with the memory of Jackson's tender touch. I tried to muster Daddy's voice to center me. *Know your place*. Every inch of my body revolted against those words. My stomach tightened, my hands and jaw clenched. I closed my eyes and tried again. *Be a good wife. Know your place*.

"No!" The yell escaped my lungs before I could stop it.

Mama gasped. "What is it? Do you hurt?"

"No!" I said again. "No, no, no! I won't *know my place*," I cried.

"I'm gettin' the doctor. She's out of it." Jimmy Lee headed for the door.

"I don't need my doctor. I need my baby. I already lost the man I love. I'm not goin' to lose the child I love, too."

Jimmy Lee's face contorted into a mess of confusion.

Mama put her hand to my forehead and I shook it off. "I'm sorry, Mama, but it's true. The baby wasn't Jimmy Lee's."

Jimmy Lee took a step closer to the bed.

"I'm sorry. I married you without knowin' I was already pregnant."

"What are you sayin'?" Mama asked.

"I was with someone else," I cried.

"You whore. Who was it?" Jimmy Lee fumed.

"Watch your mouth, that's my daughter," Mama spat.

"Who? Who was it?" he demanded.

"It doesn't matter who," I said.

"Like hell it doesn't matter." Jimmy Lee grabbed my arm and squeezed. "*You* cheated on *me*? You're nothin' but a stupid farm girl. You were charity to me! You're nothin'!"

"Get out of here!" Mama said, flat and firm. "Don't you ever talk to my daughter that way."

"Your daughter's a whore and a liar," he seethed at Mama, and then turned his anger on me. "Don't you ever speak to me again." Jimmy Lee spun on his heels and stormed out the door, leavin' a trail of vicious words in his wake.

My hands shook from relayin' details of the night of Joshua's birth to Mama. The feelin' of havin' my heart ripped from my body returned, fresh and unbearable, when I told her of our plan to pretend that Joshua had died. All I'd wanted was to protect him. Disappointment rode strong in her eyes, not from my bein' with a colored man, strange as that might seem, but for not trustin' enough to confide in her. Mama stood at my bedside now, holdin' my hand, tears streamin' down her cheeks.

Maggie flew through the doorway, out of breath and spoutin' questions. "What happened? Is she okay? Patricia said Jimmy Lee hit her. I just passed him in the hall and he looked pissed. Oh, my God, Pixie, are you okay?"

Mama let out a quick breath before answerin' Maggie. "She hemorrhaged."

"I know, I got that much," Maggie said. "But she's okay? She's gonna be okay, right?"

Maggie spoke so quickly that I could feel somethin' pushin' inside of her. The way her eyes jumped from me to Mama and back again told me she was holdin' somethin' back.

"Maggie, Mama knows," I said.

"She knows? You know?" She didn't wait for an answer. "We didn't want to lie to you. We just didn't want you to have to lie to Daddy about this, too."

Mama nodded. "You did the right thing."

"Cheatin' on Jimmy Lee? Leavin' my baby? I did the right thing?" I didn't understand how that could possibly be true.

"What you did before marryin' Jimmy Lee, that was wrong. But you know that. You don't need me to harp on you. What's done is done. And yes, you did the right thing leavin' your baby behind. Your father would have killed us both if you'd come home with a colored baby."

"But, Mama, I can't leave him. I mean, I did, I tried, but I can't leave him there. I need him. I love him."

Mama backed herself into a chair, where she leaned on her elbows and let her face fall into her hands.

Maggie took my hand and with a glint in her eye said, "Pixie, Jackson came home. He isn't dead. He's with Patricia and Joshua now."

"Jackson? Albert's brother, he's alive?" Mama looked from Maggie to me.

"Are you sure? How do you know?" *Jackson*. My world was rightin' itself. This had to be a sign. It was time I knew *my place*, only my place wasn't where Daddy thought it should be.

"Albert got word to Mr. Kane, who called me. Jackson's home. He's safe!" Maggie exclaimed.

Tears of joy sprung from my eyes. My heart beat strong within my chest, renewed energy streamed through me. I took a deep breath and did what I should have done long ago. "Mama, Jackson Johns is the father of my baby, and I love him. I love him—I love them—with all my heart." It felt so good to say those words, I had to repeat them. "I love Jackson Johns."

Chapter Forty-Seven

I felt physically stronger the next afternoon. The nurse explained that they'd pumped me full of blood, fluid, and antibiotics, and the doctor said I could go home, as long as I took it easy.

"Mama is on her way to pick you up."

I pressed the telephone receiver tight against my ear, listenin' to Maggie's concerned voice, and thinkin' about how I'd almost lost her.

"I'm gonna ask Mama to take me to see Jackson on the way home," I said.

"Pix, you can't do that. The police are patrollin' the streets. Several men are still missin'. And Jimmy Lee is on a warpath, askin' everyone in town if they knew you were runnin' 'round behind his back."

Everyone knows? I was determined to take responsibility for what I'd done and to be with the man I loved.

"You can't go near Division Street," Maggie warned.

"I gotta, Maggie. I gotta see Jackson."

"Alison, it's bad," she said. "Think about Jackson. If Jimmy Lee finds out that Jackson is the father, he'll kill him on the spot."

I assured her that we'd be extra careful.

"How do you plan to tell Daddy about the baby?" she asked.

"I'm not sure."

"Maybe I can help," she offered. "I'll feel out his mood before you get here. Daddy's feelin' the long tail of the boycott—none of the farmhands have shown up since, so he's exhausted and worried."

"Maybe it's better if we don't tell him," I said, wonderin' when it might ever be a good time to break Daddy's heart.

"We'll see. Pix, be careful if you go see Jackson. Promise me."

I promised her and waited for Mama to arrive and drive me home.

"Let's not tell your father about the baby 'til we have time to figure it all out," she said.

That made sense to me, since I couldn't go to my own apartment, and I couldn't bring the baby to Daddy's house, I didn't have many choices to consider.

"Can we stop and see Jackson and Joshua on the way?" I asked.

Mama looked at me and turned her head slightly up, in that way that said, *Oh, honey. I wish it were that easy.*

"How am I gonna do this, Mama? I love him. I want to see him and, to be honest, I don't really care who knows it. Once I tell Daddy, no one else really matters."

"You're not that naïve, Alison. You know all too well what could happen to Jackson—and to your baby."

Mr. Bingham. Mr. Green. "So, what do I do now? You tell me."

"I'm thinkin'." She drove with her eyebrows drawn together, both hands on the steerin' wheel, starin' intently at the road.

"What about if we parked behind their church and walked over?" I pleaded.

"Alison," Mama sighed.

"Please, Mama? Could you have left me, or Maggie, or Jake? Could you have forgotten a man you'd loved?"

Mama's clenched face softened, the lines on her forehead diminished.

"Please, Mama? It's all I can think about. I'm scared every minute of the day now anyway. Don't you think I worry that Jimmy Lee will figure this all out and do somethin'? Look at what he's done. He beat up kids just for bein' colored. He killed a man. He saw to the death of another. Once he knows the truth, then Jackson and Joshua—and even I—don't have a chance."

"Maggie," Mama said, as if she were thinkin' of her and the word just came out accidentally.

"What about Maggie?"

"You can stay with Maggie, you and Joshua, until you figure it out."

"Mama, have you seen Maggie's apartment? It's tiny."

"It's safe," she said, noddin' to herself. "Do you even know if Jackson wants to be with you? You're makin' a lot of assumptions about a man who just came back from the dead."

"Oh, he wants to be with me alright." For once, I knew exactly what I wanted and where I belonged. "There's no doubt in my mind. It's not an assumption. He told me."

"Even now, after all that's happened?" she asked.

I watched Mama drive past our road. "Mama? Where are you goin'?" She turned to face me. "The church."

Chapter Forty-Eight

I'll never know what possessed Mama to give in and take me to the church, because no matter how many times I asked her why she did, she just smiled and said, "It was the right thing to do."

We walked across the parkin' lot, Mama walkin' too close to me and askin' every three seconds, "Are you sure you're okay? You're supposed to take it easy. Let me know if you want to stop."

"I'm fine," I answered, and though pain pressed in on my abdomen, I honestly felt better than I had in weeks. The thought of my baby pulled me forward, the thought of Jackson pushed me faster. We reached the back lawn of their property, and I was thankful not to have to see the dark stain of my blood in the street.

Mama grabbed my arm. "Alison, listen to me. You don't have to make any decisions today. You can just visit your baby and then let that sit with you for a while."

I knew what she was doin'. What I was plannin' was scarier than anything either of us had ever gone through. My life there in Forrest Town was quickly comin' to an end, and her life, as she knew it, was too. I reached for both of Mama's hands. "Mama, you've spent your whole life worryin' about my happiness, Maggie's happiness, and Jake's. Now I've found mine. It might not be easy, and it might not be right based on this town's perspective," I dropped her hand and put my right hand over my heart, "but in here, where it really matters, it's not only right, it's perfectly clear. I've found my place."

She nodded, and we walked up the back steps of the house. Standin' on the back porch, I thought of the woman I'd become, and the sides of Mama I'd only recently discovered. She'd given up so much of her life for the good of her family—her beliefs, her interests. In a way, I was followin' in her shoes. I would have to give up everything I knew to be with my child.

My heart drummed in my chest. My nerves tingled, makin' me jumpy all over. The pain I had experienced as I walked over was masked by happiness the moment Jackson opened the door, Joshua in his arms.

The cuts and bruises on Jackson's face and the bandages around his neck silenced my joy. Jackson didn't say a word. He didn't have to. The smile that formed on his lips and the light in his eyes told me everything I

needed to know. He opened the door wide and invited us inside, handin'
Joshua to Mama, who took him without so much as a pause in her breath.

Cringin' with each painful step, Jackson took a step toward me and
opened his arms. I melted into them. The feel of the bandages beneath his
shirt saddened me. The familiarity of his chest, the way we fit together, the
warm scent of his skin, lessened my sadness. Jackson was there, he was
alive, and that was all that mattered.

Tires screeched out front. Jackson tensed.

Tinsel flew through the front door. "It's that white guy, the one who
beat Thomas!"

Jimmy Lee. Mama handed Joshua to Patricia.

The three of us went to the front of the house. Jackson told us to stay
inside as he limped out the front door and down the steps. We watched him
from the open window. Jimmy Lee stood beside his truck, parked
caddycorner across the middle of the street. He swayed, and I wondered if
he'd been drinkin'.

Jackson stood strong—legs planted firmly apart, arms crossed, biceps
twitchin'. I grabbed Mama's hand and listened, hopin' Jimmy Lee didn't
know we were there.

"Whaddaya want, Jimmy Lee?" Jackson asked.

Jimmy Lee stared at him. "My wife," he said.

I held my breath.

"She's not here. Why don't you go home and wait for her?"

Jimmy Lee took a step toward Jackson. Jackson didn't move.

"You think I'm stupid, nigger? I know she and her stupid-ass mother
are here. Parked right over at the church." He took another few steps, until
he was just a foot from Jackson. Jimmy Lee crossed his arms and looked
down his nose at Jackson. "Get out here, Alison, or I'll kill this nigger."

Mama shook her head, and mouthed, "Don't you move."

"You know I'll do it, and that Negro baby, too," Jimmy Lee
threatened.

I started for the door. Mama grabbed my arm. "Alison."

"He's not gonna hurt me, but he'll hurt them," I said with little faith
in my own words.

I pushed nervously through the screen door and stood on the porch.

Jimmy Lee started for me. "You little bitch."

"Hey!" Jackson said and took a step between us. My injured sentry.

"Jackson, don't!" I ran down the steps and stood beside him. "He's
not worth it." I stood between Jackson and Jimmy Lee. "I don't want no
trouble, Jimmy Lee. I made a mistake by marryin' you, and I'm sorry for
that, but—"

He grabbed my arm and started for the truck.

"Let go of me!" I shrieked, punchin' and kickin' uselessly.

Jackson ran into the street. Mama was on his heels. My father's truck raced down the road, slammin' to a halt behind Jimmy Lee's truck. Maggie and Jake flew out of the truck and ran toward us. My father stepped out from behind his door.

"Let her go!" Maggie yelled.

"Jimmy Lee, what the hell are you doin'?" Jake approached him and Jimmy Lee yanked me away, clutchin' my arm so tight I thought it might snap.

"You let her go now, Jimmy Lee." My father's voice left no room for negotiation. He raised the shotgun he carried at his side.

Maggie grabbed my free arm.

Jimmy Lee pulled me away from her as Jackson closed in on him.

"Step back, Jackson," Daddy said. He had Jimmy Lee in his scope, his finger on the trigger.

"Daddy," Jake said. "That'll make you no better than him."

"Shut up, Jake," Daddy said.

"You won't kill me," Jimmy Lee said. "You don't like niggers any more than I do."

My father didn't hesitate for a second. His voice was calm and fierce. "But I love my daughter." He lifted his trigger finger, then placed it on the trigger once again, the way he did when he was huntin', right before he pulled one off. "And whoever my daughter loves, I love, and she don't love you no more." He took a step closer to Jimmy Lee, the barrel of the gun inches from his cheek. "The way I see it, you've killed a man for less than what you're doin' right now. There ain't no way I'll do time. We all see you manhandlin' my daughter, and don't think I won't press charges against you for beatin' her until she hemorrhaged."

"I didn't do that," Jimmy Lee protested.

"Didn't you? I saw it, and I remember it clear as day." Patricia stood on the front porch, Joshua in her arms, a dark bruise of proof on her cheek.

"A nigger's word against mine?" he laughed.

"Somethin' tells me you got more than one nigga' after you," Daddy said.

Jimmy Lee shifted his eyes to my father, squintin' a threat in his direction and squeezin' my arm 'til I yelped. Daddy kept his gun trained on Jimmy Lee.

"Y'all are a bunch of nigger lovers." He pushed me away.

Maggie clamored forward and pulled me into her arms.

"You better watch your backs," his voice quaked as he moved backward toward his truck. "My uncle'll kill you niggers, and you, too." He pointed to Daddy. "My uncle'll make sure you don't ever earn another penny."

My father kept the gun trained on Jimmy Lee's truck until it turned the corner and drove out of sight.

I clung to Maggie. "Daddy?"

"I had to tell him," Maggie spoke with an urgency that shook me. "When I thought about you and Mama comin' here alone, I got really scared. I'm sorry, Pix."

"Sorry? You saved Jackson's life, and probably mine, too." I turned to thank Daddy and saw that he had the gun trained on Jackson, who stood with his hands up, the whites of his eyes as large as gumballs. "Daddy! What are you doin'?"

I ran in front of Jackson and held out my arms, shieldin' him from Daddy's gun.

"Step back, Alison," he said, narrowin' his eyes.

"No, Daddy. I won't." I watched Daddy's eyes. I swear I saw somethin' more than anger there—sadness? Loss of his daughter? I didn't care. "I love him, Daddy. I love him with all my heart." I pointed to Joshua, swaddled close to Patricia's chest. "That's your grandson, whether you like it or not. He exists, and I love him, too."

"Step away now," he commanded.

I remained where I was, my legs tremblin' like leaves in the wind.

"Alison Jean, your place is—"

"My *place* is wherever Jackson and Joshua are. I love you, Daddy, and I know I hurt you, and I'm sorry, but I love him, and if you love me, you'll let us be."

His shoulders dropped, just a smidgen.

"Please, Daddy?" I begged.

Mama moved next to Daddy and touched his tense shoulder. "Ralph," she whispered. "She's your daughter. You can't keep pushin' all of your children away. The world is changin', and they have a right to change, too."

My father turned to look at her, and the way he squinted and clenched his jaw, I worried he'd just explode, that we'd pushed him too far. To my surprise, he lowered the gun. There was a collective sigh of relief as Daddy turned to look at Maggie, then at me. I was so scared of losin' him, and in that moment I felt, more than saw, the transition from my bein' Daddy's little girl to somethin' else, somethin' less, maybe.

"Thank you, Daddy," I said, hopin' for somethin' more.

He swung the shotgun up the second I stepped away from Jackson, set him in his sight again, and said, "If you ever hurt my daughter I will not hesitate to kill you."

"Yes, sir," Jackson said in a respectful tone. "Sir, I love your daughter and our son with all of my heart and soul. I'd willin'ly give my life for her, but with all due respect, sir, I would rather live, and we can't do that here. Not now, and maybe not ever."

"What?" I knew he was right. We couldn't live together here. The Lovings fled the south and we would have to, also. My heart stung so badly, I felt as if it was bein' squeezed in a giant fist.

Jackson shook his head. "Alison, we'd fear for our lives, for Joshua's life, every minute of every day. I think movin' to New York, where I have a job, where interracial couples might not be the norm, but they exist without the fear of bein' killed, would be our safest move."

New York? So far away from Mama and Daddy?

"Joshua needs to be raised in a safe, lovin' environment," he continued. "We have the love, but here," he pointed in the direction of Main Street, "we have no safety. Not yet."

"You're takin' my daughter away?" My father said, liftin' his gun once more.

Mama set her hand gently on the top of the gun and pushed it down until it was pointed at the ground. "Ralph," she whispered.

My father's eyes shot darts in her direction, then softened. He wiped his face with his free hand, then stared into the field, his silence magnified the tension that hung around us. With the slightest nod of his head, he conceded.

Chapter Forty-Nine

After a month of livin' in New York, I'm still gettin' used to bein' in public with Jackson and Joshua without bein' gobbled up with fear for our safety. Sure, we still received the chin-snub from many, even some harsh comments, but a chin-snub and comments were a lot easier to take when you had friends like Darla, Bear, and Marlo, and a sister like Maggie, who snubbed and commented right back.

Although Daddy didn't allow Jake to apply to Mississippi State when he'd found the application on Jake's desk, he eventually agreed to allow him to take an art class at the community college. Maybe Maggie was right all along, and Daddy simply didn't want to let Jake leave town.

Each time I called home, I yearned to speak to Daddy. It just about killed me each time that he refused to come to the phone. He told Mama to tell me he loved me, but he had yet to speak to me himself. I prayed every night that he might come around and allow us to find each other once again. I missed him, but when I look at my baby's face, and I see the love he holds in his father's eyes, I know I did the right thing, and I have no shame about my decision or those I love.

Jackson walked through the door of our tiny apartment and asked how my day was. It was a day like any other. I woke up next to the man I loved, nursed the baby I adored, and spent the entire day with our son, just waitin' for his daddy to come home—on time, sober, and hungry to spend time with us.

"Perfect," I answered.

I hope you have enjoyed reading *Have No Shame*.

Please visit the back of the book to read the acknowledgements and about the author.

Reviews are always appreciated, though never expected.

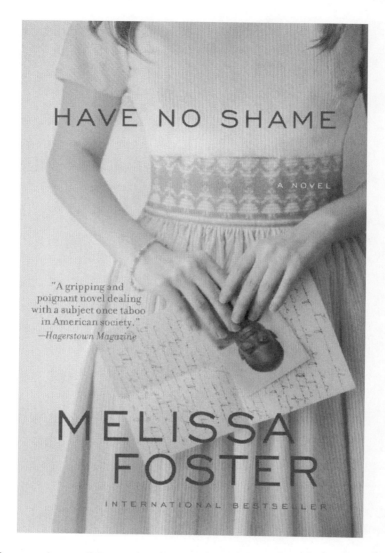

HAVE NO SHAME

A NOVEL

"A gripping and poignant novel dealing with a subject once taboo in American society."
—*Hagerstown Magazine*

MELISSA FOSTER

INTERNATIONAL BESTSELLER

This version of HAVE NO SHAME does not include the southern dialect in the narrative, however, the dialect is present in the dialogue.

Chapter One

It was the end of winter 1967, my father was preparing the fields for planting, the Vietnam War was in full swing, and spring was peeking its pretty head around the corner. The cypress trees stood tall and bare, like sentinels watching over the St. Francis River. The bugs arrived early, thick and hungry, circling my head like it was a big juicy vein as I walked across the rocks toward the water.

My legs pled with me to jump from rock to rock, like I used to do with my older sister, Maggie, who's now away at college. I hummed my new favorite song, *Penny Lane*, and continued walking instead of jumping because that's what's expected of me. I could just hear Daddy admonishing me, "You're eighteen now, a grown up. Grown ups don't jump across rocks." Even if no one's watching me at the moment, I wouldn't want to disappoint Daddy. If Maggie were here, she'd jump. She might even get me to jump. But alone? No way.

The river usually smelled of sulfur and fish, with an underlying hint of desperation, but today it smelled like something else all together. The rancid smell hit me like an invisible billow of smog. I covered my mouth and turned away, walking a little faster. I tried to get around the stench, thinking it was a dead animal carcass hiding beneath the rocks. I couldn't outrun the smell, and before I knew it I was crouched five feet above the river on an outcropping of rocks, and my humming was replaced by retching and dry heaving as the stench infiltrated my throat. I peered over the edge and fear singed my nerves like thousands of needles poking me all at once. Floating beneath me was the bloated and badly beaten body of a colored man. A scream escaped my lips. I stumbled backward and fell to my knees. My entire body began to shake. I covered my mouth to keep from throwing up. I knew I should turn away, run, get help, but I could not go back the way I'd come. I was paralyzed with fear, and yet, I was strangely drawn to the bloated and ghastly figure.

I stood back up, then stumbled in my gray midi-skirt and saddle shoes as I made my way over the rocks and toward the riverbank. The silt-laden river was still beneath the floating body. A branch stretched across the river like a boney finger, snagging the bruised and beaten body by the torn trousers that clung to its waist. His bare chest and arms were so bloated that it looked as if they might pop. Trembling and gasping for breath, I lowered myself to the ground, warm tears streaming down my cheeks.

While fear sucked my breath away, an underlying curiosity poked its way through to my consciousness. I covered my eyes then, telling myself to look away. The reality that I was seeing a dead man settled into my bones like ice. Shivers rattled my body. Whose father, brother, uncle, or friend was this man? I opened my eyes again and looked at him. *It's a him*, I told myself. I didn't want to see him as just an anonymous, dead colored man. He was someone, and he mattered. My heart pounded against my ribcage with an insistence—I needed to know who he was. I'd never seen a dead man before, and even though I could barely breathe, even though I could feel his image imprinting into my brain, I would not look away. I wanted to know who had beaten him, and why. I wanted to tell his family I was sorry for their loss.

An uncontrollable urgency brought me to my feet and drew me closer, on rubber legs, to where I could see what was left of his face. A gruesome mass of flesh protruded from his mouth. His tongue had bloated and completely filled the opening, like a flesh-sock had been stuffed in the hole, stretching his lips until they tore and the raw pulp poked out. Chunks of skin were torn or bitten away from his eyes.

I don't know how long I stood there, my legs quaking, unable to speak or turn back the way I had come. I don't know how I got home that night, or what I said to anyone along the way. What I do know is that hearing of a colored man's death was bad enough—I'd heard the rumors of whites beating colored men to death before—but actually seeing the man who had died, and witnessing the awful remains of the beating, now that terrified me to my core. A feeling of shame bubbled within me. For the first time ever, I was embarrassed to be white, because in Forrest Town, Arkansas, you could be fairly certain it was my people who were the cause of his death. And as a young southern woman, I knew that the expectation was for me to get married, have children, and perpetuate the hate that had been bred in our lives. My children, they'd be born into the same hateful society. That realization brought me to my knees.

Chapter Two

It had been a few days since that awful night at the river, and I couldn't shake the image from my mind; the disfigured body lying in the water like yesterday's trash. At the time, I didn't recognize Byron Bingham. I only knew the middle-aged colored man from town gossip, as *that man whose wife was sleepin' with Billy Carlisle.* Daddy told me who he was after the police pulled him from the river. I know now that the purple, black, and red bruises that covered his skin were not caused from the beating alone, but rather by the seven days he'd spent dead in the river. I tried to talk to my boyfriend, Jimmy Lee, about the shame I'd carried ever since finding that poor man's body, but Jimmy Lee believed he probably deserved whatever he got, so I swallowed the words. I wanted to share, but the feelings still burned inside me like a growing fire I couldn't control. It didn't help that some folks looked at me like I'd done something bad by finding Mr. Bingham. Even with those sneers reeling around me, I couldn't help but want to see his family. I wanted to be part of their world, to bear witness to what was left behind in the wake of his terrible death, and to somehow connect with them, help them through the pain. Were they okay? How could they be?

I walked all the way to Division Street, the large two-story homes with shiny Buicks and Chevy Impalas out front fell away behind me. A rusty, red and white Ford Ranch Wagon turned down Division Street. There I stood, looking down the street that divided the colored side of town from the white side. Even the trees seemed to sag and sway, appearing less vital than those in town. A chill ran up my back. *Don't go near those colored streets,* Daddy had warned me. *Those people will rape you faster than you can say chicken scratch.* I dried my sweaty palms on my pencil skirt as I craned my head, though I had no real idea what I was looking for. The desolate street stretched out before me, like the road itself felt the loss of Mr. Bingham. Small, wooden houses lined the dirt road like secondhand clothes, used and tattered. How had I never before noticed the loneliness of Division Street? Two young children were sitting near the front porch of a small, clapboard house, just a few houses away from where I stood. My heart ached to move forward, crouch down right beside them, and see what they were doing. Two women, who looked to be about my mama's age, stood in the gravel driveway. One held a big bowl of something—beans, maybe? She lifted pieces of whatever it was, broke them, then put them back in the bowl. I wondered what it might be like to help them in the kitchen, bake something delicious, and watch those little childrens' eyes light up at a perfect corn muffin. The short, plump woman had a dark wrap around her hair. The other one, a tiny flick of a woman with a stylish press and curl hairdo, looked in my direction. Our eyes met, then she shifted her head from side to side, as if she were afraid someone might jump out and yell at her for looking at me. I felt my cheeks tighten as a tentative smile spread across my lips. My fingertips lifted at my sides in a slight wave. She turned away quickly and crossed her arms. The air between me and those women who I wanted to know, thickened.

I felt stupid standing there, wanting to go down and talk to them, to see what the children were playing. I wondered, did they know Mr. Bingham? Had his death impacted their lives? I wanted to apologize for what had happened, even though I had no idea how or why it had. I realized that the colored side of town had been almost invisible to me, save for understanding that I was forbidden to go there. Those families had also been invisible to me. My cheeks burned as my feelings of stupidity turned to shame.

A child's cackle split the silence. His laughter was infectious. I couldn't remember the last time I'd heard uninhibited giggles like that. It made me smile. I bit my lower lip, feeling caught between what I'd been taught and the pull of my heart.

A Buick ambled by, slowing as it passed behind me. I startled, remembering *my place*, as Daddy called it. Daddy'd keep me right by his side if he could. He didn't like me to be around anyone he didn't know, said he couldn't take care of me if he didn't know where I was. I turned and headed back toward town, like I'd just stopped for a moment during a walk. The elderly white man driving the shiny, black car squinted at me, furrowed his brow, and then drove on.

I wondered what my daddy might think if he saw me gazing down Division Street, where his farmhands lived. Daddy's farmhands, black men of all ages, were strong and responsible, and they worked in our fields and gardens with such vigorous commitment that it was as though the food and cotton were for their own personal use. Some of those dedicated men had worked for Daddy for years; others were new to the farm. I realized, surprisingly, that I'd never spoken to any one of them.

A long block later, I heard Jimmy Lee's old, red pick-up truck coming up the road behind me. The town was so small, that I could hear it from a mile away with its loud, rumbling engine. I wondered if someone had spotted me staring down Division Street and told him to come collect me. He stopped the truck beside me and flung open the door, flashing his big baby-blues beneath his wavy, brown hair. Jimmy Lee was growing his hair out from his Elvis cut to something more akin to Ringo Starr, and it was stuck in that in-between stage of looking like a mop. I liked anything that had to do with Ringo, so he was even more appealing to me with his hair falling in his face.

"Alison, c'mon."

"Hey," I said, as I climbed onto the vinyl bench seat. He reached over and put his arm around me, pulling me closer to him. I snuggled right into the strength of him. It was hard to believe we'd been dating for two years. We'd met after church one Sunday morning. I used to wonder if Mama or Daddy had set it up that way, like a blind date, but there's no proof of that. Jimmy Lee's daddy, Jack Carlisle, was talking to my mama and daddy at the time, so we just started talking too. Jimmy Lee was the older, handsome guy that every girl had her eye on, and I was the lucky one he chose as his own. I'd been dating Jimmy Lee since I was sixteen. He was handsome, I had to give him that, but ever since finding Mr. Bingham, some of the things he'd done and said made my skin crawl. Others thought he was the perfect suitor for me. But I wondered if that, along with my daddy's approval, was enough to make me swallow these new, uncomfortable feelings that wrapped themselves like tentacles around every nerve in my body, and marry him.

I twisted the ring on my finger; Jimmy Lee's grandmother's engagement ring. In eight short weeks we'd be married and I'd no longer be Alison Tillman. I'd become Mrs. James Lee Carlisle. My heart ached with the thought.

The afternoon moved swiftly into a lazy and cool evening. I was still thinking about the women I'd seen on Division Street when we stopped at the store for a few six-packs of beer. Jimmy Lee's favorite past time. Like so many other evenings, we met up with my brother Jake and Jimmy Lee's best friend, Corky Talms, in the alley behind the General Store. I think everyone in town knew we hung out here, but no one ever bothered us. The alley was so narrow that there was only a foot or two of road between the right side of Jimmy Lee's truck and a stack of empty, cardboard delivery boxes, boasting familiar names like Schlitz, Tab, and Fanta, lined up along the brick wall beside the back door of the store. On the other side of his truck, just inches from the driver's side door, a dumpster stood open, wafting the stench of stale food into the air. Just beyond that was a small strip of grass, where Jake and Corky now sat. And behind them were the deep, dark woods that separated the nicer part of town from the poor.

I sat on the hood of Jimmy Lee's truck, and watched him take another swig of his beer. His square jaw tilted back, exposing his powerful neck and broad chest. The familiar desire to kiss him rose within me as I watched his Adam's apple bounce up and down with each gulp.

Jimmy Lee smacked his lips as he lowered the beer bottle to rest on his Levi's. His eyes were as blue as the sea, and they jetted around the group. I recognized that hungry look. Jimmy Lee had to behave when he was away at college, for fear of his uncle pulling his tuition, which I knew he could afford without much trouble. Jack Carlisle was a farmer and owned 350 acres, but his brother Billy owned the only furniture store in Forrest Town, Arkansas, and was one of the wealthiest men in town. Jimmy Lee might have been king of Central High, but now he was a small fish in a big pond at Mississippi State. The bullish tactics that had worked in Forrest Town would likely get him hurt in Mississippi, and Billy Carlisle wasn't about to be humiliated by his nephew. Jimmy Lee was set to become the manager in his uncle's store, if he behaved and actually graduated. I was pretty sure that he'd behave while he was away at college and make it to graduation, but I rued those long weekends when he returned home, itching for trouble.

"Jimmy Lee, why don't we take a walk?" I suggested, though I didn't much feel like taking a walk with Jimmy Lee. I never knew who we'd see or how he'd react.

He wrapped his arm around my shoulders and pulled me close. "How's my pretty little wife-to-be?" He kissed my cheek and offered me a sip of his beer, which I declined, too nervous to drink. I felt safe within his arms, but those colored boys were out there, and my nerves were trembling just thinking about what Jimmy Lee might do. I took my hands and placed them on his cheeks, forcing his eyes to meet mine. Love lingered in his eyes, clear and bright, and I hoped it was enough of a pull to keep him from seeking out trouble. Jimmy Lee was known for chasing down colored boys when he thought they were up to no good, and I was realizing that maybe he just liked doing it. Maybe they weren't always up to no good. Ever since finding Mr. Bingham's body, I noticed, and was more sensitive to, the ugliness of his actions.

I took inventory of the others. My brother Jake sat on the ground fiddling with his shoelace. His golden hair, the pale-blond color of dried cornhusks, just like mine, though much thicker, was combed away from his high forehead, revealing his too-young-for-a-nineteen-year-old, baby face. Jake seemed content to just sit on the grass and drink beer. He had spent the last year trying to measure up to our older sister's impeccable grades. While Jake remained in town after high school, attending Central Community College, Maggie, with her stellar grades and bigger-than-life personality, begged and pleaded until she convinced our father to send her to Marymount Manhattan College.

I wished more than ever that Maggie were home just then. We'd take a walk to the river like we used to, just the two of us, climb up to the loft in the barn, and giggle until Mama called us inside. We'd do anything other than sitting around watching Jimmy Lee blow smoke rings and think about starting trouble.

Corky cleared his throat, calling my thoughts away from my sister. He looked up at me, thick tufts of dark hair bobbing like springs atop his head as he nodded. I bristled at the scheming look in his brown eyes. He smirked in that cocky way that was so familiar that it was almost boring. With muscles that threatened to burst through every t-shirt he owned, one would think he'd be as abrasive as sandpaper, but he was the quiet type— until something or someone shook his reins. He came from a typical Forrest Town farm family. His father was a farmer, like mine, but unlike Daddy, who saw some value in education, Corky's father believed his son's sole purpose was to work the farm. Everyone in town knew that when Corky's daddy grew too old to farm, he would take over. Corky accepted his lot in life with a sense of proud entitlement. He saw no need for schooling when a job was so readily provided for him. I swear Corky was more machine than man. He worked from dawn until dusk on the farm, and still had the energy to show up here smelling like DDT, or hay, or lumber, or whatever they happen to be planting or harvesting at the time, and stir up trouble with Jimmy Lee.

Corky took a long pull of his beer, eyeing Jimmy Lee with a conspiratorial grin.

I tugged Jimmy Lee's arm again, hoping he'd choose a walk with me over trouble with Corky, but I knew I was no match for a willing participant in his devious shenanigans. Jimmy Lee shrugged me off and locked eyes with Corky. Tucked in the alley behind the General Store, trouble could be found fifty feet in any direction. I bent forward and peered around the side of the old, wooden building. At ten o'clock at night, the streets were dark, but not too dark to notice the colored boys across the street walking at a fast pace with their heads down, hands shoved deep in their pockets. I recognized one of the boys from Daddy's farm. *Please don't let Jimmy Lee see them.* It was a futile hope, but I hoped just the same.

Jimmy Lee stretched. I craned my neck to look up at my handsome giant. Maggie called me Pixie. Although she and Jake both got Daddy's genes when it came to height, I stopped growing at thirteen years old. While being five foot two has minor advantages, like being called a sweet nickname by my sister, I often felt like, and was treated as if, I were younger than my age.

Jimmy Lee set his beer down on the ground and wiped his hands on his jeans. "What're those cotton pickers doin' in town this late?" He smirked, shooting a nod at Corky.

"Jimmy Lee, don't," I pleaded, feeling kind of sick at the notion that he might go after those boys.

"Don't? Whaddaya mean, don't? This is what we do." He looked at Corky and nodded.

"It's just..." I turned away, then gathered the courage to say what was nagging to be said. "It's just that, after findin' Mr. Bingham's body...it's just not right, Jimmy Lee. Leave those boys alone."

Jimmy Lee narrowed his eyes, put his arms on either side of me, and leaned into me. He kissed my forehead and ran his finger along my chin. "You let me worry about keepin' the streets safe, and I'll let you worry about—" he laughed. "Heck, worry about somethin' else, I don't know."

Corky tossed his empty bottle into the grass and was on his feet, pumping his fists. My heartbeat sped up.

"Jimmy Lee, please, just let 'em be," I begged. When he didn't react, I tried another tactic and batted my eyelashes, pulled him close, and whispered in his ear, "Let's go somewhere, just you and me." I hated myself for using my body as a negotiation point.

Jimmy Lee pulled away and I saw a momentary flash of consideration pass in his eyes. Then Corky slapped him on the back and that flash of consideration was gone, replaced with a darkness, a narrowing of his eyes that spoke too loudly of hate.

"Let's get 'em," Corky said. The sleeves of his white t-shirt strained across his massive biceps. The five inches Jimmy Lee had on him seemed to disappear given the sheer volume of space Corky's body took up. He was as thick and strong as a bull.

I jumped off the hood of the truck. "Jimmy Lee, you leave those boys alone." I was surprised by my own vehemence. This was the stuff he did all the time, it wasn't new. I was used to him scaring and beating on the colored boys in our area. It was something that just *was*. But at that moment, all I could see in my mind was poor Byron Bingham.

Jimmy Lee looked at me for one beat too long. I thought I had him, that he'd give in and choose me over the fight. One second later, he turned to Jake and clapped his hands. "Let's go, Jake. We've got some manners to teach those boys."

"Don't, Jake," I begged. "Please, leave them alone!"

Jake looked nervously from me to Jimmy Lee. I knew he was deciding if it was safer to side with me, which would lead to instant ridicule by Jimmy Lee, but would keep him out of a fight, or side with Jimmy Lee, which would not only put him in Jimmy Lee's favor, but also make his actions on par with our father's beliefs. He'd happily fight for a few bonus points with Daddy to balance out his poor grades.

My hands trembled at the thought of those innocent boys being hurt. "Jake, please," I pleaded. "Don't. Jimmy Lee—"

They were off, all three of them, stalking their prey, moving swiftly out from behind the General Store and down the center of the empty street. Their eyes trained on the two boys. Jimmy Lee walked at a fast clip, clenching and unclenching his fists, his shoulders rounded forward like a bull readying to charge.

I ran behind him, kicking dirt up beneath my feet, begging him to stop. I screamed and pleaded until my throat was raw and my voice a tiny, frayed thread. The colored boys ran swift as deer, down an alley and toward the fields that ran parallel to Division Street, stealing quick, fear-filled glances over their shoulders—glances that cried out in desperation and left me feeling helpless and even culpable of what was yet to come.

Jimmy Lee, Jake, and Corky closed in on them like a sudden storm in the middle of the field. The grass swallowed their feet as they surrounded the boys like farmers herding their flock.

"Get that son of a bitch!" Jimmy Lee commanded, pointing to the smaller of the two boys, Daddy's farmhand. The whites of his eyes shone bright as lightning against his charcoal skin.

Corky hooted and hollered into the night, "Yeeha! Let's play, boys!"

Bile rose in my throat at the thought of what I knew Jimmy Lee would do to them, and I couldn't help but wonder if he might take it as far as killing those boys—if even by accident. I stood in the field, shaking and crying, then fell to my knees thirty feet from where they were, begging Jimmy Lee not to hurt them. Images of Mr. Bingham's bloated and beaten body, his tongue swollen beyond recognition, seared like fire into my mind.

Jimmy Lee moved in on the trembling boy. I was riveted to the coldness in his eyes. "No!" I screamed into the darkness. Jimmy Lee threw a glance my way, a scowl on his face. The smack of Jimmy Lee's fist against the boy's face brought me to my feet. When the boy cried out, agony filled my veins. I stumbled and ran as fast and hard as I could, and didn't stop until I was safely around the side of the General Store, hidden from the shame of what they were doing, hidden from the eyes that might find me in the night. There was no hiding from the guilt, shame, and disgust that followed me like a shadow. I sank to my knees, and cried for those boys, for Mr. Bingham, and for the loss of my love for Jimmy Lee.

Chapter Three

Every morning began the same way. Before sunrise, Daddy would creep downstairs, listen to the weather on the radio, and walk softly into the kitchen. I'd lay in my bed, listening to his morning noises—the refrigerator door opening and closing, a mug drawn from the cabinet, the sink water running, the kettle settling on the stove—and then, I'd roll over and fall back to sleep feeling the safety of his familiar rituals.

Mama and I were in the kitchen when Daddy came in from the fields. I swear he has a sixth sense, because every morning he came inside just as breakfast was being prepared. It wasn't until years later that I learned that Daddy watched the sun, and when it had risen to just above the roof, he'd know it was time for breakfast. Today he patted my head, as he'd done every morning for as far back as I could remember, and though I was too old to be patted, his touch brought comfort.

"Good mornin', Pix," he said. His tired eyes lit up at the smell of the warm eggs and hot, buttered biscuits. The deep lines that etched his forehead softened as he reached out and gently touched the small of Mama's back, and whispered in her ear. She turned to face him, her eyes wide. Her hand flew to her gaping mouth. All of the color drained from Mama's face.

"Mornin' Daddy," I said, watching Mama press her lips into a tight line and rub her neck. I knew better than to ask for specific details of whatever they were wrestling with, so I kept my question light; the kind of question Daddy didn't mind answering. "Is everything okay?"

"Sure is," he said. He washed his hands, then sat down at the table.

Mama set our plates on the table then wiped her hands on a dishcloth, removed the apron from her waist, and set it on the counter. Her fingers remained clenched around the fabric. She didn't make a sound. She just stood there, one hand on the crumpled apron, the other covering her eyes.

"Mama, aren't you gonna eat?" I asked. I glanced out the window. Jake's bicycle was already gone. He had class in an hour, and it was a long ride to school.

"Eat up, Pixie," Daddy said.

Mama was a quiet woman who rarely let her opinions be known, and I was used to Daddy speaking in her place. I picked up my fork and swallowed my questions.

"Is Jake at class?" I asked, just to break the silence.

My father nodded, and shoved his third biscuit into his mouth, chewing fast. "He's comin' back early. We're down one hand today. Some dumb boy got himself beat up."

I put my fork down as my stomach lurched and twisted. "Who?" The smell of the river came back to me like a bad dream.

"I dunno. One of them coloreds."

I set my napkin on the table and stared at him. "You don't know who it is, but you know he's missin'?"

My father glared at me. "Alison, know your place young lady." He took a sip of his coffee. The tension in his cheeks softened. He reached out and patted my hand. "Sorry, Pix. Albert Johns, if you must know. Why are you so interested?"

Albert Johns. I repeated his name over and over in my mind. I could no longer listen to Daddy refer to the coloreds in town, or the ones who worked for him, as "them coloreds." I'd been ignoring how Daddy'd spoken of them forever, as if they were invisible. But now, having come face to face with a dead colored man, a man who I was sure had died at the hands of a white man, I could no longer pretend they didn't matter. They were people. They had names, and families, and feelings, and thoughts.

I looked down. I'd overstepped that thin, gray line Daddy saw so clearly. "I'm just...it's just...after what happened to Mr. Bingham, I just wanted to know his name."

My father set down his fork and wiped his mouth with a napkin. I could feel Mama's eyes on me from behind. "The boy isn't dead, Pix, he's beat up. Probably did somethin' to deserve it."

"Yes, sir," I mumbled. "May I please be excused? I need to get ready to go to the library before Mama and I start bakin' for the day."

Daddy nodded. "Sure, Pix. Come over here and give your daddy a hug."

"I'll drive you in today, Alison." Mama's eyes were dark and serious.

"Okay," I said, thankful that she'd saved me from what was sure to be an uncomfortable ride with Daddy—me holding in my new feelings about the coloreds and him trying to talk to me about marrying a boy I wasn't sure I wanted to be marrying. I wrapped my arms around Daddy's neck. His earthy smell warmed me, his whiskers tickled my cheek.

"Are you sure, Hil?" Daddy only called Mama by her full name when they were in contention, which wasn't often. She was always Hil, not Hillary. Her features softened as he spoke.

She nodded. "I have to go into town for some sugar anyway. I'm makin' a cake for tonight's Blue Bonnet meetin' so we need more. Go get ready, Alison, and don't forget your sweater. It's gettin' chilly."

Mama drove faster than her usual careful pace, her left elbow rested on the open window, her fingers pressed firmly against her forehead. You'd think a small-framed blonde might look out of place driving a beat up, old, pick-up truck. I always thought she made Daddy's truck look better. Mama didn't need to drive an expensive car to get noticed. People were drawn to her natural beauty. When it was warm out, she'd whip a scarf around the front of her hair, and tie it under the back, the scarf trailing down her back. The end result looked perfectly planned. Today her waves blew free.

She hadn't said a word since we'd left home, and as we neared town I asked her if she was okay.

"Mm-hmm," she answered, then forced a smile. "I'm fixin' to stop at the drugstore first."

As I wandered through the drugstore door behind Mama, I caught a whiff of Mr. Shire's familiar aftershave. Ever since I was little, he'd worn Old Spice, a fragrance Daddy said smelled like a waste of good money. I loved the peppery-vanilla and warmed-wood smell. "Are you ready for your weddin', Alison?" he asked. Mr. Shire reminded me of any generic grandfather; a sweet, gray-haired man who tsked at the ways of youth *these days.*

"Yes, sir, almost. I'm wearin' Mama's weddin' dress, and the church is all set. We just have to coordinate who's makin' what for the reception. Thank you for askin'." Thoughts of the wedding left an acrid taste in my mouth. I glanced at Mama as she shopped and contemplated talking to her about my misgivings about Jimmy Lee, but I wasn't sure she'd understand. My own father talked about his farmhands as though they were a commodity, not individual people, and she was married to him. I decided I'd better hold my tongue for a while.

Mama returned to the counter with an armful of bandages, bottles of antiseptic, and medicated creams. She quickly slipped down the condiments aisle and returned with a bag of sugar.

"What's all that for?" I asked.

She looked at me, then at Mr. Shire. "Oh, just stockin' up. You can never be sure when you'll need first aid items."

We made one more stop on the way to the library that morning. She pulled up behind the furniture store and told me to wait in the car.

Seconds later she was up the back steps, carrying the bags she'd just purchased. She knocked on the door, her back to me. A colored woman opened the door and peeked out. Mama shoved the bag into her arms, looking behind her as she did so. The woman pushed the package back at Mama, shaking her head. Mama pushed it back into the woman's arms. *What was she doin'?* If Daddy knew that she used our money to buy things for a colored family, he'd...I don't know what he'd do, but I wouldn't want to be anywhere near the house when he found out.

The woman nodded fast and hard. Mama took the woman's hand in her own and leaned in close, saying something that I couldn't hear. The colored woman looked down, hugged the bag to her chest, and nodded.

When Mama came back to the car, I stared straight ahead. I wanted to ask her who that was, and why she'd given her the bag of first aid supplies, but I couldn't find the right words without sounding disrespectful. I had so many questions racing through my mind. *How often did she come here? Does Daddy know? How long has she known that woman? What other colored people does she know? Were they friends?* I turned to face Mama, gathering the courage to ask.

She stared straight ahead as she drove away from the store, and said, without looking at me, "Your father is never to know about this. You hear me, Alison Jean? Never."

Pride swelled within me. Mama had trusted me with a dangerous secret. "Yes, ma'am." Maybe I could talk to her about Jimmy Lee after all. I learned more about Mama in that five-minute stop at the furniture store than I had in my entire eighteen years of living in her house.

She reached out and touched my leg, her eyes focused on the road. "Good girl," she said.

Chapter Four

I sat on the deep front porch mulling over my conflicting feelings, trying to enjoy the sunshine and the gentle breeze, but the air carried with it whispers of the colored boys' cries for help. I rocked, telling myself to think of something else, but the porch creaked, reminding me of the way I impotently pleaded for Jimmy Lee to take me instead of hurting those boys. I covered my ears, wishing the memories away. Shame warmed my cheeks. What would Daddy think of me?

The sound of tires on dirt and gravel brought my eyes to Jimmy Lee's truck pulling into the driveway. Something I wasn't used to rose within me. At first, it was like I'd eaten something bad and it was stuck in my throat, pushing its way out, but then, it melted to a heat that filled my chest and spread to my limbs.

Jimmy Lee stepped from his truck, swaggering all tall and handsome across the front walk and up the steps. He wrapped his arms around me, kissed my head. "Hey there, beautiful. How's my girl?"

There it was—the sweet that evened out his sour. I stood in his arms, against the chest that was so familiar. I felt safe, and I breathed him in.

"Ready to go to town?" he asked.

We held hands as we walked to the truck. Jimmy Lee's hand engulfed mine, like Daddy's did. Daddy's hand was calloused from working in the fields. Jimmy Lee's was tainted with the blood of those boys. *Daddy would never beat up anyone.* I dropped Jimmy Lee's hand and climbed into his truck, happy to be free from the memory of the fields. "As long as we stay away from the old high school crowd. I swear, ever since I found Mr. Bingham's body, they act like I'm the one who did somethin' wrong." Jimmy Lee didn't say anything, but he patted my leg as if to say, *It's okay. I'm here.* We used to talk more, and I wanted that now. I needed it. I needed to feel his comfort and love, and try to wipe away the darkness that was creeping into my heart.

"Remember last June, before graduation? How my friends stopped hangin' out with me? I was the odd girl out because of datin' someone older? I was the literal third wheel that got kicked to the curb," I admitted, sadly.

He drew his eyebrows together and I watched tension darken his eyes. Then his gaze lightened and he said, "I remember. It's worth it though, right? You didn't need to go anywhere with them. You had me."

"Yeah," I said. "But now, it's happenin' all over again. It's as if by findin' Mr. Bingham's body, I carry some sort of bad luck. I never knew bad luck could be contagious, but others seem to think so." Jimmy Lee turned on the radio, and I continued, "Do you remember a few years back, when the Holsten's farm flooded? The neighbors helped them through, but after that year, when the next crop season began, everyone disassociated with them. I'm beginnin' to wonder about the strange relationships that our small town is made up of, and it scares me."

Jimmy Lee didn't respond. He tapped his hand on the steering wheel to the beat of the music. I tried again to bridge the gap between us, to gain his understanding.

"I feel like findin' Mr. Bingham is like that—like I'm bad luck and that's why they're shunnin' me now. I saw Sheila Porten at the store the other day and she didn't even say hello to me. We graduated together! Do you think they somehow blame me for findin' him?"

He stopped tapping the steering wheel and cast his winning smile upon me; his white teeth beaming like pearls, a sparkle in his eye. "Nah, they're just jealous that they didn't find 'im."

"You're such a jerk, Jimmy Lee. That's just awful. Who would want to see that?"

"A dead nigger? Most of the town," he laughed. His eyes danced with delight at the nastiness of his own comment.

I clenched my teeth against the unfamiliar venom that wanted to spew, and leaned against the door. In silence, we drove out to the river in the next county, which we'd done often enough for me to know what he had in mind. He had to return to school the next day, and the last thing I wanted was to be intimate with him again before he left. Sometimes I regretted giving into him the first time. Oh, I can't blame him for that. I wanted to do it just as badly as he did. He was everything I had dreamed of, strong and decisive like Daddy, and on a successful enough career track that I knew Daddy would be pleased. I just wish I had understood then what I understand now. Somehow, and I'm not sure why, sex complicated things. Sex was no longer something that we fought the urge for. Now it was expected.

Jimmy Lee reached over and grabbed my hand, a lusty look in his eyes. He hadn't started drinking yet, and he was always kinder when he was sober. I liked his gentler side and felt my heart softening toward him.

"Soon, we won't have to sneak away to the river to be alone," he said with a grin.

I feigned a smile, then turned and looked out the window, watching the town fall away. I wish I had talked to Mama about my feelings. I was battling myself, wanting to be with him and not wanting to at the same time. I wish I understood what was going on inside my crazy heart.

The wind blew the tips of the long grass this way and that, the smell of manure from nearby fields hovered in the air. Leaves rustled in the trees as we walked toward the water. Jimmy Lee carried a blanket under one arm and held me with the other. The smell of him rose to meet me, musk and pine, liked he'd rolled around on the forest floor. I felt a tug down low, and gritted my teeth against my growing desire for him.

Jimmy Lee spread the blanket out below a tree and lay down, relaxing back on one elbow. He beckoned me with his finger in a playful way. I continued toward the water.

"Can't we just walk a little first?"

"Walk?" he asked.

"Yeah, you know, one foot in front of the other? Come on." I headed down river, hoping he'd follow. The last thing I felt like doing was lying naked beneath him. I was too confused, too sickened by the way he'd viciously attacked Albert Johns, leaving the poor boy in a field, lying in pain, broken ribs and all.

Jimmy Lee came up behind me and wrapped his arms around my middle. I flushed, ashamed of how my heart fluttered at his touch.

"We don't have much time," he whispered in my ear. "I want to be with you."

It was hard to turn away from him. As much as I loathed what he'd done, I still loved him.

He took my hand and led me back to the blanket, lowering me to my knees. I closed my eyes, willing myself to be in the moment. Allowing myself to. His fingers trailed down the buttons of my blouse, unbuttoning them one by one, then caressing the skin beneath. Shivers ran up my chest, a collision of desire and the frigid air. He pulled my blouse down off my shoulder, kissing each bit of skin as it was revealed. His lips were soft and tender.

"I'm cold," I complained, partly to slow him down, and partly because it was chilly kneeling there in the breeze.

"I'll warm you," he said. The scent of him wrapped itself around me. He leaned against me, pushing me back until I was lying beneath him. I could feel him pressing against me. With one hand he reached behind his back and pulled his t-shirt over his head, his hungry eyes looking right into mine. His knees pushed my legs apart and I wanted to hate his touch, wanted to *want* to push him away because of what he'd done to those boys, but that hatred melted under his touch and I longed for him to be closer to me. His hand slid down my side and hiked my skirt up around my waist. He kissed my neck, sending a shiver down my spine. His fingers hooked my panties, drawing them down. I hated myself for wanting him.

A bird sang out from the tree, bringing my brain back to the surface. The breeze on my naked chest was causing me to shiver. I opened my eyes, listening to the flow of the river, the bristling of the leaves above us, Jimmy Lee's heavy breaths against my neck, and I began to tremble. *Byron Bingham. Albert Johns.* Thoughts tumbled like stones into my mind, knocking me out of my reverie. I must have gone rigid, because Jimmy Lee lifted his head and looked at me with a quizzical, lust-filled gaze, like he wasn't really seeing my face, but he was lost in the frenzy of what he was doing. I pushed at his chest.

"Stop," I whispered. My voice was lost in the image of Byron, strangled by the thought of Albert.

Jimmy Lee laughed, tugged his jeans down.

I turned away, a tear slipping down the side of my face. "Stop," I whispered again, or maybe I just thought it in my mind.

He thrust himself inside of me, groaning, one hand clenching my breast, the other clamped onto my hip.

"Stop, stop." I whispered. My body shook with each pounding thrust of his body. Anger rushed through me. I clawed at his back, screaming, "Stop! Stop!" I kicked and fought against him, and he pumped harder, faster, as if he didn't hear me.

"Almost," he said. "Al...al—"

"Stop!" I found my voice and screamed until my throat was raw, my nails stripped chunks of skin from his back.

He gave one last, long thrust then fell on top of me, panting. I pushed him off, crying and shaking as I did so. I thought I was going to throw up, pass out, die. I crawled away. He lay there, spent, looking at me with a stupid grin on his face.

I pulled my clothes on, sobbing, struggling to stay upright, and stumbled through the grass, toward the water. The breeze stung my skin. The birds sang out in a beautiful tune that I could not reconcile with the awful feeling blooming inside me.

"What?" he called after me with his palms held up toward the sky, confusion in his spent eyes.

Hate blinded me. I wanted to go home. I wanted to run away. I wanted to find someone to beat *him* up. The grass and trees swirled around me, pointing their branches like fingers at my guilt of knowing what he'd done. As he climbed back into his jeans, I ran past him, clambered back into the truck, and slammed the door, sobbing. Curled up against the door like a child, I covered my face and waited for him to get back into the truck and take me home. I smelled like him, like sex. I had never felt so powerless and alone.

On the way home, I remained huddled against the door. All I could think of was Mama, and how she'd kill me if she knew I was having sex

with Jimmy Lee, and how Daddy might slaughter me if I told him I wasn't
sure we should get married. Jimmy Lee kept looking over at me.

"You okay?" he asked.

I opened my mouth to answer, but all I could do was cry. How do you
tell your fiancé that he makes you sick to your stomach? Anger simmered
within me when he didn't ask me again, or try to figure out why I was
pulling so far away from him. I never thought Jimmy Lee would force
himself upon me. He'd been rough with me before, but not like this, not
like he ignored what *I* wanted. How do you tell him that the world you've
lived in for eighteen years suddenly looked different, that you noticed
sneers that you previously accepted as normal, or maybe that you—
ashamedly—had also doled out? Jimmy Lee was humming to the radio, his
thumbs tapping on the steering wheel like he was fine and dandy, while my
world was spiraling out of control and I could barely keep my head on
straight.

My father's truck was gone when we arrived home. Jimmy Lee leaned
over to kiss me but I pulled back and hopped out of the truck.

"That's it? No goodbye kiss? I'm goin' back to school. Won't you
miss me?" He looked so hurt, and the last thing I wanted was an
argument.

"Sorry," I said, and reluctantly climbed back into the truck. I
scooched across the seat and pecked his cheek.

"That's more like it," he said.

Anger bubbled up again, but this time, I found my voice. "Jimmy Lee,
I asked you to stop, and…" I saw it then, a look in his eye that said it all.
Not only was I wasting his time telling him something he didn't want to
hear, but he could no better understand what I was saying than I could
understand what he'd done to those boys. "Nevermind," I said, and
slammed the door.

As I walked toward the house, I could feel my heart breaking into a
million little pieces. I couldn't bear to face Mama. I knew I'd break down
in tears and have to tell her the truth. She'd surely kill Jimmy Lee if she
knew he'd forced himself on me. Or had he? Had I led him on? Confusion
drove me around the house to the backyard. I didn't dare look at the
windows of the house, or toward the barn or the garden. I didn't want to
accidentally see Mama. I ducked beneath the drying line hanging from the
massive oak tree in our backyard, and hurried toward the cellar doors,
thinking about how livid Daddy would be if I backed out of the wedding.
All he ever wanted for me was to be happy, like him and Mama, and I
don't think Daddy could understand how I could be anything *but* happy
with Jimmy Lee.

It was time to get my feelings in check. I pulled open the cold, metal
doors and descended the stairs into the dark dirt cellar where Mama kept
jugs of water, first aid kits, towels, and all sorts of canned supplies in case

of tornadoes. The damp, earthy smell was cold and seemed appropriate given what I'd done. I quickly slithered out of my clothes and doused a towel in water. I scrubbed his kisses from my neck, his touch from my breasts. The water was cool, raising goose bumps on my arms and across my chest. The blood rushing in my ears reminded me of his lousy, lust-filled grunts, and I cried louder, trying to drown them out as I spread my legs and wiped his chlorine-like scent from within the soft folds of my skin. In my mind, my fighting him replayed over and over, and with it came more hatred, more disgust with myself. I started scrubbing his sweat from my stomach, legs, and arms. I was pressing too hard, deserving of the pain, and hoping it would wipe all of the ugliness of the last few weeks away. I scrubbed until my skin was red and raw. By the time I'd finished, my body shook and shivered, my heart ached from loneliness, and my mind ran in circles. There was nothing left for me to do but slip my soiled clothing back on, sit on the cold step, and sob until I had no more tears to free.

I washed my face, bundled the dirty towels together, and took them with me to the burn barrel by the barn, where I hid them beneath the debris. I hoped it might even burn away the memories of the afternoon, the alleyway, and the field where Jimmy Lee had stolen precious moments of those boys' lives.

The barn loomed before me, a big, wooden structure almost as big as our house. I walked through the double doors; the familiar smell of hay and the sharp odor of stored wood and fuel assaulted my senses. Memories rushed in. Oh, how I wished Maggie was here to help me with the way I was feeling about Jimmy Lee. I could almost feel her pulling my arm toward the stall where our old cow, Hippa, used to live. Mama had painted a mother and baby cow on the wall inside of the stall. It had chipped and cracked with age, and by the time Hippa died, a few years ago, it was nearly indiscernible. I'd cried for days when Hippa died. By then Maggie was too old to be attached to a cow, I guess. She didn't cry, but when Daddy told me that it was just a fact of life on a farm, and that I should be used to it by then, Maggie took me up to the loft and held a memorial service for Hippa. Just the two of us.

Maggie went away to college while I was still in high school, and I wondered if she'd want to hang out with me anymore, or if she'd be too grown up. I longed to talk to someone about Jimmy Lee, and I had no one to turn to. Thoughts of Jimmy Lee made my stomach clench all over again. I went out the back doors of the barn and sat against one of the tractor's tires, shaded between a thick, old maple tree and the barn, out of sight from the fields and the house. I laid my head on my arms, and tried to wash away the thoughts of what I had just endured.

The calm of the breeze and the familiar sight of the newly planted rows of cotton should have filled me with ease. Instead, I grew even sadder. Nothing felt right. The life I thought I had swirled around me with the realization that Daddy, who I treasured, was treating people like machines, Mama, who I believed to be honest and good, was keeping secrets from Daddy, and my boyfriend, whose strength I used to adore, I now loathed. It was as if they all mixed together and whirred in circles, like a tornado of a mess unraveling around me. I didn't know how to move forward. I didn't want to move back. So I remained there, stiff and confused, with no outlet other than my own tears.

"S'cuse me, Miss, are you okay?"

I jumped at the unfamiliar man's voice, and pushed to my feet. I'd never been approached by a colored man before. I was even more startled because this young man wore a military uniform. He stood so straight I thought he might salute me. My stomach tightened, my senses heightened. I fought the urge to run away.

"I'm fine, thank you." I took a step backward. *They'll rape you faster than you can say chicken scratch.* I whipped my head around. My father's truck had not yet returned. I suddenly regretted my decision to hide behind the barn.

The man removed his hat and held it against his stomach with both hands. He looked down, then up again, meeting my eyes with a tentative, yet respectful, regard.

"I'm lookin' for a Mr. Tillman?" His uneasy gaze betrayed his confident tone.

"My father?"

"Yes, ma'am. I have a message for him."

I stood up straighter, suddenly feeling as though I needed to exert my strength and take control of the situation, as Daddy might. "Farmhands show up at five in the mornin'. It's gotta be seven o'clock *at night* by now. What are you doin' here?"

He smiled, then shook his head. "My apologies. I'm not a farmhand, ma'am. My younger brother is Albert Johns."

Albert Johns. The night came rushing back to me. The way Corky had egged on Jimmy Lee and Jake. *Oh, God, Jake.* What had he done? I hadn't even seen him since last night. "I...I'm sorry," I said.

"Yes, ma'am. Thank you. I came to let Mr. Tillman know that my uncle, Byron Bingham, he passed away recently, and the funeral is tomorrow. My brother Albert got beat up real bad, so he won't be here tomorrow on account of his injuries and the funeral. I wanted to come work in his place after the service, to make up for his absence."

"Your uncle?" My chest constricted. The oxygen around me slowly disappeared. I gasped for air, my heart palpitating so fast I thought I might pass out. I reached for the tractor, missed, and stumbled.

"Ma'am?" He rushed to my side, grabbing my arm just before I hit the ground, and lowered me slowly to the earth.

I waited for my breathing to calm.

"I'm sorry, ma'am. I didn't mean to—are you okay?" A flash of fear washed over him. He squinted, glancing around to see if he'd been seen touching me, and backed away quickly.

The magnitude of that one act of assistance suddenly burst before me like fireworks. I understood the fear in his eyes, and it killed me to know that if someone had seen him—Daddy, Jake, or Jimmy Lee—he'd be running for *his* life right now.

I nodded, unable to find my voice. Mr. Bingham's bloated face floated before me. My eyes dampened. "I'm so sorry," I whispered, unsure if I was apologizing for what had happened to his uncle or to his race for how his people were treated. I rubbed my arm where he'd grabbed me.

"Yes, ma'am. Thank you." He watched me with concern. "I'm sorry if I hurt you. I just didn't want you to fall."

"You didn't hurt me. I've just never been touched—I'm sorry, I've never even spoken to a colored person before." The realization of that statement sickened me. It also wasn't quite true. Once, when I was a little girl, maybe five or six, I'd seen a colored girl in the street by Woolworths. I asked her if she wanted to come in with me and get a soda pop at the counter. Mama had dragged me away. I remember crying because I had no idea what I'd done wrong. That was the instance that drove home the meaning of *knowin' my place*. I'd never spoken to a colored person again—child or adult.

He dropped his eyes, nodding his head as if he'd expected my response.

I looked behind me. If Daddy caught me I probably wouldn't be allowed out of his sight for weeks. The coloreds in town never would have spoken to me, even if I had been crying. They knew better. But this man who stood before me, he had a gentle confidence about him that made me want to know more about him.

"Yes, ma'am. I understand. I don't want to cause no trouble." He lifted his eyes to meet mine. "I heard a noise, and I thought you mighta been Mr. Tillman. I'm sorry to have startled you. I meant no disrespect." A friendly warmth lingered in the gentle way he spoke. He looked right into my eyes, as if he was interested in, even waiting on, what I had to say next. There was a little lifting of the edges of his lips, not quite a smile.

"Aren't you afraid to talk to me? You know what happens to colored men when they talk to white women, right?" I realized after I'd spoken that I'd said that because it's what was probably expected of me, not because it was something that I felt.

He pursed his lips, holding tight to his hat. "Yes, ma'am," he said. Before I could respond he added, "I know what happens here in Forrest Town when colored men speak to white women, but that's not what happens everywhere."

I knew there had been racial riots in some of the bigger cities, even if Daddy did turn off the radio the minute I walked into the room. Kids at school had talked about civil uprisings, but I'd never seen them, or, I suddenly realized, cared enough about them to ask for details. I lifted my eyebrows in question.

"Yes, ma'am. I serve with white men. Do you think we don't talk?"

"Men, not women," I smirked.

"No, ma'am. I've been to other states. My people talk to white women in other areas."

I was not accustomed to being told I was wrong by a colored man. I thought of Mama—the way she'd hidden her conversation with that woman at the furniture store, and the supplies she'd given her—and it gave me pause. Were there places where that was allowed? Why was it so wrong, anyway? I looked again for Daddy's truck, thinking about *why* I had to *know my place*. What had this man ever done to me?

"Does your mother work at the furniture store?" I asked, wanting to know if he somehow knew Mama.

He cocked his head, as if he were weighing the answer. "Yes, ma'am, her and my aunt."

"Do you know Hillary Tillman, my mama?"

"No, ma'am," he answered.

I was still mulling over my own misgivings about what she'd done, keeping a secret from Daddy and all, but I still wanted to know how Byron Bingham's family was, how Albert was feeling, and how badly he was hurt. I realized, too, that I wanted it not to be a bad thing to want to speak to this man. I measured my fear of him, not the fear that I knew I should have, but the real fear that rattled in my mind. I quickly realized that there wasn't much fear up there. The fear that did exist was driven by my father's warnings, and overpowered by my own curiosity. My chance to get the answers to all of my nagging questions about Mr. Bingham's and Albert's family was staring me in the face, and I wanted to have that conversation more than I wanted anything else in the world, as long as Daddy didn't find out.

"How is he? Albert?"

He took a step toward me. I scooted backward, still sitting on the ground.

"He's beat up real bad, but he'll be okay."

I'm sorry seemed so unsubstantial, so I remained quiet, thinking about that night, the fear I'd felt, and knowing that the fear Albert Johns had felt must've been ten times worse. I took a deep breath and asked him if he knew who had beaten up his brother.

He shook his head. "He's not talkin'."

I let out a relieved sigh, and then felt guilty for wanting to protect Jimmy Lee, Corky, and Jake after what they'd done. "What about your uncle?"

He turned away, his eyes suspiciously glassy when he turned back. His face was tighter, stronger than it had been the moment before. He stared past me, into the fields as he nodded, wringing his hat within his hands.

"I found him, you know." The words were out of my mouth before I had a chance to stop them, and they were oddly wrapped in what sounded like pride. I cringed, wishing I hadn't opened my mouth in the first place.

"That didn't come out right," I offered. "I mean, it was horrible."

"Yes, ma'am. I know you found him." This time his eyes locked with mine.

I came to my feet. Strangely, I wasn't afraid. At that moment, the only thing I felt was a need to talk about the things I wasn't supposed to, with someone who might also want to talk about them, and if that someone was a man I wasn't supposed to talk to, then so be it.

"Let's walk," I said.

He looked at me with curiosity, his eyes jetting around our property. "I'm not sure that's a good idea."

"Maybe not, but I want to talk about Albert and Mr. Bingham. I want to know how your family is, and I'm afraid we can't do that here. I don't know when Daddy will be home." I straightened my skirt. The incident with Jimmy Lee all but forgotten, I pushed away the residual anger that I felt toward him and decided to deal with those awful thoughts some other time.

The young man, who looked to be a little older than Jake, didn't follow me. He put his hat on and said, "I'm sorry, ma'am, but this is Forrest Town. I'm not sure goin' off alone is the best idea."

"Afraid?" I knew it was mean to present such a dare. Maybe even dangerous. I understood what could happen to him if we were caught, and yet, selfishly, I wanted to get my answers.

He bristled, threw his shoulders back, and said, "No, ma'am." Then he looked back up the yard toward the driveway. "Maybe a little," he confessed.

"I won't tell if you won't. C'mon." I grabbed his arm, his muscles tensing beneath my grasp. Doing something so many would see as wrong was exhilarating. I pulled him through the fields, through the line of trees that edged our property, to the creek that ran right through the outskirts of town. Maggie and I had spent hours there when we were young, throwing leaves in and following them downstream as they drifted in the water.

We walked in nervous silence, until we could no longer see the roof of my farmhouse. I pushed away Daddy's warning. My excitement about talking with him was not hampered by fear of what might happen if we were caught. In fact, just the opposite. Elation danced within me! For once I wasn't standing by Jimmy Lee's side, wondering who he'd hurt next. I didn't feel as though I had to hide my face, like I did when I ran into old friends from highschool, because I'd found a dead body. This man was fighting for our country. He wasn't fighting against our own men. He already knew that I'd found his uncle, and he didn't look at me like I was somehow tainted because of it.

"My name is Alison," I said as we walked by the creek.

"I'm Jackson," he answered. He walked a careful distance from me, and I appreciated the space. Each time I glanced at him, he was looking either down or straight ahead. He had a gentle face and full lips. Every so often, lines would form on his forehead, like he was thinking of something important. I wondered how scared he really was, and I wondered why I wasn't.

When we reached the "Y" in the stream, where it bloomed in one direction and narrowed in the other, I leaned against a tree and watched him.

"I'm really sorry about Albert," I said.

Jackson sat down on a big rock near the water's edge. He picked up a stick and poked it in the water. "Yeah," he said, shaking his head. A bead of perspiration spread across his brow.

"So you want to work for Daddy?"

"My family needs the money. I'm home for a week, so—" he shrugged.

I hadn't thought about him going back. "What's it like? The war, I mean? Vietnam?"

He turned to me and something changed in his eyes. They grew darker, more serious. "It's like havin' a million guys all chasin' you at the same time, only they have guns, and so do you, so you can kill them before they kill you. And every day you realize you're damned lucky to have survived." He turned back toward the water and tossed the stick in. "As a matter of fact, it's a lot like livin' here, only here, you're not the one with the guns."

I sat down beside him. He inched away, stiffened. We sat in silence for a few minutes.

"Sorry about your uncle," I whispered. I realized how much death this man must have seen, and it sent a shiver down my spine.

"Me, too," he said. "He was a good man."

"Do you know why he was killed? I've heard rumors about his wife's—indiscretions—but in this town you never know what's true." Rumor had her sleeping with Jimmy Lee's uncle. I had no proof of the truth of that situation, but everyone in town believed it. I leaned on my elbow, watching him fold and unfold his hat.

He nodded, glanced my way, then turned back toward the water.

I waited; each second drew my curiosity about him further toward the surface. I felt my cheeks flush. I was slowly becoming more upset with Daddy, with this town, and with the way people treated one another. This was life. This was what we were given. I knew that if Daddy was here, he'd ask me who I thought I was to think things should be any different, and I wondered what Mama would say. I thought of her face when she came back to the car behind the furniture store, her eyes fastened on the road like it was a path to escape her secret. I wondered what she was thinking at that moment. What would happen if Daddy knew? How long had she been talking to that woman? What started it? Why on earth did she trust me with such a volatile secret?

"You okay?" Jackson asked.

I looked down at my hands, clenched into fists around the edge of my skirt. "Um, yeah," I said. "I'm just thinkin', that's all."

"I got way too much time to think when I'm away."

I nodded, not knowing how to respond to his comment. "How is your aunt?" I watched him carefully, wondering if he'd get mad or lie to me.

"She'll be leavin' after the funeral. Run out of town." He stood and walked a few paces back toward my house, shaking his head.

I watched each determined step, hoping he was not going back. There was still so much I wanted to know. The muscles in his back constricted beneath his uniform. I hurried after him.

"I'm sorry. I shouldn't pry, I'm sorry."

He stopped walking. "It's not you. It's this whole thing, this town. I come back to be with my family and my uncle is dead, my brother is beaten to a pulp—"

I ached for his pain, and touched his arm out of instinct and empathy. His muscles tightened beneath my fingers. I pulled back.

"I'm sorry."

"Don't you see?" his voice rose. "You touch me and we both freeze."

I stepped back. "I'm sorry. I didn't mean anything by it."

"It shouldn't matter if you did. Don't you see that? We can't talk because our skin is different. It's crap. I have seen the other side. I've been places where I can talk to white folks. I come back here and it's like travelin' back in time. It may not be easy or perfect in other cities, but it's not—" He drew his arm wide, like he was presenting the fields beyond where we stood. "It's not like this."

I had no idea what to say, and until that week, I wouldn't have ever agreed with him. But now, everything had changed. My feelings about colored people had changed, and along with that came my inability to accept everything Daddy said as being right.

"I agree with you. It shouldn't matter."

"What?" His eyes grew wide.

"I agree with you. I mean, I'm embarrassed to say it, but I didn't used to. I was taught what everyone else 'round here was taught, that coloreds and whites don't interact—unless they're workin' for you. But I've been thinkin' about everything. You know, coloreds and whites...and it just doesn't make sense to me anymore." I turned my back to him, ashamed and angry. "Findin' your uncle changed me. I see everything differently now. When I found him, I wanted to know who his family was, and why he had to die." I didn't recognize the self-confidence in my own voice, and no matter how firmly I spoke, the words themselves surprised me. "He was a person. His family, your family—they matter."

Jackson walked toward me, each step a force of its own. I stumbled backward. He spoke through gritted teeth. "You want to know why he died? Because some white jackass wanted to sleep with my aunt, and she was too afraid to say no." His nostrils flared with anger.

He stood so close that I could feel his warm breath on my nose. His chest rose and fell, inches from mine. "You have no idea what it's like."

Time stood still. We stood like that for several minutes, listening to each other huff our frustrations away. Eventually he turned away, his shoulders rolled forward. I was too frightened to speak, though, strangely, I was not afraid of him. I was scared for the pain and anger that his family had endured.

"Tell me," I said quietly.

The air around us was quiet, save for the trickle of the creek and the rustling of leaves.

I bit my lower lip, hoping that I wasn't pushing him too far. "Tell me what it's like for you and your family. I want to understand."

Chapter Five

"You missed dinner." My father sat in his reading chair by the front door watching David Brinkley on the evening news on our small black and white television. He motioned to Jake to turn it off as soon as I came in. I usually didn't notice that small sheltering act. I was so used to it, it was like the white noise of a fan. Today it stood out like a sore thumb and I resented Daddy for the first time in my life. I heard Mama washing dishes in the kitchen, and guilt settled around my grumbling resentment toward Daddy for thinking he could keep me from knowing what's going on in the world. Between the guilt and the resentment, I felt strangled, and struggled to maintain my sense of normalcy within my family.

"Yes, sir. I'm sorry. I was out for a walk." I looked down at the worn hardwood beneath my feet and concentrated on the uneven lines between the boards.

"Your mother said she didn't see you after you came back from your visit with Jimmy Lee today. Everything alright?" he asked.

I lifted my eyes and took in Daddy sitting in his favorite upholstered chair. Daddy worked long days, and by this time of night everything looked slightly askew, from his dirty, gray t-shirt to his five o'clock shadow which grew in uneven patches of blond and brown. His hair had an indentation all the way around from the baseball cap he favored when he was out in the sun, like a halo had slipped and gotten stuck in his thick, buttery hair.

Jake turned off the television, sat back down on our plaid couch, and put an open textbook in his lap. His knuckles were black and blue. He noticed my gaze, and tucked them under his book. Working on a farm, Daddy and Mama wouldn't think anything about Jake's bruised knuckles. I knew better. Jake raised his eyebrows, as if he were challenging me to reveal what he'd done. I smirked in return, contemplating my answers. *Yes, I met a colored man and don't understand why I shouldn't talk to him.* Or, I could go with something a bit more detailed, *Jimmy Lee made me do somethin' I didn't want to, so I hid from Mama, and met a man who I know I'm not allowed to talk to, but I sure want to.* Or, I could expose Jake for what he must've done. I wondered how Daddy might react if he knew Jake had caused his farmhand not to show up for work, though I secretly feared that Daddy might praise him for what he'd see as an indiscretion. Instead, I went with a safe answer.

"Yes, Daddy. It was just such a nice night that, after Jimmy Lee dropped me off, I went for a walk. I won't miss dinner again. I'm sorry."

"It's not a problem. Just makin' sure you're okay," he answered.

Mama walked out from the kitchen, wiping her hands on a dishtowel. Mama, Jake, and I had the exact same shade of blond hair, like cornhusks kissed by the sun. Tonight hers was swept away from her face with a red and white paisley scarf. She looked beautiful, even if tired. I waited for my reprimand, and when she didn't chide me for missing dinner, I wondered how so much could have changed in the span of just a few hours. I guessed that holding Mama's secret had a few benefits that I was only beginning to discover.

"Maggie's comin' home," she said with a wide grin.

"When? Oh, Mama, can I go to get her at the train station with you, please?" I begged.

"Settle down, Pix," Daddy said. "She's not comin' until Friday, and your mama will be needin' you to help her prepare supper."

"But Daddy, I can miss—"

"Now, now. You'll help your mama, just like always. Jake'll go with me."

I bit back my frustration. I no longer wanted to be treated like a child. The world was out there and I'd had a taste of understanding what I hadn't cared enough to even think about before finding poor Mr. Bingham. Doesn't that count for something? I had to remind myself that, for Mama and Daddy, nothing had changed. Mama might have shared her secret with me, but I was still their sheltered daughter who believed whatever her daddy told her.

Mama nodded, as if to tell me to agree. I was enjoying this sudden collusion between us. Mama and I were close when it came to baking and fixing meals, but watching her and Maggie always stoked the jealousy bug in me. I was glad that I was the one Mama trusted with this secret.

"Yes, sir," I said.

Daddy reached for my hand and winked. "That's my girl," he said.

"Daddy, I have to study. I can't go." Jake purposefully shook his bangs into his eyes, hiding from looking into Daddy's eyes. He blamed Maggie for our father not allowing him to go away to school, and I knew he carried too much resentment to want to drop whatever he was doing and go pick her up. He thought that Daddy had used all of his money on her education instead of his, but to me it was clearly more than that. Maggie was more aggressive than Jake; besides having perfect grades, she possessed a mouthiness that was hard to ignore. She would've been like a caged tiger if she'd stayed here in town, whereas Jake fared just fine as a typical Forrest Town boy—from what I'd seen lately, a little too well.

I climbed the stairs to my bedroom on the second floor and thought about all that I had learned over the past twenty-four hours. I thought about Jackson, and all that he'd said. He'd described what it was like for him when he'd left; *I was scared to death of bein' in the military with them white folks.* He had no idea what to expect. Jackson only knew what he'd grown up with in Forrest Town—segregation to the nth degree. When he'd told me that, sadness took hold of my heart in a way that I never thought I'd feel for a colored boy. I just wanted to reach out and hug him, steal that fear away from him. The military had opened his eyes to the ways of the world outside of Arkansas. The white guys he'd met were from all over the world, right out of high school, like he'd been when he'd enlisted three years earlier, and some much older than him. They told him stories of integrated areas and he'd said that at first he didn't believe them. His eyes grew wide when he told me this, and he got me thinking, wondering what it would be like in those places, and if it could possibly be true. He thought they were pulling his leg, too, making fun because he was colored. He quickly came to see otherwise. He said that when they're fighting, it's as if every soldier were color-blind—unless you were Vietnamese.

Though it was cool outside, my small bedroom was warm and welcoming. My bedroom has always been a safe place for me. Probably because I shared it with Maggie for so many years. Maggie's bed was on my left when I walked in, untouched since she'd gone back to school after her holiday break. My bed was across from Maggie's, with our small desk to the right. I walked over to open the window at the foot of my bed. Then, I sat down, looking at the photographs we'd taped to our wall throughout the years, and wishing things could go back to how they were before she'd gone away. Life had been so easy. We went to school, came home and played, and were oblivious to the inequities of life. What might it be like to be so far away from home, away from the eyes of Forrest Town? I wondered. I lay back on my pillow and thought about how Mr. Bingham had died because he'd tried to defend his wife's honor. Jackson said his mama told him that Mr. Bingham had confronted Billy Carlisle and told him to leave his wife alone. That was eight hours before he'd disappeared.

Clara Bingham was also threatened that night, by Billy's wife, or at least that's what Clara told Jackson's mama. Clara had been in hiding ever since, somewhere Jackson wouldn't reveal, with plans to leave town for good as soon as Mr. Bingham's body was safely put to rest. She'd waited to hold the funeral until Mr. Bingham's brother could come into town from Mississippi.

I wondered what Daddy would do if the tables were turned, and some colored man held the power to make Mama do things she didn't want to. Would he defend her honor and die in the process? I knew the answer and the thought of losing Daddy only made my heart ache even more for Clara.

The more I thought about the family, and the impending funeral, the more I wanted to attend the service. But I knew that telling them I was sorry for their loss and standing with them, without shame, to hear the final words before his body was laid to rest, wouldn't make up for the loss of his life. Of course, I wouldn't dare attend. The chance I'd taken that evening with Jackson was ten times worse than anything I'd ever done before, and yet, it didn't feel one ounce wrong to me.

A knock on my door brought my thoughts back home.

"Come in."

My door pushed open and Mama stood in the hallway. She glanced toward the stairs, and then slipped inside, closing the door behind her.

"Hey, honey," she said, and perched herself on the edge of Maggie's bed, her hands folded in her lap. I sat up, smoothed my skirt, and crossed my ankles, as she did.

"Hi, Mama. I'm sorry I missed dinner."

She shook her head. "That's okay. I'm not here about that."

She adjusted herself on Maggie's bed, then came to sit beside me. She took my hand, and I knew for sure I was in trouble.

"Honey," she began, "you know I'd never go against your father's beliefs if it wasn't very important, right?"

I nodded, afraid to breathe. She'd let me in on her secret, now what? She began rubbing the back of my hand.

"Well, you know I love your father, no matter what I tell you, right?"

I nodded again, wanting to shove my fingers in my ears and yell, *Na na na na na, I can't hear you!* Even though I was enjoying the secret between us, I sort of wanted to keep the image of my mama as I'd always seen her, as a woman with no secrets. Learning her secrets put me in a place of keeping more secrets from Daddy. Although it was getting easier to do, I found doing it a bit scary, like I was driving a wedge between us.

She dropped my hand and lifted my chin with her finger, looking deep into my eyes. "I shouldn't have brought you with me this mornin'. I was upset. It was wrong." She took a deep breath, then continued. "The thought of that sweet boy bein' beaten—" She turned away.

I wrapped my right hand in my left, excited and nervous about this newly forged relationship that was growing between us.

"Does Daddy know how you feel?"

She looked at me again, and shook her head.

So many questions rattled around in my head, I didn't know where to start. Talking to Jackson gave me strength. He had been just as relieved to get his anger off his chest as I'd been to talk about what I'd been feeling. I took a deep breath, sat up straight, and asked Mama if she'd brought the woman things before.

"No. There was no need." Her eyebrows drew together. "Until now."

"Who is she?" I asked.

"She's Albert's mother. Millie Johns."

"How long have you known her?"

"I'm not gonna lie to you, Alison. I've known her for as long as Albert has worked for us. His mother sought me out, one day, while I was in town shoppin'. She told me that Albert was her youngest." Mama laughed under her breath, in a way that I read to be some sort of a secret joke that only another mother might understand. "Her older son was away at war, the others had moved away from Forrest Town, and Albert was all she had left."

"But why would she seek you out? Why would she do that?"

Tension drained from Mama's shoulders. She cocked her head and looked at me with so much love it made my heart ache. She brushed my hair away from my face, and said, with so much emotion that I wanted to crawl into her lap, "Because when you have children, you'll do anything to keep them safe."

Chapter Six

The next morning, I lay in bed listening to Daddy make his way toward the stairs. He peeked into my room, as he always did, and on the occasion I was awake, he winked at me. Today he blew a kiss my way and headed down the creaking stairs. I tried to go back to sleep, but half an hour later I was still too wound up from the evening before. I got up and rushed through my morning routine—showered, brushed my hair and teeth, chose my outfit.

Mama was in the kitchen when I came downstairs. "You're up early. Are you hungry?"

Only for more information. "No, thank you. Where's Jake?" I asked.

"He was headin' into town before school. He already left."

I thought of the bruises on his knuckles, the way he'd followed Jimmy Lee into that fight like a puppy vying for attention. The muscles in my neck pulled tight. "He's never 'round anymore."

"That's what happens when children grow up." Mama sounded sad. I felt bad for her, but was lost within my own emotional hayride. "Are you gonna see Jimmy Lee later, before he goes back to Mississippi?"

"No, he's leavin' too early." Guilt pushed at my heart, but I didn't let it in. Jimmy Lee had hurt me, emotionally and physically, and he was the last person I wanted to see. After what he'd done to Albert, I wasn't sure I could ever look at him in the same way.

I stood and walked to the window, staring into the fields. The farmhands were taking a break, sprawled out on the grass at the edge of the field. I thought about telling Mama about Jackson coming to work later that afternoon instead of Albert, but was afraid to reveal my secret.

"I'm goin' outside to wait for Daddy. He's runnin' me into town to pick up more of that molasses. He loved those cookies."

"Your father has a meetin' at the bank this mornin'," Mama said.

"Yes, ma'am, I know. He said I could take the bus back home. I'm stoppin' at the library anyway. He'll probably beat me back home." I kissed Mama's cheek. "Love you," I said, and headed for the door.

The morning air was chilly, and as I sat in the rocking chair, the smell of dew-soaked grass in the air, I considered the farmhands showing up at five in the morning. How cold they must have been during the fall, and scorching hot in the summertime. There must have been many times that they were too tired or sick to come to work, but out of fear of being fired, they showed up anyway. I wondered what Jackson's family was doing right then. Were they sitting around a kitchen table crying in anticipation of the impending funeral? Or perhaps they were reminiscing about the life of Mr. Bingham. I thought about Clara, hiding out wherever she might be, her life altered in a way she may never recover from.

I thought of Jackson and my stomach tightened. Could he be killed for being alone with me? I wasn't sure, though from what Jimmy Lee did to Albert—broken ribs and countless contusions—I'm sure that wasn't so far fetched. When Jackson and I had left each other the evening before, he followed the stream in the opposite direction of our property to the end of town, and I went back home the way we'd come. How hard must it be to live every moment watching over your shoulder for something as natural as just being alive?

"You're early, Pix." My father climbed the porch steps, his stained t-shirt and overalls a wicked mess of dirt. That's when the guilt hit me. As much as I disliked his disregard for the colored farmhands, I was still a Daddy's girl, and I wanted nothing more than for him to reach out and pat my head, as he always did.

He held his palms up. "Been fixin' the tractor. Think your mama will mind?" he asked.

"I think Mama'll tell you to hose off out back," I laughed.

"You're probably right," he said as he touched my head. "I'll be ready in twenty minutes."

As he walked inside, I looked up at the clear sky, glad there was no rain in the forecast. Our family's income relied on the farm, and too much rain could wipe out our crops. My father listened to the weather on the radio every morning. The familiar tinny sounds made their way upstairs to my room. Some mornings I'd lay in my bed and listen, trying to nod back off, until Mama woke me an hour later. When Maggie was still home, on really cold mornings, I'd crawl into bed with her and steal her warmth.

I spent hours milling about the library, reading the backs of so many books I couldn't keep track. I loved to sit between the rows of shelves, pulling book after book into my lap, and taking my time nosing through them, looking for the one that held voices that called out to me in a way I couldn't turn away from. I'd run my fingers over the covers imagining what I'd find inside. I was struck by how different I was from Maggie, who'd snag two or three books, leaf through the first few pages, and be ready to leave. To me, each book held the promise of a secret world, and disappearing into that world is simply delicious.

Later that afternoon, the bus dropped me off two blocks from our house. I carried my library books down the long dirt road, the tips of my shoes covered in dust. I heard the pedaling of a bike behind me, and I walked to the edge of the road to let it pass.

Jackson pulled up next to me and dropped his feet from the pedals. I whipped my head around, making sure no one was watching. If Daddy had found out about us meeting, he'd be sorely disappointed in me. I worried about him coming around the corner in his truck and scooping me right off the road. God only knew what he'd do to Jackson. The thought sent a shiver up my spine. Luckily, there was no one in sight right then. My nerves were afire with trepidation, and something else that I hadn't felt in quite some time—anticipation? As wrong as it might be, every time I thought of our first meeting, I got hot all over, like blushing gone haywire. There was no mistaking the growing attraction within me, but I knew I needed to get my feeling's in check and get back on track with what Daddy was expecting of me.

It took all my strength to continue walking. "We can't talk," I said, and walked faster toward home. The last thing his family needed was more trouble.

He stepped off his bike and hurried beside me. "Meet me later?"

I wanted so badly to know how the funeral went, if his aunt had escaped town safely. I didn't respond to him.

"Please?"

I glanced up and saw the same kindness that I'd seen the day before, the same open, hopeful smile, so different than what I'd seen in Jimmy Lee lately.

"Where?" I asked.

"Same place, by the creek. Later, after I work for your dad."

"It's too dangerous." My heart slammed against my chest. I stole a glance at him, still walking as fast as I could. His smile slowly sank, his lips pressed into a disappointed line.

"You're the first person 'round here who—oh, never mind." He climbed back up on his bike, his muscular thighs bursting against his dark work pants. "I guess you are just like everyone else."

I watched him pedal away, dirt kicking up behind him in a billowing puff of smoke. I hugged my books to my chest, wishing I'd agreed to meet him.

By the time I reached my house, Jackson was already helping Daddy in the barn. His bicycle lay sideways across the grass next to Daddy's truck. I went around the back of the house and found Mama taking clothes off of the drying line and humming a little tune. I plucked a few of the clothespins off of Daddy's t-shirts and laid them in the basket, watching her move through her chores as she had every day of my life. Had I not known her secret, I'd never have pictured Mama doing anything more than tending to our meals, clothing, and school needs. Mama was becoming someone else right before my eyes, and I wondered what other secrets she held. The more I thought about what I might not know about her, the more I wanted to share my burdens with her.

"Mama?" I asked tentatively. "What if you knew who hurt Albert Johns? Would you do somethin' about it?"

She stopped humming, her eyes shot to the barn and back. When she answered, her voice was very quiet. I leaned in close to hear her.

"That wouldn't do any good. There's no punishment for beatin' up a colored boy."

Or killin' a colored man. "But, how would you live with yourself? Knowin' what someone had done and that they didn't get punished?"

Again her eyes shot across our property. She folded the sheet she had been holding and came to my side. Mama took my hand in hers and walked me around to the other side of the house, out of sight from the barn. She reached in her apron pocket and pulled out an elastic band, wrapped it expertly around her fingers, then gathered her hair behind the nape of her neck, and fastened it in one quick movement.

"Honey, no justice will be served for this. There's nothin' we can do or say that will make this attack be justly punished." Again, she eyed the barn. "I shouldn't have taken you with me. It was wrong of me. Please, if you do one thing, please just live your life and forget about this nonsense."

"It's not nonsense, Mama, and I can't even believe you are callin' it that."

Mama remained quiet for so long, I feared I'd be punished for talking back to her. When she looked back into my eyes, I saw so much more there than anger. They were drenched in defeat.

"Honey, you're too young to understand the dangers that make up this kind of thing."

"I'm not, Mama." I paced beside her, adrenaline rushing through my veins. I had never stood up to either of my parents before, but I couldn't stop myself. "Do you think that just because you and Daddy turn off the radio I don't hear about what's happenin' in the world? Look at Mr. Bingham. He was murdered and the police didn't even care." The honesty felt good, even if it scared the hell out of me.

"Alison, lower your voice." Mama peered around the side of the house toward the barn. "Please, just keep yourself out of this mess. You have a good life ahead of you. Marry Jimmy Lee, have children, let this kind of thing work itself out."

"Work itself out? Well, can I do what you did? Can I help them?"

"No." She didn't hesitate or soften her tone. Mama grabbed my arm and squeezed tight. She'd never before laid a hand on me. She meant business, and it frightened me. "You are never to do what I did, do you hear me? Alison Jean, promise me."

I tried to pull my arm away, but as confident as I had suddenly become, I had no strength to back it up. I relented. "Okay, I promise." In my mind, I was already planning my traipse down to the creek, more determined than ever to see how Jackson's family was holding up. I knew in my heart that I was doing the right thing, and though Mama feared for me, and was probably correct in doing so, I had to do what I felt was right.

I helped Mama with the dishes, nervously looking for Jackson through the window. He had no way of knowing that I would meet him. I'd denied that I would, after all. A plan formed in my mind. While Daddy listened to the radio in the other room, and Mama finished the dishes, I stepped out on the porch where I'd left my library books. I grabbed a pencil, tore a piece of paper from my notebook, and scribbled, *I will be there.* Then I peeked in the window to make sure Daddy was still seated in his chair, which he was, and I ran out to where Jackson's bike was laying on the ground. My hands shook as I lifted the seat and tucked the slip of paper underneath. I hoped he'd understand what the note meant, and I hoped we wouldn't get caught.

Chapter Seven

The sun hovered just above the horizon, illuminating the sky in beautiful shades of blue, purple, and pink. I had been waiting for Jackson, watching the sun set, and was ready to give up when I felt, more than heard, him behind me. My heartbeat sped up and set my legs trembling. I turned around and my eyes lingered over his sweat-laden muscles pressing against his drenched t-shirt. I felt a blush creeping up my cheeks, and I was powerless to move. The air between us was suddenly thick, uncomfortable.

"You came?" he asked in a low voice.

I nodded, feeling the heat of his gaze, the same longing desire I was trying so desperately to hide. I turned away and sat down on a wide tree stump, hoping to quell the heat on my cheeks. He knelt at the creek bed and washed his hands in the fresh water.

"Did it go okay?" I asked.

He looked back and that heat of attraction hit me again. I smoothed my skirt, then patted my hair, worrying about if I looked pretty enough. I didn't know what to do with the feelings I was having. The same heart racing excitement I'd felt for Jimmy Lee so long ago, only something deeper. I wasn't only interested in Jackson's looks, like I was with Jimmy Lee at first. I wanted to know everything about Jackson. I wanted to touch him, take my time, savor the feel of his hand, our fingers interlaced. I wanted him to whisper my name in my ear and set my nerves on end. I looked away, embarrassed. What I wanted was so wrong that it was even more exciting. *What on earth was I doin'?*

"Your pop's real nice," he said.

My heart sunk. *My father will kill me.*

"Albert should be back by next week, when I leave."

Another kick to my heart. He was leaving.

Jackson wiped his hands on his pants and sat on the stump next to me. My senses were in overdrive. Goose bumps rose on my arms. My hands fiddled like nervous fish in my lap. *Stop over dramatizin' things.* Surely I was just mad at Jimmy Lee, confused, but I could not deny the desire to relax my shoulder, to let it touch his. Was I turning into one of those easy girls Jimmy Lee talked about?

"How was the funeral?" I asked, trying to stop thinking about the richness of the color of his skin, the way it glistened with sweat, so smooth I wanted to touch it.

"Sad. My aunt was there, and no one bothered her. I guess they figured they'd done enough, killin' her husband and runnin' her out of town. And now she's gone."

Reality appeared in the form of Byron Bingham's bloated face in my mind. I shivered, the former heat of attraction lost in reality. "Where will she live?"

He shrugged. "What does it matter? She's lived here for thirty years, now she doesn't." He clenched his teeth, the muscles in his jaw pulsated. "I think she went to Mississippi with my other relatives."

"Then at least she won't be alone." I had the urge to soothe him. If he were one of the guys I had known during school I'd probably have put my arm around him and told him it would all be okay, but there was an invisible line between us, and I was afraid to cross it.

He turned to face me, the sound of the water trickling fell away, his breathing filling each pulse of my heart. I was unable to resist the urge to be closer, if only by emotional pull. I turned my shoulders toward him and lifted my gaze. Our eyes held.

"True," he said, wringing his hands.

I watched his lips move, heard his words, but my mind was working what it might feel like to kiss him, what it might taste like. I stumbled over my words, finally asking, "And Albert? How is he?" A tingling sensation traveled up my arms again. I inched away from him, hoping to slow my racing heart.

"He's hurtin', but good. Scared. You know." He sighed, a long, loud sigh, his eyes looking at me, my own desires reflecting back. He pushed up from the stump, turning his back to me like he, too, was fighting an urge more powerful than he could manage. "Life in Forrest Town. It is what it is."

"So when you're done, with the war, I mean, where will you go?" I spoke just above a whisper, afraid of the answer. "Will you come back here?"

He laughed, but it wasn't a real laugh. It was more of something that I read to mean that he wasn't stupid enough to come back, no matter what he might be leaving behind. "Not if I can help it. My friend Arthur invited me to New York, said he could get me a good job there. A real job, not in the fields or maintenance work, like what I could get here."

He held his hand out to help me off the stump. I took his hand and stood, holding my breath, not knowing if I should let go or hold on. I wanted to hold on. He withdrew his hand, and I swear his eyes lingered on mine for a second. Then again, my heart was beating so hard I might have just imagined it.

We walked side by side along the bank of the creek. Each step measured, each breath calculated, so I could feel the energy that rode between us like an invisible tie.

"How's your mama doin'. I can't imagine what she's goin' through. My mama would be a mess."

"She's thinkin' that she's thankful that your mother is kind, even if your father is—" He wiped his forehead with his arm and sighed. "Even if your father is just like everyone else."

"You know about that? About my mama?"

He put his hands on his hips and said, "Sure I know. I'm real thankful, too. Your mama is a really good person."

Fear suddenly gripped my chest. "Oh no, who else knows?"

"No one who's gonna say anything."

I crossed my arms and paced, my skirt swished in the silence. "No one can know about my mama," I said. "I can't even think about what could happen to her." My voice rose, my words tumbled out fast and harsh. "You don't understand. If Daddy finds out, he'll—"

He put his hands gently on my upper arms. Even through my sweater my skin warmed beneath his palms. He looked into my eyes and spoke just above a whisper. "Hey, hey. Did you forget who you're talkin' to? I *do* understand. If anyone does, I do. My brother, Mama, my aunt. We all do."

I don't know why I did what I did next. He didn't pull me forward. He didn't push me away. My body relaxed into him and it felt like the most natural motion in the world. I leaned into his chest, my head resting on his sweat-damp shirt. He smelled of hay and perspiration. His chest trembled beneath my cheek, his hands moved slowly around me, coming to rest, hot and sure, on my lower back. I closed my eyes, feeling his heart pound against my cheek. Tears burned at the edges of my eyes. The warmth of his body and the tenderness of his touch were so different than when Jimmy Lee held me. With Jimmy Lee I was an afterthought, an imposition in his precious day, or a means to a climactic end. Jackson welcomed me, drank me in. He didn't rush my need for comfort or push me away. He didn't throw me down and push into me. He simply held me, as if I belonged right where I was.

Chapter Eight

Friday afternoon, Maggie pushed through the front door wearing clothes I didn't recognize, and an expression to match. There was tension in her smile, and her normally laughing eyes were different, more serious. I rushed into her arms, and she swung me around.

"Pixie! Oh, how I missed you." She set me down, held my shoulders, and pushed away from me, surveying me from head to toe. "Girl, you are one pretty, little thing! Gosh, look at you, all grown up!" She pushed my blond waves from my shoulder and cupped my cheek. "When you were little, one bat of those blue eyes used to get you everything you wanted from Daddy. I bet now they worry him somethin' fierce. Boys must look at you everywhere you go."

My cheeks burned. "I missed you."

She grabbed my hand and touched my engagement ring. She squeezed my hand and said, "You're sure about this?"

"Waddaya mean?" I asked, wondering if I was wearing the changes in my feelings on my sleeve. Could she see the difference in me as clearly as I could feel it?

"I haven't seen you since you got engaged. Someone needs to look out for my little sister." She squinted. "So, are you sure?"

I'd been meeting Jackson down by the creek for several days, and though we had never embraced again, I was fully aware of my growing attraction toward his gentle nature and his knowledge of the world, which was so much bigger than mine. I found myself sitting on the stairs listening to the news on the radio in the evenings. I wanted to answer Maggie with the truth: *Not really. He's different than he was, and my heart is pullin' me toward someone else.* Instead, aware of our parents watching us, I said, "Yeah, and Daddy says he has a promisin' future."

"Of course he does," Maggie feigned a smile in his direction.

"Enough of this. Come over here and give me a hug." Mama's cheeks were plumped up, pink with happiness. She opened her arms wide, and Maggie sank into them. They could have been sisters. I wished I had the beauty that they possessed. I wasn't ugly, but they had a certain something that shined through dirt, worry, and fatigue. *One day*, I hoped. One day, I'd find that beauty in myself.

"Pants?" Jake smirked.

"They're all the rage in New York, little brother." Maggie twirled in a circle, hands by her head. She looked down at her slim figure in cotton pants that tapered to the knee then flared at the bottom. "It's a whole different world out there, Jakey-poo."

Pants? Jakey-poo? It was like listening to Maggie, only bigger—more outspoken than before—and she had an air of not caring what we thought. My eyes shot to Daddy, whose arms were crossed, his right hand rubbing his chin. I had a feeling that he was trying to figure her out just as I was. I was definitely intrigued.

Mama had baked a meatloaf, fresh biscuits, and green beans. Maggie's favorite.

"Tell me about New York." I was excited to hear about the big city. She was so far away and all I could think about was how scared I'd be, moving away from Mama and Daddy and starting a life without knowing they were right around the corner.

Maggie's eyes lit up. "It's like nothin' you've ever seen. There are a million people, and I swear the noise never stops." Maggie poked at the vegetables. She had yet to take a bite.

"Do you have many friends?" I asked. Sometimes I wondered if it was easier to make new friends than to try and reignite friendships with those I'd left behind because of dating someone older. I wasn't even sure I'd want to rekindle those relationships, given how much I'd changed. Reinventing yourself to be seen as the person you wanted to be, rather than the person everyone had known since the day you were born, sounded exciting to me—and terribly scary.

"Does she ever not?" Jake smirked. My parents gave him a *not now* look. "What? Well, doesn't she?"

"That's enough, Jake," Daddy said. "Maggie, tell us about your classes. Are you learnin' a lot?"

She nodded, drawing her eyebrows together, as if she were thinking. She looked at Jake and said, "I have lots of friends. Everyone is real nice."

"That's good, honey," Mama said, and patted Maggie's arm.

Maggie tilted her eyes toward Mama and smiled.

"How about your classes, Maggie?"

Maggie set her fork down. She looked at Daddy, pulled her shoulders back, and said, "They're alright, Daddy." Her words were flat. I detected a lie.

Tension thickened in the room.

"Grades? Are you doin' okay?" he asked, staring into her eyes.

She held his gaze. "Yes, I'm doin' fine." Maggie picked up her fork again, dropping her eyes to her plate. I watched her draw in a deep breath and blow it out slowly through her full lips. "There's so much more to New York than school and grades, and there's so much more to life, Daddy."

The room grew silent. I watched Daddy's face tighten. I looked at Maggie, flabbergasted. What was she doing? I knew our parents had saved every penny to send Maggie to New York, and Daddy had fought sending her "into the big city" with ferocity. Maggie had been too much for him. She knew when to turn on the charm, "Don't worry, Daddy, I'll make you proud," and when to push, "Come on, Daddy, what's wrong with a woman gettin' an education?" In the end, I think Daddy got tired of fighting and let her go.

My father cleared his throat. "Meanin'?" he asked.

"Meanin'—" Maggie's eyes danced around the room, much to my chagrin, they settled on me. I loved Maggie but I hated being pitted between her and Daddy, and somehow, things always ended up that way. I played with my fork, holding her stare. The air electrified between us. I knew nothing good was about to happen. Maggie's lips spread into a wide grin. "There's so much goin' on out there. Music, clothin'," she grasped the edge of the table with both hands, her voice rising in excitement. "People. The people are talkin', livin' like they love life, sharin' time, information." She turned to face our father, shaking her head. "This town, Daddy," she laughed under her breath. "It's...it's way behind the times—"

"That's enough Maggie," he interrupted her.

Maggie stood up, then walked around the table and stood behind my chair, grabbing my shoulders with both hands. Her grip was strong, thrilling. "Things are happenin', Pix, big things. Things you could never imagine."

"Like you losin' your mind?" Jake laughed.

"Margaret Lynn, sit back down." My father's voice was calm, steady, forceful. Mama sat in silence, the edges of her lips slightly raised, her pride-filled eyes on Maggie, her napkin clenched in her hand. I shook in my seat, afraid of what Daddy might say. I had no idea what Maggie meant by the things she said, but I wanted to know so badly that I had to clench my teeth to remain silent.

Maggie walked around the table, swinging her hands dramatically from side to side, her chin tilted upward. "There's a whole world out there. I know you've heard about it," she lowered her chin and locked eyes with our father. "On the radio?"

"I said that's enough Margaret." If fumes could come from a person's ears, the dining room would have been filled with smoke.

"Civil rights," she said, as if she were answering her own question

Civil rights? Civil rights was not a topic discussed in the Tillman household. We knew what we heard on the radio in those moments before Daddy turned it off. Daddy was quick to shoot down our questions. *Things are just fine 'round here. We don't need no trouble brought on by some trouble-makin' coloreds. When somethin's not broke, why fix it?* I knew there were marches and speeches going on in other places, and Jake and I knew better than to ask questions or bring up what we'd heard in school or picked up by scanning the newspapers. Maggie was another story. She reveled in challenging Daddy.

Maggie leaned against her chair, watching Daddy with a dare in her eyes. Tension thickened in the small room. Silence ensued, until finally Maggie looked like she might burst.

"The civil rights movement is on, Daddy, and—" She drew out the word "on" like it was magnified.

"That's it, Margaret Lynn. I'll have no more of this disrespect." My father threw his napkin on the table and stood up.

"You can't shelter them forever, Daddy," Maggie taunted him.

I cringed.

"There's a whole world out there, and they should know about it. They should live it, Daddy."

My father grabbed Maggie by the arm and dragged her outside. We remained at the table. Mama cleared her throat, wiped her mouth with her napkin, and lowered her eyes. A piece of me wished she'd stand up for Maggie, but I knew if there was one thing Daddy didn't stand for it was disrespect, and if Mama had spoken up, Lord only knew what argument might follow. I'd been watching Mama carefully since seeing her with Albert's mother, and I'd decided that she picked her battles. She may have been one of the smartest women I knew, and at that moment, while Daddy yelled at Maggie out on the front porch, and Maggie yelled back, I wished she'd taught Maggie that same tact. I don't think I could have left the table if I wanted to. No one spoke to Daddy that way. Daddy wasn't a hitting man, but the threat of losing Daddy's favor was enough to usually keep my words in check. Being in Daddy's favor was like having the sun shine down on you, radiating with warmth and smothered in love. Mama and Jake never sassed him, either. Mama was just raised that way, and I think Jake took his cue like I did, from whatever lay behind Daddy's eyes when he was angry—a silent threat that hung in the air, and though I was never quite sure what was at the end of that threat, I was afraid for Maggie.

That evening, as Daddy listened to the news on the radio and Mama read on the couch, Maggie and I remained in our room. Maggie paced, her arms crossed, her face tight.

"As much as I love comin' home to see you, Pix, I hate comin' here because of how backwards this town is." She didn't give me a chance to respond. "Daddy wants to keep you here." She grabbed my left hand. "Marry you off." She pushed my hand into my lap and paced again. "It's just...there's so much—"

"Haven't you learned your lesson yet, sis? Daddy's gonna come up here and whoop your tail." Jake stood in the doorframe, arms crossed.

Maggie spun around. "My lesson? Is that what you think this is about Jake? You're just as bad as Daddy. Do you think I don't know what you do out there?" Her hand shot out toward the window.

Jake clenched his jaw.

"Huh? Do you? You think you're some groovy guy because you follow the other thugs in this town, beatin' up coloreds and laughin' while you walk away."

Jake came away from the doorframe and stood tall, squinting at Maggie, his jaw muscles working overtime.

"It's not right, Jake. And look," she pointed at me.

I opened my eyes wide. *Me?* As much as I loved Maggie, I didn't want Daddy yelling at me like that. *Please leave me out of this.*

"Look at her, think of her," Maggie continued. "Do you really want her to have a life like," she paused, and then continued just above a whisper, "like Mama? Caterin' to some man her whole life? Alison is smarter than that. She's got her whole life ahead of her."

"She's not that smart." His eyes never left Maggie's. As much as his comment hurt, I knew Jake was aching inside by Maggie's comment, since Daddy had kept him home. I swallowed my own feelings in hopes of the whole hurtful conversation blowing over.

"I know you hate me because they sent me to school, Jake, but the truth is, they didn't send me over you. They sent me to get rid of me. I'm nothin' but a pain to Daddy. You," she rubbed her forehead, "you're his meal ticket when he's old and can no longer run the farm. You're plenty smart enough to go to school outside of this crappy place, but he'll never let you go."

Jake's eyes changed from angry to interested in the space of a second. Maggie sat down on her bed, and covered her face. I thought she was crying, until she lifted her face from her hands and I saw her reddened cheeks and a fierce look in her eye.

"I have to get out of here." She stood up and began throwing her clothes into her suitcase.

"What? Why? You can't leave," Jake said.

I grabbed her arm, alarm bells going off in my head. I needed her. "Maggie, please don't go. You just got here. Just stay, please." *I have no one to confide in.*

She shook me off and backed onto my bed, then pulled me down beside her. Jake sat down on Maggie's bed, breathing hard, like he was ready to jump up and stop her if she tried to leave.

"Pixie, I know you don't get this, and I know you are probably scared to leave this place, but trust me, please." Her eyes bore into my heart. "You're too young to get married. This isn't Mama's generation. You can get an education, have a life other than this, more than this."

I looked from her to Jake. Deep creases ran across Jake's forehead. He fidgeted with his hands in his lap. I looked back at Maggie, not sure what I felt, what I should say. So, instead, I remained quiet. Maggie filled the silence.

"Look at me," she pleaded. "In New York, coloreds and whites talk, on the streets, in the shops. It's not like here. Women are not only homemakers or garment workers, they're secretaries and they work in the stores. They go out and dance. They don't sit around on some dirty, old farm waitin' for the next rainstorm to create chaos in their lives, or walk down the aisle at seventeen."

"Eighteen," I whispered.

"Eighteen. Pfft." Maggie drew in a deep breath and blew it out loudly. "Do you love him? I mean really love him? Does he make your stomach quake, even now, after two years? Do you long to see him when you're apart?"

I was afraid to answer honestly.

"Do you?"

I felt Jake's eyes on me, and worried that he'd run and tell Jimmy Lee if I told the truth. "I don't know."

"What?" Maggie asked.

"I don't know, okay? It's just...he's all I know." I stood up and went to the window, thinking about Jackson's arms wrapped around me. I hadn't even kissed him, and yet I still felt a longing to see him that was stronger than I'd felt for Jimmy Lee in a long time. "Sometimes, he does things I don't like," I said. *Like beatin' up Albert and makin' me do things I don't want to.* I let out a relieved sigh. It was out there in the open, someone besides me heard what was rattling around inside my head.

Jake's eyes were as wide as a child's seeing Santa Claus come down the chimney.

"Please, Jake, don't say anything. Please?"

Maggie grabbed his arm. "If you say one word, I will kill you."

"Maggie!" I said.

"Quiet, Pix. This is important. This is your entire life. If you love him and know it here," she thumped her chest, "then I'll shut up. But if you don't, there's no way you're gonna marry him, unless it's over my dead body."

"Dramatic, don't you think?" Jake pulled his arm from her grip.

"You don't get it, Jake. Once she's married, she's stuck."

Was she going to break up me and Jimmy Lee? Was she fixing to try to call off my wedding that was taking place in two months? I twirled the ring on my finger. Fear gripped my heart. My father would be furious.

"I said, *I don't know,*" I interjected. "Maybe I do want to marry him." I went back to the window, breathing fast and hard, my palms sweating against the wooden sill. The moon shone high in the sky, and my mind sought the image of Jackson, the nubby thickness of his hair, the softness of his eyes. Jackson and I had developed a system. If I were able to meet him right after he was off work, I'd leave my library books on the front porch, and if I had to meet him after supper, I left them on the rocking chair. I had done my reading on the front porch just before dinnertime, and purposely left my book on the rocking chair. Now I wondered how I'd ever get out to see him—and I wanted to more than anything in the world. My only hope of sneaking out was while Maggie was asleep, and I'm not sure she'd ever go to sleep at the rate our conversation was escalating.

"If you don't know, that means you aren't sure," Maggie said.

"Don't push her, Maggie. Just because you like it out there doesn't mean she will."

They both stared at me and I wondered how it was possible that our parents hadn't come up stairs with all the noise we were making.

"I'm so tired. Can we just be done already?" I asked.

Maggie threw her hands up. "Whatever you want, Pixie. I just want you to be happy."

"I am happy," I lied. Jake left our room, leaving me filled with guilt, which burned in my stomach like a bonfire.

"He's scared. Daddy will never let him leave."

I flopped onto my bed, staring at the ceiling. After the rush of adrenaline that carried our discussion, my body was heavy and tired. I listened to Maggie in the bathroom, brushing her teeth and washing her face. Daddy's radio silenced, and my mind ran in circles, thinking of my upcoming wedding, which I'd been so carefully ignoring.

Heavy footsteps ascended the stairs.

"Goodnight, Maggie." My father peeked into my room and smiled. "Goodnight, Pix," he said.

I listened for Maggie's response. It saddened me to know Daddy was answered with silence. "Goodnight, Daddy," I said.

Maggie came back into the room, closed the door, and climbed into her bed. She lit a candle on the nightstand, then turned off her light. "Don't let Jake make you stay, either. He's afraid he'll be left all alone." There was an edge to her voice, a warning.

I looked at her then, her silhouette striking in the flickering light. "I never said I wanted to leave."

Maggie squinted in the darkness. "Oh, Pixie, is it too late? Have they ruined you for life?"

I didn't understand why Maggie was pushing me away from Jimmy Lee and Forrest Town. Or maybe I did. Maybe what I was just starting to figure out, Maggie had figured out long ago. I was torn between annoyed and curious. "Jake doesn't care if I'm here or not," I said.

"No, he just doesn't want to seem like he needs you. Everyone needs someone, and we're all he's got right now. He hangs out with guys who do nothin' but get in trouble."

"Hey, Jimmy Lee is one of those guys."

"Sorry," she said quietly, then she sat bolt upright in her bed, mischief in her eyes. "Pix, the world is about to change more than you could ever imagine." She leaned toward me and whispered. "The white people here are assholes, Pix. The schools are not supposed to still be segregated."

She spoke so fast I could hardly keep up.

Two seconds later she was perched atop my bed, sitting cross-legged, her eyes bright with enthusiasm. "Things are happenin', and they're gonna happen here, too. There's this group, the Black Panthers, and they're just gettin' together out in California, but my friends say they're formin' in New York, too. They're gonna help the coloreds gain equal rights."

"Didn't Martin Luther King do that?"

"Look around you," she said.

I looked around the bedroom.

"Not here, out there." Maggie pointed to the window. "You tell me, did good old Mr. King fix things here in backwoods Arkansas? Can coloreds eat at the diner and go see movies in our theaters?"

Maggie was scaring me. What she said was true, it was like Mr. King's words were empty in our town—the white folks still ruled the roost. I assumed they always would.

Maggie stood up and paced, energized by her own vision. "I'm joinin' 'em, Pix. As soon as I get back to New York, I'm gonna help."

"You can't do that. It'll be dangerous. I hear about race riots on the radio when Daddy listens." I grabbed her arm. "Please, Maggie. Please don't do it."

She sat back down next to me. "I'm a woman. I'll be behind the scenes, helpin' the families and children. Oh, Pixie, I can barely walk by Division Street anymore without feelin' sick to my stomach. Those poor kids haven't a clue how they're bein' held back."

It occurred to me that Maggie wanted to fight for exactly what my heart was aching over. She hadn't said anything about white folks dating black folks, but if this whole movement went as she hoped, couldn't that naturally follow? Maybe not, and maybe never in my daddy's world. "Daddy will never let you do it." Fear prickled my arms. I couldn't stand it if anything happened to Maggie.

"Daddy won't know." She stifled my response with her glare. "Don't you care about what's goin' on 'round here?"

More than you know. I thought of Jackson standing out by the creek in the pitch black waiting for me, risking his life just to talk to me, and the excitement that chased me as I ran through the fields toward him. "I care. I do care."

"Then you won't tell Daddy."

Lying to Daddy was new to me. Before meeting Jackson I'd only lied twice—once two years ago about if Jimmy Lee had ever tried to touch me in ways that weren't appropriate (I wanted Jimmy Lee to touch me, so I didn't feel that was really a lie, or inappropriate), and the other time just the other day about where I had been when I missed dinner. I wasn't about to tell Daddy that I was with Jackson.

"Okay, but promise me that you won't do anything dangerous."

Maggie nodded fast and furious, then took me in her long, sinewy arms and hugged me tight. She pulled away and said, "Okay, good. Good." She hopped over to her bed and dove under the covers.

I lay in bed waiting for Maggie to fall asleep, and hoping Jackson wouldn't leave. The hours had passed by so quickly that I was sure he had. But still, I had to try to see him, drawn to him like a thirsty man to a river. The spark of electricity, the pull in my stomach I'd felt when Jackson held me, came rushing back and made me shiver. The right and wrong of being together made it that much more titillating. How I craved to share my secret!

I wondered if I was missing some clue, an indication that Jackson would one day become just as hurtful as Jimmy Lee. Did all boys eventually evolve into selfish, aggressive men? My father didn't seem that way, but then again, he treated his farmhands like machines. Wasn't that just as bad?

I don't know how long I laid there, worrying on the thought and craving his touch at the same time, but when I looked over, Maggie was fast asleep.

I turned to face the wall, still in my skirt and blouse, and fought the urge to see Jackson. I didn't want to put him in danger.

Ten minutes later I snuck out the back door and ran through the field, my heart thumping like a jackrabbit. *Please be there. Please be there.* I slowed as I neared our meeting spot, listening to the soft voices of nature. Inhaling the scent of the creek, my nerves pulled tight as a spool of yarn. Maggie's words and the hope of freedom for the Johns family flitted through me.

I flicked on my flashlight. "Jackson?"

Silence.

I walked toward the water, illuminating the dark night. "Jackson?" I called again. He was gone. Had he even come and waited for me? Fear shot through me like a bullet. *Jimmy Lee. Oh God, no.* I turned and ran toward home. If Jimmy Lee got wind of us, he'd kill him. My foot caught on a ditch and my body fell forward, landing on the earth with a thud. My hands and knees stung. I cried out as I pushed myself up. The darkness consumed me. I brushed myself off, praying Jimmy Lee didn't find out about Jackson.

My flashlight grew dim. I reached for it just as it went dark. Dead. *A sign?* I was too frightened to think straight. I had to find Jackson. *Please, Lord, please let him be okay.*

"Alison."

My heart jumped into my throat. I spun toward his voice. Jackson's worry-filled eyes stole my breath. He reached for my trembling body and pulled me close, one hand on the back of my head, like Mama used to do when I was a little girl, the other hand on my lower back.

"Shhh."

I shivered from the cold and couldn't stop the river of tears. The relief in my heart was too big. I opened my mouth to speak, but a coherent string of words didn't come. I'd already pictured his bloated body mirroring Mr. Bingham's and couldn't reconcile the image with the living, breathing man before me.

My palms pressed into his chest, confirming the surety of him. His heart beat hard and true against my hands. I touched the warm skin of his cheeks.

"Alison," he whispered.

I put my finger to his soft, succulent lips. Real life fell away—Mama, the farm, Jimmy Lee—none of it mattered or existed. None of it belonged to me any longer. The only thing that remained was Maggie's determination to make our embrace okay, and how deliciously safe I felt. Jackson brought his hands to the back of my head, his thumbs pressing against the hollow beneath my ears. He leaned into me, his body tense, his gaze sliding right into my soul. I put my lips to his, tasting his sweet breath. His tongue slipped slowly into my mouth, lingering inside me, caressing the roof of my mouth, the sides of my teeth. I'd died and gone to heaven. A light rain trickled upon us, dripping down our faces like tiny, little blessings.

He kissed my cheeks, my neck. "Alison."

I pulled him down to the ground, our bodies now a part of the field. He pushed my hair from my face. "Alison," he said again, lying beside me.

Desire swallowed my voice. Love poured from his fingertips as they trailed my blouse. "We can't," he whispered.

I pushed him onto his back. "We can," I said, and brought my lips to his, alighting warmth between my legs. I reached for the buttons on his pants. He grabbed my wrist, shaking his head.

I lowered my lips to his fingers, drawing them back from the ridges of my wrist, and moved them slowly into my mouth, one by one. I wanted to taste every inch of him. His body trembled in anticipation. He closed his eyes. I watched him bite his lower lip, fighting his desires. *Know your place*, my father's voice whispered. I was surprised how easily I was able to ignore it.

I pushed his shirt up around his neck and kissed his chest, gently moving his arms away when he reached for me. Tears fell onto his chest as I ran my tongue down his stomach. He sucked in a breath, lifting my head, meeting my eyes.

"I'm leavin'. In a week, I'll be gone." His eyes pleaded something between desire and fear.

"We have now."

He shook his head, and pulled me alongside him. He leaned over me. "I want more than now."

I moved beneath him. "I'll wait for you." I didn't know if I meant those words or not, but at that very second, their meaning felt as real as the ground beneath me. I reached for his cheek. He grabbed my arm and brought it between us. Our eyes met over my ring.

"You're not mine to have."

We stared at each other for interminable minutes. The rain sprinkled the ground around us.

"I am, here," I laid my hand on my heart, "where it matters."

Sadness laced his eyes. He turned away.

"I won't get married." I said, and in the heat of that moment I meant it. "When you get out of the military, we can go to New York, with your friend, and my sister."

Hope swelled between us like a heartbeat. Jackson rested his forehead on my chin. I arched my neck and kissed his worry lines away.

When he entered me, I gasped from pleasure, every nerve inside me sprang to life. He moved slow and careful, watching my eyes, asking if I was okay. His body shook, though his muscles strained beneath my hands. He kissed my cheeks, my eyes, licked my lips, in ways Jimmy Lee never had. We moved together like a perfect chorus to a familiar song. The brown of his eyes basked in love so true I could feel it wrapping around us like a blanket. Suddenly his body shivered and shook. He grit his teeth and let out a few fast, hard breaths.

My future became clear. I could no longer be with Jimmy Lee. My heart belonged there, with Jackson. No matter how wrong Daddy might think we were, and for as long as it might take until we could safely be together, I would wait for him.

Chapter Nine

I awoke in a panic Saturday morning. What had I done? How would I get myself out of my impending marriage? I ran down the stairs and bolted out the front door. I needed air.

Mama and Maggie were heading toward the house from the garden out past the barn. The morning sunlight illuminated Mama's golden hair. Her striped, blue dress hung past her knees, the only thing that differentiated her age from Maggie's. Maggie's short shift stopped mid-thigh. I wondered what Daddy might think. Maggie threw her head back and laughed. I longed for her strength and confidence.

I heard Daddy's tractor in the distance, and looked for Jake's bike. It was gone. Jake had been spending more and more time away from home, and I wasn't sure if that was a good or bad thing.

"Pixie!" Maggie's voice broke through my worry.

Heading in her direction, I yelled, "I like your boots." I'd only seen knee-high boots in fashion magazines. Maggie wrapped the crook of her arm around my neck.

"Now I'm one of the cool girls," she said with a pose.

"Until Daddy sees you. He won't let you wear those."

Mama lifted her eyebrows in confirmation.

"Come on, Pix, before we go I want to show you somethin'." Maggie grabbed my hand and ran toward the barn. She called over her shoulder, "We'll be back in a bit!"

I pulled the bottom of my skirt as low as it would go to cover the backs of my legs. The hay tickled my skin. Maggie wiggled beside me, pushing the hay flat beneath her thighs. "This loft used to be much more comfortable," I laughed.

"We're orderin' your weddin' invitations today," Maggie said.

I looked out the small window that overlooked the fields. "I know," I said.

"So, if you're gonna back out, now's the time."

"Maggie!" I swatted at her arm. "I can't back out. Mama has already booked the church. Everyone knows about it. Daddy would kill me." *Please help me back out.*

"So what?" Maggie pulled out a pack of cigarettes from her pocket and withdrew one cigarette. My eyes about popped out of my head as I watched her hold it elegantly between her lips and light the tip with a match.

"What are you doin'?" My eyes swept the entrance of the barn, afraid our parents might catch us.

Maggie took a long drag of the cigarette and held it in my direction with a nod.

"No, no way. You're gonna get in so much trouble." She exhaled and smoke wafted around us. I inched away, fanning the air.

She laughed. "I forget how young you are—and how sheltered. Everyone smokes, Pix."

Maggie looked so sophisticated, jealousy wrapped itself around my muscles and squeezed. She held her hand out again in my direction. I reached for it, fumbling to hold the cigarette the way she did, and dropped it on the hay below us. Maggie scooped it up and tamped down the embers.

"Careful! You'll burn the barn down." She held the cigarette butt toward me and I moved my lips over it, sucked in a breath of awful-tasting smoke, and hacked until I fell over on my side, my face hot. My lungs burned. I knew then that I'd never be the same risk taker that Maggie was. I spat the ashy taste onto the hay. Maggie burst out laughing, and I was only seconds behind her. The next thing I knew, Maggie had put out the cigarette and we were rolling around, throwing hay at each other.

Maggie climbed on top of me and held me down, my arms pinned beneath her knees. We were laughing so hard my stomach hurt.

"Truth," she said. "Do you want to marry him?"

"Truth?" I sobered.

"Truth."

I looked at Maggie for a long time, wanting desperately to make her happy, to side with her in whatever her dreams and goals might be. I ached to be as cool as she was, and as worldly, but I knew I didn't have it in me. I didn't even possess the strength to confide in my own sister and admit that I didn't want to marry Jimmy Lee. I shrugged.

"Uh-uh. That doesn't work, Pix." She pressed her knees harder into my arms.

"Ouch!"

"Mama and Daddy can't make your life into what you want, Pix, only you can. This is about you. Tell me."

I turned my head, gazing out the window, and praying for strength. "I don't know."

Maggie slid off of my arms. I rubbed the pulsing soreness from them.

"That's better," she sighed. "Now that we know the truth, tell me more."

"I don't know what you mean."

"Do you want to marry him? Are you sure he's the only person, the only man you want to be with? Ever?" She turned "man" into a two-syllable word.

I bit my lower lip.

"Pixie, I've been your age. I know what's goin' on in that body of yours, the way your hormones are dancin' 'round in ways Mama and Daddy would kill you for."

My cheeks burned with embarrassment.

"Yeah?" There was that mischievous smile again. "So, tell me."

"I can't," I said, moving away from her.

"Have you done it?" she asked.

My jaw dropped open. "Sheesh, Maggie. A little direct, aren't you?"

"Real, maybe," she smirked. "Come on, I'm your sister. Okay, I'll start." She crawled over to where I was sitting and leaned against my back. Maggie must have known that it would be easier for me to talk to her if I didn't have to look her in the eye. "I did it when I was your age. Remember Mr. Crantz?"

"That substitute from Mississippi?" I was mortified. "He was so old. Gross."

"He was not. He was twenty-seven, and he was adorable."

"Gross."

"Okay, your turn."

I didn't say anything.

"Pixie, what are you afraid of? That I'll run and tell Mama and Daddy? Uh, no. This is me you're talkin' to."

I locked my eyes on the tips of my fingers, tapping them up and down on the hay.

"Are you careful at least?" she asked.

I nodded against the back of her head.

"Always?"

No. "Yes." Another painful lie. My stomach tightened.

She let out a relieved sigh. "Good, because the last thing you need is to get pregnant." She spun around and in the next moment was sitting next to me. "Is that where you were last night?" The high-pitched excitement in her voice matched my fear of her knowing.

"What are you talkin' about?"

"Gosh, Pix, do you think I'm dumb? You went to bed with your clothes on. Anything you're doin', I've already done—many times over."

I doubt that. I put my head down on my knees.

"You don't have to tell me, but you know if Daddy finds out you're dead meat." She went to the window and tapped on the panes. "See the path? Daddy will see that one day and you'll be in a lot of trouble. You need to be more careful."

I looked at the flattened plantings, a clear path leading to a large flattened area where we were last night. I crossed my arms to stop them from shaking.

"Pix," Maggie said, turning my head with her hand so I was facing her serious eyes. "You can't get caught. You hear me?"

The truth in her words was more signifcant than she knew.

"Girls?" Mama's voice sang into the loft from below, stealing my chance to tell Maggie what was really going on. "Let's go."

Before we climbed down the ladder, Maggie whispered in my ear, "Don't confuse sex for love."

Chapter Ten

The pungent smell of flowers greeted us at Mrs. Watson's front door. I looked around for a vase of newly picked stems, but saw none as we walked through the threshold of the old farmhouse. Lace doilies covered every surface of the dark furniture. Mrs. Watson bustled around us in her skirt and newly-pressed blouse.

"I can't believe the big day is so close!" Mrs. Watson clapped her hands together. Though she was only in her mid-sixties, she moved slowly. Mama wondered who would take over the invitation business when Mrs. Watson no longer wanted to sell them. From her enthusiasm, I wondered if that day would ever come.

When she leaned in to hug me, I realized that the overpowering, sweet smell was coming from Mrs. Watson's perfume.

"You've grown up so much, Alison." She embraced Maggie. "Oh, dear, when are *you* gettin' married?"

Maggie looked at me and rolled her eyes, then turned on a charming smile and said, "I don't know, but I'll be sure to order my invitations from you when I do."

Mama glared at Maggie.

"Of course you will." Mrs. Watson led us to the living room, nicely appointed with braided rugs and a dark wing chair at the front, which she stood behind as she pointed to the couch. "Please, sit."

Mrs. Watson's gray hair was piled high on her head like a puff of frosting. She sat down in the wing chair, setting a thick, paper catalog on her lap and a permanent smile across her thin lips. "Alison, this is a big decision for you. Do you have a color scheme in mind?"

I couldn't take my eyes off of her nose. I had never noticed the way it pointed and turned toward the right, just slightly at the tip. I blinked away my stare. The idea of planning a wedding with Jimmy Lee turned my stomach. Instead, I thought of what I might want if I were to marry Jackson. "Yes, ma'am. Beige and white, please."

She sat up straighter and moved her feet in closer, knees so tight they could hold a penny between them. "Beige? For a weddin'?"

"Alison likes things simple," Mama offered.

Maggie kicked my foot. I looked at her out of the corner of my eyes and she mouthed, *You can still get out of this*.

"Girls, pay attention," Mama said.

I snapped my eyes back to Mrs. Watson's nose. "Yes, ma'am. I like things simple."

She said, "Well, it is your weddin', dear," but her tone said, *It will be ugly, but it's your choice.* She flipped through the catalog, sighing and glancing up at me. "We don't have much with beige." Flip, flip, flip. "I don't believe I've ever ordered beige invitations before."

I wanted to run out of the room. I didn't care what she wanted, and with Maggie sitting beside me, I couldn't stop thinking about what she said about love and sex. Maybe I was mixing up sex and love with Jackson. Ugh! My life had become much too complicated.

Finally, after what felt like an hour, but in reality was only minutes, Mrs. Watson said, "Here we go, beige," with feigned enthusiasm. She pointed to two invitations, one with brown letters and one with a lighter shade, though not exactly beige. The embossed flowers were so tiny that they looked like bugs crawling on the paper.

Maggie grabbed my hand and squeezed. "Pix, do you like these?" The laugh she held at bay bubbled behind the back of her free hand.

"I, um, I'm not sure. They're not really beige, are they?"

"Well, we could go with gold," Mrs. Watson offered.

"Gold?" Mama asked.

"Yes, gold."

"That's a little flashy, don't you think, Mama?" I said.

Maggie chimed in, "Well, you could change your whole weddin' to be gold and white. You could even put gold glitter on the cake."

The ridiculousness of the comment tickled my ribs and I stifled a snort, which spurred Maggie's laughter.

"And you could wear gold shoes!" Maggie chortled.

Laugher burst from my lips. Maggie fell over in my lap in a fit of giggles. Mama tried to rein us in.

"Girls!" she chided. "Girls, don't be disrespectful."

My belly hurt from laughter. I saw the sparkle in Mama's eyes, right before she swallowed hard and turned a stern face and a strong apology to Mrs. Watson. Maggie and I folded our hands in our laps and choked back our giggles.

We were led out the door five minutes later with instructions to return only when sincere decisions were to be made.

We drove into town in silence. Mama glanced at us every few minutes with a look of disbelief. I waited for her to lecture us, especially Maggie, who really should have known better.

Mama parked the car in front of the drugstore and turned in her seat to face Maggie. "Gold shoes?" she said, then laughed.

I held my breath, waiting for her to stop laughing, but she didn't, which made me laugh, then Maggie chimed in, "Don't forget the gold gloves!"

Mama threw her head back with a loud laugh, mouth wide, eyes tearing up. She wrapped her arm around her stomach and bent over the steering wheel in a fit of giggles. Never before had I witnessed Mama laugh so unabashedly, and though I didn't know it was possible, Mama looked even more beautiful.

"Aren't you mad, Mama?" I asked.

She cleared her throat, looked in the mirror and patted her hair, then said. "Mad? No. Embarrassed? Yes. You know the whole town will be talkin'. She'll probably pray for the two of you in her Monday night prayer group, to rid you of the evil influences that abound." Mama climbed out of the car and we followed her.

"Mama, can we wait out here?" Maggie pulled me toward a wooden bench in front of the building.

Sugar maple trees lined the sidewalk. The street bustled with Saturday shoppers from neighboring towns. Saturdays were "town" days for most local folks. Errands were run and friends visited. I watched with new interest the way the colored folks kept their eyes low and pulled their children toward them as they hurried down the sidewalk. For the first time, I noticed the glances they cast behind them as they walked toward the back of the diner, and the way the little children hung onto the front glass window with longing in their eyes. Then I noticed something that turned my stomach. The slight lift of the chin from the white folks as they passed the coloreds, a snub so small it's not surprising I missed it for so many years. A snub so small I was certain the coloreds felt it like a momentary disappearance of the air they breathed.

I thought of Clara Bingham being chased out of town, and wondered if she was missing this side of Forrest Town or if she was happy to bid farewell to the chin snubs. I hoped she'd found a better place in Mississippi, but if you only know one place for so many years, I can't imagine it would be easy to start over somewhere else.

Maggie watched a little colored boy standing on his tiptoes, begging his short and stout mother for ice cream. She tried to pull the toddler from the window, speaking in crisp whispers. Maggie's smile faded and she stood and grabbed my arm.

"Come on," she said.

In the diner, Maggie purchased a vanilla ice cream cone with money I didn't know she had. She walked back outside, bent down, and handed the cone to the boy with the enormous, dark eyes and tight, black tendrils. The little boy reached for it with a squeal. His mother pulled him out of Maggie's reach and into her arms.

"No, thank you," she said, her eyes darting from side to side.

An elderly couple slowed to watch as the mother took a step backwards.

Maggie stepped closer, the ice cream held out in front of her. "Take it. It's a gift for the baby."

The child reached for the cone, "Want it!"

His mother stepped further away from Maggie. "Thank you, ma'am," she said, her eyes on Maggie's feet. "No, thank you. Please." Her eyes begged to be left alone. A murmur rose from the bystanders.

Maggie's lips formed in a tight line. She turned to the gathering crowd. "It's an ice cream cone. He's a child." She thrust the ice cream toward the woman.

The woman hurried away. The child screamed in her arms, his hands outstretched over his mother's shoulder.

Maggie walked right up to the group of people who lingered with mumbles of "wrong" and "nigger lover."

Just as Mama stepped out of the drug store, Maggie thrust the ice cream cone at the bystanders and said through gritted teeth, "They're people. People! Not niggers or any less worthy than you." She pointed at a heavy-set man. "Or her." She pointed at a toddler in a white woman's arms.

"Margaret Lynn!" Mama's face was as red as the sunset, her eyes as angry and ashamed as if Maggie had walked outside naked. She grabbed Maggie's arm in one hand, holding a bag of groceries in the other, and pulled her toward the car repeating, "I'm sorry. I'm so sorry," to the crowd.

I followed on Mama's heels, in awe of Maggie's courage.

Chapter Eleven

The clinking of forks to plates in between stretches of chewing filled our dining room that evening. Tension mounted with every bite for everyone, it seemed, except Maggie. My father had yet to look at either of us. Jake stared at Maggie, his nose down, irises riding atop the whites of his eyes. Only Maggie ate without any noticeable tension. Her shoulders didn't ride up high, each cut of her knife was slow and careful. Every so often she looked up and smiled at me, shrugged at Daddy. I wondered what had happened in New York to make her not care about what our father thought, or what he might do. I worried that although Daddy wasn't a whipping man, he might stop paying for Maggie to come home to visit, or even worse, not pay for her to go back to New York. All afternoon she'd acted as though nothing had happened in town. She and Mama baked bread while I worked on the wedding list, which was only about twenty-five people long, because I couldn't think past the pencil-thin man in overalls who had called my sister a nigger lover. He had it wrong. I was the nigger lover.

My father sat at the end of the table with the sleeves of his t-shirt pushed up, revealing his milk-white skin beneath and the tan line that all farmers sported. He chewed slow, determined, as if each bite held his full concentration.

"Daddy, there's an art course that's gonna be given at the University of Mississippi that I'd like to take. I could work off the money on the farm." Jake's eyes were hopeful.

My father looked at him, then wiped his mouth with a napkin and set it on the table next to his plate.

Jake looked at Maggie, then shifted his eyes to his plate. "One of my teachers told me about it," Jake continued. I had a feeling it was Maggie who told Jake about the class, but I knew better than to ask right then.

My father looked at me, then back at Jake. "Art class? What a waste of money. Art class," he laughed. "What on earth can someone do with an art class under his belt? Draw cartoons?"

"No, sir." Jake sat up tall. "I can do lots of things. I can learn to design buildin's or—"

"Pipe dreams, son. You stick with your business courses. You'll do just fine."

"Daddy, what if Jake doesn't want to be a—"

My father cast harsh eyes on Maggie. He leaned forward, his elbows on the table, and said in a serious, dark tone, "I know what's best for my children, includin' you."

Maggie set her fork down and crossed her arms, meeting Daddy's stare.

"I heard about you today, little missy. Disgracin' the family like that. You should be ashamed of yourself."

Maggie looked at Mama, who had conveniently begun clearing her plate, avoiding Maggie's pleading look.

My father shook his fork in Maggie's direction. "I don't want you girls goin' into town while Maggie's home. There's no good gonna come from what you did today."

"No good? Ashamed? Daddy, please, I tried to give a child an ice cream." Maggie picked up her fork and poked at the green beans on her plate.

My father stabbed a piece of meatloaf. "You listen to me, Margaret. You will not go into town. You're leavin' tomorrow night, and I don't need anymore strife from you."

Maggie pushed her chair from the table. "It was an ice cream. He was a child, a little boy no different than Jake was as a child. How dare you—"

"How dare I?" Daddy yelled. His chair shot out behind him as he sprung to his feet. A lump grew in my stomach heavy as lead.

Please stop, Maggie, I silently pleaded.

"Those people are not the same as Jake, or you, or me, or any of us." He swung his arm around so hard I thought he might hit her. "Don't you sass me, young lady." He stood with his face two inches from Maggie's.

Tears burned in Maggie's eyes. "Know my place, right Daddy? I'm a white girl so I should act like one?"

Shut up, Maggie. Shut up! I clenched my hands into fists, praying as hard as I could for Maggie to stop needling Daddy. She didn't catch my prayer.

"I've seen other parts of the world, Daddy. I know about civil rights and I know that this damned town you live in is ass-backwards, and I'll do whatever I can to fix that."

My father's hand connected with Maggie's cheek with a crack so sharp she stumbled backward. Mama flew between them, arms spread out wide.

"Ralph! Stop!" It was a command, not a plea. She pushed Maggie behind her with the order to go upstairs. When Maggie remained, too stunned to move, a pink mark blossoming on her cheek and hatred glowing in her wide eyes, Mama said in a strong, even tone, "Go."

My father reached for Mama's arm. I watched in horror as Mama's eyes narrowed. Fear laced every fiber of my being. I couldn't watch Mama get hit. Jake's hands were on the table, elbows bent, like a cat ready to pounce.

Mama lifted her chin just as those white folks had on the street, casting a silent warning between them that could only be read by husband and wife. My father hesitated, then lowered his hand. His chest heaved up and down, his teeth clenched. To my relief and sorrow, he stormed out the front door. I flinched when the screen door slammed against the frame, making a mental note to bring my books indoors before bed. There would be no sneaking out tonight.

That night Maggie and I lay atop her blanket, our hands entangled, our breathing matched, the silence of the house pressing in on us.

"I'm scared," I whispered.

"You shouldn't be scared, Pix. You should be angry." Maggie spoke with little to no emotion, as if she'd accepted the anger that had replaced our previously happy family.

"I don't know what to feel. Ever since I found Mr. Bingham, my whole life has gone crazy."

"What was it like? Findin' him?" she asked.

I thought about the moment I realized that what I'd thought was a lump of refuse was really a body. The memory seeped back in from the crevices of my mind where I'd tucked it away. I cried as I told Maggie about the bruising, his bloated body, and the way his eyes looked up toward the sky with a permanent shock of terror that I couldn't look away from. I must have squeezed Maggie's hand, because she yelped and turned on her side, facing me. She took her finger and moved my hair off of my forehead, the way Mama used to do.

"I'm sorry you found him, Pixie. That must have been horrible."

A tear slipped down my cheek.

"I wish I could bundle you up and take you back to New York with me. I hate leavin' you here."

The weight of my life tumbled around me. Jackson swam in my heart and Jimmy Lee clawed at my mind. Maggie was pushing herself out of our family faster than a chicken chased by a fox, and Mama was standing up in ways I'd only imagined in my dreams—and it all felt so wrong. I put my hands on Maggie's arms and curled into her, wishing I could climb beneath her skin and soak in her strength. She wrapped me in her arms and held me as I sobbed.

Maggie didn't ask me why I was crying, she didn't try to fix what was wrong. She honored my sadness with patience, allowing me to lie against her beating heart until my eyes were red and swollen, with no more tears to shed.

Chapter Twelve

By mid-afternoon, Mama was already wrist deep in apple peels. The kitchen was alive with the aroma of cinnamon and baked apples. It was Wednesday and Jackson would be returning to his military service on Friday. I needed something to keep my mind off of him leaving. Three days had passed since Maggie returned to New York with promises of weekly letters and being home before the wedding. And it had been exactly four days since I'd seen Jackson. I just couldn't muster the courage to sneak out after what I'd witnessed between Daddy and Maggie. My heart pulled and fought me to see Jackson again, and I cringed with sadness every time I thought of him looking for my library books on the porch. He must hate me by now, I was sure of it. But after the rift between Maggie and Daddy became a fissure that I wasn't sure would ever close, I knew I wasn't ready to take a stance and chase away my Daddy's love to be with Jackson.

Mama focused on the apple she was slicing. She sighed, long and low.

I pretended not to notice, figuring she'd tell me what was wrong when she was good and ready.

She finished coring and slicing the last apple, then removed the first batch of baked apples from the oven. I mixed the brown sugar, cinnamon, and honey in a big bowl, dipping my finger in for a taste of the sweet nectar before adding the butter.

While Mama mixed the apples and the sauce together, I leaned against the counter, licking my fingers and wondering what I could do to mend Maggie and Daddy's relationship.

"Honey, wash your hands, please."

I turned on the water and glanced out the window over the sink. Albert had come back to work, although he wasn't working in the fields yet. He and Daddy stood by the barn. My father pointed to the tractor, and I looked in that direction, catching sight of Jackson coming in from the furthest field alongside several other colored men, their arms heavy with containers of DDT, their faces glistening with sweat. Smiles lifted their lips as they chatted back and forth, throwing a rag like a ball between them. They stopped their playful banter as they neared the barn.

"Mama, shouldn't we bring those boys some lemonade?" Seeing Jackson opened the door to my heart that I'd closed out of fear.

"Your father has water for them."

"But, couldn't we bring them lemonade? On a day like today it might be more refreshin'." I eyed the bowl of lemons on our counter.

Mama put her hand on my shoulder and said, "It's probably best if we don't."

I spun around and asked her why.

For a long time she just looked at me, measuring her response. "Well, when you were younger, your father didn't want you takin' them anything, because he worried for your safety; but I think if we do it together, it'd probably be just fine."

I made quick work of cutting and squeezing lemons into several pitchers of ice water, dousing them with sugar, and making sure the end result was sweet and refreshing. We put the pitchers on trays and carried them outside just in time to greet the men as their day came to an end.

I didn't trust myself being too near Jackson for fear of blushing. I knew Mama would see the desire in my eyes. Fifteen young colored men grabbed glasses of lemonade. I was too young to be called ma'am, and yet these men, some just about my age, with fatigue in their eyes and sweat on their brows, treated me as if they knew the place Daddy had spoken of so often—my *place*.

Some of the men were as slim as the day was long, holding their glasses out for more of the cool drink. Their long arms bubbled with baseball-sized muscles. They gulped down a full glass worth in one swallow and set their glass back on the tray with a sincere measure of gratitude.

Jackson stayed a respectable distance from me, accepting a glass from Mama's tray with a generous thank you. I watched him out of the corner of my eye. His eyes were cold and distant, locked on the fields beyond the house. *Our fields*, as I'd come to think of them. I swatted at a bug, awkwardness grasping at my movements. *What had I done?* Four days was too long. I hadn't talked to Jackson since we'd made love, and now I worried that I'd never have a chance.

I coughed, played with my hair, spoke too loudly, and still he didn't look over. I told myself that Jackson would never take a chance of being caught eyeing me, then worried that he hadn't wanted to. There was no secret smile, no symbolic gesture, and the absence of even the smallest acknowledgment hurt like a paper cut, swift and deep. Today, my books were going on the rocking chair.

Chapter Thirteen

As soon as the house was silent, I tiptoed to my parents' room and peeked in. They lay still, Daddy's arm arced over his head, the other across his stomach. Mama slept with her back to him. I made my way silently downstairs and out the back door. As soon as the night air hit my lungs, any hesitation I'd felt the days before turned to determination. I might not be ready to give up Daddy's love, but the hurt I felt that afternoon when Jackson shunned me made me realize that I wasn't ready to give him up, either.

The rows of plantings were thick and soft beneath my feet as I ran toward the creek. When I finally reached the end of the field's grasp, I saw Jackson sitting on a rock beside the water, his back to me, his strong frame hunched forward. I ran to him, brushing his shoulder. He flinched beneath my touch.

"Hi," I said, out of breath.

He nodded. He didn't move toward me, he didn't reach for my hand.

I crouched before him and touched his knee. "Hey, you okay?" When he didn't answer, I said, "I missed you."

He nodded again, then sat up tall. "I'm leavin' tomorrow."

"Tomorrow? That's only Thursday. I thought you were leavin' Friday." It was too soon. *One day.* One day wasn't enough.

He shrugged. "Tomorrow, Friday, what's the difference?"

"A day. A full twenty-four hours."

He stood and crossed his arms. "Right, and what's the big deal about that?"

I shook my head. "What do you mean? Don't you want to be with me?"

"Me?" he raised his voice. "Yes, I want to be with you, but you've made it clear how you feel. I haven't heard from you in days."

My stomach tightened. I touched his arm, desire warming my throat. "I'm sorry." It was the truth, I was sorry. "I couldn't get away." *I'm too weak.*

"I'm sorry? Is that all it takes for you? Well I don't know how you treat Jimmy Lee, but that's not enough. We…" He lowered his voice and pulled his shoulders back, like he was recovering from saying Jimmy Lee's name and bringing him into our conversation. "We were close, and then you disappeared. How do you think that made me feel? I look at your porch everyday, hopin' your books are there, and everyday I'm shut down like a used-up mule."

Hearing him say Jimmy Lee's name was strange. I hadn't thought about Jimmy Lee in days. I was too busy worrying about how to keep my family together, and the steps I needed to take to protect myself from losing them.

"I'm sorry. I really, truly am. I've been confused."

"Yeah, well you'll have four months to get unconfused, because that's how long I'm gonna be gone, and when I'm out of the service, I'm goin' straight to New York."

"Wait, I thought we were goin' to New York together?" I heard the falseness of my words as they left my lips. I wouldn't run away with him and leave my family behind. I couldn't.

He touched my arm, then, and said softly, "Alison, you're not goin' anywhere. You're one of them. What we had—"

Hot tears fell down my cheeks. He wiped them away, and I grabbed his hand and brought it to my lips. I kissed his palm, then rested my cheek on it. "I love you."

"Maybe, but if this is how you love, it's not enough for me. I've been oppressed my whole life, held back by the ropes of color. I want to love for real. I want to know that whoever loves me will love me regardless of my color, regardless of what others think, and you can't do that, not here."

"I could lose my family."

"I know." He leaned down and kissed my forehead. I grabbed his waist and held on. His words were true, but they didn't stop the ache in my heart. The cool night air stung my lungs as I sucked in a deep breath, hoping to dislodge the lump from my throat. "I can do it. I do love you."

"I know you do, but I watched you these last few days, avoidin' the fields, avoidin' me. I couldn't think past your name, Alison. I can't eat, I can't sleep. It's killin' me."

Our bodies trembled, mine from the fear of being without him, and his, I was sure, from the truth his words carried.

"No," I cried, shaking my head and pulling away. "I want to be with you. Maybe I can do this."

"Alison, you're gettin' married in a few weeks. *Maybe* means you can't do this."

"No," I cried. "Be with me, I'll show you. One more time, before you leave?"

He shook his head. "You're not mine. You never will be."

"It hurts too much. I want to be." I wiped my eyes with my arm. "Will you write me? Through Albert? We can find a way, like my mama does with your mama?"

Again, he shook his head. I dropped to my knees, the harsh sting of rejection stealing my strength. "I just made a mistake. I should've given you a message. I should've met you. I'm sorry. I was afraid. My sister had a fight with Daddy, and I was afraid he'd tell me to leave, too, if he found out."

"You're right. He would have, and I would never forgive myself if he did. I love you. I will always love you. But I won't steal you from another man, and I won't be your hidden lover." He came down on his knees. His lips met mine, soft and delicious.

When our lips parted, my eyes remained closed. I knew that the moment I opened them what we had would be forever changed.

"I don't blame you one bit," he whispered.

I opened my eyes and saw tears in his.

"Maybe I'll see you when I visit Maggie?" I knew it would never happen.

"Maybe," he said. He held my hand and we sat there, on the side of the creek, the trickling water moving by like the past few days, sure and steady.

I touched his face, his eyes, his hair, his ears. I wanted to memorize every bit of him. His musky smell, his taste, sweet and ripe, the feel of his palms, soft like butter, yet peppered with callouses across the tops. I let my hands drop to his wide, solid hips. His hands moved down my shoulders, my arms warm beneath his touch. Moonlight streaked through the umbrella of trees, illuminating the grass beside us. I wanted to fall asleep there beside him, and wake with his gentle caress. I wanted to make baked apples for him, and to take his mother a batch without having to hide. More than anything, I wanted our love not to be forbidden.

He pulled me to my feet, our chests touching. I pressed into him and felt his desire firm against my hip. He kissed away my tears.

"You deserve a beautiful life," he said. He turned and walked away, following the creek toward town.

"Jackson," I called after him. He turned, and our eyes met. Mine, pleading for him not to go, his knowing he had no choice. I blew him a kiss. He reached toward the sky and caught it, then put his hand to his heart. *Run after him.* My legs were rooted to the ground by my Daddy's love. He disappeared into the darkness, taking a piece of my broken heart with him.

Chapter Fourteen

The weeks before the wedding passed painfully slow, like molasses from a Mason jar. Each breath took an insurmountable effort to push past my feeling of loss. I had created my own darkness by pushing Jackson away instead of following my heart, and God knew how much I loved him, but I held a mantra in my mind that it was the right thing to do.

I found myself longing for Maggie's presence, but she hadn't returned home from college at the end of her term. She stayed in New York to work as a secretary for a law firm. She'd written me a letter and confessed that she'd joined the Black Panthers, as she'd hoped to, and that the law firm that she was working for was really into making changes with civil rights. She made me promise not to tell Daddy. She said she was making a difference, and I was happy for her, but every time I looked at her empty bed or brought up her name at the dinner table, a wave of despair settled in around me. Daddy wouldn't even say her name, and in his silence, sadness pressed forward. The blue in his eyes dimmed with hurt. I couldn't imagine what it would feel like to have him feel that way because of me.

One day I snuck over to the side of the field where Albert Johns was working, and I'd asked him if Jackson had sent any letters for anyone. He'd taken two steps backwards, whipping his head around like we were doing something against the law—in a way we were, though the law was unwritten. Albert looked at me like I was crazy for talking to him, and that's when I knew there would be no letters. As much as I missed Jackson—and I surely did—I thought I'd made the right decision, no matter how sad it made me.

With my love for Jackson put on hold, and without Maggie around to sidetrack my thoughts, I finally gave in and chose a light pink for our wedding invitations, which seemed to please Mrs. Watson. Jimmy Lee had graduated from college, and although I was too sick the morning of his graduation to attend, I was proud of him. I had high hopes that once he returned and was a working man instead of a schoolboy, he'd stop his crazy antics and settle down.

Chapter Fifteen

The morning of my wedding arrived with a bout of nausea. Mama said it was just my nerves, and Maggie, who'd arrived the evening before, held my hair back as I threw up the previous night's dinner. My father had yet to say two words to her.

"You're sure about this, Pix?" she whispered when Mama left the bathroom.

"I'm not you. This is best for me." The inability to see Jackson made it that much easier to convince myself to start fresh with Jimmy Lee. Even if I didn't love him the way I loved Jackson, and maybe I never would, I knew it was best if I stayed in my safe cocoon of a life. I didn't have what it took to be on my own the way Maggie did. The comfort I drew from Daddy's warm embrace, and his conditional admiration, no matter how unrealistic, was something that I cherished. There was no doubt in my mind that I needed Daddy in my life.

We moved into the bedroom to prepare for my wedding. I sat at the dressing table with my puffy eyes and pink nose, soaking in the tenderness of Maggie's efforts as she combed through my hair.

"Okay, but you know, the offer is still open for you to come to New York with me." There was a sparkle in her eye that made me want to follow her anywhere. The thought of seeing Jackson in New York excited me, then saddened me. I'd made my bed, and it was time to sleep in it.

"I'm good, thanks, though."

"Will you at least visit me?" she asked.

"Right after we're settled."

"Promise?"

"Promise." And so it was set. I'd take the train to New York at the end of the summer. I was sure Jimmy Lee wouldn't mind. He knew how close Maggie and I were. Maggie told me all about her job with Mr. Nash's law firm. He was a civil rights activist and had warned Maggie about the Black Panthers, but she assured me that they had never done anything violent, he just worried they might. She said she'd remain safely behind closed doors with the families.

"I won't protest, don't worry. I just want to do my part," Maggie said.

"I wish I could do somethin' like that here, help the colored families to do little things, like eat in the diner."

"Little things?" Maggie said sarcastically. "That's a huge thing, Pix."

"Girls, need any help?" Mama came into the bedroom in a flurry, nervously looking around the room. She looked gorgeous in her blue dress with her hair brushed shiny and full away from her face.

"We've got this, Mama," Maggie said, zipping up my dress.

I stood in the middle of the room in Mama's wedding dress, which was less like a frilly wedding dress and more like a long, white ball gown. She'd hemmed it, and it fit like a sleeve, though noticeably tighter than it had when I'd first tried it on.

"Is it too tight?" I worried.

Mama ran her hand down my side, trailing the silky gown's seam. "You're just carryin' five pounds of happy," she said. "Brides gain or lose weight right before their weddin', because they're happy. They've caught their man and they relax a little bit." She patted my cheek. "Glory be, you are a sight, Alison. Jimmy Lee is one lucky man."

Why the statement saddened me, I wasn't sure. I thought I had moved past my indecision—or maybe I just hoped that I had.

"Yes, he is, and he'd better remember that every day of your long life," Maggie smirked.

Mama embraced me. "My little girls are all grown up. Why, I'll have no one left 'round here."

"We're only movin' into town, Mama. It's not like you'll never see me. Besides, you have Jake here, remember?"

A shadow crossed over Mama's face, and I wondered what she was thinking just then. She kissed my cheek and said, "I'll go make sure your Daddy is ready. He's all thumbs when it comes to tyin' his tie."

There are times in our lives when everything comes together and we know we are exactly where we are supposed to be. My wedding day was not one of those days. I stood at the altar, facing Jimmy Lee, handsome in his black suit and crisp, white shirt. My stomach quivered as I looked into his eyes, reciting my vows. "I promise to love, honor, and cherish..." *Love, honor, cherish.* I could love him, yes, I knew I could. I had before, and once he stopped chasing down innocent boys, I'd surely love him again. *Honor.* I respected Jimmy Lee, well, at least most of the time I did. We'd had a long talk last week about how I felt that day at the river, when he was too rough, and he apologized and I could tell he meant it. It was easy to forgive him, we'd been together for so long that he knew just how to say all the right words to make me feel better, even if he didn't do that unsolicited anymore. Did anyone after two years? Yes, I could honor him. *Cherish* was a more difficult concept for me to wrap my heart around. The pulse of my heart fought me on *cherish*. When I thought of the curved edges of that word, they were Jackson's arms I felt around me. When I said the word out loud, I'm reminded of Jackson's soft lips on mine, the way his body felt against me, the way he moved in slow, careful movements, looking at me, not through me. *Cherish* was not a word my heart embraced with Jimmy Lee, but I said it all the same. It was my place, after all, as his wife.

Jimmy Lee slipped the ring on my finger and my marriage became real. I was no longer Daddy's little girl or Maggie's little sister. I was Mrs. James Carlisle, and when Jimmy Lee kissed me to seal our union, I prayed to feel the same rush of love I felt for Jackson. I prayed for the heat to rush from the center of my stomach up to my chest and down my thighs. I hoped the kiss might rekindle the spark I once felt for him. I came away from that kiss, that start of our marriage, wondering how I would ever find what I was hoping for.

Chapter Sixteen

We didn't take a honeymoon because his uncle said Jimmy Lee needed to begin training for his position with the furniture store. Jimmy Lee hoped to plan a trip to Niagara Falls once we had enough money saved. I didn't mind waiting. I knew it would be forever before we could afford it, even if his uncle was fixing to pay for half of the trip.

We fell into our married life like two kids playing house. Every morning Jimmy Lee went to work and I cleaned, baked bread, planned dinners, and quickly grew bored. I wondered how Mama did it for all those years. After a few weeks, Mama suggested that I think about getting a job in town, where I could walk to work, something part-time.

"I make enough money," Jimmy Lee argued. "You don't need to work."

We were eating dinner at our small kitchen table. I had spent the entire day inside, and I wasn't used to being so confined. I was tired all the time and hardly ever felt like eating. I was sure that it was because I missed the activity of daily life. I stared at the same white walls of our apartment day in and day out. I tried taking walks, but it wasn't enough. I needed something more to pull me out of the funk I'd fallen into. Some days, it was hard for me to climb out of bed and when I finally made it to the kitchen to fix Jimmy Lee's breakfast, the smell of his eggs cooking made me sick to my stomach.

"I know you do. I just need a little somethin' to do, Jimmy Lee. I'm in this apartment all day and night."

"Mama doesn't work. Your mother doesn't work." He took a bite of the biscuits I'd made the evening before, which weren't nearly as flakey as Mama's, but he didn't seem to mind.

"I know yours doesn't, but mine does, on the farm, and besides, they had us to take care of. It's just me here, all day, by myself."

"We're not havin' no baby, Alison. Not yet, at least."

I sighed. Why didn't he ever listen to me? "I don't want a baby, Jimmy Lee, I just want a part-time job where I can talk to people and get out of the apartment for a few hours each day." Nausea rose in my throat. I swallowed against it. *Nerves.*

He wiped his mouth and stood to leave. "Do what you want to, but just make sure you're home every night early enough to make dinner. I work hard. A man needs to eat."

Already planning my outfit for my day of applying for jobs, I agreed. Even his chauvinistic comment couldn't damper the renewed energy the idea brought with it.

Each store held the promise of something new and exciting. My legs were tired as lead, but as I looked in the windows of each shop, new energy filtered in. I looked back toward our apartment and wondered what Daddy would think of my working part time. I asked myself, *What would Maggie do? Maggie wouldn't have thought about Daddy in the first place.* I checked my blouse and hair in my reflection in the window of the diner, thinking about the little boy and the ice cream cone he wasn't allowed to accept. I took a deep breath to quell my nerves, and walked through the door, and nearly bumped right into Mrs. Tempe, who was holding an orange and black Help Wanted sign.

"Oh, I'm so sorry."

"Alison! Why that's okay, darlin', I was just headin' up front to hang this old sign. Marla left on account of her movin' outta town next week." Her yellow and white waitress uniform fit snug against her thick curves. Her short, brown hair curled so perfectly in tiny rings around her face it was like she had invisible rollers holding them in place.

"I didn't mean to run you over like that," I said.

"Oh, honey, you couldn't run me over if you tried, you're such a tiny, little thing." She waved her hand up and down. "I guess I oughta call you *Mrs.* Carlisle now, huh, sugar?"

"It's strange, havin' a new last name. I'm not really used to it yet."

"By the time you get used to it you'll be over it. That's how fast it happens. One day you wake up and you realize that you didn't notice the switch, when you went from Alison Tillman to Alison Carlisle. Those few days you have to think before you sign your name pass faster than castor oil through a baby." She patted my arm. "What are you here for today? A nice cake for that handsome husband of yours?"

"A job." The words slipped out before I could form a proper response.

"A job?" She leaned in close and whispered. "Are you havin' money troubles already?"

"Oh, no." Worry soared through me. Is that what people would think? I couldn't embarrass Jimmy Lee like that. "I'm just bored, really. Jimmy Lee is at work all day and I've got nothin' to do in that tiny little apartment."

She drew her eyebrows together. "Yes, that does happen, doesn't it?" She looked around the diner. "With Marla gone, I am in need of a capable set of hands, and yours'll do just fine. It's only a few hours here and there."

"That would suit my needs perfectly. Thank you!" I bit back my enthusiasm and asked tentatively, "Do you think people will really think we're havin' money trouble? I don't want people talkin' like that."

She waved her hand in the air. "What do you care what others think? A young, pretty girl like you?" She put her arm around my neck and said, "Better to have a little sanity break every now and again than to lose your mind worryin' about small town gossip, right?"

There was a knock at the back door and I waited as Mrs. Tempe gathered the wrapped food that was spread across the counter, placed it in a paper bag, and headed for the door. I sat down next to a heavyset man on one of the orange stools at the counter. The stools spun if you pushed them hard enough. I had driven Mama crazy on those stools more times than I could count.

I watched Mrs. Tempe at the back door. A small colored boy, who couldn't have been more than eight years old, dug deep into his pockets. His spindly arms were all elbows and wrists. He handed her a fistful of money and stood on his tippy toes, peering around her. His eyes caught mine, and I couldn't read what they held—embarrassment? Curiosity? He looked away quickly, leaving me feeling embarrassed for being *inside* the diner. Jackson sailed into my mind. The thought of him standing at the back door of any diner bothered me. I'd been pushing away the thoughts of him so effectively that the memory took me by surprise.

The door thumped shut, jolting me out of my own mind and back to the present. Mrs. Tempe's hips swayed from side to side with her hurried gait as she picked up dirty dishes from the booth where two women sat. They whispered among themselves, and Mrs. Tempe's lips pressed into a firm line. She slapped a check down on the table, spun around with determination, and carried their dishes behind the counter, where she passed them wordlessly to Joe, the cook, who masterfully slid them out of sight.

She punched numbers into the cash register, mumbling about *hoity toity* women and the nerve of them. "Those people have to eat, too," she whispered to me with a speck of frustration.

The coloreds in our town had always gone to the back door of the drugstore and the restaurants. I had known that my whole life, but until that moment, I hadn't felt suffocated by the knowledge. I blinked several times, trying to make my thoughts of Jackson go away, but they remained as present as the floor I stood upon. There was no denying my growing discomfort. My eyes were opened to the segregation around me and I knew I had to do something to help those who where treated differently. *Maggie would be proud.*

Mrs. Tempe must not have noticed my momentary lapse of focus. She gave my wrist a sweet squeeze and said, "Can you start tomorrow? Ten a.m.?"

Chapter Seventeen

All dolled up in my prettiest dress, with Jimmy Lee's favorite meal in the oven, I was ready to break the news of my being employed. *Employed*. A thrill rushed through me. I'd never held a job before, besides helping out on our farm. Dinner was perfectly timed. At exactly five forty-five the table was set just so, candles were lit, and my speech was practiced. I tapped my foot as I watched the minutes tick by. *I'll save every penny towards our honeymoon*, I rehearsed. Anticipation made me jumpy, and I paced our small kitchen.

By six fifteen my back ached and I knew the biscuits were gonna be too soggy for Jimmy Lee to enjoy, so I quickly piled his meal into a bowl and set new biscuits in a separate dish. I'd lather the chicken, vegetables, and gravy on top when he walked through the door.

By six thirty my frustration had stolen my pleasant mood and I felt too sick to eat. I blew out the candles, and wrapped Jimmy Lee's dinner.

The sun dropped from the sky and I closed the curtains against the darkness. I thought about walking down to the furniture store, but I knew Jimmy Lee would worry if he came home and I wasn't here. I curled up on the couch and read, until my eyes became too heavy to remain open.

The key jiggling in the lock woke me from where I'd fallen asleep on the couch. I stood too fast and my head spun. I grabbed the side of the couch as Jimmy Lee stumbled in through the door and toward the living room. The stench of alcohol was so thick I turned away.

"Where have you been?" I asked.

Jimmy Lee staggered backward and sat down at the kitchen table. "Where's dinner?" he slurred.

I looked at the clock; it was one thirty in the morning. I could not tame my spiteful snark. "I put it away."

"I told you a man gets hungry." He took his jacket off and tried to place it on the back of his chair. It missed, landing on the floor.

I folded my arms across my chest, breathing hard. "Why didn't you tell me you were goin' out?"

"Why should I?"

Why should you? "Maybe because we're married, and I made your favorite dinner." *Damned tears.* I swiped at them with my hand. "I lit candles and everything."

"So light them again," he slurred.

I stomped into the kitchen and pulled his dinner from the oven, removed the foil wrap, and dropped it before him with a *clank*. He flinched.

"Where were you?" I asked again.

Jimmy Lee shoveled the food into his mouth like he hadn't eaten all day.

"Jimmy Lee?"

He stopped his hand in mid air and lifted his eyes, still hunched over his food like a protective animal.

"I got a job," I spat.

He shoved the food into his mouth, his eyes locked on mine. He chewed slow and solid. I sat in a chair to stop my legs from trembling.

"At the diner, part-time."

He dropped his eyes to his plate and ignored me.

I stewed, too tired to argue. "I start tomorrow," I said over my shoulder as I went to the bedroom. Tears streamed down my cheeks. It seemed that's all I did lately. Cried. I paced the bedroom floor, wondering why I ever wanted to get married in the first place.

It wasn't until the next morning, after Jimmy Lee had gone to work and I was separating the laundry, that I noticed the bloodstains on his shirtsleeves and the thighs of his pants. Fear gripped me by the throat. *Which colored boy paid the price of his drinkin' this time?*

Chapter Eighteen

I'd been working at the diner for three weeks, much to Jimmy Lee's chagrin. He'd taken to coming home late several nights each week, complaining about my needing to wash my uniform in the evenings, and yapping about me working at all. Although I enjoyed my job, I was tired all the time. A knock came from the back door. Jean (Mrs. Tempe asked me to call her that, *Makes me feel younger,* she'd said) still wouldn't allow me to bring food to the colored folks. She said the white folks could get feisty if their food had to wait, and she didn't want any trouble for me. I watched with a longing to be involved each time she handed over the meals, wrapped tight and kept warm, into the waiting and thankful dark hands. The more I witnessed them calling at the back door, the more I wanted to help them get rights to the front. I called into the kitchen for Jean, gripping my stomach. The smell of eggs was particularly strong, and I bit back my breakfast from making a second showing.

"She ran to the market. We're out of paprika." Joe's basketball-shaped, bald head poked through the food window, which hid his plump body.

Another knock came from the rear of the diner. Joe handed me a big, brown bag and said, "Take this to them, will ya'?"

I swallowed against the dizziness that seemed to plague my too-fast movements lately. The heavy door swung in and I stepped aside. Albert Johns' mother stood before me. I remembered her gentle face from the furniture store. I must have looked surprised, because her eyes changed from smiling to concerned.

"Sorry it took so long," I said, and handed her the paper bag.

She stood with her frowning lips pressed tightly together.

I held my hand out to receive her money, and wondered what I'd done wrong when she didn't offer payment. *Great, my first time takin' food to the coloreds, and already I messed it up.* "Ma'am? You're supposed to pay now," I whispered, flush warming my cheeks.

She slipped a hand into her dress pocket, then pressed the money into my palm, and gripped my hand. Hard.

I looked down at my hand, then back at her.

She whispered, "You hurt my boy."

My throat tightened. *Jimmy Lee*. I shook my head. "No, ma'am, I never touched Albert."

She stared at me with the darkest eyes I'd ever seen. "Jackson."

The world spun before me. I held tight to her hand as the world went black and cold. Everything moved in slow motion, my legs gave way. I saw the concrete step coming too close, too fast.

"Pregnant?" Mama's voice hung in the air. Dr. Davis stood beside me, his white hair and spectacles coming slowly into focus. I tried to sit up, but my head felt like it'd been run over by a truck.

"Mama?" I whispered through the haze that clouded my mind.

"Jean called me. She said you passed out," Mama explained.

"Lay back, Alison," Dr. Davis said, gently pressing my shoulders back down on the couch. "You knocked your head pretty hard when you passed out."

"Passed out?" I asked. I realized that I was in the office of the diner.

Mama leaned over me, her eyes wet with tears. She leaned in close to my ear and asked me when I'd had my last period.

I blinked, not sure I'd heard her correctly. Understanding sent me bolt upright, ignoring my throbbing head. "You think I'm pregnant?" *Oh no, Jimmy Lee will be so upset.*

"Well, when was your last menstrual cycle?" Dr. Davis asked.

"I don't know. It's hard to think. With all the stress of the weddin' and all, I guess it was sometime before the weddin'."

"Why don't you come by my office this afternoon and we'll do a quick blood draw."

Mama lifted her eyebrows. "Have you been sick in the mornin's? Tired?"

Oh, God.

Two days later Mama drove me to Dr. Davis's office to discuss the results of the blood test. I prayed that I was just sick or tired, anything but pregnant. There we sat, on metal chairs in his claustrophobic office, the two of them speaking as if my pregnancy was a good thing. My mind spun in circles. I hadn't slept in days, the sight of food sickened me, and the thought of telling Jimmy Lee I was pregnant nearly sucked all the air from the room.

"You can eat like you normally do, but try not to gain too much weight. The baby needs you to be healthy, so be sure to drink your milk and eat plenty of protein."

"Crackers will help with the nausea." Mama squeezed my hand, a glint in her eye. "Oh, honey, wait until Jimmy Lee finds out."

"Are you sure, Dr. Davis?" I asked, picking at my fingernails.

"Sure as the day is long."

Mama rattled on the whole way home about how she'd make me maternity clothes, and we'd have a baby shower when it was time. I could use my old crib if I wanted. She had it stored in the attic. I lay my head back on the passenger seat headrest and wondered how on earth I was gonna tell Jimmy Lee.

"I know you were fixin' to see Maggie, but I think I'd wait a bit. You're just three months pregnant, and it's probably best to wait another month or two. Just to be sure everything is okay."

I wondered if Maggie would be disappointed in me.

"But then I can take the train to New York?" I needed to hear her say it again. I needed to be sure. I didn't want to miss seeing Maggie.

Mama laughed. "Of course. You can do anything when you're pregnant, but it's best to wait until you have some of your energy back. The first three months can be very tryin'."

"You're tellin' me? I just passed out and konked my head."

Mama squeezed my hand. "Will you quit your job now? So you can rest?"

My job? I hadn't thought about quitting my job to rest. I loved my job. "No, actually, it really helps keep me sane. I can't stand bein' alone all day in the apartment."

"Well, you won't be alone much longer."

I knew she meant well, and I could feel the light radiating from her with the thought of being a grandmother. Mama loved babies. I, on the other hand, couldn't help but worry about being a mother. I was barely able to hold my marriage together. How would I ever care for a baby?

That evening, before Jimmy Lee came home, I drafted a letter to Maggie and walked it down to the post office.

"We talked about this. How could you let this happen?" Jimmy Lee wasn't drunk, but the smell of alcohol on his breath was becoming the norm.

"This wasn't all me, Jimmy Lee." I sat on the couch, my feet curled under me, watching him pace across our small living room floor.

"How? When? We're careful."

He was right. Since we'd been married, we'd been more careful than ever.

"I don't know, okay? It just happened. We are havin' a baby, Jimmy Lee, and we just have to deal with it."

Jimmy Lee lit a cigarette and sat down beside me. I pulled back. Even his cigarette smoke bothered my stomach lately. He took a long drag and turned his head to blow the smoke in the other direction.

"Okay," he said, and leaned back against the couch.

"Okay?" I asked.

"Yeah, okay. You're gonna have to deal with it. It's not like we have a choice."

I'm gonna have to deal with it? "Maybe you can come home earlier some nights?"

He turned angry eyes toward me. "And do what? Leave Corky to hang out alone? I'll do what I see fit," he snapped.

The memories of the afternoon he'd forced himself upon me came rushing back, followed by a shiver of a memory of being with Jackson, then a rush of fear from the confrontation with his mama. She was right. I'd hurt her son. I only wish she knew how much I'd also hurt myself. None of that mattered anymore. That part of my life was over. I was Mrs. James Carlisle, and a mother-to-be. I vowed to try to be the best mother ever.

Chapter Nineteen

I'm not sure what disappointed me more, the extra weight that went to my boobs and made them heavy instead of perky, or Jimmy Lee's increased drinking. Several weeks had passed since I found out I was pregnant, and all of my clothes were too tight. Mama altered the larger waitress uniforms Jean gave me, but I still felt like a packed sausage as I waddled through the diner.

There was a knock at the back door, and ever since I saw Jackson's mother, I had steered clear of answering it.

"Can you get that, hun?" Jean hollered from the office. She'd been giving me more and more responsibility lately. *You're gonna be a mama. You can handle anything now.*

With not a single patron in the diner, I had no excuse not to answer it. I grabbed the paper bag from the counter and headed for the back door. What if it was Jackson's mother again? The metal doorknob was cold beneath my sweaty palm. I peered slowly around the edge of the door. To my relief, a small boy stood on the step with his hand outstretched and three dollars and fifty cents in his tiny palm.

"Hi, sweetie. Here you go," I said, and handed him the bag.

A gap-toothed smile graced his lips. Before I could say anything more, he turned on his heels and ran away, his pencil legs moving as fast as they could down the alley, disappearing around the corner.

A week later the same little boy showed up, and I realized that his father bought lunch from the diner every Friday. The third Friday, I was ready. When the little boy put the money in my palm, I pressed a cookie into his.

Later that afternoon I was walking through my parents' house thinking about the smile on that little boy's face, when Daddy took me in his arms and squeezed me so tight I could barely breathe. "Pixie! Look at you, plump as a mother hen."

"Thanks, Daddy. I think."

"Are you sure you want to go to New York in your condition? It's a lot of travelin'."

"Yes, Daddy. I haven't seen Maggie in ages and I miss her."

Daddy kissed the top of my head. "I worry about you is all. Don't let her put those crazy notions of hers into your sweet, little head, ya' hear?"

"Don't worry, Daddy. I'll come back just as I left, as your perfect, little, pregnant girl." As I said those words I wondered, not for the first time, if being Daddy's perfect girl was the right kind of girl for me to be. I used to be filled with pride about being his perfect, little girl, but now I realized that being that girl meant not helping the coloreds, and my heart battled that stance at every turn.

"Woman," Mama interrupted.

I sure didn't feel like a woman. Jake sidled up next to Mama.

"I thought I heard your voice," he said, and hugged me. "Look how fat you are."

I punched him in the arm. He laughed. Behind us, the farmhands piled into a rusted and dented truck. Albert looked back over his shoulder before climbing into the back with the rest of them. The way he shook his head made my heart sink. I wanted to run over and tell him that I didn't mean to get pregnant by Jimmy Lee and that I wished it was Jackson's baby, but I knew that even thinking that thought was wrong.

"I got somethin' I wanna show you," Jake said, and I followed him into the house, hiding my face behind the curtain of my hair.

Upstairs in his room, he opened a notebook and showed me a sketch of the inside of the barn, complete with mine and Maggie's feet hanging over the loft, and the crack in the window.

"Oh, Jake, this is wonderful. How did you get such detail? Every strand of hay is perfect. I can practically smell the DDT on it."

He shrugged.

"Did you show Daddy? I'd bet if you do, he'll let you take those art classes you want."

"No way," he said and snagged the notebook back from me.

"But—"

"You've seen what he does. You saw how he treated Maggie. No way will I go up against him. No way." He tucked the notebook into his desk and changed the subject, asking me what it felt like be pregnant.

"I feel like a fat girl. Don't change the subject."

He laughed.

"Seriously. Nothin' fits, I waddle, and I can't do anything about it." If he could change the subject, so could I. Maybe Jake could help me figure out what to do about my husband disappearing every night. "Jake?"

He stood with his back to me.

"Jimmy Lee is drinkin' all the time, and he comes home late every night. Are you hangin' out with him and Corky?"

He turned around and sighed.

"Jake, you can tell me. I won't get mad at you. Promise."

He shook his head. "Corky hasn't been out in two weeks. He cut his hand at the farm and is on some big time medicine. Can't drink while he's on it, so he just stays inside at night."

"So, have you been with him?"

Jake shook his head. I suddenly felt like there was a lead balloon in my stomach instead of a baby in my womb. I lowered myself to sit on his bed. "Jake, what's goin' on? He said he's been out with Corky all this time."

Jake shrugged, and started for the stairs.

I couldn't tether my rising voice. "What's goin' on? What's he doin'?"

Mama opened the front door and hollered up the stairs. "Is everything alright up there?"

I stood with my arms crossed, staring at Jake.

"Fine," I said to Mama. I heard her step back onto the porch as I pushed past Jake and hurried down the steps.

All I could think about on the way home was where Jimmy Lee was going and what he was doing. I stopped at the furniture store, something I hadn't done in the weeks since we'd been married.

"Why, Alison, what a nice surprise."

Mr. Kelly had worked at the furniture store forever. A widower who had a gift for making himself seem important, he stood before me in a crisply-pressed, three-piece suit, his shoes perfectly shined. His chin maintained a constant tilt up, as if he was always looking down his nose at you.

"Hi, Mr. Kelly. Thank you. Is Jimmy Lee here? I'd like to talk to him."

He cocked his head as if I'd asked him if he had seen a five-legged cow. "No." He offered no explanation.

"Do you know when he'll be back?" I asked, biting back my mounting anger.

"I think you'd better ask his uncle."

His uncle? "Okay. Is Mr. Carlisle here?" The storeroom door opened, and Jackson's mother stepped into the showroom. Her eyes dropped to my ever-expanding belly. She dropped her eyes to the floor and clasped her hands in front of her waist, waiting silently for Mr. Kelly's attention.

"Yes?" he said, chin lifted.

"I'm sorry, Mr. Kelly, sir. I was just comin' to tell you I was leavin'," she said.

My legs locked. I fumbled with my purse and forced myself to move clumsily toward the door. "Thank you. I'll...I'll find him. Thank you."

Chapter Twenty

The empty shoebox lay on the bed, the lid on top of my clothing, which was strewn across the floor. My belongings were scattered around the bedroom like we'd been robbed. Jimmy Lee sat on the bed with his back to me, Maggie's weekly letters unfolded on the pillows like public newspapers.

"What's this shit?" he spat.

Maggie's letters spoke of the ways she was helping the colored folks, and the things she was planning. I never thought Jimmy Lee would actually rifle through my belongings, and yet, maybe I did, and that's why I'd felt the need to hide them. "What are you doin'?" I hurried to the bedside and grabbed at Maggie's letters, pulling them toward me. "You had no right."

He grabbed my wrist. "No right? I'm your husband. What is all this shit?" He pushed me away. My back hit the dresser. He grabbed one of the letters and read it aloud, "I'm so happy that you want to know what you can do to help with the civil rights movement." He turned scorn-filled eyes toward me. "Civil rights? What are you doin', Alison?"

I clamored for the letters. "Give me those. They're my private letters. This is none of your business." I hated myself for not throwing the darn things away, but the thought of discarding anything from Maggie saddened me. Now, I wish I hadn't been so darned sentimental. I'd never make that mistake again.

He pushed me again; my back slammed against the wall and I fell to my knees, protecting my stomach, and crying out in pain.

"This *is* my business. You wanna help those niggers? You? *My* wife?" He gathered the letters in his arms and tossed them in a bag. "You're not goin' to New York. You can forget it."

I pushed to my feet, holding the dresser for support. "I'd rather be there than here with you," I cried. "I'm goin' to see my sister, and you can't do a darn thing about it. My father already bought the ticket."

"I never should have married you! You're a…a…charity case."

"Charity case?" A lump lodged in my throat like a baseball. "My family has more class than yours ever will, the way you beat up those poor kids." I pushed past the hurt in my back and the fear that made my entire body quake, and gathered my courage like a shield. "I know you and your uncle killed Mr. Bingham, too." It was a guess, a weighted guess based on the things I'd learned about my husband and his uncle in recent weeks. I had hoped it wasn't true, but the moment the words left my lips there was no question.

He was on me in seconds, pinning me to the bed, my belly between us like an unwelcome border. Through gritted teeth he said, "Don't push me, Alison. You don't know shit. That nigger deserved to die."

I struggled against his weight. "Get off of me. You'll hurt the baby."

"My wife ain't gonna help no cotton-pickin' niggers. You got it?"

Hate soared through me. My wrists felt like they were ready to snap beneath his weight.

"Got it?" he hollered. His knees dug into my thighs. "Or it'll be the last thing you ever do."

I had to do something—to get out of there before he hurt the baby. "I got it. Okay, I get it," I seethed.

He pushed his knees deeper into my thighs, until I cried out in pain. Then he climbed off of me with one last thrust, grabbed the bag of letters, and left the bedroom. I curled into a ball, my arms around my belly, and cried, wondering what in the hell I should do next.

Chapter Twenty-One

I sat on the porch of my parents' house the next afternoon thinking about my life, and how it was spiraling out of control. I spent my days avoiding being alone and my nights avoiding my drunken husband who thought I had to *deal with* having our child on my own, like he wasn't planning on helping at all. I felt so alone. I searched for my daddy's truck and found it parked near the fields. It was almost quitting time. I longed for him to call me his little girl and hug me tight. I needed to talk to Mama. She'd know what to do about Jimmy Lee. Loneliness was strangling me, and I needed to find a lifeline before it was too late.

The farmhands walked toward the barn in pairs. I watched Albert, wondering if Jackson was out of the service yet, and then felt guilty for wanting to know.

The screened porch door creaked open behind me. "Daddy's got your train ticket purchased and ready for your trip next month. Are you waitin' to see him?"

"No, actually. I wanted to see you." We sat on the rocking chairs, side by side. "Mama, do you still see Albert's mother?"

She looked out at the field, then down at her lap. When she finally lifted her eyes toward me, she said, "Yes, and Alison, I know Jimmy Lee and Jake hurt that boy. No doubt they were egged on by Corky or some other troublemaker."

"You know about Jake?"

She nodded. "Surely you noticed how little time he's spendin' at home these days. I had a long talk with him." She pressed the wrinkles in her dress against her thighs. "Jake tries to please your daddy, but he battles himself, too. He's a sensitive boy, always has been. He knows what he did was wrong, but inside," she put her hand over her heart, "he's all confused. And now he's avoidin' me for settin' him straight."

"But what about Daddy?"

"Your father doesn't know, and Jake isn't gonna run to your father. He's...more sensitive than that." She inhaled and blew it out slowly.

"He's just like Daddy."

"No, he isn't. Jake's nothin' like him. He just doesn't know any way to connect with your father other than followin' in his shoes."

I didn't understand. If she knew about Jake and Jimmy Lee, why did she allow me to marry him?

"So, you just overlooked what Jimmy Lee did altogether?"

"No," she said. "I was very upset, and I had a talk with his mother. But, the truth of the matter is, that here, in this town, things aren't gonna change anytime soon, and in life, we must pick our battles."

I got up and paced the front porch. "But you let me marry him, so what you really mean is turn our backs on what's happenin', right?"

Mama stood behind me, her hand on the small of my back. "No, I mean do what we can, but not ruin our families in the process. You love Jimmy Lee, who am I to ruin that? We can't change how people like your father and Jimmy Lee feel about equal rights. We can't change how Jimmy Lee was brought up, but we can stop the cycle. We can make changes in the next generation and be kind on the other end of things."

I turned toward Mama, my eyes wet. "I am the next generation."

"Yes, you are."

"But what if that's not enough? I can't look past it. I hate my husband more every time I see him." My hands flew to my mouth, covering it before anymore could slip out, and hidin' the shame I felt for having admitted my secret.

Mama reached out and took my hand in hers. "Alison Jean, you don't mean that."

A tear slipped down my cheek, falling onto my blouse as I nodded my head. "Yes," I whispered. "Yes, I do."

"You must learn to deal with that hatred. Think of what he provides for you, what made you fall in love with him in the first place."

"Mama, I keep thinkin' about Maggie. She's makin' a difference, and workin' hard at bein' involved, and I'm here in this…this…cocoon of a town, pretendin' things aren't goin' on around me." I turned and watched the men at the barn. "My husband is hurtin' boys, and men, just because their skin is a different color."

"Oh, Alison. You're not Maggie. Maggie is a different woman all together. She could no sooner settle down and have a baby than you could go to New York and change the world. You're sewn from different fabric."

Maybe Mama was right. Maybe I was just dreaming, and I didn't actually have the strength to do anything or evoke any changes in life.

"I guess." I sighed, resigning myself to the life I'd created. "How do you get past it, Mama? When you are with Daddy, how do you forget how he treats them?"

"Your father isn't beatin' up anyone. He treats them fairly, he gives them secure jobs. He just holds them at a different social level than us. That's very different."

"Is it?" I asked.

Chapter Twenty-Two

I had looked forward to the train ride to New York, but after several hours of traveling, the movement made me sleepy. I dozed on and off, thankful that there was not a passenger sitting next to me, though we picked up more at each stop along the way. The nearer we came to New York, the more color the leaves boasted. Glorious red and orange leaves waved from their branches. The crisp sky looked less dense than the Arkansas sky, and I wondered if that was because of the heat that seemed to linger in the south, or if it was just the unhappiness in me lifting itself off my shoulders. Jimmy Lee fell silent after our fight. He didn't argue about me going to see Maggie, and I didn't press him about going through my personal things. It was like there was a silent agreement between us to leave each other alone for a bit, and for that, I was thankful.

When I first stepped on the train, I was scared of traveling so far by myself. I wasn't sure what to expect, though Maggie had assured me that no one would bother me. I brought a few books and when I wasn't gazing out at the pretty landscape, I was nose down, escaping into the private world of John and Abigail Adams. *Those Who Love* had been recommended by Maggie, and I found myself enthralled with the love in those pages.

Each time the train stopped, I'd look around at the people going off and coming on the train, and I'd wonder where they were heading. I didn't dare talk to anyone. All in all, I found the train relaxing, like I was in the pages of my own adventure book.

Mama had sewn a small pillow for me to rest my head on, and another for my lower back, and surely I would have been in worse shape without them, but still, I was achy and uncomfortable as we neared my destination. I was surprised to see two colored men board the train and sit in the same car as me. I couldn't help but keep glancing at them. *Were they worried about sittin' where the white folks sat?* I didn't think so. That must be what Jackson and Maggie had been talking about. Things were different up here.

It was no wonder Maggie didn't come home more often—by the time we reached New York, the twenty-two hour trip felt as though it would never end. Crowds of people disembarked, walking fast, as if they all knew exactly where they were going. I felt as out of place as a pig in a horse trailer, and as lost as a blind cow.

"Pixie!" Maggie's voice carried through the station like a familiar embrace. I saw her running toward me, dropped my bags to the floor, and fell into her open arms. "Let me see you!" She ran her eyes up and down my swollen body. "You are so beautiful," she said.

My feet hurt, my belly was as big as a house, and I knew how awful I must have looked. Though I'd been trying to ignore it, looming on my shoulders was Jimmy Lee's rage. Even the relief of seeing Maggie and her compliments didn't take away the hurt of my life.

"Come on," she said, gathering my bags. "Let's get you to my place. I wanna hear all about your new married life."

Cars raced by as we walked block after block toward Maggie's apartment. Her hair had grown shaggier, and her skin shone bright. The walk didn't seem to dampen her energy one bit, though it zapped what little I had left quicker than I realized. I had never seen so many people in one place. Several times I stopped and stared, in awe of the mixing of the races, and the sheer number of people on the street. Maggie tugged me forward, anxious to get to her apartment. I felt like a cow being herded toward a barn. Everyone seemed to be going somewhere in a hurry. I didn't notice the chin-snub that was so common back home, and that, more than anything else, made me wonder about this new place Maggie had made her home.

When we finally flagged down a streetcar with the money Daddy had given me, I fell into the black vinyl with a long-overdue sigh of exhaustion and took it all in. I ran my hands along the smooth, shiny seats. I'd never seen anything like it before. Daddy would be mad that we gave money to someone to drive us around. I could just hear his voice, *That's what God gave you legs for.* I smiled to myself, missing him but knowing I'd have to keep yet another secret about what we used his money for. We took the streetcar for several blocks, and I marveled at the height of the buildings. Never before had I seen anyplace with so much concrete. Everything here was new to me, and I tried to make sense of this world that Maggie lived in. There was hardly any grass anywhere. Where did all those people get their eggs and beef? Maggie explained that in New York, everything came from markets, and there was no farmland in the city. I couldn't wait to tell Mama about everything. I soaked it all in, memorizing the way the buildings looked, and even the insane honking of the horns. Every building seemed to have a stream of people walking in and out. Cars' engines revved and lights flashed, and I was drawn into the energy of the area. By the time we reached Maggie's apartment building, my reservation had been replaced with curiosity.

We climbed five flights of narrow stairs up to the top floor of a very old building. Plaster peeled from the walls, from cracks wider than my pinky finger, and snaked around the corners.

"Maggie, are you sure this is safe?" I asked, out of breath as we neared the top of the staircase.

"You're such a farm girl," she laughed. Maggie unlocked three locks and let us into an apartment, which was about the size of our bedroom back home. There was a tiny stove and refrigerator to the left of the door, and a window that looked across a span of about ten feet, and directly into the brick wall of the building next to us.

"My view of New York," Maggie laughed. "Pix, wipe that pity off of your face. This is the most freedom I've had in twenty years."

"It's just that it's…"

Maggie twirled around, her arms almost hitting the wall. "Small? Old? Ugly? I know, and I still love it!"

I sat down on the only piece of furniture in the room, a ratty, old couch. I sank all the way down to metal.

"Careful, that's our bed you're sittin' on," she said.

I stood and Maggie lifted the cushions to show me the convertible sofa. "The guy next door was givin' it away when I moved in. It suited my purpose just fine." Maggie poured us each a glass of lemonade and sat down beside me.

"Wow, you really are pregnant." She rested her hand on my stomach.

"Yeah, I guess I am."

"I guess I had you pegged wrong, Pix. I got the feelin' you weren't even sure about gettin' married to Jimmy Lee. Are you happy? Does he treat you right?"

I nodded, feeling the burn in my cheeks, trying to feign a smile. My sister saw right through my façade. She squeezed my hand and put an arm around my back.

"Oh, Pixie," was all she said. I laid my head against her shoulder and breathed in the floral scent of her perfume. Tears bubbled up from within my chest and I tried to bite them back, tensing my muscles and swallowing the sound of my sobs. I must have cried for a full five minutes before I pulled back and wiped my eyes, sniffling, my cheeks growing redder by the second.

"What is it? You can tell me, Pix."

"He found your letters. He—" I couldn't bring myself to tell her about him attacking me. She'd be furious. She'd never have been that weak.

Maggie brushed my hair off my shoulders and held my hand. "Okay. Okay, so he knows…what? You're involved? I'm involved?"

"I don't know. That you're involved, and that I wanna be."

"Damn." Maggie drew in a breath and let it out quickly. "Well, then, we gotta figure out what's next. Do you think he'll tell anyone? This could be very dangerous if they know what's comin'."

"What's comin'?"

"Pix? Did somethin' else happen? Did he do anything to you?" Maggie skipped right over my question.

I turned away.

"Pixie, if he touched you, so help me."

I nodded with my back to Maggie.

"Damn him. Well, you're not goin' back there. No way, Pixie."

I spun around. "I have to go back. He's my husband. Mama and Daddy are there."

"What kind of husband hurts his wife?" Maggie paced, her arms crossed. She stopped and put her hand to her chin. When she got that determined look on her face it could only mean one thing. The wheels of her mind were churning, planning.

"He didn't really hurt me. He just, he...he held me down and called me a Negro lover."

"Oh, I'll show him a Negro lover all right," Maggie fumed. "I can't let you go back there."

"I'm goin' back, Maggie. I have to." I laid my hand across my stomach. "I'm havin' his baby. It's my duty."

"Damn it, Pixie, now you sound like Daddy. Your place is not to be held down by an ignorant redneck."

In my heart I knew she was right, but in my mind, I couldn't take his baby away from him even if he didn't want it. He'd grow to want it. Mama said all men did, that they were just scared of the responsibility, but once they see the little baby's face, they melt like butter. I was learning that marriage was hard, and staying in my marriage was what was expected of me by Mama and Daddy, no matter how much it hurt or how hard it was. I found myself stuck between running from a man I no longer loved or respected and confessing my failure as a wife to Daddy, or sticking with my wedding vows, for better or worse, and remaining the sparkle in Daddy's eyes.

Maggie stomped across the floor and took my face in her hands. I had nowhere to look besides into her angry eyes.

"Pixie, you listen to me. I know you, and you know this isn't right. It's not okay for you to be treated this way."

"He was just angry. It'll pass. He's never hurt me before." *At least not physically.*

"It'll pass? Pix, you're not a little girl anymore. You're gonna be a mother. You need to think about more than just yourself." Maggie put her hand to her eyes. "What happened? How did he go from sneakin' out with you to this?"

If only she knew.

"Promise me that if he touches you again, you will leave immediately. Go stay with Mama and Daddy. Come here. Hell, go anywhere you need to, but do not stay with him. I swear to God I will kill him if he touches you again."

I gave her my word, then wondered if I were strong enough to keep it.

Maggie pulled a flyer out from beneath a stack of papers. "There's a meetin' tonight about the boycott in Forrest Town."

"Wait, you didn't tell me about a boycott there. You said they were makin' headway with civil rights, but you never mentioned Forrest Town. Maggie, I said I wanted to be involved, but a boycott, where I live? I don't think that's smart."

"I didn't tell you because I thought you'd cancel, Pix. They've been workin' on this for months. They were gonna have the meetin' last month, but I asked them to wait."

"You tricked me!"

"No, I opened a door so you could make a decision for yourself. You don't *have* to do a damn thing. There are groups comin' from all over; Mississippi, Chicago, New York. Pix, this is huge. They'll be boycottin' the major stores and—"

"Wait," I said, panic thumping against my chest. "Boycottin' the major stores? Why? Jimmy Lee's furniture store? It's the biggest store in town. Why are you doin' this to me?"

"Oh, my God, Pix, have you lost your mind? Doin' this to you? Think about it, they don't let coloreds work in the showroom, only in the stockroom, and for peanuts!" She paused, letting her words settle on my shoulders like a weight. "Hell, they don't even let them shop in the front of the stores or eat in the diner. If we don't take a stance now, when will it happen? Do you see any changes occurrin'? Do you see Jimmy Lee openin' his shop to Division Street families?" Maggie ran her hand through her hair. "Do you want your baby to grow up like we did? Afraid to talk to the little colored girls in town? Come on, Pixie, do the right thing."

The tiny room was closing in on me. *Jimmy Lee's store, boycotted?* "If the coloreds boycott, how will that help make any changes?"

"Not just coloreds, Pix. This is bigger than you and me and Division Street. There are whites from all around who are takin' part in enforcin' integration." Maggie spit her words out fast, smacking the back of her hand in her palm for emphasis, as if everything she said was the most important. "Think about it. No one will come from other cities to shop there. People will be afraid to cross the picket lines, afraid of fights and trouble."

"Maggie—"

"I know what you're thinkin'. Not trouble like violence trouble, but trouble like yellin' and name callin'."

That didn't feel right. I'd heard about the riots, the fights, coloreds getting beaten. "How can you say that? You don't know," I said. "You have no idea what might happen, and you know what they do to coloreds there, for nothin' more than breathin'—this could cause all sorts of trouble for them. And what about you? What will you do in all of this?"

Maggie sat down and crossed her long legs, her short skirt barely covering her thighs. "Alison, listen to me. You can live in your little daddy bubble all you want, but I can't. I thought you wanted to help."

I sat next to her. "I did, but—"

Maggie shook her head. "You did when it was removed from where you were, when you could hear about it, but not really be affected by it. I get it, you know? I was that person. But now," she looked around the apartment. "Things are different. I have friends who are colored. I have met wonderful men and women who are colored. I can no longer turn a blind eye to things. Even if things are better here, and in bigger cities, I can't pretend they're that way everywhere."

I closed my eyes and just breathed. I couldn't make any decisions, my mind was too full of information, right and wrong, segregation and integration, tangled together like a convoluted web of confusion.

"Why don't you rest for a few hours before we leave for the meetin'."

Nothing could have sounded more inviting at that very moment. I closed my eyes and drifted off to sleep.

Chapter Twenty-Three

The only thing that separated night and day in New York was the color of the sky. There were just as many people walking around the streets at night, coming in and out of stores and restaurants, as there were during the day. Some were dressed in fancy clothing, others wore everyday jeans. Coming from a family where going into town was a big deal, seeing children milling about at eight o'clock at night with their parents made me wonder what type of parents those people were. Children sat in restaurant windows, their parents smoking at the dinner table. Daddy would have none of that. Daddy was all about family being home, safe, together. Forget the fact that we couldn't afford fancy restaurants. Even if we could, I think Daddy would want Mama's down home cooking warming our bellies.

"Don't these kids have to get to bed? Don't they go to school?" I asked

Maggie laughed at my ignorance. "Of course. It's just different here." She pointed to a brightly lit sign above the restaurant that said, *Anyone with cash is welcome.* "You don't see that back home, huh?"

Maggie pulled me down an alley and then down two more quieter streets. I began to worry when I realized we were suddenly alone. The noise of the city fell away behind us, and suddenly everything seemed too big. Two colored men came around the corner, heading in our direction. I grabbed Maggie's hand.

"Relax," she said with a smile. "You're not in Arkansas anymore."

I watched them descend a stairway and disappear, and then I let out a breath I hadn't realized I was holding.

Two minutes later, we were heading down the same set of stairs. I clung to Maggie's arm, begging her to turn around. "Trust me," she answered. The stairway led to a small, dead-end alley. Maggie knocked three times on a dark-green, wooden door. She knocked two more times in rapid succession, and the door swung open.

A colored man with an enormous Afro and crooked, yellow teeth stood before us. Maggie embraced him. I closed my mouth tight, my eyes darting around the inside of the building. The alley behind me was dark, the room before me was not much lighter. I wanted to run, to find a modicum of something familiar, but there I stood, mesmerized by the sweet and pungent aroma that filtered out the door.

"Marlo, this is my sister, Pixie. Pixie, Marlo."

"H...hi." My voice shook. It took all of my will to follow Maggie into the dark, low-ceilinged room. Cigarette smoke and something more acerbic filled the air. Music played low in the background, the beat fast and inconsistent. My hand was glued to Maggie's arm. She pulled me forward, embracing each person, colored or white, introducing me as her little sister. I'm not sure what I expected, but the closeness of the coloreds and whites, sitting on the same couches, white girls with their legs stretched across the colored girls' laps, passing cigarettes back and forth, took me by surprise.

"Drag?" A stick-skinny, dark-haired girl held out some sort of thin cigarette toward me.

"No," Maggie said, and pushed her arm away. "Darla, this is Pixie, my little sister. She just 'bout choked when she tried smokin' with me." Maggie winked at me. "She's not smokin' and she never drinks, so she won't be playin' any of those reindeer games." They laughed like schoolgirls.

"Sit down. Take a load off," Darla said. I wiggled in between her and the end of the couch. The biggest colored man I'd ever seen came over and sat on the arm of the couch. I leaned toward Darla, my heart going *thump, thump, thump* real hard.

"That's Bear," she said, and tapped Bear on the back.

"You're scarin' her. Move your ass," she said.

Bear grinned at her, then turned very serious, threatening eyes toward me. "I scare you?"

I swallowed hard, instinctively reaching for Darla's arm as if she were Maggie.

"Relax," Maggie smacked Bear's arm. "He's teasin' you, Pix."

"I thought I was gonna have a heart attack," I whispered harshly to Maggie, which only made Bear laugh harder than he already was. I inched closer to Darla.

"She's straight off the train from Arkansas," Maggie explained. "Be nice, will ya'?" Maggie sat at my feet and said, "He's sweet as a teddy bear, hence the name Bear. Nothin' to worry about, Pix."

I grabbed Maggie's shoulder and hung on tight. Bear got up to answer the door, and I breathed a sigh of relief.

"Can we go home, please?" I whispered to Maggie.

Maggie squeezed my hand and shook her head. "I'm here, you're fine. Trust me."

The door opened and I heard it slam closed. Several colored men blocked the doorway, murmuring something, then making a hole between them. Two white men in business suits entered the room, moving toward the front of the crowd. All eyes were on them, including mine. I wondered if they were courageous or stupid. In Forrest Town this mixing of the races, where there were more coloreds than whites, might render these men in trouble. They showed no fear, which made me wonder again if this was the type of thing Jackson had been referring to.

Marlo held his hands up and shushed the crowd. "Let's come to order, please, we have a lot of ground to cover today. Mr. Nash and Mr. Grange are here to fill us in on what we can expect, legally, from the boycott."

We listened as the lawyers described violent riots, with protesters of all races being beaten, some near death, colored men going missing, and even reports of women being manhandled. Arrests, they said, were sure to happen, by the hundreds. I clawed Maggie's shoulder. She put her hand on mine and patted it. I could feel her digesting all of the dangers as her shoulders tensed beneath my fingers. Darla reached over and laid her hand on top of ours. I looked at her, and she mouthed, *It's okay. Change is good.*

There was beauty in the mixing of the races in the room. I sensed a meshing of strength and hope. What was missing was fear. The coloreds in Forrest Town carried fear in their tentative gaits, embarrassment clear in their rearward glances when they headed toward the back doors of the buildings. The lack of that type of fear was evident in that jam-packed room where I sat clinging to my sister's shoulder. I still didn't trust this change, though the enormity of the hope rose above the horrific odors of perspiration and cigarettes that lingered like thick fog in the tiny room. I laid my hand across my belly, and slowly came to realize how much I wanted my baby to grow up in a world of hope, not a world of oppression—even if that oppression might not be pushed upon a white child, it still had an unforgivable impact.

"We're scheduling the boycott for Forrest Town for late fall. As you know, the white children go back to school in September, but the colored children are forced to pick cotton in the fields, and they don't return to school until after picking season. We want to hit at a time when those white folks *need* the colored labor. The goal is to stop all purchase power in the white stores and all picking power on the farms. This will have the greatest impact." Sweat glistened on Mr. Nash's forehead, the pits of his white shirt soaked through.

His words hit home, and I worried about my daddy's farm, and how he would make it through the winter without his income from the fields. There had been years when he had to borrow money for cotton seed, and I remembered those years with less food on the table and restrictions on how often we could go into town with the truck. One year we all helped Daddy cut down all the trees in the lower five acres of our property and brought it to the mill to sell. My memory of that year was dull. I scarcely remember anything more than constant fatigue. I worried about Jimmy Lee's job and his uncle's furniture store, but that worry was too cloudy with hurt to be anything more than an obligatory thought.

"Forrest Town families rely on the income from the fields, both colored and white families. Retailers rely on the income stream from neighborin' towns. Without it, the stores will shut down."

The voice came from behind me and stole my very breath. *Jackson*. I turned toward his proud voice, my hand slipping from between Maggie and Darla's safe grip. I stared into a thick crowd of bodies, my heart slamming against my ribs, and I wondered if I'd somehow merely wished his voice. Then, the crowd split, and Jackson, in all his handsomeness, stood before me. His eyes were locked on the lawyer in the front of the room. Each step he took brought with it a memory; his scent, his touch, the thick deliciousness of his kiss. The urge to reach for him was strong. I clasped my hands in my lap, hoping to quell my sinful thoughts. The love that I thought I had given up, forgotten about, maybe even only dreamed existed, reared its powerful heat within me.

"There'll be coloreds who won't take part. They won't work against us, but they'll be too 'fraid of what comes with fightin' segregation." He stood beside Mr. Nash, his shoulders and chest thicker than when I'd last seen him, five months ago. His face was stronger, his eyes more determined and focused than I'd remembered. Under my hand, something in my stomach moved. *My baby*. Jimmy Lee's baby. The doctor estimated twelve weeks when I had the blood drawn. Twelve weeks. My wedding night. There was no turning back, now just shy of five months. I'd made my choice, and now I felt sick to my stomach instead of excited by the first movements of the child that grew within me.

"Are you okay, hun? You're shakin'." Darla put her hand across my shoulder.

Maggie spun around. "Pix, you alright?" she whispered.

I didn't mean to shake my head instead of nod, but that's what happened. Maggie helped me stand from my perch on the couch. Darla put an arm around my waist as they led me away from the group. I turned and looked over my shoulder, meeting Jackson's confused eyes.

The small bedroom in the back of the apartment where the meeting was taking place smelled like cigarettes and hummed from the voices outside the door. I laid on the bed, Maggie and Darla crouched beside me.

"What's goin' on? Do you need a doctor?" Maggie asked.

"No, I'm just tired. All that travel must have worn me out worse than I thought." Their concerned stares were too much to take. How could I tell my sister about my secret love for Jackson? I was sure that even the thought would get me a one-way ride to hell. "Can we just go home?" I asked.

Maggie shook her head. "It's a really long walk. I think we're better off restin' here until after the meetin' and bummin' a ride. I don't have fare for a streetcar."

I closed my eyes and listened to the noises of the meeting, reminding myself that I was supposed to love Jimmy Lee. *I love Jimmy Lee. I love Jimmy Lee* played in my mind. I turned toward the dirty, gray wall and thought, *I love Jackson Johns. I love Jackson Johns. I'm in so much trouble.*

The door opened and when Jackson's voice floated over my back and into my ears I held my breath. "Is everything alright?"

I couldn't turn and face him. I was afraid to be that close to him. I didn't trust myself.

"Yeah, my sister just got here from Arkansas. She's exhausted." Maggie rubbed my back, then said, "Hey, Jackson, do you know Alison? You worked on our farm a bit when you were home, remember?" She tapped my shoulder. "Pix? Turn around and say hi."

No, no, no!

"Uh, no, we never met," Jackson lied.

Maggie pulled my shoulder and turned me just enough to see him. I blinked back the love that wanted to drip from my eyes. I covered my belly, ashamed of the child that grew within me, ashamed of what that child represented between us—my weakness, the love I threw away to save face with my own father.

Jackson walked over to the bed and looked down at my stomach. I thought I had forgotten the hold that look of desperation had on my heart. His dark brows furrowed, his eyes softly taking me in. Behind the concern of his serious cheeks, I felt a warmth, a caring smile that dared not show for fear of revealing whatever emotions lie in wait. "When is your baby due? Alison, right?"

I nodded.

"She's due in March. Little Pix here got pregnant on her weddin' night!"

"Maggie!" I flushed.

"Yeah?" Jackson crossed his arms. His next words were caressed with sadness that I think only I noticed. "You are certainly blessed."

"Hey, Jackson, do you want to meet up with us tomorrow, after Pixie, uh, Alison, is feelin' better? I want to talk about what she can do back home, in town, to help prepare."

"Maggie? What if I'm not feelin' better?"

"I can come to your apartment," Jackson offered, holding my gaze.

"Yes, perfect. We'll figure it out then," Maggie agreed.

Jackson reached for my hand. "Until then, Alison?"

I shook his hand, in the eyes of Maggie and Darla, the hand of a caring stranger. Warmth spread through my body, and I knew I was in trouble.

Chapter Twenty-Four

The next afternoon, trepidation pinched my nerves. By noon I had already cleaned Maggie's apartment, washed down her counters and bathroom, and still had more nervous energy than I knew what to do with.

"What is with you, Pix? One minute you're shaky and weak, the next you're like Mama, only hyper."

"Nervous, I guess. I'm not sure this boycott is the best idea." I kept my back to her as I wiped down the inside of the front door.

"It's scary, but just think of the families you will help. For generations to come, people will talk about the ones who made it happen."

"But, arrests? Missin' men? I mean, it sounds pretty scary to me. You know what Jimmy Lee and Daddy will do if they find out I'm helpin', right? They'll lock me in the cellar for good." My mind drifted back to the day Jimmy Lee found Maggie's letters and the attack that followed. I shivered.

"They'll never know."

I turned to face her. I swear my belly had grown overnight. It protruded like a small watermelon carried by my widening hips. "Yeah? Jimmy Lee already thinks I'm wantin' to be involved in civil rights, remember?"

"We'll have to go covert, then. Can I send you letters at work instead of at your apartment?"

I thought about that route. "Maybe."

"And as for Daddy, well, why would he find out? Daddy stays on the farm. He's not a busy body or attune to town gossip. Jimmy Lee might be a different story. You'll probably have to figure out a way to meet with some of the colored supporters without Jimmy Lee findin' out."

"Supporters? Division Street? Do you really think that's a possibility?"

"Jackson's mama has been coordinatin' the meetin's. She works at the furniture store, in the warehouse, too. And since Albert works for Daddy, maybe you guys could meet at one of their houses."

"Oh, yeah," I smirked. "I can just see me waddlin' down toward that end of town. People would notice me from a mile away."

"What about outside of town?"

"How would I get there?"

"What about at the river, that's not far from the apartment, you could say you're takin' a walk, or do it while Jimmy Lee is at work."

I could do that.

By the time Jackson arrived, a knot had tightened across my shoulders in anticipation of his visit. Maggie let him in and I busied myself pouring lemonade and setting out the cornbread I had baked.

"Smells like my mama's kitchen," Jackson said as he sat on the couch.

Seating would be a problem. The couch was small and there were no other chairs. I set the tray on the small table and lowered myself to the ground facing the couch.

Jackson stood, "Please, sit here."

"I'm fine," I said. "I'm pregnant, not injured."

"Alison!" Mama's shock rode on Maggie's face. She turned to Jackson. "I'm sorry, her manners must have slipped away with her pregnancy."

Jackson laughed, and it brought warmth to my cheeks. I felt like a schoolgirl experiencing her first sip of moonshine, only I'd already tasted the sweet nectar and longed for more. *Would I flush every time I was near him?* I wondered, or was it the old everyone-wants-what-they-can't-have syndrome that Mama had warned me about so many times?

"I'm sorry. Thank you, Jackson," I said.

Jackson and Maggie concocted a way for me to communicate with the families. Jackson would call his mother, and she'd spread the word among them. She'd get a message to me through the back door of the diner, and so the system was born. I couldn't take my eyes off of Jackson. I could feel him purposefully not looking at me, and when he did stray my way, his eyes met mine, never lowering to my stomach, never letting on that he had any feelings for me whatsoever. I couldn't blame him. I had been the one to throw away the brief, albeit immense, love we shared. I'd been the one to marry a man I didn't truly love, and now I'd have his spawn. I loved the baby inside me, or at least I thought I was loving it more and more with each passing day. It still didn't feel very real to me. But that love was tamped down the moment I saw Jackson. The baby felt like a bridge between us that I knew we could never cross. I must be losing my mind, because I had no business thinking in those terms at all.

"How does that sound, Alison?" Maggie asked.

I had been so busy wallowing in self pity that I had no idea what they'd been talking about.

"Um, what part? The river?"

Maggie laughed. "The whole thing. I know how you feel about the river."

"We're worried that with findin' Mr. Bingham," Jackson's voice softened, "it might bring back too many hard feelin's." He looked at Maggie. "Maybe we should choose another location. I don't feel really safe with her goin' there anyway."

"No, I'm fine," I said, knowing full well that it would be harder than milking a horse to return to the river. Not only did Mr. Bingham's body linger in my mind, but a shadow of Jimmy Lee's nastiness remained. "Actually, can we meet at the creek at the end of our property? It runs parallel to the apartments behind the woods. I think it's even closer than the river, so it might be easier for me." Maybe it was bad of me to suggest the creek, since it was where Jackson and I had spent our first afternoon together, but I couldn't help it. I wanted to see how he'd react, and besides, it was more convenient.

Jackson shot a look at me and rearranged himself on the couch. The way he twitched in his seat told me that, like me, he was thinking about the first time we walked down by the creek. As cruel as that might seem, it warmed my heart to see him squirm. He couldn't forget our time together any better than I could. "I don't—"

"I think we should do whatever will make Alison feel safest," Maggie looked at me protectively. "Pix, do you remember Mr. Kale? The old man who used to run the post office?"

"Sure. Candy Kale the lollipop man? Why?"

"His son is part of the Panthers' support group and he'll be there at each meetin'."

"Is that safe for him? I mean—"

"Yes," Jackson answered. "He's well protected. I worry more about you, Alison. You're with child. I'm not sure this is the best thing for you to take part in."

"I want to do this. I want my baby to be born into an integrated world and brush arms with everyone, not be afraid to play with other children just because of the color of their skin. Every time I see a white water fountain and a colored water fountain it makes me sick. Don't get me wrong, I'm petrified to do this, but I think I have to." I took a deep breath and said, "I can't be weak any longer. It's time Daddy knew what I believed in." I wanted to prove to Jackson that my feelings still rode deep, and that I was going to make a change in my priorities. I realized that as soon as Daddy knew what I was fixing to be a part of, there'd be no keeping those thoughts from Jimmy Lee, and I was slowly coming to realize that my baby being born into an integrated lifestyle did not go hand in hand with Jimmy Lee raising this child. I had no idea what I'd do about it, but the thought was riding heavily on my shoulders.

"Whoa, Pix, you can't tell Daddy what you're doin'. No way."

I knew she was right. "I know, okay. I didn't mean that literally. Sheesh, he and Jimmy Lee would kill me." Jimmy Lee's name slipped out before I could catch it, and Jackson looked away. "I meant that I want to do this. I've been a coward with all of the important aspects of my life, and I don't wanna be anymore."

Maggie ran her eyes over my belly, then gave me a look that said she was proud of me, but also...that it might just be too late. I twisted the wedding ring I wished I wasn't wearing.

On the way out the door, Jackson hugged Maggie, and then she went to the kitchen to wrap up a piece of cornbread for him to take home. Jackson pulled me close and whispered, "Even with his child inside you, I still love you."

Too shocked from the embrace to reciprocate, I stood there like an idiot, paralyzed by his admission. Maggie returned and handed him the cornbread. "We should do this again," she said.

I couldn't tell if the tiny flutter in my belly was caused by butterflies or the baby.

"There's a get together Thursday night. A bunch of people are holdin' a live performance of enactin' desegregatin' America."

Jackson caught my worried look. I saw him searching my eyes for a response to his confession, but I had no words to say. They were tethered to my aching heart and refused to break free.

"Don't worry, the word isn't out," Jackson finally said. "There are just about thirty of us and it's in the projects. There's music, but there'll be no words. I'd love for you to come see it."

"What are the projects?" I had so much to learn.

Jackson lifted one eyebrow, and smirked. "It's like Division Street back home."

"Is it safe?"

"Safer than Division Street." Again, his sarcasm cut me like a knife.

"I promised to work late Thursday night—big court day Friday. But you should go, Pix. Jackson, will you take good care of her?"

"No, really. I would feel funny."

"Nonsense. I'll pick you up at eight." His tone left no room for negotiation.

Chapter Twenty-Five

"You're goin' tonight, Pix. This is good for you, to break out of that small town fear. I was scared the first time I went, but really, Jackson will take good care of you."

That's what I'm worried about. Maggie wasn't buying my fake sick routine. She was going to work and I'd have all day to stew over being alone with Jackson.

"Besides, remember when we used to walk by the church near Division Street on Sundays and the gospel just pulled us in? Remember how we moved to the music, and if anyone drove by we'd pretend we were just messin' around? You don't have to do that anymore. Now you can enjoy it. I promise you, you'll return a changed woman."

I think I already am.

The knock on the door made my heart leap into my throat. My hands trembled as I reached for the knob.

I pulled the door open. *I can do this.* Jackson stood before me in a dark-green t-shirt and jeans. His eyes met mine, and I swear a current of electricity passed between us.

"You look radiant," he said.

I looked down at my maternity blouse and skirt, feeling like an overgrown balloon, and turned to hide my blushing cheeks. "Let me grab my bag," I said.

Jackson came inside and closed the door behind him. He stood in the entryway, respectfully giving me space.

"I'm glad you agreed to come."

"Mm-hmm." My voice was caught in my throat. It took all my courage not to fall into his arms.

"Listen, we should talk," he said. "The way we left things, I'm really sorry. I understood where you were comin' from. Things were too dangerous for us." He paused. I listened with my back to him as I put Maggie's house key in my purse. "You did the right thing. I'm happy for you."

"Don't be." *Oh, my goodness, where did that come from?* I spun around and fumbled for words. "I mean, don't be happy. No, not that, it's just...oh, I don't know how to say it."

Jackson took a step closer to me. I could smell his aftershave, a different, sexier scent than the smell of him after he'd worked all day.

"What is it?" he asked. He placed his hand on my upper arm, and my heart swooned with its warmth, inciting memories of his tender touch as we dropped to the field months before. I could still feel his body trembling under my hands, his muscular thighs bare against my own.

I looked down at the floor, hiding my blush. He lifted my chin with his finger. "Alison, you can tell me anything. I won't think poorly of you. I won't try to take you away from the life you have."

"But—"

"I meant what I said, that I love you even if you are carryin' Jimmy Lee's baby. I haven't been with another woman since we parted, and I don't want to. It's you who touched me with your open heart."

He touched my cheek, and I closed my eyes again, relishing in his touch. When I opened them, he was smiling.

"I believed what I told you, that things needed to change. I was goin' in this direction anyway, but I didn't really have the courage then to do what I'm doin' now. You gave me that courage. You made me realize that no matter what I thought in my heart, no matter what I might have felt, this issue was so much bigger than that. Love can't conquer all."

"I was afraid to lose Daddy," I explained.

"Shh," he said, and dropped his hand. I wished he hadn't. "I understand. Your father, your family, that's your world. My world isn't backwoods Arkansas. My world is everywhere. I want to know that anywhere I go, I can go with the one I love."

"I'm sorry."

"Don't be. You helped me to understand myself better. I know I can't have a partial relationship." He rubbed his hands on the thighs of his jeans, then said, "Alison, there was a big Supreme Court case in June, and it, combined with our boycotts and protests, has the ability to change everything."

"What do you mean? Martin Luther King tried to change everything and Forrest Town is still segregated."

"Come, sit." He guided me to the couch. "The Lovings, they're an interracial couple who married in '57 in Virginia."

My eyes grew wide. "That was ten years ago."

"Illegal, right? Well, they were sentenced to a year in prison in '59, but it was suspended for 25 years if they agreed to leave the state. Mildred, the wife, she wrote in protest to Attorney General Robert F. Kennedy. Kennedy referred her to the American Civil Liberties Union, and that's when everything started to change.

"The ACLU filed a motion on their behalf, and a slew of lawsuits followed, eventually reachin' the Supreme Court. Get this, five years later, the Loving's case still hadn't been decided, so they began a class action suit in the D.C. district court—and even that was shot down."

"I really don't understand all this legal stuff."

"What it comes down to is that they didn't give up. They appealed, and in June, the 12th of June to be exact, the court overturned their convictions, dismissin' Virginia's argument that the law was not discriminatory because it applied equally to, and provided identical penalties for, both white and colored people. The Supreme Court ruled that the law against interracial marriages violated several clauses in the Fourteenth Amendment. They won. They won, Alison, and they've opened doors for more interracial couples."

"But what does that have to do with Arkansas?"

He grabbed my hands. "Things are changin'. Maybe not now, maybe not tomorrow, but they are. Look around you. You've seen how different New York is from Arkansas."

"Yeah, it scares me a little," I admitted.

"It scared me, too, when I first got here, but I can't ever go back to livin' how it was in Forrest Town."

I tried to process what he'd said, but Mr. Bingham's dead body kept floating into my mind.

"I can't imagine Forrest Town ever bein' any different."

"Baby steps. That's all we can do. We can try, and if we fail, we fail."

"But what if failin' means you get killed?" The reality of that possibility loomed between us, thick and uncomfortable.

"I fought for this country. Doesn't it make sense that I'd fight for my hometown, where my family lives?"

We walked through the dark streets of the projects, passing old men and women sitting on the concrete steps, cigarette smoke clouding around them, open bottles of alcohol by their feet. Children moved about, carefree and seemingly undaunted by what I found desolate and depressing. There were small clusters of young colored men and women hooting and laughing. I grabbed Jackson's hand, then wrapped my free arm around my belly protectively.

Jackson leaned into me. "Don't worry, nothin's gonna happen."

We turned down an alley and entered a courtyard with a small, grassy area. Eight or ten men and women were performing, their arms swayed in the air and they jumped about with great, dramatic flair, but they didn't speak. I had never seen such a performance. Some moves were as graceful as a dancer's, while others were sharp and angry. The crowd moved to a strange musical rendition of guitars and tambourines.

People sprawled on blankets on the grass or leaned against the building. Many held cigarettes, and I recognized the same sweet aroma that I'd smelled at the meeting, which Maggie explained was marijuana.

The moon shone down on the performers like a spotlight, and we sat on the grass and watched the performance unfold. It seemed everyone held either a can of beer or a bottle of alcohol, and it reminded me of the night that Albert was beaten, further confirming my desire to be part of the Forrest Town desegregation efforts.

Darla came and sat next to me, pulling me into her thin chest in a deep embrace. "So glad you made it, Pixie," she said with a coy smile. "I hope you don't mind, Maggie shared your nickname with me. I love it. It suits you perfectly." She touched my belly. "You're such a tiny, little thing."

"I don't feel so tiny," I answered. I wasn't used to people touching my stomach. I'd lived such a solitary life with Jimmy Lee that my shoulders relaxed, the knot in my stomach loosened, and it felt good to let Darla in. It had been so long since I'd had a friend, that I was almost afraid to believe in it.

"Aw, come on. You're a pixie. It suits you." Darla sat next to me and began swaying, her arms held high above her head. I turned to find Jackson staring at me. He nodded, and then put his own arms up in the air. I followed, tentatively, letting the soothing guitar rhythm move me.

"Pix, you made it! Groovy to see you!" I opened my eyes to find Marlo, yellow teeth and big hair, crouched in front of me. His stringy arms hanging by his side.

Darla shrugged. "I said Pixie suited you. So I shared, shoot me."

"It's okay, Darla," I said, covering my blushing cheeks.

"Nah, don't be embarrassed. Know why they call me Marlo?"

"Uh, it's your name?" I said.

"Are you kiddin'? My parents would never call me that. My name is Martin Riley Logan, after my pop. Never been called Marlo 'til I met these fine folks. They gave me an identity all my own."

I liked that. Maybe it was time I had my own identity.

"Right on, sista'," Marlo went off to greet another friend.

I turned toward Jackson. "Thanks for bringin' me. I'm really glad I came. This is so different than anything I've ever been around."

"This is the new world, Alison."

He wrapped his arm around my shoulder. I stiffened.

"I'm sorry," he said, withdrawing his arm. "I didn't mean anything by that. I just got too comfortable."

I looked at Darla, worried she'd seen and would think I was some sort of loose woman. Her eyes were closed, her hands wrapped around a beer bottle. She swayed back and forth, seemingly oblivious to the rest of us. Completely absorbed by the music.

"I overreacted," I said. "I just don't want to cause undue trouble. That's all."

In protecting my own emotions by trying to remain at a distance from him, I'd hurt his feelings. I reached for his hand. To hell with what others thought. Jackson was my friend, and if this wasn't someplace we could show that, there would never be a time or place where we could. Even if for only a few minutes, I wanted to feel the sense of being with him, alive, in public. Jimmy Lee was so far away that it was like he existed in some dream I'd conjured up long ago.

After the performance Jackson and I held hands as he walked me home. My back and legs were tired, but I felt free from the shadows of the past. Strangely, I didn't feel as though I was cheating on Jimmy Lee by holding Jackson's hand, and the worry of what Daddy might think was fleeting rather than all-consuming. I did wonder what Mama might think, if she saw me now. She'd be disappointed, of that I was certain. Not because the color of Jackson's skin, but because of the vow that I had taken with Jimmy Lee.

We stopped at a coffee shop, and I waited out front at a small, round table while Jackson went inside to grab two cups of hot chocolate. Car horns honked as they passed. How different New York was from Forrest Town. If I were home, I'd be sleeping beside Jimmy Lee, waiting for the next uneventful day to unfold. A cool breeze wrapped itself around me. *Jimmy Lee.* I was having his baby. What was I doing here with Jackson? I watched him through the glass storefront, paying for the hot chocolate. He looked over and smiled. I turned away. Why was life so complicated? Why had I not stood up for what I felt back home, all those months ago? How would I ever get out of the pickle I was in? Maybe I couldn't. I'd chosen my life, what right did I have to try and change that now?

"Here you are," Jackson said as he set down the hot cocoa. "You alright? You look kind of, I don't know. Sad?"

I sipped the cocoa, letting the warmth of it soothe my worries. "I'm alright. This is all so new to me."

"That it is," he said, and reached for my hand.

I looked around. No one there knew me, no one would run back home to tell Jimmy Lee that they'd seen me, but I worried about Maggie—what would she think? I withdrew my hand.

"Alison, I don't want you to get the wrong impression. I'm not tryin' to take you away from your husband."

"You're not?" *Now I feel stupid.*

"I love you. I do, but I'm not a kid. I know what trouble it would cause for you to leave your husband and come to New York, or for me to come back to Forrest Town—I'd never survive. It'd be my body they found next in the river."

"Don't say that," I said.

"It's true."

How we'd gone from being apart to being this close in one evening, I had no idea. We drank our hot cocoa, then walked the rest of the way home in silence. The lights were on in the apartment. Maggie was home. A relieved sigh blew through my lips. I didn't want to be in the position to have to decide where to go from there.

Jackson took my hands in his.

"What now?" I asked.

"Now, we work to make things better for the folks back home."

"Right, through your mama. But—"

Jackson put a finger to my lips. "Don't. I know what happened. She told me."

"But you told her—about us? How could you?"

"How couldn't I? I trust Mama. She raised me. She loves me."

"She hates me."

Jackson shook his head. "She hurts *for* you. She knows there was no way we could be together, but I needed to tell someone." He looked down, rubbed the back of his neck. "The hurt was so deep, Alison. I wasn't eatin', wasn't sleepin'. Mama knew without me tellin' her. All I did was confirm who I was pinin' for."

I wanted to run away and hide in a hole. His mother knew how much I had hurt him. I was just as bad as Jimmy Lee. I'd hurt one of her boys. What would my own mother think?

Jackson touched my cheek. "Alison, now we go back to our lives. You have your baby, I have my life."

I was thrown right back into that night at the creek, when I chose Daddy's love over him. Fear tiptoed up my nerves and clasped around my heart. That all-consuming emptiness I'd felt as he walked away shrouded around me. I squeezed his hand; my heart pulling my lips toward his, my mind telling me to beware. I shook my head. "I don't want to lose you again."

His eyebrows drew together. Jackson shook his head, his confusion stretching between us like a bridge I wanted to cross.

I pulled him gently toward me and kissed him, long and slow, like he'd kissed me all those months ago. His hands slid around my waist, my pregnant belly pressing against him. I ran my hands up the back of his neck, feeling the pulse of his heart against me. The world fell away. "I want to be here with you," I whispered.

He kissed my cheek, my neck, then whispered in my ear, "Don't make promises you can't keep."

"I can't promise, but I can try," I whispered. All I knew was that I wanted to be right there forever. I never wanted to go back to Forrest Town. I didn't want to see, much less be with, Jimmy Lee. I didn't want to watch Jake vying for Daddy's attention, or see the hurt look in Daddy's eyes when I spoke of Maggie. I didn't want to think about Clara being forced into a sexual relationship with Jimmy Lee's uncle, that would lead to the death of her husband and her fleeing her family and friends to save her own life. I wanted to remain in New York, in Jackson's arms, far away from the reality of life that scraped at my very being every second of the day.

The doorknob rattled, startling me out of my fog. I stepped away from Jackson.

"There you are, Pix!" Maggie was dressed in an oversized t-shirt I didn't recognize and cotton pants. "I was worried. Jackson, did you take good care of my little sis? Wanna come in?" She swung the door wide open.

My cheeks burned as I slipped by her and into the apartment. I sat on the couch, my arms wrapped around my middle, and my heart tied in knots.

Chapter Twenty-Six

The week after I returned from New York, I was setting out the chocolate pie Jean had made, when there was a rap at the back door of the diner. It was Friday, and I grabbed a lollipop from the counter and headed toward the door, looking forward to the one happy moment in my world of disappointment. Jimmy Lee hadn't asked me about my trip, and he hadn't been spending much time at home. Seeing the little boy's face light up would be a real treat.

I pulled the door open and Mrs. Johns stood before me, her thick middle bubbling over the belt of her dress. I blinked a few times, looking from side to side, our previous confrontation rushing back. My heart slammed against my chest as if seeking escape.

She dropped her eyes to my swollen middle.

I put my hand over my belly. "Ma'am?"

She reached into her purse, shaking her head and pursing her lips.

Oh, God, oh, God, oh, God.

She took a step toward me, leaning in so close that I could smell the coffee on her breath. She took my hand in hers, then curled my fingers around something and pressed in tight. "Be careful," she whispered. She turned and hurried down the steps, disappearing around the side of the building.

"Was there an order?" Jean asked from behind me.

I slipped my hand into the pocket of my uniform. "Uh, no, she was mistaken. Her husband didn't order anything today, I guess." I kept my back to Jean, worried my eyes might reveal my lie.

As Jean's footsteps retreated, I hightailed it into the bathroom and locked the door. The sealed envelope was small and stained. I ran my fingernail along the underside of the flap and withdrew the single-paged letter. I brought the paper to my nose and inhaled, hoping for a scent of Jackson. There was none.

Dear Alison,

I know you're scared, afraid you'll be caught writing to me, or that Mama will be caught giving you the letters. Have faith. Be strong. I will wait as long as I have to, until your trying can become your promise.

Love, Jackson

Jean jiggled the doorknob. "Alison? I gotta go, hun."

"I'll be right out." I looked around the tiny bathroom and saw no place to hide the letter. Afraid of being caught with it, I tore it into tiny pieces, wrapped it in toilet paper, and flushed it down the toilet.

For days I'd wished I'd kept the letter, if only to see the easy slant of his handwriting or to be sure I remembered each word correctly, but getting caught weighed heavily on my mind. I watched the face of every person who came into the diner, and watched Jean for an inkling of her knowing the truth.

Main Street was empty as I walked toward my apartment. I had no idea if I could safely send letters to Jackson, but it didn't matter. I was high on the fact that he hadn't forgotten about me or moved on, or even hated me for what I'd done before.

Mama was expecting us for dinner at five thirty, and Jackson's letter had filled me with purpose, strengthening me over the days since receiving it. I felt as if I might finally be becoming a woman rather than a little girl going home to see Mama and Daddy.

Chapter Twenty-Seven

Six o'clock came and went, with no sign of Jimmy Lee. I phoned Mama to let her know we'd be late, and she said she'd hold dinner for us. Each passing minute fueled my annoyance. Between Jimmy Lee's drinking and his disregard for me, I'd wondered if he'd show up sober for the sake of my parents. I hadn't thought he would not show up at all.

I dialed the furniture store's phone number and asked Mr. Kelly if I could speak with Jimmy Lee.

"Oh," he said with surprise. "Hold on just a moment, please."

Silence stretched long and painful. Just when I thought he'd forgotten about me, Mr. Kelly came back to the phone. "Alison, did you speak to Mr. Carlisle the last time you came in?"

"No." I tried to keep the annoyance out of my voice, and failed miserably.

"I think you need to speak with your husband about his whereabouts."

What did he think I was *trying* to do? "Yes, thank you. Is he there?"

"No, he's not." He paused, then hissed into the phone, "Perhaps you should try The Waterin' Hole."

The line went dead. *The Waterin' Hole?* I stared at the telephone, as if it held the answers of my husband's whereabouts. The Watering Hole was the nastiest bar around. Located at the edge of town, it was rumored to be where bored husbands went to fill their sexual needs with some of the dirtiest, lowest women in Forrest Town. It was too far to walk at that time of night, but even if it was closer, I wouldn't stoop so low as to go traipsing after my husband like the pathetic wife, even if I was starting to feel that way. No, I couldn't believe it. There was no way Jimmy Lee would lower himself to that. He wasn't bored. I was home all the time, with dinner ready, and a clean house. I wasn't sure what made me feel sicker—that I was always home waiting for him or that he might actually be with another woman.

I dialed my parent's' number and told Mama we would not make it for dinner after all. I feigned fatigue and said Jimmy Lee was working late. The more I thought about where he might be, the easier it became to believe him that he'd been spending time with Corky. They both like to drink and chase coloreds. That thought didn't sit any better in me than him being with some nasty other woman.

"Do you want me to come by with some dinner for you?" Mama asked.

"No, I'm just gonna go to bed."

"Are we still bakin' tomorrow?"

Damn, I'd forgotten. "Yes, of course. I'll be there 'round noon."

That night, I penned my first letter to Jackson. I had no idea if he would receive it or not, and I knew if Jimmy Lee found out, we'd both be dead. But with hurt coursing through my veins, and nowhere else to point my anger, I let it fuel my writing.

Dear Jackson,

I'm changing. I can feel it in everything I do. When I serve meals at the diner I can barely look into the eyes of the men who I know have made things hard for the people of Division Street. When I inhale, there's a charge of hope in the air that I'm sure only I can feel, and that pulls me forward and takes me to the next task at hand. I want things to be different for my baby—I want things to be different for me, and yet, I know how selfish that sounds, but as much as integration will change things for coloreds, it carries over into a freedom that impacts everything in life for all of us, and I look forward to that change.

I'm seeing Daddy this weekend, and I pray I'll be strong enough to start being myself, instead of his little girl. I'm not sure if you can understand that, but I don't know how else to say it.

Stay safe.

Love always, Alison

Chapter Twenty-Eight

The faintest outline of dark circles shadowed Mama's eyes as she rolled the crust for the pecan pie.

"Mama?" I asked.

She stopped rolling, wiped her brow with her forearm, and lifted her eyebrows in answer.

"Can I talk to you about somethin'?"

Mama set down the roller and pulled out two chairs from the kitchen table. I sat down, fidgeting with a dishtowel. My father's tractor roared as it neared the house. Jake sauntered into the kitchen.

"Alison, wow, you're as big as a house," he said, and grabbed an apple from a bowl on the counter.

"Thanks," I said, wishing he hadn't come in so I could talk privately with Mama.

"Hey, what do you think of this?" Jake placed a hand-drawn picture of our farm on the table, every detail precise, from the cracks in our front porch to the perfect dips and mounds of plantings in the fields. He'd drawn the entire picture with a pencil, shading each crevice to the nth degree.

I picked up the paper and looked closer. "Jake, this is amazin'."

Mama sat back with a smile across her lips. "He's good, isn't he?"

"More than good. Jake, how did you learn to do this?"

He shrugged. "Mama showed me a few things."

"Mama, really?"

Pride filled Mama's eyes. "He's a natural. I just showed him a thing or two, tweakin', you know. He's really gifted."

"Have you shown Daddy?" I asked.

I caught a wave of discomfort pass between them. Jake reached for the picture as the noise of the tractor quieted. Jake folded his drawing and shoved it in his back pocket as the screen door creaked open.

My father crossed the kitchen and lifted me to my feet, then bent down and hugged me close. "I've missed you. You look radiant. How's my grandchild?"

I blushed. "Fine, Daddy."

"You look just as beautiful as your mother did when she was pregnant with you."

Mama pushed her hair behind her ear, revealing a flirty grin, then went back to work on the pie crust.

"Thanks, Daddy."

He smacked Jake on the back. "About ready to go into town?"

Jake's mouth tightened.

"Daddy, have you seen—"

"Alison, come help me," Mama interrupted.

"Uh, okay," I said, confused.

Jake gave me a harsh look. "C'mon, Daddy, let's go."

"Wait. I gotta get a drink for the crew." My father grabbed a , plastic pitcher from the cabinet and ran the water in the sink.

"I've got ice water ready for them in the fridge," I said.

"This'll be fine," he said.

"Daddy, why don't you give 'em the cold water? They'd probably appreciate it." I spoke before thinking, and Daddy turned and looked at me like I'd spoken another language all together. "I mean, it's not that cool out, and they've probably been workin' for hours and all."

"Why don't you let me worry 'bout the farmhands, and you worry 'bout the pies, okay?"

"Okay, Daddy. Sorry."

Mama shook her head. If I hadn't been looking to her for support, I might have missed it. I mixed the sugar and butter in a large bowl, annoyance tightening my nerves until I had to speak.

"Daddy, why don't I take the water out? I don't mind gettin' the water with ice."

"Alison Jean," Daddy said, leaving no room for negotiation.

I stirred the butter until it was creamy, faster, harder, pouring my energy into it as I gathered the courage to take a stance. I took a deep breath and turned to face Daddy, holding onto the back of a chair for support. "Daddy, they deserve ice water. It's just ice. It's not like you're cookin' 'em dinner."

Mama set her hand on my shoulder, pressing gently.

My father narrowed his eyes. I thought of Maggie, and Jackson, and every person in the Panther meeting, and I held his stare, white knuckles wrapped around the edge of the chair.

"What's this about, Alison?"

"About? Nothin', Daddy, it's just," I dropped my eyes. *Be strong.* I wrapped my arm around my middle. "They're people, Daddy, and now that I'm havin' a baby, I'd hate to think of someone not givin' my child a drink of cold water when he or she needed it. It just seems…unnecessary."

Mama squeezed my shoulder. "Honey, why we'd better get this pie ready, or we won't have any for dinner."

My father walked out of the kitchen with the pitcher of tepid water and a frown on his unshaven cheeks.

"Sheesh, sis, what the heck?" Jake hissed.

"Me? How about you and your picture? Why can't Daddy see it?" Going up against Daddy left my nerves full of adrenaline, and maybe even anger, but I had done it. Maggie would be proud of me. Heck, I was proud of me.

"You know how your father is," Mama said. She put a hand on Jake's arm. "He doesn't want to see Jake waste his time. He knows Jake's talented, but your father believes self-worth comes from hard work, and in his eyes, art isn't hard work."

Jake pulled his arm free and headed for the door.

"Jake!" She stopped him with her tone. "I know it's hard work. Your father's just old school. You can't teach an old dog new tricks, is all."

"Right." Jake pulled the picture from his pocket and tore it into shreds, throwing it behind him as he stormed from the house.

"Mama, I didn't mean to cause trouble," I said quickly.

Mama just shook her head. Creases formed across her forehead. She put the spoon she was holding down and leaned on the table.

"It's not you, honey. All you're doin' is what's right."

All you're doin' is what's right. Mama's confirmation fed my confidence. With Daddy and Jake gone, I willed myself to speak a little more openly with her.

"Mama, what do you think about this whole civil rights movement?" I kept my eyes on the bowl before me.

She sighed. "Another boy was beaten last night. It's really gettin' outta hand."

I wanted to spill my hurt over Jimmy Lee not coming home, and connect the dots that it might just be him beating those boys, but given that everyone in my family seemed to be having issues of some kind, I thought it best to hold my tongue.

"A fourteen-year-old," Mama continued. "He was walkin' home from the drugstore with aspirin for his mother." She rubbed her arms as if she'd suddenly gotten a chill. "I think in general, it's a good thing. It's a dangerous thing, but a good thing." She walked to the window and watched Daddy drive the tractor toward the barn. "You know, Alison, we haven't talked about Maggie. Tell me about Maggie. How is she?"

When Mama turned back to me, I understood the shadow in her eyes that I hadn't been able to decipher earlier—she was lonely. How empty her life must feel with the house so empty, all at once, losing both your daughters, and having a son who did everything within his power to stay away from home.

"She's good. She likes her classes, and her job. She's involved in things that keep her busy."

Mama took my hand and led me to the table, where she sat with her elbows propped up beside the bowl I'd been using. Then she sat back and folded her arms across her chest, then set them in her lap.

"You're as jumpy as Jake was with Daddy. What's wrong?"

"I miss her, you know? I mean, she and your father, they never saw eye to eye, but me and Maggie—"

"She drives him batty, that's for sure."

She nodded. "She knows what she wants and I admire that. Maggie's not afraid to go after her dreams, no matter what it involves."

"Or, who's in her way," I said.

"Right, or who's in her way."

"Or, who she might lose," I added.

Mama nodded. "I didn't think I'd miss you girls so much," she admitted. "One minute the house is full of laughter, little feet scamperin' up and down the stairs, my name bein' hollered, then the next minute, Maggie's off to school and you're sneakin' out of the house."

She lifted her eyes and caught me by surprise.

"You knew?"

"I'm your mother. I know everything."

"But, why didn't you—"

"I was young once, too. I remember what it was like, your heart poundin' so hard in anticipation of that secret kiss. Oh, yes, I remember. I wouldn't have taken that away from you for anything in the world."

Embarrassment softened my voice. "Thank you. I'm sorry."

"Don't be sorry. Although, you do owe me. There was one time, just before your graduation, when your father woke up as you came in the door, and I had to convince him it was the wind." Mama took my hand and said, "It's not easy bein' a mother, Alison. I worried sick over you, even before you started sneakin' out. I worried about you walkin' down our street, headin' to the store, while you were at school. And now, I worry about you workin' your way through your life without me by your side."

The way Mama looked at me made me wonder if she knew what was going on with Jimmy Lee. The more Jimmy Lee didn't come home, the less I cared. But nagging and pulling at my mind was the thought of him beating up colored boys. I didn't have proof, and even if I did, there wasn't anything I could do about it, so I kept it tied inside my mind like a bug in a web begging to be set free.

"Do you think I can do it? Be a good mother I mean? Like you?"

"Like me?" she laughed. "I'm not a very good mother, Alison."

"Yeah, Mama, you are."

"I'm weak. I let your father make the rules." She folded the edges of a napkin.

"You have to. You can't fight him." I thought about Daddy, his ability to define our lives without any force or harsh words. Daddy's leer was enough to let you know your place, and his loving smile was enough to want him to remain on your side.

Mama shook her head, the edges of her eyes damp. "I'm so thankful Maggie did what she did. I should have stood up for her long ago. I should have stood up for Jake, and you."

"Me? Mama, I've had a great life. I don't think you did anything wrong."

"Alison," she took my hand in hers and lowered her voice, "I let your father teach you to believe that you *had a place*, and that's just wrong." She looked away and then back at me. "I let him push away my dreams, and that was okay, that was a different time all together, but then I let him push away Jake's dreams, and your own blessed thoughts."

"I don't know what you mean." I swear my heart stopped and the world silenced as Mama searched my eyes for the truth. I knew exactly what she meant, but I didn't dare tread down that path. I wanted the illusion of Mama being happy to remain in my heart forever.

She patted my hand. "Okay, well, I should have stepped in and made you realize that such a *place* should not exist."

What are you tellin' me?

"Alison, how are things with Jimmy Lee?"

Mama wasn't a nosey woman. The fact that she was asking me meant that she'd caught wind of something. I shrugged. "Okay, I guess. He works a lot."

She looked deep into my eyes and drew my tears right out. I held my breath. *Don't cry. Don't cry.*

"Oh, Alison." Mama wrapped her hand around the back of my neck and pulled me to her bosom. "Shh."

"It's so hard, Mama. He's never home, and when he is, he's drinkin', and I just don't know what happened, how things went so wrong."

She stroked the back of my head. Telling her the truth brought my shoulders down where they belonged and air to my lungs. I breathed like I hadn't breathed in months, with lungs so full of oxygen I felt like my brain worked for the first time in forever. I pulled back from her and wiped my eyes. "I'm sorry. I shouldn't have said anything. That was very unwifely of me, but Mama, it's so hard. Some days I feel like I might burst, sittin' in that apartment waitin' for him, not knowin' if he'll be drunk or if he'll even come home before midnight."

Mama listened, without interrupting me.

"I don't even think he loves me anymore, Mama. Most days I'm not even sure why I married him."

"I know why you married him, Alison. You'd have done anything to keep peace within this house. I just shouldn't have let you do it."

I stood and paced. "You couldn't have stopped me, Mama. I was runnin' from myself as much as tryin' to keep peace. I was afraid of what I might do if I didn't marry him."

Chapter Twenty-Nine

So much had happened over the past few weeks that I felt like everywhere I turned a crisis was waiting on me. Though it felt good to unload my marital worries on Mama, I wondered if putting that burden on her was fair. I knew she'd worry about me now more than ever. I was feeling so alone lately, maybe I secretly wanted that worry. Did that make me selfish? I wondered.

The morning rush had eased into a calm afternoon at the diner. I was putting in a few more hours than I usually did, but I figured it's better than sitting home worrying about my husband's whereabouts. When the knock came at the back door, I was happy for the distraction.

I opened the back door of the diner and shivered against the trickling rain. A gust of wind blew through the alley and up my legs. I handed the large, brown, paper bag to Jackson's mother, his letter tucked deftly inside between two napkins.

"Tonight, eight o'clock," she whispered from beneath her umbrella.

I nodded, and as I turned to go into the building, she touched my hand. When I turned to look at her, fearing an outburst about how I'd hurt her son, she looked at me with a smile behind her eyes. I retreated back inside the diner and closed the door, leaning against it as I calmed my racing heart.

My eyes jumped from one customer to the next. I half expected them to jump up and point at me, yelling, *"Negro lover!"* I smoothed my uniform over my burgeoning belly and went back to work.

As I walked home that afternoon, I wondered how I would get out at eight o'clock. Maybe Jimmy Lee wouldn't even be home yet. With the way things had been going, that was a real possibility. I decided to face the problems with Jimmy Lee head on. I turned around and headed for the furniture store, knowing that there was a good chance he wouldn't be there. I just kept hanging onto the hope that he did show up for work on most days, and that I was just asking on the days he'd skipped out. If he was there, I was fixing to ask him if he'd be home on time, and if not, then he needed to fess up to whatever was going on to keep him away from home. I walked seven blocks in the pouring rain. By the time I reached the parking lot I was determined that if Jimmy Lee wasn't at work I'd walk down to that godforsaken bar and find my husband. There wasn't an ounce of jealousy left in me concerning Jimmy Lee, but the notion that he would choose to be with those heathens instead of me set my feet in motion. Even with my umbrella, my sneakers were soaked through to my toes, and my legs were frigid.

I peered around the corner of the building, looking for Jimmy Lee's truck. Relief brought a laugh to my lips. Maybe Mr. Kelly was wrong after all. Jimmy Lee might drink, but maybe he wasn't doing those other things behind my back.

The metal door on the side of the building squeaked open. I ducked around to the front and leaned against the brick beneath the green and tan awning. The side door slammed, echoing against the rain.

Yelling filled the air. I strained to hear what was said, but between the now sheeting rain and the distance, I only caught angry tones—and those angry tones belonged to Jimmy Lee and his uncle. I hurried back down the street toward the diner. I heard Jimmy Lee's truck start, so I turned into the alley beside the drugstore and waited for him to pass.

Wheels squealed on the wet pavement. Jimmy Lee's truck sped past. I breathed fast and hard, panicked. Jimmy Lee would arrive home and I would not be there. I went into the drugstore and searched for something to use as an excuse.

"Hi, sweetie, what can I get for you today?" Mr. Shire's wrinkled face was too happy for the frantic worry that raced through me.

"I, um, gee, I can't really remember," I said.

"Oh, honey, that happens a lot with pregnancy. You just take your time. Here, let me get you a paper towel to dry off." He disappeared behind the counter and returned with a handful of paper towels. "It's a wet one today, isn't it?"

I wiped the rain off my arms, chest, and face. My eyes searched the shelves, finally landing on a beautiful, pink bottle of Pepto Bismol. "That's what I came for, a bottle of Pepto." I reached for it while Mr. Shire rattled on about his wife's stomach ailments when she was pregnant.

"Are you gonna be alright walkin' home in this mess? You're welcome to wait here for a while ' til the rain lets up."

And deal with Jimmy Lee's wrath when I get home even later? "No, thank you. I'll be fine."

Jimmy Lee's truck wasn't in the parking lot when I arrived home. I went upstairs and found the apartment just as I'd left it. A warm shower served to chase away the chill that had settled in my bones. It was already three thirty and I prayed the rain would stop before the evening arrived.

I answered the phone on the second ring, hoping it would be Jimmy Lee.

"Alison? This is Mr. Kane. I wondered if I might escort you tonight to the meetin' of the Blue Bonnet Club."

"The Blue Bonnet Club?" Had I missed something?

"Yes, the *women's guild* meetin' tonight? My wife Mitzi will be goin' and she suggested we pick you up along the way." He lowered his tone when he said *women's guild*, and I realized that he was covering for the meeting at the creek later that evening. I felt as dumb as a stump.

"Yes, of course, that would be lovely. Thank you."

"We'll pick you up at seven forty-five."

The rain had stopped, leaving the creek running high and the surrounding ground soft and mucky. I stood in my rain boots among a growing crowd, some of whom I recognized, and some I did not. Since Jimmy Lee didn't return home, I left him a message and decided that what I was doing was far more important than worrying about where he'd sped off to.

Mr. Kane stood beside me in his hunting coat, his rifle in his right hand, pointed at the ground. I questioned the safety of my very presence as the din around me grew louder and more people emerged from the woods. I worried each one would be Daddy, or worse, Jimmy Lee.

Mitzi Kane stood beside me, her fleshy arm around my shoulder, a constant source of comfort and confidence with her whispers of encouragement, "We're doin' the right thing. This has to change. Maggie would be so proud of you."

Mrs. Johns came through the crowd with two boys in tow. I recognized Albert, a light-colored scar led from the corner of his eye to his hairline, a painful reminder of what my husband and brother had done to him. I wanted to reach for his hand, touch his arm, do something that would let him know that I cared, but I didn't dare. We might be among mixed races, but this was not New York, and I thought I'd be better off keeping my hands to myself than making waves. I moved from Mitzi's grasp and stood before Albert.

"I'm sorry," I said softly. "I'm sorry they hurt you."

He nodded, his eyes cast toward his feet.

Jackson's mother put her arm around the other boy, who I recognized as my Friday afternoon lollipop boy.

"This is Tinsel," she said. "And I'm Patricia."

How I had wanted to know Jackson's family, to sit at their kitchen table and talk with his mother about her children, cooking, and life, as I did with my own mother. Jimmy Lee's parents rarely spoke to me, and I longed for the warmth that I saw in Patricia's eyes, so different than when we had met at the diner.

My voice shook. "It's a pleasure to meet you both." Fear and happiness coalesced, creating a bubble around us, in which I wanted to stay. I wanted to get to know her better, but stronger than my curiosity was my desire to right the wrongs done by my race, in Forrest Town.

A young girl stood behind Patricia and, behind her, a man who must have been six foot five rested his hand on her shoulder. When he looked into my eyes it was Jackson's image that was staring back. My heart skipped a beat.

He nodded. "Ma'am."

"I'm Alison," I said.

"Michael Johns," the man said, in a voice so deep it startled me.

It took all of my concentration to look away from Jackson's father, when what I really wanted to do was give the man a hug and tell him that I was sorry for hurting his son. Instead, I cast my eyes to the left, recognizing the clerk from the department store, the gangly man who ran the gas station, and the always-smiling librarian, Lilly. I was thankful for the distraction. The moonlight shone down on the sea of people. Most of the men carried weapons, spinning around every few seconds to scan the woods.

Mr. Kane sidled up beside me. "There are more comin'. We have scouts on the other side of the woods, they'll send someone in if there's any hint of trouble brewin'."

"Alison?"

I had a difficult time reconciling Mama's voice to my surrounding's. I turned slowly, and found her standing behind me, her eyes wide, her hair perfectly combed. She wore her Wednesday night Blue Bonnet best.

Suddenly, I no longer felt afraid.

Chapter Thirty

"What are we gettin' at the market, again?" Jimmy Lee was driving me to the store to buy fixings for dinner.

"I'm makin' chicken and biscuits."

Jimmy Lee had come home after me the evening of the meeting, and we'd barely spoken in the days that followed. I lived in constant anticipation of receiving Jackson's next letter, and there was no avoiding the guilt that followed the rush of excitement. I was a married, pregnant woman, and even if I'd married Jimmy Lee for the wrong reasons, even if I didn't love him, I had to know in my heart that our marriage wasn't failing solely because of my love for someone else—a warped need to not let Daddy down on all accounts. He'd be devastated if our marriage ended, but if it were my fault, he might never get past it.

"Nice." Jimmy Lee reached for my thigh and gave it a squeeze. "You look pretty today." That was the first compliment he'd given me in months, and I hadn't realized how much I missed the soft edges that he hid so well. I realized then, that even with him being kinder to me, I still yearned to be with Jackson.

"Thank you," I said, running my fingers through my hair. "Do you wanna go to your parents' house for Thanksgivin' or mine?"

Jimmy Lee didn't answer.

We passed the diner, and I longed to go inside, march right to the back door, and whip it open. I longed for Patricia to hand me another letter. A quick note, some sort of acknowledgment that Jackson had received my letter.

"Alison!" Jimmy Lee fumed.

"Gheez, what, Jimmy Lee? You scared me."

"I asked you three times. You were off in La La Land. I said, I have to go out tonight, so have dinner ready early."

"Where are you goin'?" Annoyance pecked at my nerves.

"It doesn't matter," he said.

"It does matter. We're married, and I never see you." I crossed my arms over my chest, biting back my hurt.

"You see me. I'm here now, aren't I?"

"That isn't what I mean. Ever since we got married, we never hang out anymore, we never go on dates, we never do anything but wake up together."

He eyed my belly. "I think we do more than that."

I rolled my eyes and turned away. Then realized it was now or never.

"Jimmy Lee, where do you go at night, when you go for drinks? Where are you goin' tonight?"

We stopped at a red light and Jimmy Lee turned toward me, one hand on the steering wheel, the other resting on his open window. "What I do does not concern you." He faced forward, then said in a cold, even tone, "Someone has to keep these streets safe."

Chapter Thirty-One

Women huddled by the butcher, whispering among themselves. The cashier leaned in close, whispering to the customer in line when I walked by. I glanced out the front window where Jimmy Lee was lighting a cigarette, and then headed for the frozen vegetable aisle. I neared the butcher counter and the gossiping women quickly dispersed.

"Hi, Charlie," I said to the butcher as I passed.

"Alison. Where's that husband of yours?" He looked up and down the aisle.

"He's waitin' outside."

What was going on? Did everyone know about the meeting last night? *Oh, God.* I hurried through the store and picked up the groceries I needed, then headed for the cashier.

"Hi, Millie." Millie Lapas, a thin-lipped girl who'd been in my English class, looked me up and down.

"How are you, Alison?"

I patted my belly. "Fat and happy, I suppose."

She smirked, darting her eyes at the women who were now huddled by the dairy aisle.

"How are you really doin'?" she whispered.

"Fine?" *What on earth?*

"I just figured, with that boy pressin' charges and all that, you know?" She raised her eyebrows.

I shook my head in confusion.

"Oh, it's none of my business. I'm sure it wasn't Jimmy Lee." She swatted the air.

"What wasn't Jimmy Lee?" I asked. Jimmy Lee leaned on the front of the truck, cigarette in hand.

Millie stopped ringing up my items and leaned across the counter. "You know, that boy he beat up?"

Albert? I wrapped my arm around my belly, wanting to protect my baby from hearing whatever might come next.

"You don't have to hide it, Alison. Everyone knows he beat up that colored boy, Thomas Green. Left him near 'bout dead."

My knees grew weak. "Wh...what?"

What had he done? Good Lord, everyone knew? I looked around the store, the eyes of every patron were cast on me like fishing hooks.

"Can you hurry, please?" I scrambled to pay, grabbed my groceries, and rushed out of the store, one hand around my burgeoning belly, the other carrying the bag of groceries, as I crossed the parking lot toward the truck.

"Get in quick," I urged Jimmy Lee.

He didn't budge while I climbed in and set the bag of groceries strategically between him and me. "Get in, Jimmy Lee, now!"

He stamped out his cigarette under his foot and lackadaisically stepped into the truck. I covered my face and motioned with my hands with him to hurry.

"What has gotten into you?" He started the truck and I ducked down in my seat to avoid the glares of the women who stood peering out the window of the market.

"What did you do, Jimmy Lee?"

He laughed. "Smoked a cigarette."

"You beat up another boy, didn't you? All those people in the store, they said you beat up a colored boy and his family is fixin' to press charges."

"Shit, that kid? He was just some scrawny Negro."

"Well that scrawny Negro is a person. He has feelin's, Jimmy Lee, and he hurts just like you an' me. Besides, that poor sufferin' boy will get you put in jail."

Jimmy Lee sped toward home. I turned my back to him, my hands and jaw clenched tight.

"My uncle'll hire the best attorney in town. Ain't nobody gonna touch me."

"Your uncle? Is that what you think, Jimmy Lee? Uncle Billy's gonna get you out of this mess? How about me? How about our baby? I'll be shunned by everyone."

"Not the people who matter."

Tears of anger stung my eyes. "You're so selfish! Can't you see what you've done?"

He skidded to a stop on the side of the road and leaned so close to me he spit on my cheek as he spoke. "You listen to me. I'm the same man you married. All I did was take out the garbage."

Too frightened to move, I leaned hard against the door, the handle pressing into my side. I had to find a way out of my marriage.

Chapter Thirty-Two

The letter came three days later. The date had been set. The boycott would take place on November 6, a Tuesday. I held the letter against my chest and silently prayed that no one would get hurt. I thought of Thomas Green and Albert Johns, and wondered how many other people my husband had hurt. Jimmy Lee's hate-filled eyes consumed my thoughts. What would he do if he found out I was engaged in the civil rights movement? I leaned against the bathroom wall and wrapped my hands around my belly.

"Don't you worry," I whispered to the unborn child that I was becoming more and more attached to. "I won't let Daddy hurt you." I vowed not to let him hurt me, either. I couldn't keep him from hurting others, and I couldn't keep tabs on his whereabouts without a vehicle, but I could damn well make sure he never touched me again.

Mama and I sat on the front porch of our farmhouse. We regarded each other with caution. I knew better than to speak of what was going on, and Mama knew better than to tell me not to. The dynamic between us had changed the night of the meeting. She learned that I was an adult, and in the silence that had stretched between us when we were surrounded by that hopeful and determined mix of races, I learned that she was far more than a quiet participant in her marriage. I wondered what my grandmother would think, if she were alive. She'd groomed Mama to be a loyal and submissive wife, and until that night, I thought that Mama had followed suit. I now understood the pride she held in Maggie for doing all the things in her life that Mama had only dreamed of.

"I've heard the rumors, about Jimmy Lee," she said.

No response would change the situation.

"They say he and his uncle are also responsible for the death of Mr. Bingham."

I had been harboring that worry for so long, and to hear confirmation out loud made my heart ache. I looked at Mama with the hope that she could make the situation go away, or at least lessen the ramifications, but I knew she could not. I wished I was twelve years old again, and that my biggest worry was what skirt to wear or which cookies to help her bake.

"Alison, these are serious allegations," she said solemnly.

"His uncle and his daddy will get him off." I hated myself for parroting my vicious husband.

"I raised you better than that."

I flushed. "I don't know what to do. He's a monster. He was a monster before I married him. Mama, what do I do?"

"I can't tell you what to do. I can only tell you that you need to make sure that you and that grandchild of mine are safe. That's your job, Alison."

I don't know what I expected, but it sure wasn't such a hands-off approach. I wanted her to give me the answers.

"What would you do?" I asked.

Mama took a deep breath and blew it out slowly. "Come, let's walk," she said, and we headed out toward the edge of the property.

"I thought he might change after we were married," I explained. "I thought he was just, I don't know, bein' a schoolboy or somethin'. But he's only gotten worse."

"Alison, what we're doin', it's terribly dangerous. Not just because your father or your husband might find out, but most folks around here, they're just fine with the way things are. In fact, they want things to remain exactly how they are."

"I know that."

"Jimmy Lee's uncle, Billy, he's the ring leader. I didn't know 'bout this before you married Jimmy Lee, and I'm not certain 'bout it now, but I think he might even be part of the KKK."

"The KKK? Are they even around here?" I'd heard about the KKK in other towns, but not here, not in Forrest Town. If Mr. Carlisle was part of that awful group, then chances were, so was Jimmy Lee. It was falling into place like pieces of a puzzle. Jimmy Lee disappearing, boys getting beat up. Of course, Mr. Carlisle would cover for him. I shook my head, but the awful reality clung to my mind like meat to a bone.

"Oh, yes. Mr. Carlisle doesn't wear a white hood and carry a burnin' cross, he's more clever than that. He goes undetected, but let that leave no question. They kill people—and leave them in rivers to rot." The look in her eyes made me shiver.

"I'm gonna be sick." I leaned over and coughed, holding onto Mama's arm.

"Sit down, here, under the tree."

I settled in beside Mama, my back against the tree, my head on her shoulder.

"So you really think Jimmy Lee killed Mr. Bingham? Mama, I can't go back to him. I can't sleep next to him in that apartment."

"You have to."

I looked at her as if she was crazy.

"If you leave now, he's gonna figure it all out. He'll track your every move, and his uncle will be sure of it. Right now, you're protected. You're his wife. He thinks you'll cover for him no matter what it takes, and you will."

"But—" I must be thick headed, because it struck me then that if Jimmy Lee and his uncle were involved with the KKK, then chances were, so was his father.

"But nothin'. Listen to me. This is real, Alison. This is life and death. If Mr. Carlisle thinks we're plannin' to help the colored folks, he'll take us all out. I have no doubt."

"That sounds really paranoid," I said.

"Maybe, but think about it. Jimmy Lee found your letters from Maggie."

"How do you know that?"

"Maggie told me."

"Oh, God."

"She was worried about you," Mama explained.

"So, you knew what Maggie was up to this whole time?"

"I've known what Maggie was up to since she was five. Why do you think I encouraged your father to send her to New York? I have friends there who keep an eye out for her."

Who is this woman? "You have friends in New York?"

Mama blinked, her cheeks flushed, as if a fond memory had wormed its way into her mind. "A friend who relocated there after high school. If Maggie had stayed here, she'd have gotten herself killed, or put in jail. She was a wildfire waitin' to burn. Once she sets her sights on somethin', she pushes until she's right in the thick of it. In New York, she can burn all she wants and people will rally around her—she's one of thousands, not a seed in the miniscule flowerbed of Forrest Town."

The truth of her words hung between us. I realized that what I'd seen of her was merely what she wanted me to see. I wondered if she worried that once the outside layer was removed, the others might unravel.

I knew that, when Mama was young, she had painted beautiful pictures, like the one inside the barn, but she'd given that up before I was born, and I'd never seen her pick up a paint brush a day in my life. Now, I wanted to know how that felt—giving up something you loved. I wondered if it were strangely like how I had felt about Jackson, the night at the creek when I'd let him go.

"Mama, why'd you give up paintin'?"

Mama stared off into the fields. "Oh, honey, I wasn't that good, not like Jake, and things were so different then. Women didn't go traipsin' off to some big city to follow their dreams."

"Couldn't you follow them here? Take classes, continue to paint?"

She shook her head, and looked at me as she had when I was a little girl dreaming of things that were far more magnificent than I would ever see. "I tried. I painted a bit when Maggie and Jake were younger, but life takes over, and Daddy and I had no money. Grandma and Grandpa left us some, but not much. Sometimes what you want to do isn't really what you're meant to do. I like my life just fine. Besides, I'm old, honey. Now it's your turn."

"Old? You look like my sister." We laughed, and it felt good to let down my guard for a minute. Lately it felt like I was hiding behind a coat of armor. Mama's forehead grew tight again, and I knew our moment was over.

"Listen, Alison, you need to be very careful. Stand by your husband. Don't give him any reason to believe that somethin' bigger than what he's already goin' through is goin' on. To everyone in town, you are the wife of a wayward husband—to your husband, you're his savin' grace. Men fall hard, and he will. He might get mean, and if he does, you leave immediately. Call me and I'll come get you, but I don't think he's gonna go in that direction. Most bullies—and that's what he is, a bully who beats up kids—they turn into whiny babies. Once the seriousness of this comes forward, he'll cling to you like a child, and the town will rally around you out of pity."

"No, they won't. You should've seen the spears they shot at me in the market. You'da thought I was the one who beat up Thomas Green. And besides, I don't want pity."

Mama leaned back against the tree, again. "There are bigger things on the horizon. Pity isn't so bad. You're young, you're just startin' out in your life. Pity will endear them to you and you will come out on top."

"Are you worried, Mama? About the boycott?"

Her eyes darted back toward the house and fields. She nodded. "Yes, but you and I, we aren't gonna be in it. We're behind the scenes, and we'll stay there. Maggie's gonna stay in New York. I'm more worried about someone findin' out about it ahead of time. If anyone finds out we're involved," her eyes met mine, and held them, "well, let's just not let them."

"Then why should I stay with Jimmy Lee? Can't I come home? I feel like a lamb tied to a tree."

"I'm not givin' you up like a sacrificial lamb," she laughed. "If you support Jimmy Lee, he'll have no reason to doubt your motivations. If you argue with him, work against him, leave him, he'll have reason to be concerned and may go nosin' around. The last thing you do to a snake is hit it with a rake. It'll turn on you faster than you can run away." She leaned forward and softened her tone. "You know I love you, and I'd bring you home today, but there are many lives at stake here, and we're too deep in to turn back."

"Do you wish you could? Turn back, I mean?"

"From bein' involved? No, but with other things—"

"Meanin'?" I could see something else festering in the worry of her hands on the edge of the rocker.

"I wish I could turn back time and stand up for my children more."

Chapter Thirty-Three

The hammer came down a week later, swift and skillful. Mama came into town and was having a cup of coffee at the diner when we heard shouting outside.

"What are those boys up to now?" Jean said as she walked toward the front window. "I swear, there's more fightin' in this town—" She peered out front and called for me, waving her hand to hurry me along.

"What is it?" I set down my order pad and excused myself from my customer. Mama got up from the counter and followed me to the window.

Down the street, Jimmy Lee stood red-faced, chest heaving, before two men in dark suits who stood in front of Mr. Mackey's law office. Mr. Carlisle was rushing up the sidewalk from the direction of the store. Jimmy Lee's voice rang out, echoing between the buildings. I could not make out the words, or maybe I didn't want to.

"Oh, sweetheart, your man's in a bit of trouble, isn't he?" Jean took my hand and walked me toward one of the booths.

I glanced at Mama. *Pity. How could she have known?*

"It's okay, Alison. You just sit here and we'll find out what's goin' on." Jean looked at Mama.

"Yes, right. I'll go see if I can calm things down."

"Mama?" I worried that Jimmy Lee might get upset if she intervened. Mama held her hand up, as if to say she had it under control. She pulled her shoulders back and walked out the door toward the ruckus.

Customers rose from their seats and gathered in the front window, watching the scene unfold. I remained seated, my head bowed. I would accept that pity with grace, just as Mama had advised.

A knock at the back door startled me.

"I've got it, hun. It's gonna be Tinsel, come for his daddy's food. He's so cute." She hurried off and I knew that if it wasn't Tinsel, if it was Patricia, I'd have missed my chance at a letter from Jackson. I sat and listened to my husband's life falling apart out front and my worry mounted about what was transpiring out back. Mr. Bingham's ravaged body came to me, strengthening my resolve. My husband deserved whatever they doled out to him.

The bell over the door jingled as Mama came back into the diner. She walked strong and tall toward the booth, and slid in across from me. She leaned in close and whispered, "They're pressin' charges for what he did to Thomas Green. Those are attorneys, here to meet with Thomas' family. I didn't hear too much, but from what I gathered, Jimmy Lee caught wind of their visit and, well, you know, sort of lost it."

"What should I do?"

"Nothin'. You do just what you're doin'. Tonight, don't bring it up. Let him stew. He'll talk when he's ready. Be as invisible as you can. The more you pry, the angrier he'll get. He needs to know you believe in him and that he's not alone."

"But I don't believe in him. What he did was wrong."

"I know." She took hold of my hand. "Now is not the time to show your strength, now is the time to make your husband love you."

The shouting outside the diner quieted. Jean moved toward the front of the diner. "Okay, people. Sit down and eat. The show's over." She wrangled customers back to their seats and brought me a cup of tea.

"I'm okay, Jean, really."

"You have a lot on your family's dinner plate right now, Alison. Why don't you take the afternoon off and go relax."

"Relax?" I no longer knew what that word meant.

Before I even got inside the apartment that afternoon, Jimmy Lee was asking me questions.

"Finally. Where have you been?"

I set my purse on the table and stood by the door, weighing his mood. "I was at work." It took all my strength not to let him know how embarrassed I was, or how angry.

"Those niggers hired lawyers."

Should I act surprised? I was glad he'd been caught. I didn't have a clue how to respond, but I didn't have to decide, because in his next breath, he told me everything.

"They're pressin' charges for beatin' up that little shit, Thomas Green."

And Mr. Bingham?

"My uncle's lawyer says it'll never stick," he fumed.

His eyes were glassy, open wide like a crazed animal, his hair disheveled. I almost felt sorry for him—until I thought of Mr. Bingham, Albert, and Thomas. I walked over to the couch where he sat and lowered myself down on the far end. I hoped the charges would stick, and I swallowed the urge to tell him so.

"So, now, I go to work and I come home. He said they'd be watchin' me, or some shit like that."

"Okay," was all I could manage. *Home?* At least he wouldn't be at that dirty bar, if, in fact, that was even where he'd been hanging out.

"Alison, I know I haven't been the best husband in the world, and I'm sorry."

How did Mama know? "It's okay," I whispered.

"No, no it's not. I haven't been home, and you're all pregnant and everything. I promise I'll be better. No more goin' out for drinks, no more late nights. I'll be home every night on time."

Because you have to be.

Jimmy Lee sprang to his feet when someone knocked on the door, his eyes wide and fear-filled. Every muscle in his body clenched.

He looked out the window. "Police."

Police! I hadn't thought the situation through. Of course they'd come for him. Panic pounded in my chest and the tiny hairs on the back of my neck prickled. "What do we do?"

He put his hands on his hips, then crossed them over his chest, and blew out a long breath. "Answer the door."

We stood a foot apart, eyes locked on each other. He reached for me and I clamored into his arms, unexpected tears filling my eyes.

"I love you," he said.

"I love you, too." I was shocked by my need to hold onto him. I felt like a piece of me was being arrested with him. He pulled away from me and went to the door.

"Ma'am." Officer Chandler stood in the doorway, nodding at me as he spoke; his partner stood silently beside him. "Jimmy Lee, we gotta take you in."

Jimmy Lee nodded. I ran to his side and wrapped my arms around him. I might not be in love with him, but at that moment, I realized that I did love him, and it hurt like hell to listen to Officer Chandler give him his Miranda Warning, and to see Jimmy Lee's shoulders roll forward and his head hang low.

Jimmy Lee stared at the floor. "Yes, sir. I understand. Yes, sir." He spoke without looking at me. "Alison, call Uncle Billy."

I picked up the phone as the door closed behind them. I stood with the phone in my trembling hand, the magnitude of what he'd done pressing in on me. I was married to a felon. My husband was going to jail.

Chapter Thirty-Four

"Mr. Carlisle? This is Alison. Jimmy Lee's just been taken to the police station." Tears flowed steady and warm down my cheeks as I pressed the phone to my ear. Why was I so darn upset? It made no sense. I should be happy that he was out of my way. There would be no threat to me as long as he was gone, and still, I was torn, and scared, and alone.

"Thank you. We'll take care of it," he answered.

"Should I go to the police station?" I was already thinking ahead about calling Mama and having her drive me there.

"No, you stay put. We'll take care of it and bring him home." Jimmy Lee's uncle spoke confidently.

I hung up the phone and called Mama.

"Hello?" My father's voice caught me off guard.

"Daddy?"

"Pixie?"

He knew. I could hear it in his tone. "Hi, Daddy, is Mama there?"

"Are you okay? Do you want me to come get you, bring you home for a bit?"

Yes, God yes! "No, I'm okay. I just need to talk to Mama."

"They'll get him off, Pix, you know they will. He'll be back home before you know it."

That's all I need. Daddy was being positive because that's what he thought I wanted. I felt guilty accepting Daddy's careful coddling when I knew I should be fessing up to the truth of my feelings.

"Those damn Negros, they're biting off more than they can chew with Jimmy Lee Carlisle."

"Daddy! They didn't do anything wrong." *Damn it. Why can't I do what Mama told me to do?* I listened to Daddy's heavy breath come through the phone. "Sorry, Daddy, I mean, I don't know what I mean. I'm all confused. Can I please just talk to Mama?"

My father didn't say a word. He set down the phone and I listened to his heavy footsteps retreat on the wooden floor.

"Alison? Are you alright, honey?"

"Yes. I think I made Daddy mad, though. They arrested Jimmy Lee. They took him in!" My words fell fast and panicky from my lips. "He told me to call his uncle, Billy, which I did. What should I do now?"

"Alison, take a deep breath. Calm down. It's gonna be fine."

"Okay," I said, and then did as she asked.

"What's his uncle doin'?"

"He told me to stay home and he'd take care of it. I have no idea what that means—get a lawyer, I guess. Mama, Jimmy Lee is in *jail*." I rubbed my belly. "I'm not ready for this. This is too much."

"Alison, grab a chair and sit down."

She waited while I settled myself onto a kitchen chair.

"Now, listen to me. You let Mr. Carlisle handle this and you go along with your life just as if Jimmy Lee was still home. You eat breakfast and lunch, go to the diner, whatever it is you do, do it."

"But, everyone knows. Daddy already knew!"

"Yes, they do, and that won't change no matter what you do, so the best thing to do is just go on with your daily life. Do you want me to come over?"

"No. Daddy needs you there. I'm just scared, Mama. I feel like I'm caught in a trap. I've got all this stuff goin' on behind his back, and now *this*. I wish I could just go to sleep and wake up to everything bein' normal again."

I pictured Mama pushing her hair behind her ear and crinkling her forehead, stuck between wanting to take care of her daughter and telling her to do the right thing. I didn't look forward to that kind of maternal quandary.

"Normal wasn't great, Alison, it just felt that way because you were blissfully ignorant, like we all were. We walked around with blinders on, but you do have a choice." She lowered her voice. "You don't have to be involved in any of it. You can turn away and never look back."

She wasn't being condescending or making me feel like I was weak. Mama was doing what any mother would—offering genuine support that carried through her tone and wrapped itself around me like her loving arms. Even so, she didn't know how wrong she was.

Chapter Thirty-Five

My heart leapt with the ringing of the phone. I sat up in bed, still encased in a sleep-induced fog.

"Pixie, are you alright? Mama told me about Jimmy Lee." Maggie didn't give me time to respond. "About time, huh?"

"Maggie." I sat up and tried to wrap my mind around why I was hoping it was Jimmy Lee. "He's my husband. This isn't really *good* news." *Except, it kinda is.*

"I'm sorry, you're right, but it does clear the path. The boycott is right around the corner, and it'll be easier with him out of the way."

"You shouldn't be callin'. You can't afford it," I said.

"This is different, Pix. It's one phone call. I'd go into debt to make sure you're alright. Don't ya' know that yet?"

I was comforted by Maggie's words, and wishing I could chance a phone call to Jackson. Maggie's call was one thing, but a call to Jackson would leave a trail that could only end in trouble when Jimmy Lee saw the phone bill.

"The meetin' went well. We've got a system set up to disseminate information, and I don't think anyone knows about the effort. Mr. Kane was brilliant. What's happenin' up there?"

"They're plannin' a march in South Carolina over the weekend, to help integrate one of the schools. I'm thinkin' about goin'."

"Maggie! You promised you wouldn't do anything dangerous." I threw my legs over the side of the bed. The apartment was silent around me, the sun peerin' in through the bedroom curtains. I thought of Jimmy Lee sitting in a jail cell, and though I had been emotional about him being taken away yesterday, I felt no sorrow today. I didn't miss him. I didn't worry. I knew his uncle would take care of him. I finally began to see how little room there had been for me in his life from day one of our marriage, and now I no longer cared.

"It's fine, Pix. I won't go if it looks like there's gonna be trouble."

"There'll be trouble alright, Maggie. Hey, you knew about Mama. Why didn't you tell me?"

"I was worried about you. You and Daddy are so close."

"Were so close."

"Oh, Pix, no. What's happened?" I pictured Maggie's eyebrows coming together, and that worried look passing over her face.

"Nothin' *happened*, really. I'm just not the same little girl I once was, and some of the things Daddy does, well, they're irkin' me more and more. I'm havin' a hard time keepin' my mouth shut."

"Oh, no, Pix. Don't do what I did. It's not worth it. Daddy doesn't mean to be the way he is. He's just doin' what he was brought up to do and to believe. Don't let this come between you." She paused. "I miss him. I miss our family."

"I know. I do, too," I said, and I meant it. "I wonder if they're gonna nail Jimmy Lee for beatin' up Albert too, or killin' Mr. Bingham?"

Maggie was silent for a moment. "I hope they do," she said, then quickly added, "I'm sorry. I know he's your husband, but—"

"It's okay. I'm so conflicted about all of this, but if I weren't married to him, I'd want the right thing to happen. How's Jackson?" I squeezed my eyes shut, praying she wouldn't think too much about why I'd asked.

"He's doin' really well. He's goin' to the march, too. He's enmeshed more deeply than I am on the outside, so he keeps us all up to date on the movements he attends."

My heart sank. "He goes to marches and things?"

"Yeah, he goes to most of them. He's got a huge followin' and he's really rallied the folks across five states. Who knew a leader would come out of Forrest Town? Crazy, right?"

"Yeah, crazy. Hey, Maggie, I gotta run. Patricia is bringin' me the meetin' information when she picks up her husband's lunch today at the diner. Love you, and call me the second you get back from the march. I know you can't really afford it, but just a quick call. I wanna know you're okay."

The order for lunch wasn't called in that morning, and I was surprised when there was a knock at the back door. I swung the door open, expecting to see Patricia, but she wasn't the one who showed up that afternoon. A middle-school-aged boy with darker skin was bent over, leaning on his knees, panting like he'd been running for too long. He looked up at me with eyes so big and white they were unsettling.

"Mr. Green, the father of the boy who was beat up, is missin'," he said.

"What do you mean missin'?"

He stood, pushing his hands into his sides as he panted out an answer. "Didn't come home last night. Everyone's worried."

Oh, no. My heart slammed into my ribs, chasing a chill up my arms. "Where's Patricia?" I asked, then looked back over my shoulder for Jean, who was busy at the cash register.

"She's at home, 'fraid to leave. Everyone's lookin' for him." He looked frantically up and down the alley. "I gotta go." He ran away, leaving me staring after him, frightened and feeling useless. I prayed that Mr. Green was okay, but I knew otherwise. *Mr. Bingham. The river.*

"Jean," I called as I made my way to the front of the diner. "I'm not feelin' so well, do you mind if I go?"

She was at my side in seconds. "Are you okay? Want me to get Joe to drive you home?"

"No, I'm okay, just a little off. I think I need to rest. This whole thing with Jimmy Lee has me tied in knots." *Jimmy Lee.* If something happened to Mr. Green, then at least this time it wasn't at the hands of my husband.

"Sure, sugar, you go. You don't work again 'til Monday, so you rest up."

Chapter Thirty-Six

Please don't be there. Please don't be there. I didn't see anything along the way to the river—literally. I didn't notice if there were cars going down the street or people milling about in town. I had tunnel vision, clouded by the image of Mr. Bingham, and my nerves remembering the fear that consumed me when I found him. I shook and trembled as I made my way through the woods, passing trees and stepping over logs as if on autopilot. *Please don't be there.*

I don't know what made me think that I'd find Mr. Green in that same location, or why I thought I'd find him at all, but something told me I would. I pushed through the last bush and into the clearing. Tears burned my eyes and I squeezed them away. *Please don't be here.* Scenarios raced through my mind. What if I found him? Who would I tell? Would we all be next, everyone who was at the meeting?

The river flowed steady and fast from the recent rains. I climbed over the rocks to the edge, flashes of memory coming at me hard and fast. I looked down river, then up. A tangle of something massive in the branches of a tree that sprouted from the water's edge sent a stab of fear through me. *Please don't be him.* I moved cautiously towards it. *Please don't be him.* Twigs and grass covered a mound of something brown. I stopped dead in my tracks. What was I doing? I can't do this again. I can't take it. I turned toward the woods, but knew I had to continue on. Adrenaline pushed me forward, fear made each step like walking through quicksand. I crouched by the water's edge, praying it wasn't him. I poked at the mass of muck and twigs. The mass didn't budge. I used the stick to clear away a spot in the center of the mass, revealing brown fur. I dropped to my knees, covering my face with my hands, and let the tears fall. I glanced back up at the mass, and it was then, through my blurry eyes, that I saw the long, thick neck craned backward, the horse's head positioned at a painful angle, buried deep under the water.

I walked down river, away from town, partially to get closer to where the woods met my apartment, and partially to calm my revved up nerves. I wished Jackson was there. What I needed more than anything was someone to hold me and tell me everything was going to be okay, because as it stood, I couldn't see anything being okay any time soon.

Vultures circled overhead, giving the white sky and chilly air an ominous weight. I stopped at the edge of the woods, listening to the flow of the river and the birds cawing overhead. I placed my hand on my expanding belly and closed my eyes, trying to envision what my life would be like once my baby came. Darkness prevailed. I saw my lonely apartment, and Jimmy Lee's drunken comments and disheartening absence. I took a deep breath and blew it out slowly. I put my other hand on my belly and envisioned what my life might've been like if I had gone to New York with Jackson—if the baby within me had been his. The glow of his face filled me with warmth and comfort, his soft and supportive eyes danced with light, a smile graced his plump lips. The smell of his sweat came back to me, the feel of his hands on my body gave me goose bumps. Beneath my fingers, my baby moved, bringing with it renewed thoughts of security. I wanted my baby to have what I had growing up—two parents who loved each other, safe goodnight kisses, and a sense that the world was safe. I wanted that more than I wanted to breathe fresh air. I opened my eyes, reality all around me in the place I stood, the reason why I was there. I had to decide once and for all, before it was too late. Was I staying with Jimmy Lee, as Mama said, to help with integration efforts, for the greater good of the community, and for all babies who would come forth after that time, or could I close my eyes and walk away, without a care for what happened outside my own thin walls?

I pondered that thought as I navigated my way through the woods, toward home.

Street noises filtered in through the trees as I neared the apartments. A blood-curdling scream came from somewhere off in the distance. I stopped. Listened. More screaming. Footsteps rushing through the brush. All at once people were running into the woods, hollering in the direction of the outcry. I followed the panicked trail toward the screams.

A deep voice hushed the screaming woman and broke through the panic. "Get back. Everyone, get back."

I peered past the group of people and followed their craned necks up toward the umbrella of trees. Mr. Green's limp body hung from a rope like a deer bleeding out. I turned away, grabbing a nearby tree for support. *Why did this have to happen?* Fear pierced my thoughts—was it because of our meeting? Did someone know? I racked my brain trying to remember if Mr. Green was at the meeting, and came up empty. Jimmy Lee had beat up his son. A shudder ran through me as comprehension of what was sure to be the truth set in.

A young mother turned away, hurrying out of the woods with her child in her arms. Two white men turned and walked away at a calm, even pace, one muttering, "Got what he deserved."

Every muscle in my body stiffened. I willed myself not to run up to those men and smack them across their pompous cheeks. Enough was enough.

A colored man scurried up the tree and cut the rope, dropping Mr. Green's limp body into the arms of three colored men waiting below.

"There's a note," one of the men said. He pulled a piece of paper out of the pocket of Mr. Green's flannel shirt. His dark eyes scanned the note, and then he dropped his hand to his side without uttering a word. The man standing next to him took the note from his hand.

"It's a warning. It says, '*Back off or you're next.*'"

"Back off what?" a colored woman asked.

Back off? Of the charges to Jimmy Lee? Of the boycott? I turned and ran home as fast as my pregnant body would carry me. Mr. Green's lifeless body solidified my decision. There was only one way that I could ever move forward with my life without living in regret's unforgiving shadow.

Chapter Thirty-Seven

I flew in the apartment door, grabbed the phone from the table, and dialed Maggie's number. Her phone rang and rang. I hung up and tried to reach Mama. There was no answer. I walked in circles, wishing I could go to the jail and talk to Jimmy Lee. His uncle said he'd take care of it. I lowered myself to the couch. *He'd take care of it. Mr. Carlisle. Of course.*

"The same way you took care of Mr. Bingham for your brother?" I stomped across the floor. *The hell with this.*

I yanked open the bedroom closet door. The shoebox, where I used to keep Maggie's letters, sat empty on the top shelf. I dug the bag of summer clothes out from the back and emptied it onto the bed. I found the pair of dark blue shorts and unzipped the tiny pocket, then withdrew the small piece of paper, and walked back to the phone. Staring at the receiver, I gathered my courage, remembering the morning after I'd returned home from New York. After Jimmy Lee had gone to work I'd hidden Jackson's phone number in the closet. I couldn't bear throwing it away, and Jackson had made me promise to use it if I was ever in trouble. I reached for the receiver, and unclenched my shaking hand. The slip of paper fluttered down onto the bed. I dialed Jackon's number, watching the rotary move painstakingly slowly back to zero with each pull of a number.

"Hello?"

My voice stalled in my throat. *What was I doin'?*

"Hello?" he said, again.

"It's…it's me," I said softly.

He was silent for a beat. "Alison?"

"Mm-hmm."

"Alison, what's wrong? We said we wouldn't take the chance of callin'. Are you alright?"

"They killed another man. Jimmy Lee got arrested for beatin' up Thomas Green and now Mr. Green's been hung." Tears streamed down my cheeks. I held the receiver so tight my knuckles hurt. "There was a note in his pocket that said somethin' like, 'Back off or you're next.' And his uncle, Billy, he told me not to go to the jailhouse." I spoke so fast I could barely breathe. "He said he'd take care of it, but Jimmy Lee didn't come home, so I guess he's still in jail, and I have no idea what else Mr. Carlisle might have meant. I thought he meant he'd get a lawyer or somethin'. Oh,

God, Jackson, what should I do?" I gasped a quick breath. "I think Jimmy Lee had him killed."

"Okay, okay. Damn it. But you're alright? Where are you?"

"I'm fine. I'm at my apartment."

"Maggie and I are leavin' in an hour to go to South Carolina. Damn it. Can you call Mr. Kane? Let him know what's goin' on? Alison, how can you be sure this isn't because they caught wind of the boycott?"

"I can't, but I've wracked my brain and I don't remember Mr. Green bein' at the meetin'. I'll call Mr. Kane. He'll know if he was there. He knows everyone who attends."

"Can you go stay at your mother's?" Jackson asked.

"I don't know."

"Alison, I don't want you to be alone. If there's any chance that Jimmy Lee knows what we're up to, you'll be in danger."

He was right. "Okay, I'll stay at my parents'. I wish you were here." I wished so hard, my stomach ached.

"Me too, but we couldn't be together anyway, so what good would it do?"

"Why do you have to be so practical?" Wishing that, just for once since leaving home, someone would make everything in my life okay.

"Because I want to stay alive."

Chapter Thirty-Eight

"Life got you a little freaked out, sis?" Jake asked when he came to pick me up in Daddy's truck.

"A little."

"Want me to take you to see Jimmy Lee?"

It hadn't dawned on me that going to see him was an option. I was still the obedient, little girl Daddy raised. I didn't really want to see Jimmy Lee, but part of me thought it was my wifely duty to act as if I cared, and another part of me wanted to try and figure out what was going on in his head.

"You'd do that?"

Jake drove toward the jailhouse and handed me a paper he'd had tucked under his leg.

I unfolded the paper and was surprised to find an application to Mississippi State. "Where'd you get this?"

"Mama got it for me."

"No, she did not."

Jake grinned. "Daddy doesn't know. She said it wouldn't be easy to get in, and I'd have to work to afford it, but she said they had great art courses."

"Jake, what will Daddy say? You can't leave him." *We can't all leave him.*

"I probably won't even get in, but Mama says I have to try. I don't know what's come over her, but she's been different since you left."

"How do you mean?"

"I don't know, just different. She's all…like, tellin' me to follow my dreams, and she takes pies she bakes outside to the field hands and stuff." Jake laughed, then said, "You shoulda seen Daddy's face the first time she took them a snack. He shot her a look, and she just went on like she didn't see it."

I couldn't believe Mama was taking such blatant strides. I wondered what other changes I might find when I got back to the farm.

The jail smelled like old leather and summer sweat. I wrapped my arms around myself as I sat and waited to be taken back to see Jimmy Lee.

Jake leaned in close beside me. "You okay?"

I nodded, unable to speak. What would I say to Jimmy Lee? What if his uncle came in and saw me? I shuffled my feet and clasped my hands together.

"Would you really go to that school?"

Jake shrugged. "Maybe. I don't know. I want to."

My world was changing, and I was either going to change right along with it, or remain in an unhappy marriage and raise my child with a racist husband.

"Mrs. Carlisle?" A bald, overweight officer spoke with a stern voice as he held the door open. His eyes dropped to my pregnant belly.

"A woman in your condition shouldn't have ta worry yourself none. None of us want your husband in here. He was just cleanin' house."

Cleanin' house? Was the entire police department corrupt?

"He'll be out of here soon enough." He turned and winked.

The door closed with a *clank* behind us as we made our way down the narrow, gray hallway. At the end of the hall, we turned right and the officer stopped in front of a solid door with a small glass window. He opened the door and stepped aside.

Inside, Jimmy Lee sat at a metal table. He wasn't wearing handcuffs, as I'd imagined. He didn't look especially tired or even unhappy. He stood and opened his arms.

"Alison," he said, and pulled me close.

"You're okay?" Completely taken aback by his warmth, I gently pushed away.

"Sheesh, yeah, I'm fine. Piece of cake."

The door closed, leaving us alone in the stark room.

Jimmy Lee sat down and I lowered myself into the cold, metal chair across from him.

"Your uncle told me not to come, otherwise, I woulda been by yesterday."

"That's okay. It won't matter. There won't be a case by tonight," he said smugly.

"Whaddaya mean?"

"We took care of things. I don't think the Green's will be botherin' us anymore."

The room began to spin. *Took care of things.* I didn't want to believe it. I grasped for some other explanation. "They're droppin' the charges?"

"In a way."

I held my purse in both hands to keep them from shaking. "In what way? Either they're droppin' the charges or they're not." *Tell me you didn't have him killed. Please, lie to me if you have to, just please tell me.*

"Oh, they'll drop the charges all right. Stupid niggers."

The word made my skin crawl. "Do you have to do that?"

"What?" He held his palm up toward the ceiling, as if he had no idea what I was referring to.

"That— callin' 'em stupid." *Shut up. Shut up. Shut up.* I knew I was traveling down a dangerous path. My life was speeding out of control, like a train wreck waiting to happen. My pulse raced, my hands worked at fraying the edges of my purse, and I wanted to jump up and run from the room—heck, I wanted to run from Arkansas.

"They are stupid," his voice escalated as he rose from the chair. "Dumb niggers think they can keep me down? No way would Daddy or Uncle Billy let that happen."

Your father? Your uncle? How long can you rely on them to take care of you? Had I relied on Daddy takin' care of me for too long? On some level, was I still relyin' on the security of him too much? I forced my emotions inside, and asked when he'd be coming home.

"I'll be out by midnight."

"Midnight?"

"They're settin' bail tomorrow, but I think somethin' is gonna change that plan."

Mr. Green's dead body.

"I'm stayin' at Mama's tonight. I don't really wanna be alone."

Jimmy Lee nodded. "Okay. I'll get you when I'm out."

"Not at midnight."

"In the mornin', then."

"Yeah, mornin'. Okay." I let Jimmy Lee take my hand in his. My stomach twisted and turned. My husband was responsible for a man's death, and I had to keep my mouth shut. My Daddy's voice haunted me— *Know your place*—but the image of Mama sneaking up to the back door of the furniture store rivaled that thought.

Chapter Thirty-Nine

Jimmy Lee didn't come to collect me the next morning, and my phone calls home went unanswered.

"Let the man be. He'll come when he can," Daddy said dismissively. "He's in a mess of trouble. He might be meetin' with lawyers or somethin'."

"I guess, but he coulda called," I said.

My father sat at the head of the kitchen table eating his eggs as quickly as he could. "Are you alright, Pix? You don't look very well."

"I'm just tired. My husband is in jail, Daddy, and Mr. Green is dead." I watched his eyes narrow. "Aren't you affected at all by Mr. Green? I mean, he was hung from a tree, Daddy. I saw him. It was awful." I pushed my plate away.

He went to work on his biscuit. "It's not my business," he said between bites. "And it ain't yours, either."

Mama walked behind my chair and set a glass of orange juice in front of me, patting my shoulder, reminding me to go easy. My entire life was spent going easy. No wonder Maggie blew up.

"My husband beat that kid, of course it's my business." I set my eyes on Daddy, ignoring the heat from Mama's stare.

He set down his fork and looked up at Mama, but spoke directly to me. "Your husband did whatever he felt he had to do. Know your place, Alison. Don't cause undue trouble. There's enough of that goin' 'round right now."

I stood and paced, then threw my napkin on the table. "Right now, Daddy, I'm so sick of knowin' my place that I could puke." I stormed out of the house and sat on the front porch.

Five minutes later, Mama joined me.

"Mr. Kane called. The Blue Bonnet meetin' is scheduled for tonight instead of Wednesday."

A silent message passed between us; *Mr. Green's death had sent up alarms.*

Twice as many people showed up that night as had the previous week. Mr. Kane explained that supporters from other towns were already arriving, with others on their way. Many had already arrived in neighboring towns. The boycott had been rescheduled. We had three days to prepare.

Mr. Kane leaned on his shotgun and announced with a low, serious tone, "Now, we're suggestin' that women and children stay inside their homes durin' this protest. We don't know what we'll come up against, but if Mr. Green is any indication, it may be very dangerous."

"How many is comin' from other towns?" A short colored man asked. The crowd murmured in agreement with his question.

"We don't know, but it looks like hundreds of protesters, includin' the Black Panthers."

The Black Panthers? Maggie? I hadn't heard from her since she'd left for South Carolina. How would they make it here in three days? I wondered how the South Carolina protest went.

"What can we expect, in town, I mean?" my voice quaked.

"We're gonna march down Main Street with signs and picket the businesses. None of the supporters are fixin' to show up at work, at least none that are takin' part in the protest."

"They'll shoot y'all. You know that. They hung Mr. Green; the police, they're all part of it. I saw it. I heard it with my own ears." Mike Taylor, who worked in the lumber mill, pulled at the straps of his overalls.

"Shot? We can't be part of that!" The voice came from the back of the crowd.

Mr. Kane nodded. "Now, now, settle down. Mr. Taylor, you're right, but there are a few police who aren't tainted. And Mr. Nash is bringin' the press, so everything will be documented. People will know."

"But people know about everything that's goin' on. That doesn't stop it from happenin'," someone else called out.

Albert came bursting through the woods and into the center of the group. He bent over, out of breath. "South Carolina, the march. It—" he panted, catching his breath.

"What?" I urged him.

He turned to face me. "It went real bad. Six people died. More injured."

"Maggie? What about Maggie and Jackson?" I asked, fear snagging hold of my emotions and my voice.

"Don't know. I don't think it's good, though. Several men are missin'. A ton got arrested."

A collective gasp came from the crowd, followed by a shouting of questions and worried comments.

I grabbed his arm, then let it go quickly. "How'd you find this out? We have to find them."

"Pastor Peters got a call. They're tryin' to track down everyone. The Panthers showed up with guns. Everything went haywire. That's all I know."

I grabbed hold of Mr. Kane's arm. *Guns!* "What should we do? We can't do this."

Mama stood before Albert and set her hands on his shoulders. "Albert, listen to me. You tell me any information you get, do ya' hear me?"

"Yes, ma'am." His forehead glistened with sweat, fear shadowed his eyes.

"How, Mama? How can he do that?"

"Calm down, Alison." She turned back toward Albert. "He knows how."

Albert nodded.

I understood that there was much I was not privy to.

"Listen, Alison, we're goin' home. You are not to leave the farmhouse—understood?" She turned to Mr. Kane. "Are the others ready for this?"

"Chicago, Mississippi, DC, yes, they're all ready."

Mama nodded, then faced the angry group. "Then so are we. Change isn't easy, and it's not a game. But if we're gonna make this happen, now's the time."

I couldn't believe what I was hearing. Her daughter was missing and she was telling everyone to risk their own lives? Why? I couldn't see the value in the protest if death would be the outcome.

On the way back to the farmhouse I argued with Mama. "How can you tell them to do this?"

"Maggie and Jackson will be fine. Maggie promised that she wasn't gonna get involved if things got violent. She and Jackson probably took off when things got ugly."

Her words were confident, but in her eyes, worry swam.

"What if they didn't? What then, Mama? What if they find Maggie and Jackson hangin' from trees?" A cramp strangled my belly like a vice. I called out in pain.

"What is it?" Mama pulled the truck over and slammed it into park.

"Nothin', just a cramp. I'm okay." I breathed deeply and leaned far back in the seat, giving my baby as much space as I could in my tight ball of a stomach.

"Alison, this is too stressful for you. I don't want you comin' to these meetin's anymore."

"I'm fine. Let's just get home." Another cramp called my attention, this one not quite as strong. I closed my eyes and took a few deep breaths until it subsided.

By the time we reached my parents' house a dull pain the size of Mississippi had formed in my lower back. Mama helped me inside and reminded me not to mention Maggie to Daddy. She assured me that she would let me know as soon as Albert was in contact with her.

My father was sitting in his chair beside the front door when we arrived. "Did Jimmy Lee call?" I asked him.

"Nope. How was Blue Bonnets?" he asked.

Mama leaned down and kissed his cheek. "Oh, just fine. You know how we women like to gab."

"Pix, you look green around the gills, you okay?"

"Yeah, too much pastry," I lied. "I'm gonna go upstairs and lie down." I started up the stairs then turned and asked, "Daddy, can you please call the jail and ask if Jimmy Lee was released?" I didn't care so much about talking to him, but I did wonder if he was out of jail yet.

"Oh, he was released alright. He's just takin' care of things, I'd imagine."

"How do you know?" *And why the hell didn't you tell me?*

My father called over his shoulder to me. "I don't rightly know. I just assume his uncle got him out, and frankly, it's none of my business."

"Urgh!" I stomped upstairs, frustration consuming my ability to think clearly. I went into my bedroom and shut the door.

Jake opened it behind me and slipped in. "I know where Jimmy Lee is," he said, and closed the door behind him.

"Where?" I was too worried about Maggie and Jackson to really care where Jimmy Lee was, but I had to look like I cared, just as Mama had said.

"There's gonna be a boycott or somethin', and Jimmy Lee and his uncle are pullin' together their men to snipe them as they come into town."

Chapter Forty

Two days had passed without a word from Jimmy Lee. Mama had alerted Mr. Kane about Mr. Carlisle's plan to shoot the protesters before they even made it into town, and he alerted the supporters, both local and out of town. I was so nervous that I could barely see straight. I jumped at every noise, and worried that Jimmy Lee had found out what I'd been up to, and I'd be the next body they found hanging from a tree. Without a word from Jimmy Lee, it was like waiting for the shoe to drop. I called Jean and asked for a bit of time off work.

"You take all the time you need, sugar," she answered.

No sooner had I hung up the phone than it rang again.

"Alison?"

"Mr. Kane?"

"Yes, can you come over to my house with your mother? Now?"

I looked outside. Daddy was in the lower end of the fields picking cotton. Mama was in her garden. "Yes, I think so. What's happened?"

"Not on the phone. Come quick."

I hung up the phone and went outside. My stomach began to cramp as I waddled down the hill toward Mama's garden. I stopped to catch my breath and called out to her. Thankfully, she heard me and came running to my side. She dropped her basket when she saw me grasp my stomach.

"What is it? The baby?" She put her arm around me and held me up.

"Yes, no. Mr. Kane called. We have to go to his house right now."

"What on earth for?" She scanned the fields.

"Daddy's down there." I pointed to where the men were working.

"Okay, I'll leave him a note. Let's get you inside. You can wait here."

"No, I'm goin'."

"Alison, you really need to get off your feet."

"I'm goin'."

Mrs. Kane hurried us to a small guestroom off the kitchen.

"Mama?"

Maggie! I spun around and saw Maggie's swollen, black and blue face. Her right eye ballooned so big she could barely open it.

"Oh, my God, Maggie!" Mama and I ran to her. She fell into our arms and cried.

"What happened? Who did this to you?" Mama asked.

"Where's Jackson?" I asked.

Maggie looked up as a tear fell from her good eye. Her lips trembled as she tried to find the words to tell me what her look already had.

"No, oh, God. No," I sobbed, crumpling onto the sofa like my bones'd gone soft.

"I'm sorry, Pixie!" Maggie reached for me.

"No!" I shoved her away. "I don't believe it. It can't be true," I cried. I wrapped my arms around my belly and rocked forward and back, forward and back. "No. No," I repeated.

Mama sat beside me on the small, brown sofa and wrapped her arms around me so tight I couldn't escape her grasp. "Shh," she soothed. "Shh, baby, shh."

If hearts could shatter, I'd have shards of mine littering every inch of my insides. I collapsed against Mama's chest, the beat of her heart against my tear-soaked cheek.

"Maggie," Mama said. "What happened? Tell me everything."

Maggie sat down on Mama's other side. "We were marchin', and it was all very civilized, ya' know? Blacks and whites, we had our signs, children even marched. Then, suddenly, from nowhere, the police came at us with these...these shields, tellin' us to get back." She looked up at Mama. "I swear, Mama, I stopped. Jackson did, too, but one of the Panthers, he drew a pistol. God, I had no idea they even had one; then, suddenly, there were several of 'em with guns, and the police were beatin' people, and I got trampled."

"Oh, Maggie." Mama let me go and pulled Maggie to her chest. "My poor girl."

"What about Jackson?" I asked again.

"I don't know. They dragged me into the woods and tied me up, said I was a nigger lover, and they...they beat me, and—" She collapsed into sobs.

"Shh, Mag, no more. You don't have to say it."

She pushed out of Mama's arms. "Someone came and untied me, a woman. Then she ran off. I don't know how long I was in the woods. I finally made my way to a shack, and this couple took me to my friend's car. I asked if they'd seen anyone else in the woods, but they hadn't. I went into town and asked around, but no one knew where Jackson was. There were so many people who disappeared. Some even killed. It was horrible."

"What if he's there, tied up, and hurt?"

Maggie shook her head. "Remember Marlo? He had a group of people search everywhere. He checked the jail, they checked the woods, the river. He said anyone who was missin' was probably—" she choked on the last word, "dead."

I collapsed beside her. *Dead. Jackson's dead.* My body trembled. "But he's still there? Marlo? Just in case? Right? In case they show up?"

Maggie nodded.

"Why didn't you come home?" I asked.

"Daddy," she said sadly.

Of course.

"What if Jackson is tryin' to get home and can't find Marlo?" I asked through my tears.

Maggie gave me a pity-filled look.

"We need to get you to a doctor," Mama said.

"No, no way. They'll figure out where I was. We can't chance it. The boycott is tomorrow!" Beneath the battered face of my sister, determination shone.

"Oh, no, young lady. You are goin' nowhere near that boycott." Mama looked from her to me. "You, too. There is no way in hell any of us are goin' anywhere near it."

"Doc Warden is on his way over." Mrs. Kane stood in the doorway, a mug of hot tea in her hands and concern in her eyes.

"Doc Warden?" I asked.

She nodded. "He's one of us."

"You said the Panthers were safe," Mama said to Maggie. "You promised."

"I had no idea. Really, Mama. I didn't know they had guns." Maggie's bravado had been stolen from her, and it scared me.

Mama shook her head. "I never shoulda allowed this. Maggie, I'm so sorry, and now poor Patricia has to deal with losin' Jackson."

I felt like I was underwater. All I could hear was the slamming of my own heart against my ribcage. Every breath took effort. A cramp seized my belly and a crushing blow hit hard to my lower back.

"Mama?" I cried and bent over in pain. "Oh, God, Mama!"

"Lay back, Alison. It's too early for the baby. This is your body reactin' to the stress." She turned toward Mrs. Kane. "How long 'til Doc Warden gets here?"

"Any minute."

Doctor Warden opened the door and motioned Mama back into the room. "I think Alison had a panic attack," he explained, "which set off some minor contractions. Her baby is fine, but she needs rest. She has another four or five weeks to go, and I want her off her feet—completely. I gave her a mild sedative to calm her down."

Mama gave me an *I told you so* look.

"If she's anything like you, that's what it will take to keep her down. Now, let's take a look at Maggie, shall we?" Doctor Warden was a short, thin, bespectacled man with wisps of gray hair along the sides of his head. He squeezed my hand before leaving the room. I listened to their hushed voices and prayed for Jackson's safety as I drifted off to sleep.

Light streamed through the blinds, filling the tiny room where I'd fallen asleep. I sat up, my mind still groggy. The events from earlier came back in bits and pieces. Maggie, badly beaten. Jackson gone. *Dead.* I lay back down. Tomorrow was the boycott. None of it seemed to matter anymore. My husband was out preparing to kill even more people as they rallied around Forrest Town to try and make things better. *Better for who?* I wondered.

Maggie opened the door. She wore a patch over her eye, but looked surprisingly better than she had earlier. "Hi, Pix." She sat on the sofa next to me. "Are you okay? I was so worried."

"About me? Have you looked in a mirror lately?"

"Yeah," she whispered. "I'm sorry I got you into this." She played with a bracelet she wore on her left arm. "I can't believe Jackson is gone. We never woulda gone if we'd known."

Mention of his name brought tears. I squeezed my eyes closed against them. I was all too aware of the anger growing from the pain of losing Jackson.

"Oh, Pix. I'm sorry to upset you. Jackson was my friend, too. We'll all miss him."

I shook my head. "How do we keep those people from bein' shot by Jimmy Lee and his uncle's posse?"

"You mean the KKK assholes?" Maggie's wit must have come back with the light of day.

I nodded.

"The network is gettin' word out. Mr. Kane has a group goin' miles up the highway to stop 'em before they get close."

"Have you talked to Patricia?"

Maggie shook her head. "Mr. Kane did."

"How is she? I can't stand this," I cried. "Maggie." I longed to tell her how much I loved Jackson. I wanted to tell her about how we used to meet by the creek, and the things he said, and the way he touched me. I wanted to pour my heart and soul into her lap and have her hold it there, safe, forever.

"Are you girls hungry?" Mrs. Kane appeared in the doorway carrying a tray of soup.

"No, thank you, ma'am," I said, wishing she'd go away. I swallowed my emotions and knew I'd forever hold my secret.

"Yes, ma'am, I'd love some," Maggie said, and took the bowl of soup from the tray.

Mrs. Kane disappeared back into the kitchen.

"What were you gonna say, Pix?" Maggie asked, and took a sip of the soup.

"Nothin'. I'm just scared for everyone, and now we're stuck here doin' nothin'. Where's Mama?"

"She had to go home. She's tellin' Daddy that you're back at your apartment."

"Are we stayin' here?"

Maggie nodded. "She thought it was safer than goin' back home and raisin' questions with Daddy."

"Do you think they'll reach 'em in time?" I sat up next to Maggie and leaned against the back of the sofa.

"Yeah, they will."

"But what then? Will they call it off?"

Maggie shook her head.

"But—"

"Mr. Kane said they'll let 'em believe the boycott is called off, and then they'll show up."

"But it's too dangerous!" I envisioned Mr. Nash getting shot in his car, Bear and the others dead in the backseat. "Is Darla comin'?"

Maggie nodded. "Everyone's comin'."

"Except Jackson," I said, and closed my eyes against the now familiar wave of sadness before it swallowed me whole.

Chapter Forty-One

Maggie and I had been ordered to remain at the Kane's house until Mama came for us, when it was safe. We sat in the living room listening to Mr. Kane on the telephone, as he gave directions to the contacts for each of the traveling groups. Mr. Kane's long-time friend was one of the police officers who arrested Jimmy Lee, and he'd confided in Mr. Kane about the timing of the sniper-style massacre that awaited the protesters.

"That's right, they're expectin' you at ten o'clock, three hours from now. Hang back 'til at least five in the afternoon. By then, they'll figure you gave up, and I'll make sure that's what they think." He paused. "Mm-hmm. Tell them, too. Any word from South Carolina?" Mr. Kane sighed. "Okay, yeah, we have that covered."

"What's gonna happen to everyone here? Did they go to work today?" I felt out of the loop since losing half the day to sleep yesterday. Maggie's bruises were turning a ghostly green and yellow. The swelling around her eye had gone down significantly from the ice Mrs. Kane had insisted upon.

"They're actin' like it's a normal workday. When the protesters come, that's when they'll leave."

"What about Patricia?"

His eyes softened. "She's angry and scared, but more than anything, she's grievin'. There's been a lot of death around that poor woman lately. Mr. Green was a close friend of their family's."

Mrs. Kane stood with one hand on the couch, one hand on her ample hip.

"Before the ruckus starts, I'm headin' into town to load up on a few necessities. Do either of you girls need anything?"

We shook our heads. "But can we come with you? We promise not to stray. We just want one last look at the town the way it is," Maggie pleaded. It hadn't taken long for her spirits to rise.

Mrs. Kane looked Maggie up and down, a frown on her lips.

"I'll say I fell down. Please? No one knows where I've been," Maggie begged.

Mrs. Kane flattened a wrinkle in her dress and sighed. "I don't know. Your mama would have my hide if anything happened to either of you." She came around the couch and stood before us. "Alison, you heard Doc Warden. You need to rest."

"Yes, ma'am, but—" Even I could hear that my conviction toward goin' to town wasn't as strong as Maggie's, but Maggie was not leaving me behind.

"I'll stay right with her. We won't get into any trouble. I promise," Maggie piped in.

Mrs. Kane looked at the clock and I held my breath, half praying she'd allow us to go along and half praying she wouldn't.

"I suppose if we hurry, that's fine. We'll be back here in an hour, safe and sound."

The morning sun lit up Main Street just as it did most days. There were people milling about, and it appeared no one was the wiser to the impending boycott. While Mrs. Kane ran into the General Store, Maggie and I went into the diner.

"Oh, sugar, there you are safe and sound." Jean hugged me close. Her jaw gaped when she spotted Maggie behind me. "My word, what on earth happened to you?"

Maggie put her hand up to cover her split lip. "I tripped in the street. I'm a klutz." Maggie was a terrible liar. Her cheeks flushed and her eyes skitted nervously around the diner.

"That musta been some fall. You girls want some coffee? Tea?"

We sat at the counter and I apologized for asking for time off. I explained what the doctor had said. Jean leaned over the counter and whispered, "With all that's goin' on today, I think y'all should scoot on home right quick."

I grabbed Maggie's hand under the counter and feigned ignorance. "Whaddaya mean?"

Jean rolled her eyes. "Do you think I don't know that you know? Come on, Alison."

"What?" I shot a concerned look at Maggie. "Who else knows?"

"My Aunt Katherine went to the meetin's. I would go if I could, but you know my husband would have me tied to the porch if he had his way. Now you girls get outta here before somethin' happens." Jean came around the counter and put her hand on my shoulder. She whispered in my ear, "Get home and be safe."

Outside the diner, I grabbed Maggie's arm and pulled her into the alley. "What if others know? We could be in real danger."

Maggie held my hands and looked into my eyes in that calming way she had about her. "Pixie, no one knows. We're fine."

Suddenly, from across the road, a crowd broke through the trees—black men I didn't recognize, dressed in tank tops and t-shirts, their muscles glistening in the sun. There must have been thirty of them carrying something at their sides. I grabbed Maggie's arm. Maggie's eyes danced wildly up and down the road.

"Wicked smart," she said under her breath. "It's the boycotters. "

"Maggie, let's go. We gotta go!" I said, pulling her arm toward Mrs. Kane's car. "Why are they here? They'll be shot." I looked all around for the snipers, expecting to hear shots ringing out any second.

"No," Maggie said, as if in a daze. "They're brilliant. The police are all on the highway." Maggie ripped her arm from my grasp and ran toward them, yelling over her shoulder, "Pixie—find Mrs. Kane! Go! Now!"

I ran toward the drugstore, the heft of my baby weighing down each step. By the time I reached the store, Mrs. Kane and nearly every store owner on the block had come outside. There were three trucks full of coloreds coming from the direction of our farm. Alfred was on the bed of the largest truck, along with a mass of other men.

"Good Lord," Mrs. Kane said. "Come quick, child. We must go!" She hurried toward her car.

"I can't leave Maggie!" I ran into the street toward the crowd that now held up signs: *Equality Everywhere; Freedom; Racial Dignity; Stop Racial Wars.* I put my hands under my belly and lifted my girth to alleviate the mounting pressure in my groin. "Maggie!" I yelled. The trucks had parked and now there were people everywhere I looked, in the road, marching down Main Street, standing on the sidewalks. I was swept away with the pushing of the crowd.

"Maggie? Maggie?" I yelled again, frantically searching for her through the crowd.

Someone pushed me forward and I stumbled, grabbing onto the man's belt in front of me. He turned around with angry eyes, then softened when he saw me struggling to stand. He helped me to my feet and asked if I was okay. We moved down Main Street as a loud, determined group. I worried about the police mowing us down with bullets. Maggie's voice came from the outside of the crowd. I pushed my way toward her.

"Maggie!" I yelled.

"Pixie! Go home!" She yelled through the tangle of arms and legs.

I was lost in a sea of bodies. Angry store owners retreated behind locked doors. A heavy white woman ran into the street and got in the face of the colored men who led the charge.

"Get out of our town! We don't want you here!" She spat on him and the crowd pushed past her, leaving her screaming into the uncaring air.

Police sirens sounded in the distance. Cars came from the direction of the farms at the far end of town. Whites joined the march. Angry shouts came from the sidewalks, and within the marching crowd came a beat of footsteps on pavement and strong voices, "Equal rights, equal pay, equal freedom. Equal rights, equal pay, equal freedom."

I found myself swept up in the cadence and the energy of the crowd. I thought of Jackson and tears stung my eyes. Words thrust from my lungs, "Equal rights, equal pay, equal freedom!"

Suddenly a colored man burst from the crowd and sprinted for the diner. He swung the door open and yelled, "Let our people eat! Let our people eat!"

I stared in amazement, waiting for Jean to slam the door shut. Jean came out and stood on the sidewalk, arms crossed, a shock of red lipstick across her smiling lips. Joe's fleshy body filled the doorway, his face set in a harsh, nasty glare. The colored man continued his chant. "Let our people eat! Let our people eat!" Joe shook his head and wiped his hand on the white body apron he wore, then he walked away, spurring on the man in the doorway. "Equal rights! Equal Freedom!"

The crowd chanted, "Let our people eat!" Sirens blared, growing louder by the second until they were almost upon us. Three squad cars skidded to a halt, blocking Main Street and halting the yelling crowd. "Equal rights, equal pay, equal freedom!"

I caught sight of Maggie pushing her way through the crowd. I recognized Albert and young Thomas Green's swollen face a few feet from where I stood. They chanted and sweat, their eyes serious, unwavering. Thomas limped against a wooden crutch, one arm in a cast. The veins in Albert's neck swelled thick like snakes as he yelled in unison with the group. He turned my way and caught my stare. *Jackson.*

Marching toward us was a group of white-capped klansmen carrying thick sticks. One carried a fiery torch. "Niggers, go home! Niggers, go home!"

I stood, slack jawed, watching the group of them stomp down Main Street, the white drapes they wore flapping in the breeze. Eye holes cut in pointy, white hats that rose far above their heads and covered them clear to their chests. *Mama was right.* Would they kill us all? I scanned the crowd quickly—there was no sign of Maggie. I had to get out of there. I looked for Mrs. Kane, but she, too, had been swallowed by the chaos. How did things go so wrong? I was pushed along with the boycotters toward the KKK, their angry words booming louder, above the din of the crowd.

The police stepped from the cars, their nightsticks slapping hard against their palms. Officer Chandler planted his legs hip width apart. "Y'all break it up now, ya' hear?"

"Niggers, go home!" the KKK chanted.

The crowd continued, "Equal rights, equal pay, equal freedom!"

I spotted Maggie pushing through the front of the crowd. She crossed her arms and nudged her chin up. I knew that stance. Maggie stood eye-to-eye with Officer Chandler.

"This is a peaceful movement. We aren't hurtin' anyone. We're makin' a statement," Maggie shouted.

"Step aside, Maggie. This doesn't concern you," Officer Chandler commanded.

"Yes, it does," she said. Maggie turned toward the people ogling from the sidewalk and yelled, "This concerns you!" She pointed at two women coming out of the furniture store and gawking at her. "And you, and you!" Maggie pointed at a white man, then another, standing angrily and sneering at the crowd. "This is our town, and you should all be ashamed."

One of the klansmen moved toward Maggie, his large white fist—the only visible piece of his skin—clasped around a thick stick. Officer Chandler held his arm out, protecting her. The klansmen moved around the police car and pushed a short, stout, colored picketer. Suddenly there was a rumble of white caps and colored men. Blurs of white sheet flew against flashes of black, spots of red appearing on the sheets as men were beaten to the ground. I was pushed to and fro, stumbling to remain upright. Someone grabbed my arm and pulled me back away from the fighting and into the depths of the group. I heard Maggie's voice rising and falling in an argument with Officer Chandler, as the police moved in on the crowd, pushing them back down Main Street the way they'd come.

Several cars raced into town, screeching to a halt. People piled out of the cars and shouting ensued. Blacks, whites, old, young, men, and women, there were more people than I'd ever seen on Main Street. I pushed toward the front of the crowd, yelling for Maggie. A sharp pain raced through my lower back and I cried out in pain. The police formed a line and were pushing the crowd back, the KKK yelled angry barbs, "Coons, go home! Niggers, retreat!"

The raging pack of klansmen set their sights on a group of colored men, staring them down through the eyeholes in their ridiculous—and ominous—caps. Suddenly there was a swarm of fists, arms and legs upended, and a rumble on the ground. It was hard to decipher where one white-caped man ended and the next began. I had to look away. The police ignored the beatings, fueling the rage of the group that swarmed the streets. A shot rang out, followed by a hush of the crowd. Then, as if the clouds had suddenly burst upon us, another shot rang out and the coloreds barreled into the police, taking them down and mauling the KKK.

I caught my breath and felt a strong hand pull me toward the sidewalk. I was being pulled and dragged, disoriented as I passed shouting people, punches flying in all directions. Someone kicked me in the side and I screamed, careening forward toward whoever was pulling me away. I clamored along the ground until we were away from the crowd, and I looked up to find Patricia's terrified eyes, wide-set and serious.

"Get up! Get up!" she hissed.

I stumbled to my feet and she pulled me along, pressure mounting in my belly, each step a painful, determined force. She pulled me deep into the woods toward Division Street.

"Maggie!" I yelled through my tears.

"I can't help her, but I can help you," she said, and put her shoulder under my arm, bearing most of my weight as she hurried me away from the fighting. Shouts and cries drifted away behind us, two more shots rang out.

"I'm sorry, I'm so sorry about Jackson," I said.

"Quiet," she said.

She brought me through the woods and we came out across the road from Division Street.

"Hurry now," she said, and urged me to walk toward her house.

"I can't." Every step felt as though my baby would fall right out of my body. "It hurts."

"It's gonna hurt a lot more if they catch us. Now think of your mama and get your ass movin', child."

We stumbled across the road. Tinsel ran up beside me and turned his wide eyes up to his mother.

"She okay?" he asked, his little arms flailing up and pointing at my chest.

I concentrated on breathing, keeping myself moving forward.

Patricia didn't answer, just huffed as she helped me toward the house.

Tinsel prodded. "She gonna get us killed? She gonna have dat baby?"

"Tell Arma to boil water," she snapped. "Now!"

Tinsel ran the last fifty feet toward the house.

Chapter Forty-Two

Eight children huddled around the kitchen table, and three women stood by the sink. Worried eyes ran over me, whispers spoken behind close hands as I was led through the tiny kitchen and laid on a mattress in the smallest bedroom I'd ever seen. The walls, adorned with five pictures of young children, nearly touched the sides of the double bed. My eyes were drawn to a picture of a young boy whose kind eyes I'd recognize in the dark. *Jackson.* A deep pain began in my back and slipped across my belly like two giant hands, squeezing as strong as they could. I wrapped my arms around my stomach and pushed against it.

Patricia rushed from the room, immediately attacked by harsh whispers and strong inquisitions. *Who's that? Why's she here? Dangerous! Too big a chance.* I couldn't take my eyes off of Jackson's face. I cried out as every muscle pulled together, squeezing my baby within me. Patricia rushed back to my bedside carrying a pot of steaming water and towels.

I lifted my head and saw sixteen eyes, wide and curious, in the doorway.

"Get back!" Patricia swatted at them, pushing the door partway closed. She skillfully pulled my legs apart and said, "You're gonna have this child, and you need to pay attention now."

I couldn't look at her. The pain ran so deep and debilitating that I clenched the bedside and grit my teeth, straining the muscles in my arms until they rocked my shoulders. "It's too early!" I cried, shaking my head from side to side.

"Child, you don't decide when this baby comes. This baby is gonna come whether you like it or not, and I'll tell you, you'd better give in to it or it's gonna rip you apart."

I blew fast hard breaths through my teeth. "What about Maggie? My mama?"

"I ain't leavin' your side. Not with my son lookin' down on me." She felt my belly like she'd done it a hundred times before. "Your baby's just about ready. Don't think my boy don't tell me things. I know all 'bout you two." She looked up at the picture of young Jackson, and swallowed hard. "He loves you...he loved you. So, I love you. It's the way it works with kin."

Another hard contraction gripped my body.

"Breathe, child, breathe. You gotta get air to that baby. That's right," she said. "Breathe in, and out, in and out."

"It hurts too much. I gotta get this baby out," I cried.

"Not yet, darlin'. You just let this baby come when it's ready. Don't force it."

"It's too early. Somethin's wrong. I'm not due for another month."

The front door opened and there was a flurry of voices. *Maggie.*

"Maggie!" I yelled, then clenched with another contraction. "Maggie," I said through clenched teeth. "Help me."

Maggie came into the tiny room and climbed around me to the other side of the bed. She sat next to me. "Breathe, Pixie, breathe. That's a girl. In and out."

She thanked Patricia, who made a *what-else-was-I-to-do* face.

"It hurts so much," I whined through the pain.

"I know, Pixie. Think of somethin' good. Think of the barn, and the fun we've had. Think of your weddin' day."

I glared at her.

"Oh, right, no don't think of that." Maggie looked at the photos on the wall, and I watched as she swallowed hard, like she was willing tears away. "Is that Jackson?" she asked.

Patricia nodded.

"He was a good man."

"Don't count him as gone yet. Not 'til we find him."

Maggie nodded, and then brushed my hair from my sweaty forehead.

"Jimmy Lee's out there with his uncle. They're right alongside the Klan. They're not wearin' white robes, but they're givin' 'em orders. The police have gone haywire."

"That ain't no peaceful march, that's for damn sure," Patricia said.

My belly squeezed and I grabbed Maggie's hand so hard she yelped.

"Can't we do anything for her?" Maggie asked.

"We just gotta let this baby do what it's gonna do."

"What about a doctor? Doesn't she need one? Doc Warden? He might help." Maggie said.

"Doc Warden won't go near that nightmare of a street. He's the only doc we got, and he's too smart to get hisself killed."

The door creaked open and a set of little eyes peeked in. *Tinsel.*

"Boy, you better get your butt outta here. Arma!" Patricia called. A teenage girl came to the door and took Tinsel's hand, leading him away.

"Sorry, Mama. I'll keep him out here," she said and blinked her thick, long eyelashes. She closed the door behind her.

"Now, I'm gonna have to take a look down there," Patricia said in a way that left no room for complaint, just as my mama woulda done.

I closed my eyes as she pulled my pants off and then removed my panties. "Oh, child," she said. "You in luck. This baby wants out and soon."

Maggie laughed, and pain tore through me, stealing any coherent thoughts I might have had. I clenched my eyes shut.

"Breathe, child, breathe!" Patricia commanded. "You gotta breathe or you'll pass out."

"I gotta push. I gotta get it out. It hurts. Please!" I cried.

Patricia used the hot water to wash me down there, and she spread clean towels underneath me.

"Arma!" Patricia hollered. Arma peered into the door with a scared look in her eyes.

"Tell Sharon to heat the towels."

"Yes, ma'am." The door closed with a hurried *clank!*

"How did you," *pant, pant,* "know where I was?" *pant, pant,* I asked Maggie.

"Albert told me he sent someone to tell Patricia that you were sick, and when I couldn't find you, I knew she'd taken care of you." Maggie kissed my forehead. "Pixie, I would never have let you go if I'd known that was gonna happen."

"That's what happens when brothers get angry." Patricia kept one hand anchored to my calf. "I heard that they were the group from up north. They were tryin' to get a jump on the snipers. I guess the jump was on them." Patricia shook her head. "This nonsense has gotta stop. There's gotta be a way."

"This will help. I'm sure of it. There's only a handful of police in this area. They can't hold everyone back." Maggie said.

Another contraction sent the baby's head down between my legs. "Get it out!" I screamed. I could feel Patricia pulling and prodding the baby, wiggling its shoulders until suddenly there was a burst of freedom and the baby slid out from inside me with a whoosh of relief.

"Jesus, Mary, and Joseph." Patricia stared down at the baby.

"What?" I cried. "What? What's wrong?" I grabbed Maggie's hand. "Is the baby okay? I can't hear it. The baby's not cryin'!"

I held Maggie so tight she couldn't move to see the baby.

"Child, you in trouble now." Patricia worked down below cleaning the baby. She called for Sharon, who rushed in with fresh towels in her arms.

"Goodness!" Sharon shrieked. She handed the towels to Patricia, who caught her eyes and frowned.

"That's enough now," Patricia said in a harsh tone.

Sharon looked at me, then back at the baby. "I heated the towels with the iron, they're nice and warm."

Patricia bundled the baby and told Sharon to come into the room and close the door. "It's a boy. You've got a son," Patricia said. I sensed fear in her tone.

"What's goin' on?" I demanded. "Maggie!" I dropped her arm and struggled to sit up.

Maggie slid off the end of the bed next to Patricia. The baby's cries came in quick, sharp bursts.

"Oh, thank God. Thank God." I cried, and fell back on the pillow.

"Pixie?" Maggie said. She squeezed behind Patricia and Sharon and leaned down to speak to me, inches from my face. "Pixie, who is the father of your baby?" she whispered.

Had she lost her mind? "What kinda question's that? Jimmy Lee is the father!"

"Look at me, Pix. It's me. You can trust me. Who is the father of this baby?" She turned her head toward Patricia and I followed her gaze to my bundled baby held close to Patricia's chest. Patricia leaned forward, and my baby's jet black hair, and skin as smooth and dark as cocoa, came into view. I didn't fully understand what all the fuss was about, until Patricia brought the baby closer to me, and I saw my baby's wide-set nose and full lips. Even through the tiny slit of his eyes I saw the resemblance to his father.

"Girl, you cannot take this baby home. They'll kill you, your baby, and the baby's father." Patricia put her hand on the baby's chest and whispered, "A blessin' and a life sentence, all in one."

"They can't touch his father. He's already dead."

Chapter Forty-Three

Even with the madness taking place just a mile down the road, with Joshua at my breast, I felt the pieces of my life come together in a way that I never understood they could. The baby I had carried and felt was separate from me, a being made not of love, but of duty, had instantly latched onto my heart and made me whole. This wasn't a baby of duty at all. Joshua was made from the very essence of love.

Maggie sat on the side of the bed, her hands on her knees, her face a mask of worry. "I don't understand, Pixie. How? When?"

"Before I got married," I admitted.

Maggie shook her head. "Then, why did you marry Jimmy Lee?"

"You can't blame her," Patricia said. "Love can only endure so much. Imagine your father if she said she was in love with a colored man. Imagine her life. Girl, there was no way this could've come to be." Patricia had cleaned up the baby, and she'd sent Sharon out back with a plastic bag containing the bloodied sheets, towels, and the afterbirth. She was to bury the whole mess in the back yard.

"You can't take this baby home, Pix," Maggie said. "Jimmy Lee will kill you, you know that."

"What am I supposed to do, leave my baby here?"

"Pixie, remember Mr. Bingham? His wife? Remember what's goin' on down the street? No way, Pix, no way you're leavin' this house with that baby."

"I'm not leavin' my Joshua."

"Joshua?" Maggie asked.

"Joshua."

Maggie leaned against the wall, arms crossed. "You can't even support a baby alone, and what do you think's gonna happen? Jimmy Lee's gonna raise another man's baby? A colored man's?" Maggie covered her face and let out a long, frustrated, guttural groan. "This is a mess."

"That's my grandson. You leave that baby with me. You go on home and tell your husband your baby died."

"Died? No, I won't do it." I held Joshua close against me and cried. "No way. No."

Patricia sat next to me on the bed. "Now you listen here, I have lost one child to this backwards world and I'm not losin' a grandson—or you. Jackson loved you. Do you think he wants you to die because of his seed?"

No. I can't do it. I can't leave him.

"Look into that baby's face. Is that the face of a white baby?" Patricia asked.

I lowered Joshua from my shoulder and looked at his beautiful, dark eyes, the too-dark shade of his skin. I touched his cheek and I felt complete, happy.

"Maggie, I can't do it," I pleaded.

Maggie shook her head as if, for once, she didn't have an answer. She climbed back onto the bed beside me and put her arm around me. I laid my head against her chest, Joshua in my arms, and cried. Maggie brushed my hair away from my face.

"Shh," she soothed. "We'll figure this out."

I shook my head. "How? There's no figurin' this out. Jackson's dead, Jimmy Lee is just plain awful, and—" *Daddy. What about Daddy?* He'd disown me for sure.

"I'm gonna leave you two to discuss this, but our time is short. That nonsense goin' on out there ain't gonna last all day, and someone's gonna be lookin' for that pregnant girl."

Chapter Forty-Four

When I told Jimmy Lee that our baby died, I think he was relieved. He didn't ask to see him. He sat on the couch staring straight ahead, not looking at me, not holding me, just staring ahead like he was watching a picture show.

Maggie had come up with a plan to pretend to bury the baby in our family plot on Daddy's farm. She said we couldn't bring Mama into the plan, because we'd be putting her in the terrible position of having to lie to Daddy, and two liars in the family were enough. Mama was shouldering enough burdens for any woman. I didn't want to do it—keep the secret from Mama or pretend to bury Joshua—but I didn't see any other way around the situation. Maggie bundled a doll that belonged to one of Patricia's children, put it in a cardboard box, and taped it up; then, wrapped the box in blue paper, and even sealed it with a bow. She'd gone back home the night of the boycott to tell my parents what had happened. She said Daddy lugged his biggest shovel down to the plot and dug a hole, stopping often to wipe tears with his sleeve. Maggie sat in the truck and watched him, holding the box safely on her lap.

Mama showed up at my apartment twenty minutes later.

"Oh, my baby. My poor baby," she cried, holding me so tight I could barely breathe. Her wet cheek pressed hard against mine, her chest heaving with sobs. She pulled back, fresh tears in her eyes. I thought I had no more tears left in me, but seeing Mama's tears, and knowing that my lies had caused them, made my tears flow like a river.

She reached out and touched Jimmy Lee's shoulder. "Are you okay, hun?" she asked.

Jimmy Lee shook his head. "I'm not sure we were ready for a baby anyway."

"No one's ever ready, but that doesn't make it hurt any less when you lose your child."

He turned to her and said, "I'm not sure. Maybe it does." He stood and walked into the bedroom, leaving Mama's jaw hanging open in dismay. When the bedroom door thumped shut, Mama whispered, "Oh, honey. I'm so sorry. He's...ugh...forget about him. What can I do to help you?"

Let me love my baby.

Chapter Forty-Five

The next day after Jimmy Lee went to work, I went outside and walked to the edge of town. Every muscle in my body ached. It felt like a basketball had been ripped out from between my legs. My breasts were full and achy, and I longed to see Joshua. I wanted to hold him in my arms and tell him how much I loved him. I wanted him to hear how much I loved his father, and to know that, even though I could not be with him right then, that I did not abandon him, and above all, that I was not ashamed of him.

Main Street stretched before me with broken windows in the storefronts, glass and debris in the road. I couldn't help but feel like I'd let Jackson down. I looked down at the ground, my arms hanging uselessly at my sides, and I cried. What kind of difference did we make? I saw no evidence of change, just a haunted street that would forever hold the ghosts of beaten men, and the smell of fear and hatred.

I turned toward the direction of Division Street and my feet drew me forward, as if they were guided by someone other than me.

Joshua.

I ignored the pain and pressure in my lower abdomen, the noise of passing cars. I had tunnel vision, and at the end of the long stretch of darkness was my baby. *My baby.* The thought of him sent a searing pain through my breasts. I crossed my arms over them and pressed them against me.

The corner of Division Street was upon me, calling me forth. I never looked back. I didn't care who saw me. My baby needed me. To hell with Jimmy Lee. He didn't care. He'd never cared. He'd kill Joshua, and he might even kill me. I was never going back there. I knew that with all my heart and soul. I. Would. Not. Go. Back.

As I stumbled down Division Street, the houses spun around me. An engine roared behind me. I held onto a tree for support. My legs weakened, my vision blurred. I had the sensation that something wet was dripping down my legs, but was unable to look down without feeling like I'd pass out.

Patricia's front door opened, and I saw her standing on the porch, Joshua bundled in her arms.

"Joshua," I whispered. I barely registered screeching wheels behind me, a slamming truck door.

"Alison!"

Jimmy Lee? I turned my head slowly, as if in a fog. Fear ran through me like an electric shock. "Gettin' my baby," I said with as much determination as I could muster, and stumbled toward Joshua.

Jimmy Lee grabbed my arm and held onto me, his fingers digging into my skin. "Alison! Stop!"

I pulled and kicked and tried to break free. "My baby! I want my baby!" I cried. I looked at Patricia's house, less than fifty feet away. It felt like a million miles. "Please, my baby, I want my baby," I sobbed.

He dragged me backwards. I kicked and flailed blindly toward him. "Joshua!" I yelled. The world faded in and out.

Suddenly Patricia was there beside me, yelling, "What are you doin'? She's bleedin'!" Her capable hands pulled at my other arm. I was being stretched like taffy, my head lolling back and forth, the world spinning around me—bits of conversation filtered into my ears, muffled as if under water.

"My wife—"

"You'll hurt her!" Patricia's voice was a thin thread, miles away.

My baby wailed incessantly. *Joshua.*

"... stupid nigger!"

Patricia came into focus just as the back of Jimmy Lee's hand connected with her cheek and she tumbled to the ground. I wrenched myself from Jimmy Lee's grasp and crawled along the gravel toward the blurry bundle before me. Joshua lay screaming within Patricia's grasp.

"My baby!" I reached for him as Jimmy Lee tugged me backwards, leaving a warm trail of blood beneath me. My fingertips connected with Joshua's blanket and I pulled, hard, until I had him in my arms and tumbled backwards. "Joshua," I whispered over and over. I pressed my cheek against his as he cried and fought me with all his tiny might.

Jimmy Lee's truck roared to life, tires squealing and comin' to a halt beside me. I felt Joshua ripped from my arms. *My baby!* Hands grabbed me roughly and tossed me into the truck. As we sped away, my baby's cries, and the world around me, faded to black.

Chapter Forty-Six

A light haze filtered in through my eyelashes, as if I were looking through gauze. An endless rhythm of beeps surrounded me. I blinked away the haze, my head pounding out a painful beat.

"Oh, thank God." Mama's tight face came into view. She gently touched my arm. "I was so worried," she said. "It's okay, you're in the hospital. Jimmy Lee brought you."

"Joshua," I whispered.

Mama dropped her eyes. "I know, baby. I know. He's gone, remember?"

I shook my head, my eyes instantly filling with tears. Memories trickled back to me. Patricia lying on the ground. Joshua in my arms. Jimmy Lee. *Oh, God, Jimmy Lee.*

"Where's Jimmy Lee?"

"I'm here," he said from the doorway. "I was just talkin' to the doctor."

"What happened?" I asked.

"I saw you walkin' down the road and I was yellin' to you, but it was like you didn't even hear me. Then I saw the blood drippin' down your leg, and you must have been delirious because you headed down Division Street and you grabbed some woman's baby."

"Joshua," I whispered.

Jimmy Lee looked at Mama. "She must still be out of it."

I shook my head. Mama rubbed my arm. "She lost so much blood," she said. "Alison," she said softly. "You hemorrhaged, from the delivery. They were able to stop the bleedin', but you have to take it easy." She closed her eyes against the tears pooling in her eyes. When she opened them, she touched my cheek. "I'm so sorry, baby. Thank goodness you're alive. We almost lost you."

"Joshua," I said again.

"He died, remember?" Jimmy Lee spoke sharply, then turned and paced. "Can't they do somethin'? Make her go to sleep or somethin' so she doesn't torture herself like this?"

I grasped the edges of the mattress, the IV line in my arm pinched my skin. "I'm not torturin' myself."

"He's dead, Alison," Jimmy Lee insisted. "Dead, okay? He's not comin' back."

I shook my head against the pillow.

"Alison, we buried him in the family plot, remember? You rest, honey." Mama turned to Jimmy Lee. "Why don't you go home and rest, too, Jimmy Lee. You've been through a lot lately. "

"I'm not leavin'," he said.

I could still feel the soft weight of Joshua in my arms. My baby didn't know me. He might not ever know me. My breasts ached, engorged with milk my baby would never drink. I looked at Jimmy Lee and felt the same disgust I'd felt since the day he forced himself upon me at the river. I turned away, my mind burning with the memory of Jackson's tender touch. I tried to muster Daddy's voice to center me. *Know your place.* Every inch of my body revolted against those words. My stomach tightened, my hands and jaw clenched. I closed my eyes and tried again. *Be a good wife. Know your place.*

"No!" The yell escaped my lungs before I could stop it.

Mama gasped. "What is it? Do you hurt?"

"No!" I said again. "No, no, no! I won't *know my place*," I cried.

"I'm gettin' the doctor. She's out of it." Jimmy Lee headed for the door.

"I don't need my doctor. I need my baby. I already lost the man I love. I'm not gonna lose the child I love, too."

Jimmy Lee's face contorted into a mess of confusion.

Mama put her hand to my forehead and I shook it off. "I'm sorry, Mama, but it's true. The baby wasn't Jimmy Lee's."

Jimmy Lee took a step closer to the bed.

"I'm sorry. I married you without knowin' I was already pregnant."

"What are you sayin'?" Mama asked.

"I was with someone else," I cried.

"You whore. Who was it?" Jimmy Lee fumed.

"Watch your mouth, that's my daughter," Mama spat.

"Who? Who was it?" he demanded.

"It doesn't matter who," I said.

"Like hell it doesn't matter." Jimmy Lee grabbed my arm and squeezed. "*You* cheated on *me*? You're nothin' but a stupid farm girl. You were charity to me! You're nothin'!"

"Get out of here!" Mama said, flat and firm. "Don't you ever talk to my daughter that way."

"Your daughter's a whore and a liar," he seethed at Mama, and then turned his anger on me. "Don't you ever speak to me again." Jimmy Lee spun on his heels and stormed out the door, leaving a trail of vicious words in his wake.

My hands shook from relaying details of the night of Joshua's birth to Mama. The feeling of having my heart ripped from my body returned, fresh and unbearable, when I told her of our plan to pretend that Joshua had died. All I'd wanted was to protect him. Disappointment rode strong in her eyes, not from my being with a colored man, strange as that might seem, but for not trusting enough to confide in her. Mama stood at my bedside now, holding my hand, tears streaming down her cheeks.

Maggie flew through the doorway, out of breath and spouting questions. "What happened? Is she okay? Patricia said Jimmy Lee hit her. I just passed him in the hall and he looked pissed. Oh, my God, Pixie, are you okay?"

Mama let out a quick breath before answering Maggie. "She hemorrhaged."

"I know, I got that much," Maggie said. "But she's okay? She's gonna be okay, right?"

Maggie spoke so quickly that I could feel something pushing inside of her. The way her eyes jumped from me to Mama and back again told me she was holding something back.

"Maggie, Mama knows," I said.

"She knows? You know?" She didn't wait for an answer. "We didn't want to lie to you. We just didn't want you to have to lie to Daddy about this, too."

Mama nodded. "You did the right thing."

"Cheatin' on Jimmy Lee? Leavin' my baby? I did the right thing?" I didn't understand how that could possibly be true.

"What you did before marryin' Jimmy Lee, that was wrong. But you know that. You don't need me to harp on you. What's done is done. And yes, you did the right thing leavin' your baby behind. Your father would have killed us both if you'd come home with a colored baby."

"But, Mama, I can't leave him. I mean, I did, I tried, but I can't leave him there. I need him. I love him."

Mama backed herself into a chair, where she leaned on her elbows and let her face fall into her hands.

Maggie took my hand and with a glint in her eye said, "Pixie, Jackson came home. He isn't dead. He's with Patricia and Joshua now."

"Jackson? Albert's brother, he's alive?" Mama looked from Maggie to me.

"Are you sure? How do you know?" *Jackson.* My world was righting itself. This had to be a sign. It was time I knew *my place*, only my place wasn't where Daddy thought it should be.

"Albert got word to Mr. Kane, who called me. Jackson's home. He's safe!" Maggie exclaimed.

Tears of joy sprung from my eyes. My heart beat strong within my chest, renewed energy streamed through me. I took a deep breath and did what I should have done long ago. "Mama, Jackson Johns is the father of my baby, and I love him. I love him—I love them—with all my heart." It felt so good to say those words, I had to repeat them. "I love Jackson Johns."

Chapter Forty-Seven

I felt physically stronger the next afternoon. The nurse explained that they'd pumped me full of blood, fluid, and antibiotics, and the doctor said I could go home, as long as I took it easy.

"Mama is on her way to pick you up."

I pressed the telephone receiver tight against my ear, listening to Maggie's concerned voice, and thinking about how I'd almost lost her.

"I'm gonna ask Mama to take me to see Jackson on the way home," I said.

"Pix, you can't do that. The police are patrollin' the streets. Several men are still missin'. And Jimmy Lee is on a warpath, askin' everyone in town if they knew you were runnin' 'round behind his back."

Everyone knows? I was determined to take responsibility for what I'd done and to be with the man I loved.

"You can't go near Division Street," Maggie warned.

"I gotta, Maggie. I gotta see Jackson."

"Alison, it's bad," she said. "Think about Jackson. If Jimmy Lee finds out that Jackson is the father, he'll kill him on the spot."

I assured her that we'd be extra careful.

"How do you plan to tell Daddy about the baby?" she asked.

"I'm not sure."

"Maybe I can help," she offered. "I'll feel out his mood before you get here. Daddy's feelin' the long tail of the boycott—none of the farmhands have shown up since, so he's exhausted and worried."

"Maybe it's better if we don't tell him," I said, wondering when it might ever be a good time to break Daddy's heart.

"We'll see. Pix, be careful if you go see Jackson. Promise me."

I promised her and waited for Mama to arrive and drive me home.

"Let's not tell your father about the baby 'til we have time to figure it all out," she said.

That made sense to me, since I couldn't go to my own apartment, and I couldn't bring the baby to Daddy's house, I didn't have many choices to consider.

"Can we stop and see Jackson and Joshua on the way?" I asked.

Mama looked at me and turned her head slightly up, in that way that said, *Oh, honey. I wish it were that easy.*

"How am I gonna do this, Mama? I love him. I want to see him and, to be honest, I don't really care who knows it. Once I tell Daddy, no one else really matters."

"You're not that naïve, Alison. You know all too well what could happen to Jackson—and to your baby."

Mr. Bingham. Mr. Green. "So, what do I do now? You tell me."

"I'm thinkin'." She drove with her eyebrows drawn together, both hands on the steering wheel, staring intently at the road.

"What about if we parked behind their church and walked over?" I pleaded.

"Alison," Mama sighed.

"Please, Mama? Could you have left me, or Maggie, or Jake? Could you have forgotten a man you'd loved?"

Mama's clenched face softened, the lines on her forehead diminished.

"Please, Mama? It's all I can think about. I'm scared every minute of the day now anyway. Don't you think I worry that Jimmy Lee will figure this all out and do somethin'? Look at what he's done. He beat up kids just for bein' colored. He killed a man. He saw to the death of another. Once he knows the truth, then Jackson and Joshua—and even I—don't have a chance."

"Maggie," Mama said, as if she were thinking of her and the word just came out accidentally.

"What about Maggie?"

"You can stay with Maggie, you and Joshua, until you figure it out."

"Mama, have you seen Maggie's apartment? It's tiny."

"It's safe," she said, nodding to herself. "Do you even know if Jackson wants to be with you? You're makin' a lot of assumptions about a man who just came back from the dead."

"Oh, he wants to be with me alright." For once, I knew exactly what I wanted and where I belonged. "There's no doubt in my mind. It's not an assumption. He told me."

"Even now, after all that's happened?" she asked.

I watched Mama drive past our road. "Mama? Where are you goin'?"

She turned to face me. "The church."

Chapter Forty-Eight

I'll never know what possessed Mama to give in and take me to the church, because no matter how many times I asked her why she did, she just smiled and said, "It was the right thing to do."

We walked across the parking lot, Mama walking too close to me and asking every three seconds, "Are you sure you're okay? You're supposed to take it easy. Let me know if you want to stop."

"I'm fine," I answered, and though pain pressed in on my abdomen, I honestly felt better than I had in weeks. The thought of my baby pulled me forward, the thought of Jackson pushed me faster. We reached the back lawn of their property, and I was thankful not to have to see the dark stain of my blood in the street.

Mama grabbed my arm. "Alison, listen to me. You don't have to make any decisions today. You can just visit your baby and then let that sit with you for a while."

I knew what she was doing. What I was planning was scarier than anything either of us had ever gone through. My life there in Forrest Town was quickly coming to an end, and her life, as she knew it, was too. I reached for both of Mama's hands. "Mama, you've spent your whole life worryin' about my happiness, Maggie's happiness, and Jake's. Now I've found mine. It might not be easy, and it might not be right based on this town's perspective," I dropped her hand and put my right hand over my heart, "but in here, where it really matters, it's not only right, it's perfectly clear. I've found my place."

She nodded, and we walked up the back steps of the house. Standing on the back porch, I thought of the woman I'd become, and the sides of Mama I'd only recently discovered. She'd given up so much of her life for the good of her family—her beliefs, her interests. In a way, I was followin' in her shoes. I would have to give up everything I knew to be with my child.

My heart drummed in my chest. My nerves tingled, making me jumpy all over. The pain I had experienced as I walked over was masked by happiness the moment Jackson opened the door, Joshua in his arms.

The cuts and bruises on Jackson's face and the bandages around his neck silenced my joy. Jackson didn't say a word. He didn't have to. The smile that formed on his lips and the light in his eyes told me everything I needed to know. He opened the door wide and invited us inside, handing Joshua to Mama, who took him without so much as a pause in her breath.

Cringing with each painful step, Jackson took a step toward me and opened his arms. I melted into them. The feel of the bandages beneath his shirt saddened me. The familiarity of his chest, the way we fit together, the warm scent of his skin, lessened my sadness. Jackson was there, he was alive, and that was all that mattered.

Tires screeched out front. Jackson tensed.

Tinsel flew through the front door. "It's that white guy, the one who beat Thomas!"

Jimmy Lee. Mama handed Joshua to Patricia.

The three of us went to the front of the house. Jackson told us to stay inside as he limped out the front door and down the steps. We watched him from the open window. Jimmy Lee stood beside his truck, parked caddycorner across the middle of the street. He swayed, and I wondered if he'd been drinking.

Jackson stood strong—legs planted firmly apart, arms crossed, biceps twitching. I grabbed Mama's hand and listened, hoping Jimmy Lee didn't know we were there.

"Whaddaya want, Jimmy Lee?" Jackson asked.

Jimmy Lee stared at him. "My wife," he said.

I held my breath.

"She's not here. Why don't you go home and wait for her?"

Jimmy Lee took a step toward Jackson. Jackson didn't move.

"You think I'm stupid, nigger? I know she and her stupid-ass mother are here. Parked right over at the church." He took another few steps, until he was just a foot from Jackson. Jimmy Lee crossed his arms and looked down his nose at Jackson. "Get out here, Alison, or I'll kill this nigger."

Mama shook her head and mouthed, "Don't you move."

"You know I'll do it, and that Negro baby, too," Jimmy Lee threatened.

I started for the door. Mama grabbed my arm. "Alison."

"He's not gonna hurt me, but he'll hurt them," I said with little faith in my own words.

I pushed nervously through the screen door and stood on the porch.

Jimmy Lee started for me. "You little bitch."

"Hey!" Jackson said and took a step between us. My injured sentry.

"Jackson, don't!" I ran down the steps and stood beside him. "He's not worth it." I stood between Jackson and Jimmy Lee. "I don't want no trouble, Jimmy Lee. I made a mistake by marryin' you, and I'm sorry for that, but—"

He grabbed my arm and started for the truck.

"Let go of me!" I shrieked, punching and kicking uselessly.

Jackson ran into the street. Mama was on his heels. My father's truck raced down the road, slamming to a halt behind Jimmy Lee's truck. Maggie and Jake flew out of the truck and ran toward us. My father stepped out from behind his door.

"Let her go!" Maggie yelled.

"Jimmy Lee, what the hell are you doin'?" Jake approached him and Jimmy Lee yanked me away, clutching my arm so tight I thought it might snap.

"You let her go now, Jimmy Lee." My father's voice left no room for negotiation. He raised the shotgun he carried at his side.

Maggie grabbed my free arm.

Jimmy Lee pulled me away from her as Jackson closed in on him.

"Step back, Jackson," Daddy said. He had Jimmy Lee in his scope, his finger on the trigger.

"Daddy," Jake said. "That'll make you no better than him."

"Shut up, Jake," Daddy said.

"You won't kill me," Jimmy Lee said. "You don't like niggers any more than I do."

My father didn't hesitate for a second. His voice was calm and fierce. "But I love my daughter." He lifted his trigger finger, then placed it on the trigger once again, the way he did when he was hunting, right before he pulled one off. "And whoever my daughter loves, I love, and she don't love you no more." He took a step closer to Jimmy Lee, the barrel of the gun inches from his cheek. "The way I see it, you've killed a man for less than what you're doin' right now. There ain't no way I'll do time. We all see you manhandlin' my daughter, and don't think I won't press charges against you for beatin' her until she hemorrhaged."

"I didn't do that," Jimmy Lee protested.

"Didn't you? I saw it, and I remember it clear as day." Patricia stood on the front porch, Joshua in her arms, a dark bruise of proof on her cheek.

"A nigger's word against mine?" he laughed.

"Somethin' tells me you got more than one nigga' after you," Daddy said.

Jimmy Lee shifted his eyes to my father, squinting a threat in his direction and squeezing my arm 'til I yelped. Daddy kept his gun trained on Jimmy Lee.

"Y'all are a bunch of nigger lovers." He pushed me away.

Maggie clamored forward and pulled me into her arms.

"You better watch your backs," his voice quaked as he moved backward toward his truck. "My uncle'll kill you niggers, and you, too." He pointed to Daddy. "My uncle'll make sure you don't ever earn another penny."

My father kept the gun trained on Jimmy Lee's truck until it turned the corner and drove out of sight.

I clung to Maggie. "Daddy?"

"I had to tell him," Maggie spoke with an urgency that shook me. "When I thought about you and Mama comin' here alone, I got really scared. I'm sorry, Pix."

"Sorry? You saved Jackson's life, and probably mine, too." I turned to thank Daddy and saw that he had the gun trained on Jackson, who stood with his hands up, the whites of his eyes as large as gumballs. "Daddy! What are you doin'?"

I ran in front of Jackson and held out my arms, shielding him from Daddy's gun.

"Step back, Alison," he said, narrowing his eyes.

"No, Daddy. I won't." I watched Daddy's eyes. I swear I saw something more than anger there—sadness? Loss of his daughter? I didn't care. "I love him, Daddy. I love him with all my heart." I pointed to Joshua, swaddled close to Patricia's chest. "That's your grandson, whether you like it or not. He exists, and I love him, too."

"Step away now," he commanded.

I remained where I was, my legs trembling like leaves in the wind.

"Alison Jean, your place is—"

"My *place* is wherever Jackson and Joshua are. I love you, Daddy, and I know I hurt you, and I'm sorry, but I love him, and if you love me, you'll let us be."

His shoulders dropped, just a smidgen.

"Please, Daddy?" I begged.

Mama moved next to Daddy and touched his tense shoulder. "Ralph," she whispered. "She's your daughter. You can't keep pushin' all of your children away. The world is changin', and they have a right to change, too."

My father turned to look at her, and the way he squinted and clenched his jaw, I worried he'd just explode, that we'd pushed him too far. To my surprise, he lowered the gun. There was a collective sigh of relief as Daddy turned to look at Maggie, then at me. I was so scared of losing him, and in that moment I felt, more than saw, the transition from my being Daddy's little girl to something else, something less, maybe.

"Thank you, Daddy," I said, hoping for something more.

He swung the shotgun up the second I stepped away from Jackson, set him in his sight again, and said, "If you ever hurt my daughter I will not hesitate to kill you."

"Yes, sir," Jackson said in a respectful tone. "Sir, I love your daughter and our son with all of my heart and soul. I'd willin'ly give my life for her, but with all due respect, sir, I would rather live, and we can't do that here. Not now, and maybe not ever."

"What?" I knew he was right. We couldn't live together here. The Lovings fled the south and we would have to, also. My heart stung so badly, I felt as if it was being squeezed in a giant fist.

Jackson shook his head. "Alison, we'd fear for our lives, for Joshua's life, every minute of every day. I think movin' to New York, where I have a job, where interracial couples might not be the norm, but they exist without the fear of bein' killed, would be our safest move."

New York? So far away from Mama and Daddy?

"Joshua needs to be raised in a safe, lovin' environment," he continued. "We have the love, but here," he pointed in the direction of Main Street, "we have no safety. Not yet."

"You're takin' my daughter away?" My father said, lifting his gun once more.

Mama set her hand gently on the top of the gun and pushed it down until it was pointed at the ground. "Ralph," she whispered.

My father's eyes shot darts in her direction, then softened. He wiped his face with his free hand, then stared into the field, his silence magnified the tension that hung around us. With the slightest nod of his head, he conceded.

Chapter Forty-Nine

After a month of living in New York, I'm still getting used to being in public with Jackson and Joshua without being gobbled up with fear for our safety. Sure, we still received the chin-snub from many, even some harsh comments, but a chin-snub and comments were a lot easier to take when you had friends like Darla, Bear, and Marlo, and a sister like Maggie, who snubbed and commented right back.

Although Daddy didn't allow Jake to apply to Mississippi State when he'd found the application on Jake's desk, he eventually agreed to allow him to take an art class at the community college. Maybe Maggie was right all along, and Daddy simply didn't want to let Jake leave town.

Each time I called home, I yearned to speak to Daddy. It just about killed me each time that he refused to come to the phone. He told Mama to tell me he loved me, but he had yet to speak to me himself. I prayed every night that he might come around and allow us to find each other once again. I missed him, but when I look at my baby's face, and I see the love he holds in his father's eyes, I know I did the right thing, and I have no shame about my decision or those I love.

Jackson walked through the door of our tiny apartment and asked how my day was. It was a day like any other. I woke up next to the man I loved, nursed the baby I adored, and spent the entire day with our son, just waiting for his daddy to come home—on time, sober, and hungry to spend time with us.

"Perfect," I answered.

Acknowledgments

While it was a joy to research this story, it was also very painful to hear about the realities of segregation from those who lived through it. I could not have written this book without the insight from Maxine Johnson, who was generous enough to share her family's history. Details were also gathered from Joe Easter, Mary Easter, Sandy Barnes, and my good friends, G.E. Johnson and Emerald Barnes. Without such friends, the southern way of life and dialect could not have been so well depicted. I know that it is hard to imagine that in the late sixties there were small southern towns that were so far removed from the integration that was happening at that time in larger cities, but what I have conveyed is as true to the stories I was told as I was able to write.

As an author, I write stories for my readers, but my stories would not shine without the thoughtful, diligent, and professional efforts of my editors and proofreaders, who are kind and patient beyond words. Warm hugs of gratitude and respect to Kristen Weber, Colleen Albert, and Dale Cassidy.

A hearty thank you to Stephen and Sandra Foster, Patricia Fordyce, Kathleen Shoop, Kian Vencill, Tammy Dewhirst, and everyone else who took the time to help me through the specifics of my story and my drafts. Thank you to all of my wonderful beta readers. I could not have made it through the toughest days of writing without my World Literary Café staff, each of whom are there hashing out storylines and supporting each other daily. Thank you, Stacy, Amy, Bonnie, Gerria, Emerald, Clare (my formatting genius), Natasha, Christine, and Wendy. And to my sisters on the Women's Nest who cheer me on, thank you.

Lastly, thank you to my mother, my husband Les, and our children. I love you all and appreciate your support.

About the Author

Melissa Foster is the award-winning author of four International bestselling novels. She is a community builder for the Alliance of Independent Authors and a touchstone in the indie publishing arena. When she's not writing, Melissa teaches authors how to navigate the book-marketing world, build their platforms, and leverage the power of social media, through her author-training programs on Fostering Success. Melissa is also the founder of the World Literary Café, and the Women's Nest, a social and support community for women. She has been published in Calgary's Child Magazine, the Huffington Post, and Women Business Owners magazine.

Melissa hosts an annual Aspiring Authors contest for children and has painted and donated several murals to The Hospital for Sick Children in Washington, DC. Melissa lives in Maryland with her family.

Melissa welcomes an invitation to your book club, meeting, or event.

www.MelissaFoster.com